Cruel Truths

Eastern High Series Book Two

Eve Campbell

ISBN- 9781923416277

Cover Design- Dolores Dezigns

Chapter 1

SAM

Every time I walk the halls of Eastern High, I remind myself this place is just a stepping stone. I turned eighteen at the start of the school year. I keep my grades high, my dreams higher, and my mouth shut when the whispers follow me down the corridor.

"Virgin tease."

I hear it every time. Nicole doesn't bother whispering it anymore.

I shift my books higher in my arms and keep walking, my boots clicking against the tiles. They're scuffed and beaten-up, nothing like her designer knock-offs. She's got another sucker on her arm today. Some junior with hopeful eyes and a hard-on.

She leans in with fake sweetness, her eyes fixed on him as if he's the only one that matters. But she's already scanning the hallway for someone better, someone bigger, someone who will give her the attention she truly desires.

That's Nicole's game.

When she's not turning it on for the boys, she turns it on me. The second their attention drifts or someone prettier walks past, she sharpens her voice and points it at my throat. Petty digs in the hallway. Back-handed compliments that sound sweet until you actually listen. Snide laughs shared with whichever girl is standing closest, always just loud enough to be heard. She doesn't need a spotlight to feel powerful—she only needs someone to burn. And for as long as I can remember, I've been her favorite.

Red hair means fire crotch.

Not having a boyfriend means something must be wrong with me.

Talk to a guy and I'm a tease.

Don't sleep with him and I'm a prude.

It doesn't matter what I do. They've already made up their minds. And there's no version of me that ever comes out clean.

I turn the corner, and my stomach twists—just like it always does when he's around.

Reece Wilson is pressed against some girl at his locker. Her back is arched, lips parted, and his hand sits low enough on her waist to make it clear he'll get whatever he wants. His grin is lazy and dangerous, the kind that makes a girl forget her own name. He doesn't care who's watching. He never does. He's one of Noah's boys, and around here, that makes him untouchable. Rules don't apply to them. Hearts aren't off-limits. And Reece? He breaks both without flinching.

I hate that I notice the way his fingers graze her hip, slow and possessive. I hate that he leans in, lips brushing her ear, not kissing her but close enough to make her legs go weak.

And above all, I hate that he catches me staring.

His eyes lock onto mine. Blue. Sharp. Full of heat he never even tries to hide.

He smirks, as if he knows exactly what he's doing.

"Hey, Red," he calls out, loud enough to make heads turn.

Nicole's laugh pierces the hallway, shrill and fake—her way of pulling the spotlight back onto herself. It's always the same game with that bitch.

I roll my eyes at the sound of his voice and pick up my pace. My cheeks burn.

Reece Wilson will never get under my skin.

Not again.

Jace, the asshole next to him, leans against the wall like he's God's gift to women. His mouth is already moving. "Looks like your little ginger's got it bad."

Reece doesn't look at him. He lets out a rough laugh, the kind that gets under your skin. "She wishes."

I don't give them the satisfaction of reacting. That's the rule. If you flinch, they win. So I keep my face blank, shoulder-check the nearest doorway, and slip into class without a backward glance. My heart's doing its usual traitor routine—too fast, too loud—but I pretend it's just the caffeine.

Reece Wilson is chaos in ripped jeans and last year's sneakers. He's all crooked smiles and fuck-me eyes, the kind of boy who can ruin you with a look and never lose sleep over it. He doesn't keep trophies. He flirts, he conquers, he forgets. And somehow, every time he glances my way, I'm the one left standing in the wreckage.

Every single time.

They all think I'm immune.

Liz with her color-coded calendars. Lola with her snack stash and her laugh that echoes through walls. And Aubrey, so in love she floats when Noah's near.

They look at me and see control, poise, and intelligence before boys—red hair and rolled eyes. They think I don't care.

Maybe that's my own fault. I built this armor. I perfected the polished smile. I made sure no one could see how much those throwaway lines sting, how much the heat in Reece's voice turns to ice when he uses it on someone else.

They don't know it gets hard to breathe when he looks at me and laughs, all teeth and heat, like I'm the setup to a punchline he never finished. Or when he throws out that one word... "Red" as if it means nothing to him and everything to me.

They don't realize that every time Nicole calls me a tease, a prude, or a virgin, it sinks into my skin and stays there.

I keep my chin high and my voice steady, pretending none of it ever lands. I tell myself their words bounce off, that his laugh doesn't hit bone. But I feel every bit of it. And then I bury it deep where no one can see.

The classroom's half-full, sunlight slicing across chipped desks and half-dead posters peeling off the walls.

I see Liz near the back, phone in hand, typing with the kind of fury that means someone's about to get a very aggressive reminder to attend Student Council.

She looks up from her phone. "Please tell me that flustered look is because you tripped over your own shoelaces and not because Reece winked at you again."

I sigh as I settle into the seat. "Yeah. You know. Just another Monday where I question all my life choices."

She doesn't pause. "Ah yes. Monday. Where Nicole calls you a tease and Reece decides the hallway is his personal strip club. Very peaceful."

I snort. "You missed the part where Tia tried to kill me with her eyes. I'm pretty sure she's still manifesting Aubrey's downfall so she can steal Noah back."

Liz finally looks up, unimpressed. "Tia's just bitter Noah fell for someone who didn't spend two years fake-tanning and terrorizing freshmen."

"And Nicole?" I ask.

Liz shrugs. "Oh, she's bitter no one's fallen in love with her yet."

Right on cue, the classroom door swings open.

Aubrey walks in with that flushed, just-kissed glow she probably doesn't even notice. Her hair's loose, falling over her shoulders, an effortless beauty that doesn't need a filter. She heads toward us, her hand already reaching for Noah's. He catches it without missing a beat.

Noah used to be a fuckboy. Cold smile, hot hands, and a reputation that followed him into every room. He played girls the way Reece and Jace still do—easy, careless, never sticking around for the fallout. All sharp edges and zero apologies. He used to be untouchable. Unreachable.

Until Aubrey.

Now he walks beside Aubrey with his hand wrapped around hers, and you can see the shift in him. The way his eyes never leave her. The way his body moves in sync with hers, ready to shield, ready to strike. Now he bends for her.

And when he looks at her, it isn't soft.

It's brutal. Possessive.

The kind of look that imprints itself into memory and refuses to fade once the moment's over.

It says touch her, and you're dead. Cross that line, and he won't hesitate.

They sit down in the seats across from us. Aubrey raises her hand and waves. I wave back, relaxed, casual, pretending the knot in my chest isn't tightening.

I really am happy for her. I am. She deserves it. After everything she's been through, she fucking deserves this peace, this love, this boy who would torch the earth just to keep her warm.

But still... something twists. It lingers there, just behind my ribs.

It's not envy. Not exactly.

It's that quiet, unbearable ache that hits when you see someone else get everything you act like you don't want. It's wondering what it would be like if someone looked at me the way Noah looks at her, as if she's already home. Like the war's over and she's the reason he made it through.

To be truly seen and still be chosen.

Not for the way I look. Not for the red hair or the body they think I haven't given away yet.

But for me.

Lola charges through the door as if she's late to her own drama. She holds a half-eaten muffin in one hand, her bag barely hanging on her shoulder, with crumbs trailing behind her like confetti.

"Don't ask," she groans, dropping into the seat in front of me. "I stepped in gum, spilled my coffee, and got hit in the face by my locker door. The universe is out for blood."

"You've always been cursed," Liz mumbles, still glued to her phone. "Today's just extra."

Lola spins around to face me, eyes narrowing. "Alright. Spill. Did Reece finally grow a soul and make a move, or is he still acting like the emotionally stunted man-child we all know and love?"

I exhale through my nose, the tired kind. "Still playing."

She beams. "Love that for you. Nothing says romance like unresolved sexual tension and deep-rooted trauma."

"Thanks, Dr. Phil." I roll my eyes at Lola's comment as Tia walks into the room.

She's alone.

No backup dancers. No smug parade of cheerleaders snapping gum at her heels. Only her, and the flick of her eyes, scanning the room for one person.

Noah.

She spots him easily, seated next to Aubrey with their heads close. But it's not him that hurts, it's Aubrey. The girl who shattered Tia's perfect little world in two. The one who didn't back down, even when Tia charged at her claws first.

Aubrey didn't just steal Noah; she stole the entire narrative. Now, because of that, Tia walks in without anyone bowing. They just watch.

It's strange to see Tia like this—quiet. This is the same girl who used to own hallways like a runway, whose laugh could turn heads and ruin reputations instantly. The one who once had girls begging to sit at her lunch table and boys lining up just to be ignored.

Now?

Nobody looks up. Nobody gasps. Nobody even blinks.

She walks past our row without a single glance. Not a glare. Not a smirk. Nothing. And somehow, that hits harder than any insult ever could.

Tia doesn't ignore people. She breaks them down.

Her quietness isn't surrender. It's the storm gathering strength before it strikes. She's not finished. She's watching. Waiting. And when she fights her way back to the top—because girls like her always do—someone's gonna bleed. And it won't be her.

Tia barely takes her seat before the next act walks in.

Nicole saunters through the doorway, gum snapping between her teeth, her skirt riding too high, and that voice already grating on my nerves. She walks as if the floor was made for her heels, as if the rest of us are just scenery.

She tosses her hair with dramatic flair, as if she's practiced in front of a mirror a thousand times. She dramatizes dragging her freshly manicured nails across Reece's desk as she walks by.

He doesn't even blink.

He leans back, legs spread, one arm draped over the back of the chair. That stupid silver ring glints on his thumb as he twirls his pen between his fingers, all casual sin and zero shame.

Nicole slows down, eyes narrowing as she tracks the direction of his gaze with sharp focus.

And then she notices it.

Sees me.

Her mouth twists, but I hardly notice because now I'm the one caught.

Reece is watching me. Not just in passing or by accident.

Really watching.

My pulse wavers. I quickly look away, pretending I didn't notice it. That slow crawl of heat up my neck, the twist low in my stomach, the ache I've spent months trying to hide.

His eyes stay fixed on me anyway. I can feel them dragging over my skin.

Nicole doesn't speak, but her silence is heavy. She hates it—hates that for once, the attention isn't on her.

That Reece isn't looking at her or any of the other girls who chase him through the halls like he's some messed-up prize. Because Reece Wilson, the resident heartbreaker and certified bastard, is staring at me. And my body's betraying every rule I swore I'd follow.

I hate that he makes me feel seen. I hate that I want him to keep looking, and I really hate that Nicole knows it.

"Still wasting your time on the virgin?" Nicole purrs, voice loud enough for the whole room to catch it. "Thought you went for girls who actually knew what the fuck they were doing."

The words hit harder than I want to admit. My breath catches, and for a moment, I freeze.

Reece doesn't even blink; he just twirls that damn pen as if he's bored out of his mind.

"Maybe I'm into slow burns," he says.

A few of the guys snicker behind us. Someone mutters "shit" under their breath. Nicole's smile twitches because she wasn't expecting that.

I give him a glare.

He meets it head-on, eyes locked with mine, piercing through the walls I've spent years building. He holds the stare and doesn't give me a moment to breathe.

I don't know what this is. This slow, cruel game he keeps dragging me into. All I know is I never come out the other side whole. He plays, I break. I bleed, he walks away untouched. Nicole's glare cuts across the room, aimed straight at my throat.

"Don't," Liz murmurs beside me. "The bitch is begging for a reaction."

"She always is," I whisper, voice tense.

Lola leans over the back of her chair. "Her jealousy's louder than her perfume, and that's saying something. She needs a hug, a nap, and a reality check. In that order."

I try not to laugh. Lola always chooses the worst moment to say the dumbest stuff. I swear she couldn't read a room if the instructions were stapled to her forehead. But I love her. Fiercely. Stupid jokes and all.

Nicole opens her mouth, caught up in the sound of her own voice, soaking up the attention as if it's hers to hold.

But then Noah shifts in his seat.

One look. That's all it takes.

His tone cuts through the noise, sharp enough to draw blood.

"Sit the fuck down, Nicole," he says. "And know when to shut your mouth."

The air becomes still.

Every head turns. No one breathes. Because when Noah speaks, people listen.

Nicole's eyes go wide. She blinks slowly and in shock, as if she wasn't expecting Noah to say anything—let alone pick a side. Especially not mine.

The room stills.

Even Reece stops, his smirk fading as his pen halts in midair.

Nicole hesitates, frozen for a second, then moves. She slides into the seat behind me, the scrape of the chair loud in the silence. Her breath ghosts across the back of my neck, sticky with sugar and venom.

"You'd be real pretty if you weren't such a stuck-up little tease," she murmurs, voice low enough only I can hear. "You walk around acting like you're above it. Like they only want you because you're different. But here's a reality check, Sammy—every guy wants the same thing. And none of them stick around after they get it."

I clench my fists in my lap.

I don't need this crap today. Not when I've got college applications waiting at home and just one shot to get out of this place for good. Let them keep playing games in a town they'll never leave. I'm already halfway gone.

Mrs. Whitman sweeps into the room exactly on cue, clutching a stack of papers and a travel mug that probably contains both regret and espresso. She claps her hands once, and the room falls into the bare minimum of order.

I straighten up in my seat and take a deep breath. I try to hide that I'm still trembling from Nicole's whisper and Reece's stare. The only battle I want to fight today is against the clock.

But peace doesn't last long here. Not with the ex-queen bee sitting three rows over, and the new contender sharpening her claws behind me.

Tia raises her hand five minutes in, all polite smile and fake humility. "I just wanted to ask about the upcoming homecoming court nominations," she says, sweet as poison in a glitter bottle.

Of course she does.

The moment the words leave her lips, I feel Nicole stiffen behind me, tension spilling off her shoulders like she's gearing up for a duel. It's not about the votes. It never is. It's about image. Power. Legacy. Who gets to wear the crown and whose name gets erased from history.

Tia may have lost the boy, but she's not giving up the spotlight without a fight.

And Nicole? She's willing to burn the whole school down before she lets Tia take center stage again.

The war isn't beginning. It has never ended. They're just switching weapons.

Mrs. Whitman attempts to bring the room back to something educational, but it's too late. The air is already thick with ego and glittering tension. Tia throws a smug glance at Nicole.

The rest of us just hold our breath and act like we're not watching.

Ten minutes before the bell, Mrs. Whitman decides to ruin my life. She claps her hands, all business, and starts rattling off partner names. Then I hear it—my name.

And his.

"Samantha and Reece."

My stomach drops.

I blink once.

Twice.

The world doesn't stop spinning, but it definitely slows down.

Did she really say that out loud?

What the fuck?

There has to be some kind of cosmic glitch happening. Some cruel little glitch coded by the universe just to mess with me. Maybe it's karma, taking advantage of something I forgot I did.

I glance over at Reece.

He doesn't hide the smirk forming on his face. One eyebrow raised, eyes shining with amusement, posture exuding arrogance. He's leaning back in his chair, relaxed and smug, as if this is the best news he's received all day. His fingers toy with the edge of his desk, tapping out a slow, steady rhythm that mirrors the tension building in my spine.

Then he moves.

His chair screeches across the floor, drawing attention along with it. Every eye in the room shifts. They know this is a show. And he's about to put on one.

He stands, stretches, and walks toward me with all the time in the world.

I sit frozen in my seat, jaw clenched, fingers gripping my pen as if it could save me.

"Oh shit," Lola breathes, loud enough to sound like a public service announcement. Her head swivels between Reece and me, back and forth, back and forth, as if she's watching a car crash in slow motion and can't decide which angle hurts more.

Liz is already gone, traitor that she is, slipping into the chair next to Sofia without even pretending to hesitate. Of course, she's got Sofia. Calm. Normal. Safe. The kind of partner who uses highlighters properly and doesn't stare at you like they might ruin your life for fun.

Why couldn't that be me?

Why couldn't I be working with Sofia, quietly filling out worksheets and counting down the minutes until the bell, instead of sitting here waiting for disaster to slide into the chair next to me?

Lola leans in closer, lowering her voice. "If you survive this, I'm buying you fries."

I snort despite the nerves fluttering under my skin.

And then he's there.

I keep my eyes locked on the notebook in front of me, pretending I don't feel the air shift when he moves. Pretending I don't already know that if I look up, I'll see that smirk. The one that melts logic and short-circuits my entire nervous system.

He doesn't wait; he simply drops into the seat beside me with the confidence of someone who knows exactly what he's doing. His knee bumps against mine, hard enough to jolt but gentle enough to feel like it's deliberate.

"Looks like you're stuck with me, Red."

I grit my teeth. "Lucky me."

"Could be worse," he says, eyes burning into the side of my face. "Could've been Nicole."

"Please." I keep my tone flat. "You'd love that."

He leans in, his breath brushing the curve of my cheek, and I swear the universe is intentionally doing this.

"Maybe," he murmurs. "But she doesn't look nearly as pretty when she's pissed off."

I shove the worksheet at him, the one someone left on my desk while I was busy spiraling through the seventh circle of emotional hell. "Shut up and read."

He laughs, a sound that hums in your blood long after it stops.

And I hate that it hits me right in the stomach, heat curling slowly, striking a match I never asked for.

We sit in silence.

Or... I try to.

Reece treats silence the same way he treats rules: he ignores it completely.

He shifts next to me, all relaxed limbs and smug confidence.

"Don't look so miserable, Red," he says, voice full of that lazy charm he uses when he's trying to get under someone's skin. "We used to get along, remember?"

I don't look at him because I do remember, and that's the problem.

We used to talk, once. Back before the parties, all his hookups. Before his fuck count got high enough to earn him a reputation and a whole damn scoreboard.

Back when he was just Reece, he had no swagger or smirk. No trail of girls wondering why they were never enough. He was simply a boy with sea blue eyes and a crooked smile who knew how to make me laugh effortlessly.

There was a time—long ago—when we sat in a circle in someone's basement, giggling over a bottle we were too young to drink. It spun around. Slowed down and landed on me.

He was my first kiss.

It was awkward. Too fast. Barely more than a breath. But it stayed with me anyway, the way firsts always do.

I glance up. "That was years ago. You hadn't learned how to be an asshole yet."

"Admit it, Red, you liked me back then." His grin widens.

I snort. "I had a crush. I also had braces and thought cutting my own bangs was a smart idea. Let's not trust past me."

He leans back, arms loose, mouth full of trouble. That confidence rolls off him, warm and suffocating, filling every inch of space between us.

"You're cute when you're mean."

I don't flinch. Don't let the flutter in my chest show.

"Yeah?" I say, reaching for the worksheet. "You're tolerable when you shut the fuck up. Let's just do the damn worksheet."

He taps his fingers on the desk with a slow rhythm. Each tap challenges me to respond.

"Fine, Red," he says. "You want me to play nice, I'll play nice."

It's a lie. Every word he says is just a game. Every look is another move on a board only he seems to understand.

Before I can respond, the bell rings loudly through the room.

I shove my belongings into my bag so quickly that my notebook nearly rips in half. Pens clatter to the floor. I leave them. I can't stay here even for a second longer. Not with him still watching me. Not with my pulse pounding like I just lost a fight I didn't agree to take part in.

I bolt. Down the aisle, out the door, through the hallway.

I don't slow down until the sunlight hits my face outside. I grip the strap of my bag. My heart's still pounding in my chest, all scrambled and loud, as if it hasn't realized that I'm free.

This year was supposed to be the best I could get.

Not perfect or like a fairytale. Just something that finally worked in my favor for once. One chance to get straight grades, walk across that stage, and move on to something better than this town has for me. I want more out of life.

This assessment counts for forty percent of our final grade. Nearly half my grade depends on one sheet of paper and a few weeks of partner work I never asked for. I need every single point I can get if I want to pass.

So no, I'm not letting Reece Wilson—human distraction, chaos in sneakers, walking red flag with a six-pack—screw that up for me. He can keep his grin, that flirty voice, the lazy charm that makes half the school fall over themselves just to be the next name he forgets.

He's not ruining this for me.

CHAPTER 2

REECE

It's her fucking hair. That's where it starts. Always. That red, too bold to ignore, too dangerous to touch without getting burned. It glows in the sun, turns molten under the fluorescents, and makes my brain short-circuit every time it brushes her shoulder.

Sam Carter doesn't own the hallway. She doesn't strut. She doesn't perform. Most people don't really see her, not the way they should. She keeps her head down, shoulders squared, moving through the noise instead of feeding it.

But I see her, and that's the fucking problem.

Sam Carter is the kind of girl who makes tight jeans, and low cuts seem desperate. She doesn't cake herself in makeup or pout in bathroom selfies. She exists and nothing more. Effortlessly. Beautiful in a way that's real. Natural.

Some days she shows up in a hoodie and jeans and still manages to make every fake bitch in this school look like they're trying too hard. Because they are. Tia with her stripper lashes. Nicole and her please-look-at-my-tits top.

Sam... She doesn't try. Doesn't lick a straw like it's a skill. She's everything. Messy hair, sleeves too long, lips soft and unbothered, and somehow I'm standing here wondering how they'd feel wrapped around my...

Focus.

I mean, sure, I've imagined it. Once. Maybe twice. Fine. Every damn time she opens her mouth and tells me to fuck off. Those lips are pure fucking trouble—smart enough to ruin me, soft enough to make me want it. The kind of lips that stay in your dreams for a moment, enough to wake you up hard, irritated, and one bad choice away from a hand job you're not even proud of.

It's humiliating, honestly.

She rolls her eyes, mutters something and suddenly I'm spiralling, wondering what those same lips would do if she wasn't using them to verbally dismantle me. If she wants me the way my body wants her.

Which is aggressive, always at the worst possible time.

I've heard Jace talk about her. It's crude shit. Locker-room garbage. Running his mouth about her ass, her body, what he'd do if she ever let him. I laughed it off in the moment because that's what I do. But my jaw was locked so hard I thought I might crack a tooth.

I almost punched him.

Not because he was wrong, she is hot as fuck. But because she wasn't his to talk about.

Sam doesn't smile at me the way the others do. No fluttery lashes. No lip bites or giggles. Hell, I'm pretty sure she'd rather set herself on fire than be in the same room as me.

She rolls her eyes when I wink. Crosses her arms when I talk. Looks at me like I'm static she learned to ignore years ago.

But I see it.

It's the twitch in her jaw when I get too close. The split-second hitch in her breath when I call her Red, as if I'm saying something filthy. The way her fists curl like she's deciding whether to punch me or drag me somewhere dark and lock the door.

She acts unfazed. Almost bored.

But I see it. I always fucking see it. I get under her skin. Scratch that. I fucking live there.

Although she'll never admit that, but that's half the fun.

She fucking loves it almost as much as I do.

She makes me want to ruin her mood. Hell, maybe her entire year.

Whatever perfect plan she's got in that pretty little head? I want to fuck with it. Just enough to make her snap.

This isn't a crush. That shit's for freshmen and idiots who fall for the first girl that looks their way. This is something else. Something darker. Deeper. A fixation that's carved itself into my ribs and made a fucking home there. A fever that simmers beneath my skin every time she walks past, every time she opens that mouth and tells me to fuck off.

I won't name it, because the moment I do, it becomes real. And if it's real, it owns me.

So I leave it where it is—in the glances I steal when she's not looking. In the smirk I wear to rile her up. In the heat that curls low in my gut when she squares her shoulders and goes toe-to-toe with me.

I may hook up with other girls while she walks by. Maybe I make sure she sees it. Maybe I get off on the way her face tightens before she snaps it back into place.

I lean back against the brick wall out front, and Shantel presses up against me. She's already got one hand on my chest, the other sliding lower like we've got five minutes before the bell and she plans to use every one of them.

If we weren't standing in front of the school, she'd be on her knees by now. Wouldn't be the first time. It wouldn't even be the third.

She's easy. Always has been. Ever since I bent her over behind the gym, she's been stuck to me like a bad fucking habit. One she doesn't try to kick. I ignore her texts, purposely call her the wrong name, treat her like an afterthought. But it doesn't matter. She keeps coming back like she's wired for it. Always ready. Always begging for another round.

Her lips are on mine, hot and sloppy, and yeah, my cock's getting hard. But it's not for her.

It's for the redhead who just stepped out of her car. Tight high pony-tail swaying with every step, bag slung over one shoulder. She's scrolling her phone, oblivious of what she is about to stumble on.

But she's coming this way. Past the wall where I've got Shantel pressed against me, her tongue in my mouth, her hand halfway to my belt as if she's on a damn mission.

This moment it's calculated. Deliberate. I want her to see it. I want Red to look up from her phone and spot me with someone else's lips on mine. To roll her eyes and mutter something under her breath because she's pissed and doesn't know why.

I live for that because the more she hates me, the deeper I crawl under her skin.

And fuck, I love it there.

I pull back just enough to tuck a strand of Shantel's hair behind her ear. It's my signature move, the one that makes them think I'm sweet before I remind them I'm not. My fingers linger, thumb brushing her cheek as if I give a damn, as if this isn't just theater.

I hear the telltale click of boots on concrete. Sam. Right on time.

So I lean in and kiss Shantel again, soft at first, then deeper. Open-mouthed and drawn-out, the kind of kiss you'd expect in some high school softcore fantasy. She moans, loud enough to echo, as Sam walks past.

Perfect.

I hear it. The hitch in her step. That tiny pause in her usually bullet-proof stride. She doesn't look over, doesn't break pace, but I feel her feel it.

When I pull back, I keep my eyes on Sam's retreating figure. Red ponytail swinging. Shoulders squared. Walking with that nothing-touches-me strut, even though I know I do.

This isn't about getting laid.

I could get off with any girl in this place.

I already have.

But Sam?

She's the only one who makes it worth the chase.

I let Shantel kiss me again. Harder this time, messier. She's all tongue and lip gloss, and I let her think it's doing something for me. It's not. My mind's already miles away, somewhere between the front gate and the swing of a red ponytail.

When I pull back, I wipe my mouth on the back of my hand. No shame, no apology.

Just a smirk for the effort.

She pouts, lower lip shoved out like she expects me to kiss it better. "You're such a tease," she says.

I cock my head. "Takes one to know one."

"You want to hang out?" she asks.

Not a chance. I'd rather watch paint dry.

"Nah," I say. "Got better things to do." Which is code for: I've already used you for what I needed, so now it's over.

She huffs, tugs at her too-short skirt like modesty suddenly matters, and storms off toward the courtyard. "Asshole," she mutters under her breath.

She's not wrong.

I move through the school gates, backpack slung low, swagger set to cruise control. Noah's already waiting near the flagpole, Jace beside him with that smug grin that usually means trouble or tits. Sometimes both.

We fall into step, cutting through the chaos. First bell hasn't even rung, and the place is crawling with try-hards and hormone-choked wannabes.

Jace sparks a cigarette he won't finish. One of those crusty teachers will be on his ass before the filter burns. But Jace... he lives to stir shit. The more rules he breaks, the harder he grins.

"Shantel blew me behind the science block this morning," he says, dragging in deep and exhaling through his nose. "So technically, you're tasting me right now."

I freeze mid-step, dry-heaving like I've been poisoned. "What the actual fuck is wrong with you?"

He shrugs, all cocky shoulders and zero shame. "Thought you deserved to start your day with something memorable."

"You're fucking feral."

"I aim to please. She swallowed," Jace adds with a wicked grin. "Begged for it too. Said she hadn't eaten yet."

Noah chokes, gagging so hard he actually stumbles. "You're fucking sick."

"I'm just generous," Jace says, smug as hell. "Feeding the hungry and shit."

Noah rolls his eyes, shoving his hands into his pockets. "Do you guys wanna hang out later? Might hit the courts after school."

I'm about to answer, but Noah's gaze sharpens ahead, zeroing in. Aubrey.

She's cutting across the quad, head down, hair loose, books clutched to her chest. And just like that, Noah forgets we exist.

"Later," he mutters, already moving toward her.

Jace watches him go, snorts, then turns to me. "Pussy whipped."

I snort. "You're one to talk."

"Only when the pussy's worth it." He grins, all sharp teeth and zero shame.

"Classy."

"Always."

Jace grinds out his cigarette with the toe of his boot, sending ash skittering across the concrete. We push through the front doors, and the noise swells. Laughter too loud. Shoes squeaking. Some idiot slamming a locker shut just to hear it echo.

A group of girls turn as we walk in. Whispers. Bites of giggles. One of them tucks her hair behind her ear, angling her body toward Jace with that desperate smile he never returns.

I barely notice them.

I'm scanning the hallway. Eyes moving over heads, searching for Red. She's not here, and neither are her friends. Not that I care. I just look.

Jace and I head for our usual spot near the back hallway, where no one goes unless they're cutting class or dealing with something they shouldn't be.

Jace's eyes land on a guy who's practically dry-humping his girlfriend in front of the vending machine. It's all hands and tongue, no shame, right there next to the Doritos.

He nudges my elbow. "Think if he fucks her hard enough against the glass, a Snickers'll fall out?"

I let out a laugh and lean back against the wall, letting the noise fade around me. Girls walk past, tossing glances. Jace laps it up. I don't even see them.

My eyes are still on the hallway. Waiting for red.

Nicole appears from around the lockers. Tight skirt. Black tank. Eyes sharp as glass and hungry for witnesses. She makes a straight line for Jace and hooks her arm around his elbow, claiming him in public because that's how girls around here measure worth.

"Morning," she says, all sugar-sweet and loud enough for every girl within earshot to hear. The bitch is venom wrapped in lip gloss.

She presses into him, hand already sliding over his chest. "What are you doing?" she asks, batting her lashes.

It is always a performance.

Everyone knows it.

Tia and Nicole have been locked in some pathetic bitch war ever since Aubrey knocked Tia on her ass.

Now the two of them take turns parading guys around, proving who still has power. Last week it was Tia hanging all over Jace, whispering promises and letting everyone see.

This week, it looks like it's Nicole's turn. By Friday, they'll probably decide to share him and call it a strategy.

Jace never says no. Attention and action are his favorite drugs. The guy practically runs on ego and blowjobs.

Nicole tips her chin up, lips parted, already imagining the win, already planning how she'll brag to Tia at lunch.

Her mouth hovers just above his.

"What the fuck are you doing?" Jace shoves her back with one hand.

Not hard, but hard enough.

She stumbles, catches herself on the locker behind her. Faces turn. Eyes lock on the scene as if blood's been spilled.

Jace doesn't kiss. Everyone knows that. It's the one line he won't let a girl cross.

Nicole stands frozen, trying to claw back her pride, but Jace's voice slices through her before she can grab it.

"You really thought I'd kiss you?" He says. "Your mouth's been on more dicks than the boys' locker room bench."

Nicole's face goes white-hot.

"You're a fucking asshole," she hisses.

"Yeah," Jace says, grinning. "But at least I don't pretend my mouth is a personality trait."

She storms off, heels stabbing the floor with every step.

"Real smooth," I say.

Jace shrugs, eyes trailing Nicole's retreat. "She'll be back. They always come back. Must be the charm."

I roll my eyes and shift my weight.

And everything else fades. Real quick.

Because my gaze is already locked across the hallway.

There she is.

Sam.

Standing with Lola and Liz, arms crossed, chin tilted, that little smirk teasing the corner of her mouth.

Aubrey's probably off with Noah doing the whole heart-eyes, I'd-kill-for-you-baby bullshit that somehow works for them.

Jace follows my line of sight. "You gonna fuck her or write her poetry?"

I don't answer.

He grins. "Thought so. Bet she's got claws. The quiet ones always do. Rip your heart out and wear it for earrings." Jace elbows me again, harder this time. "You better move quickly." He jerks his chin forward.

Some guy I've never bothered to learn the name of is already looking her way. One of those preppy dickheads who wears his backpack over both shoulders and thinks gel makes him look edgy. His eyes are locked on Sam, and I see he's unsure if he should approach her.

"He can have her. I'm not interested," I say, turning my head away as if I didn't just mentally plan the guy's funeral.

Then Jace grins. "Then let's go fuck with her. Cockblock the asshole."

I don't argue. We move in sync, cutting through the hallway. The guy spots us coming and stiffens.

Good.

He knows who the fuck we are.

Lola spots us coming and groans. "Oh great, here comes the dick parade."

"You say that like you're not dying to ride the float." Jace throws her a wink.

"Please. I'd rather do squats on a cactus." She cocks a brow.

"Kinky," Jace says. "Just say the word, I'll grab the pot plant."

Lola smirks. "Why don't you grab a clue instead."

Jace laughs, and even I crack a grin. Lola's the only one who can roast him and live to tell the tale.

Lola's come out of her shell since Tia stopped making her life hell. You can see it in the way she is now—shoulders relaxed, head up, as if she's finally allowed to exist without apology.

"Hey, Red!" I say. I can't fucking help myself.

She doesn't blink. Just looks at me like I'm gum on her shoe and she's deciding whether I'm even worth scraping off. Then she steps around me and keeps walking down the hall.

Lola takes a step forward. "Wow. Good chat, Romeo." Then she trails after her.

I don't say anything. Just watch Sam walk away, that glorious fucking red hair catching the light, the curve of her spine a middle finger carved in motion.

<hr>

CHAPTER 3

SAM

<hr>

The house is already too alive by the time we arrive.

The party is in full swing. Music pulses through the walls, shaking the floorboards, bass hard enough to punch through my ribs. Laughter rings out from the back somewhere close.

The air is a fever dream, humid and buzzing, heavy with heat and hormones and that reckless, end-of-week energy that turns normal people into chaos junkies.

Every hallway's stuffed wall-to-wall with people who look like they live for nights like this—glossed lips, sweaty necks, hands grazing hips with the kind of casual confidence that only ever happens after three drinks and a lie.

Someone has killed the living room lights and replaced them with strands of tangled fairy lights that cast everything in a soft, flickering gold. A spinning LED disco thing throws red and blue across the ceiling as if it's recreating a crime scene in slow motion. It's dizzying and disorienting. Which is probably the point.

The kitchen's a mess. Red Solo cups litter the counters and the floor, one tipped sideways and still leaking onto someone's abandoned phone. There's a haze of burned food still clinging to the air. Maybe a frozen pizza someone forgot in the oven, or microwave popcorn nuked past the point of saving.

No one seems bothered. In fact, someone's dancing in front of the open fridge with the door alarm blaring and a slice of cake in their hand, frosting smudged across their cheek.

Girls pass by in groups of three, trailing glitter and whispers, weaving around guys with cocky smiles and eyes that scan for someone to entertain them.

Lola grips my hand as we move further inside. Her eyes are lit with a wild, reckless spark. She loves nights like this where the music's too loud, the hallway's too narrow, and the tension hums as if it's wired into the walls.

Noah's ahead of us with Aubrey tucked against his side, cutting a clean path through the mess of bodies, parting the crowd without saying a word.

Liz trails behind, hunched small, as if shrinking might make the night less sharp. Her shoulders are pulled tight, and her arms are wrapped around herself.

She told us the news on the way here. In the driveway, before we walked in, her voice cracked in a way that makes your own throat sting in sympathy.

Liz couldn't look at any of us when she said it. She stared at the steering wheel, fingers locked so tight around it that her knuckles went white, and turned off the engine as if she were trying to stall the moment.

Her dad's transfer came through. Out of nowhere. Another state. Another school. End of everything. No warning. No vote. Just a conversation behind closed doors and a decision handed down like a sentence.

No choice.

Now she's supposed to pretend everything's fine while the ground's already slipping out from under her feet. She's supposed to dance in someone else's house, fake a smile, laugh at inside jokes she won't be around to hear for much longer—all while her whole world burns quietly in the background.

Aubrey doesn't know yet. She rocked up with Noah, still glowing from whatever they were doing before this. Her hand's in his back pocket, her mouth close to his ear. They missed the driveway breakdown. Missed Liz's voice cracking and the way she kept wiping at her face when she thought we weren't looking.

I want to say something comforting to her, but the words won't come. Something like... "Hey, it'll be okay. We'll figure something out."

But there is no figuring this out. Not when her whole life's been rerouted by a decision she didn't get to be a part of. And especially when everything she knows is being packed up and shipped off, and all she gets is a weak "you'll adjust" and a deadline.

Even Lola didn't know what to say, and she never shuts up.

She sat there in the back seat, eyes wide, mouth opening and closing, but nothing came out. For once, the girl who talks the head off anyone within a ten-foot radius, especially now that Tia's stopped treating her like a chew toy, had nothing to say. That's a first these days.

We end up dead center of the room, too exposed, too visible, exactly the kind of place I never used to stand. That's the problem with hanging out with people like Noah. Once you're part of the orbit, you can't simply disappear. Eyes follow. Whispers chase. There's no place to hide.

I grab a soda from a half-melted cooler. Cold bubbles rush up and bite at the back of my throat. It's fizzy and pointless. Sugar and noise falsely appearing to be something more powerful. But it keeps my hands busy. It keeps me from folding.

Across the room, Reece is already prowling.

He leans against the kitchen counter, red cup dangling from his fingers, head tilted enough to make it look effortless as he laughs at something Jace says.

He's entirely too aware of the way every girl within a ten-foot radius keeps glancing his way when they think no one's looking. He drinks it all in as if attention's his oxygen.

No doubt the second he spots Noah, he'll drift over.

That's how it works now.

We're all orbiting the same damn planet lately, pulled in tighter ever since Aubrey and Noah got together.

I watch him for a second longer.

His eyes roam the room, lazy, practiced. They skim, linger, move on. Until they lock onto me.

His grin retreats enough to make my stomach turn because I know that look. That stillness that says he's just found something worth breaking.

My stomach drops. That low, twisting free-fall kind of drop that says "run", but my feet refuse to move. My fingers tighten around the soda bottle, nails digging into the plastic.

I turn away.

"You good?" Aubrey murmurs beside me when she notices the shift in me.

"Yeah," I lie. "Just hot."

She nods but doesn't push.

I let the lie hang between us.

Nicole drifts past with two of her loyal little bitches, the same ones who thought it would be hilarious earlier to corner me in the school corridor and announce, nice and loud for an audience, "Red hair, fire crotch, and still nobody is brave enough to fuck her."

Tia's stationed near the hallway, arms crossed tight over her chest, watching the room with that smug half-smile she wears when she thinks she still runs the place.

Something's going down. I can feel it. It's in the way Lola's been giving a running commentary for weeks now, reporting every hallway whisper like a scandal analyst with a grudge. She's been tracking the shifts in power, the fake smiles, the dirty looks, the not-so-accidental shoulder bumps.

When Tia's eyes catch mine, the smile drops. Her gaze sharpens. It's a warning. A reminder. So I don't forget who she is.

I look away before she can decide to make it worse. Tonight is already loud enough without her trying to prove something.

Liz presses closer to me, her voice barely cutting through the noise. "I hate this place."

"I know," I say, turning to face her. "We can leave whenever."

"Give it some time," Lola says, eyes tracking something across the room.

Reece chooses that exact moment to drift closer. I feel him before I see him. The way the air shifts. The way the noise seems to bend around him.

Jace strides up to Noah, already a little drunk, and smacks a hand against Noah's chest. "There he is. The King of Eastern High. Thought you'd finally outgrown these scenes."

Noah raises an eyebrow. "Didn't realize I needed your permission to show up."

Jace laughs, slinging an arm around his shoulder like they're best friends and not two seconds from pissing each other off. "Relax, golden boy. I'm surprised you're not off being wholesome somewhere. You know, babysitting puppies, reading to orphans or making out with Aubrey."

Noah shoves him off. "Are you done?"

Jace smirks. "Not even close." His eyes slide sideways and follow a girl in a short skirt. "But don't worry, I'll behave. Probably."

Jace turns to Reece, but Reece is already stepping into my space.

I take another sip of my soda, completely ignoring him.

His gaze drops to my drink, then rises slowly.

His mouth curls. "What is that? Cola?"

I don't answer.

"Figures," he says. "Too much of a good girl to taste anything real."

Jace laughs behind him, already amused.

Reece's eyes stay locked on mine.

He wants a reaction.

Wants to rattle me, throw me off enough that I fall right into any game he is engaged in.

I take a slow sip, and meet his gaze, steady.

"Why don't you go use your little words on someone who'll actually trip over them?" I say coolly. "Because here, they're background noise to a life you'll never get invited into."

Reece's smile sharpens, all swagger and sin. He steps in closer, gaze dropping to my mouth.

"Careful, Red. Keep looking at me like that and I'll start thinking you want to be the reason my sheets are a mess."

I don't blink. "The only mess I'd ever make in your bed is lighting it on fire," I say sweetly. "While you're still in it."

Jace chokes on his beer. Reece's grin grows wider.

The sick bastard probably liked it.

The crowd keeps thickening, noise rising with it until the walls feel too tight and the air too hot. The music blares through cheap speakers. Someone starts chanting along with the chorus, off-key and too loud, dragging a few drunk voices with them until it turns into a sloppy anthem.

A couple grind against the wall near the staircase, mouths locked together, hands roaming like they forgot where they are. Someone tosses a pillow at them from across the room, but they barely flinch.

More bodies press in. Solo cups are being refilled. Laughter spikes in the hallway. A guy stumbles backward through the archway, catches himself on the doorframe, and throws his arms up like he scored a goal.

Reece and Jace left us a while ago, and I can finally breathe. The air feels lighter without their egos sucking up all the oxygen.

Aubrey checks her phone before looking up with a grin tugging at her mouth. "Hey. Noah and I are heading out to the lake."

Lola looks at her. "Now? It's dark outside."

Aubrey shrugs. "Exactly. Best time of the night. No people, no noise, just stars and a boy who can't keep his hands to himself. I'll see you guys later." And with that, she is gone.

"I think we should go too," Liz says, her voice flat, eyes dull. She hasn't enjoyed a single second of this night, and after the news she got earlier today, she never should've come.

"Yeah," I nod, touching her arm gently. "I need to use the bathroom first. I'll meet you and Lola in the car, okay?"

She nods once, already grabbing Lola by the arm and pulling her towards the door.

I turn and walk away, ducking past a group of guys doing shots, one of them yelling something unintelligible as lime juice drips down his wrist.

Two people are making out against the wall—his hands on her ass like he owns her.

A few feet later, I step over a guy passed out cold on the carpet, a half-empty solo cup still in his hand, his legs splayed like he didn't quite make it to wherever he was going.

I keep moving.

Past the half-open door where two people are arguing in sharp whispers.

The further I go, the more the sound dims, music fading into a background thump, laughter bleeding into white noise. The air turns cooler, clearer, like the house itself is finally breathing again.

And then I hear it.

Two voices.

I know them now—too well—thanks to Noah keeping them in our orbit.

My feet slow on instinct. Breath-catching. Heart punching into my ribs. I press myself into the wall. The music thumps somewhere far behind me, but here... it's quiet.

Reece's voice hits first. Lazy and somewhat amused. "I told you," he says. "Red bites. That's what makes it interesting."

Jace lets out a low laugh. "So, you like them angry now?"

There's a pause, just long enough to stretch tight.

"I like them breakable."

The words land like spit in my face. I flinch.

I stare down the hallway. The bathroom door is only a few steps away. I should keep moving, I tell myself. Walk away. Go in, lock the door, splash water on your face and pretend you never heard any of this.

"She hates you, man," Jace says. "She'd never let you touch her. Let alone fuck her."

Reece's snort is soft, derisive. "Hate's not the problem," he mutters. "Hate's just foreplay when you know how to play it right."

I squeeze my eyes shut for a second. My fingers curl into a fist at my side. I want to scream. Hit something, or maybe disappear into the floor.

But instead I stand there, frozen in place, learning something I wish I didn't know. My stomach twists hard as if something rotten has just bloomed inside me.

"You really think you can fuck her?" Jace asks, as if this is a game, and I'm some faceless conquest in the lineup.

Reece's voice follows. "Have you ever known me not to get them spread out, ready for me to take?"

There's laughter. A pause.

"Yeah," Jace says, "but she's different. She doesn't fall for your shit."

Reece doesn't hesitate. "Two hundred says I will. Before graduation. She'll beg me for it."

The words hit like a slap—open palm, full force. My chest caves in around them, breath bottling somewhere too deep to reach. Heat floods my face, all humiliation and rage and something else I can't quite name.

"You're on," Jace says. "But there is no way in hell that virgin's letting you stick it to her."

Reece laughs. "Relax. I'll be gentle."

They laugh again, loud, careless, and cruel.

My vision goes blurry around the edges. The soda I drank swirls sick in my stomach. I feel as though I might throw up. Or scream before I shove both of them against the wall and rip them a new one. God help me, I am so goddamn tired of being someone's fucking game.

Something in me fractures and I step out of the shadows.

Their heads snap toward me, and for once, Reece seems not so sure of himself.

"Say it again," I spit, slamming a hand against his chest hard enough to shove him back until he hits the wall with a dull thud.

Reece's mouth curves, as though he received a present with a fuse. Jace pales as if he's seen a ghost.

"I heard you," I say, voice trembling but loud enough to leave a bruise. "Every. Fucking. Word."

Jace's hands lift in surrender. "I'm out," he mumbles, backing away, disappearing down the hallway without even pretending to defend himself.

Fucking coward.

Reece pushes off the wall and steps into my space.

"Do you always listen to other people's conversations?" he drawls, eyes glittering with something dark and unholy.

"You always bet on girls like we're scratch-and-win cards?" I snap back.

He shrugs, all smug. "People bet on sure things."

My laugh is sharp enough to slice open his ego. "I'm not a fucking thing to bet on, Reece."

"No," he says, eyes locked on mine. "Oh, but you are a challenge."

My smile is all teeth. "Then I hope you like losing, you fucking asshole."

I slam my shoulder into his chest, knocking him back hard enough to make a point. He stumbles—only half a step—but it's enough. I don't wait for him to find his balance, don't wait for the comeback already loading behind that smug mouth of his.

I turn, shove through the hallway as if I've got steel in my spine, not jelly for legs.

My boots hit the floor too loud, too fast, my pulse racing ahead of me as I charge toward the bathroom as if it's a finish line. I twist the handle, shove the door open, and slam it shut behind me. Lock it with fingers that won't stop shaking.

Now it's just me and the mirror and the girl I don't want to be.

Flushed cheeks. Red-rimmed eyes that don't dare spill. Lips pressed tight to hold in the scream clawing its way up my throat. I grip the sink so hard my knuckles blanch, breathe through my nose, trying to hold the fury in.

I will not cry. Not for him. Not here. Let them fuck themselves on their own egos. I'm done being the thing they pass between them like a dare.

A soft knock breaks the silence.

One tap. After that, I hear Lola's voice.

"Sam, are you in there? You've been gone for a while."

I don't answer. Simply twist the lock and pull the door open.

Lola's eyes skate over my face, before shifting to the way I'm gripping the doorframe. She doesn't speak right away, but her brows pinch together and her mouth pulls into a line she's biting down hard on.

"Did one of those bitches say something to you?"

"No," I mutter. "Let's go."

The second I step onto the porch, the cold air hits. It slaps the heat from my cheeks and makes everything inside me ache sharper. The night hums... music spilling out the front door behind us, voices raised in laughter that feels miles away from where I'm standing. The stars hang carelessly overhead, scattered like they don't give a shit about anything happening down here.

I keep walking. Fast. Focused. Trying not to fall apart.

Lola's boots scrape the gravel behind me. "Are you sure you're, okay?" she asks, racing to catch up. "I think Liz is about to lose it. She's barely said a word since we got into the car. I think we should take her to the Sugar Spoon. She doesn't want to go home yet."

I nod once, not trusting my voice.

Because going home...

That sounds worse than staying out. Going home means quiet. Means being alone with my thoughts and letting everything he said replay itself again and again until it buries me.

Ice cream at midnight with Liz and Lola doesn't fix what happened. But perhaps it's enough to halt the bleeding. For the time being.

The car door slams behind me, loud enough to rattle something loose in my chest. Liz starts the engine. Lola leans out the window and flips the house off without a word, her expression set in stone.

As we pull away, the glow of the porch lights disappears in the side mirror. The road ahead stretches out, lined with houses that blur past in silence.

The sound of Reece's voice claws at the back of my mind, twisting deeper with every mile. I can still hear the smug tilt of it, the way he said it as if I was a game he planned to win. The humiliation clings, now impossible to shake.

I turn my face to the window; forehead nearly pressed to the glass. Something shifted tonight. I sense it in my bones. In the hollow behind my ribs. Reece Wilson crossed a line, and I won't forget it.

He can rot in fucking hell.

I am done with him... completely.

I will not give him another second of my time, another ounce of attention. Not a single fucking inch. He can keep his smirks and bets and cheap arrogance for girls who mistake noise for confidence. I am not one of them. I never was.

He is a fuckboy who treats people as entertainment. I am not built that way. I'm someone who works for what I want. I earn it and don't play games with bodies or hearts simply for dominance.

And it hits me.

The assessment.

The one I am partnered with him on.

I let out a breath that tastes bitter.

Fucking perfect. Another thing I will have to endure with my head high and my temper locked down tight. I will survive it, though, because I will not sink to his level.

And if he so much as breathes the wrong way in my direction and fucks with my life... God help him, because I am done playing nice.

Chapter 4

REECE

There's a buzz crawling under my skin the moment she walks in, the kind that makes it hard to sit still. Chin held high. Shoulders back. That red skirt brushes her thighs with each step, riding just enough to make my teeth grit. I can't stop tracking the sway of her hips, the quiet confidence in how she owns the room without asking permission.

Fuck.

My body reacts before my brain catches up. My dick goes hard, standing to attention as if it thinks this is a game it wants in on. I shift in my chair, annoyed at myself for letting her do this to me without even trying.

She doesn't look at me. Not once. No glance, not even a flicker of irritation.

She walks straight past, eyes ahead, treating me as if I'm nothing more than a desk she has to work around.

That's the fucking part that gets under my skin.

I've made girls lose their shit over me. Cry in bathrooms. Blow up my phone. Show up places they weren't invited just to see if I'd notice them.

I know how to provoke, to push until they snap. But this... quiet dismissal or being stripped of my presence and reduced to nothing. It fucking burns.

I want her to be mad. I was counting on it, honestly. After what she overheard at that party—the crap Jace and I were saying—I expected fury. That quick flash in her eyes tells me I've got under her skin. I know how to handle anger. I thrive on it. Hate is easy. It shows she's paying attention and means I still matter enough to make her angry.

But this?

This calm indifference feels wrong.

She moves through the room as if she has already won, as if the power I believed I had over her has slipped away the moment she decided I wasn't worth the bother. There's no tension in her shoulders, no stiffness in her stance. She isn't braced for a fight. She isn't waiting for me to poke the wound again.

She's already moved on.

And that terrifies me more than her temper ever could.

My fingers curl around the edge of the desk, knuckles whitening as I hold on a second too long. The grin I wear for everyone else slides into place out of habit, but it doesn't sit right. It's hollow. As if it belongs to the version of me she refuses to see anymore. I'm not built for this waiting game. I don't chase reactions. I get them, provoke them. I own the fallout.

Lola drops into the seat beside her in a rush of movement and noise, already leaning in, already whispering before her bag even hits the floor. Sam tilts her head, enough to listen, lashes lowering, attention pulled somewhere that isn't me. Her mouth twitches, and my focus locks on it like a target.

I remember that mouth. That party all those years ago, and the way the world seemed to shrink to her standing in front of me. Kissing her cracked something open that night. It burned its way straight into my chest. It set a standard I never intended to keep chasing, but here I am.

I remember the feeling of her, the way she froze for half a second before kissing me back. No matter how many mouths I've had since, no matter how many chicks I've fucked, nothing ever hits the same.

She wasn't just my first kiss; she was the one who spoiled all the others.

She smiles at something Lola says, small, and private, and it shouldn't matter. It shouldn't hit this hard. But it does. Because that smile isn't for me. It's soft. Untouched. And the fact that she's giving it to someone else while pretending I don't exist makes my chest tighten in a way I don't recognize.

I act before I think, before I can stop myself.

I cut past her aisle, close enough that she should feel it.

She doesn't even acknowledge the space I steal as I pass her.

I stop and glance at the jackass slouched in the chair behind her. He's got his legs stretched out, tapping his pen on the desk as if he didn't unknowingly sign his own death warrant.

Five fucking seconds.

That's all I give him. My stare does the talking, the kind that promises violence without a word.

He lasts three.

He mutters something under his breath, scrambles out of the chair, grabs his bag and bails quickly. Smart fucking choice. I drop into the seat he vacated, spreading my legs and twisting my silver ring around my thumb, again and again, needing something to do with my hands. She's pulled her hair back today, and it annoys me more than it should. I miss the way it curls over her shoulders, soft and loose. I know it's stupid. It's borderline unhinged. But all I can think about is burying my hands in it, tangling my fingers until she has to tilt her head back for me. Finding out the sound she makes when I pull.

I lean forward regardless.

"Morning, sweetheart," I murmur, close enough that my chest brushes the back of her chair, so if I breathe in deep enough, I could work out what conditioner she uses.

She doesn't reply, and that silence hits harder than her anger ever did.

I know exactly why she's pissed. What she heard the other night, the laughing, the bet Jace and I never thought would reach her ears. That I would fuck her by the end of the year. Turn the good girl into a prized fuck, to prove a point, as if she was a challenge. A prize.

Now she treats me that way.

It hurts more than I'm happy to admit.

But I notice the way her shoulders stiffen slightly, and there it is. The crack. The proof she's still listening even when she pretends she isn't. I grin, because if ignoring me is her weapon, I've got no problem playing hardball.

I move my mouth closer to her ear.

"I'd die to get between those thighs," I say softly. Filthy. "Tell me you haven't imagined me there, my mouth on you where you pretend you don't want it."

Her breath catches. Just once.

Her thighs press together under the desk, muscles tightening, and I feel the shock of it running through me. That's what I needed. Proof I still affect her. That I'm not invisible.

I smirk and lean back in my seat, letting the chair creak enough to say I've finished crowding her space. For now.

My fingers stretch towards my notebook, and I tear out a sheet of paper.

I don't think. I write.

Messy black ink. Slanted. Rapid. The kind of handwriting that reveals just how wired I am.

You can sit there and pretend you're not doing dangerous things to me.

I'd ruin that skirt in under a minute if you let me, drag you onto my cock and make you forget why you're mad.

Tell me your body didn't give you away long before your mouth ever would.

I fold it once, then flick it forward with just enough force to make it arc over her shoulder and land right on her desk.

It slides to a halt, just inches from her hand.

She sees it. Her spine stiffens, shoulders tense, and her breath becomes shallow in a way she probably thinks no one notices. Her fingers remain perfectly still.

Beside us, Liz groans dramatically and mutters something about forgetting the stupid textbook again. Lola offers hers without missing a beat, already giggling as she scrolls through her phone, whispering about some TikTok she saw last night. In the corner, Aiden and Mason are mid-argument about last weekend's football match, voices overlapping, both convinced they're right.

The room hums with a dull, half-awake noise that settles in before a teacher arrives. Chairs scrape. Someone yawns too loudly. Pages flip without anyone actually reading. Everyone's here, bodies present, minds elsewhere. Distracted. Restless. Killing time.

No one's paying attention at all.

Except me.

I watch the paper sit there, untouched. Watch her pretend it doesn't exist the same way she's pretending I don't exist.

She's got my blood pumping, my pulse out of sync, my thoughts dirty and loud, and she's treating me like I'm nothing but dust on the floor. Something to step over.

I turn my ring around my thumb again, more slowly this time, eyes fixed on that folded piece of paper.

I tear another piece of paper from my notebook. This one isn't thought through. It doesn't get softened. It comes straight from the ugly, needy part of my mind that's sick of being ignored.

The pen scratches firmly against the paper.

> *Bet you taste better than you talk. I'll eat that pussy until you forget every lie you tell yourself about me. I promise I won't disappoint.*

It's cocky... just the sort of thing a good girl shouldn't want and definitely shouldn't be reading in a classroom.

I don't bother folding it. I lean forward and let it slip from my fingers, watching it fall onto her desk in plain sight.

That sparks a response.

Not from her hands. She still doesn't touch it. But her shoulders lock up, stiff as stone.

She reaches out and crushes the note in her fist. Doesn't even read it, just crumples it up then drops it onto the floor next to her desk, as if it is nothing.

I chuckle loudly and unapologetically. "That's the game you want to play, Red?"

She turns halfway in her seat towards me. Calm on the surface, but eyes sharp as hell. "Don't fucking talk to me."

Fuck me. That voice. I want to hear it crack on my name, breathless and shaking, cursing me while she's grinding down on my cock and hating herself for how good it feels. I want to show her exactly what being bad does to a girl who thinks she's above it all.

I smirk, recognising it now. The crack in her control.

"So what do you say, Red," I murmur, voice pitched low enough to crawl. "You want to sit on my face later and see where I can take you."

The words hang there. I'm already riding the hit, with the tension snapping tight between us.

And before I get to enjoy it—

She slaps me.

Hard.

Open palm.

Right across the face.

The sound cracks through the room.

My head snaps to the side, heat exploding across my cheek, skin burning as if she branded me. My pulse roars, blood rushing hot and fast, and for a split second, everything goes white.

Lola gasps loudly.

Mason lets out a laugh he tries and fails to hold back.

Someone swears under their breath.

I lean back slowly, my tongue pressing against the inside of my cheek.

I watch her turn back around in her seat, spine straight, chin lifted, as if she didn't just light me the fuck up in front of half the class.

"Jesus," Liz mutters. "You deserved that."

The slap still stings. My cheek throbs, heat radiating each time I move my jaw. But my smile remains. Crooked and dark, because her cold shoulder I can handle. But that slap... That's fucking foreplay.

Sam doesn't acknowledge me for the rest of the class, but she's tapping her pen hard enough to crack the table. Her leg won't stop bouncing.

She's not unaffected.

And that's the thrill I live for.

I spend the next forty minutes pretending I don't care, which is complete bullshit.

My knee won't stop bouncing, and no matter how hard I try to focus, my eyes keep drifting back to her. To the back of her neck. That pale strip of skin between her collar and her hairline feels obscene in how much it pulls at me. I keep imagining what it would be like to press my mouth there, to see if she gasps or if she breaks and lets out a quiet moan she can't stop.

Lola passes her a note, sliding it across the desk with a grin, and they snort quietly together. Lola leans in, whispering something under her breath that makes Sam smile.

Mrs. Whitman drones on about thesis statements and structure, her voice blending into background noise I can't latch onto.

Pens scratch. Pages flip. I don't write a single fucking word. My notebook stays blank, open to a clean page that mocks me every time I glance down.

Sam fills an entire page. She underlines something twice, pressing hard enough that the pen almost tears the paper. She cares about school. About things that don't include me, my mouth, my cock, or the mess I want to make of her.

Because while everyone else is half-asleep and checked out from hearing the teacher drone on, she's fully present.

The bell rings, and the room bursts into movement. Chairs scrape loudly as students jostle to get up. Bags zip shut. Voices rise sharply as everyone pushes towards the door. Sam is on her feet immediately, her bag already slung over her shoulder, moving with determination. Lola's at her side, Liz close behind, the three of them weaving through the crowd.

Behind me, Jace stands. "You done poking the bear or what?"

I look up at him. "She's not a bear."

He grins. "Sure. She's more dangerous."

I should laugh. Normally I would. This is the part where I'd toss something back, shrug it off, act like it's all good fun. But my eyes drift to the doorway where Sam disappeared.

Jace and I linger, watching the room empty around us.

Papers litter the floor. Mrs. Whitman's already gone, heels clicking down the hall.

Jace nudges my shoulder as we finally make our way to the door.

"You should pay up now," he says, smug as ever, that bullshit smirk glued on. "No way in hell you're fucking that wildcat."

I meet his gaze.

"Just watch me," I say. "I'll get there."

"You're serious," he snorts.

"Dead serious. Have you ever known me to fail?"

Jace eyes me for a second; his grin fades slightly before it snaps back into place.

"There's a first time for everything," he says.

The next day at school drags on. Midday classes are already boring as hell, the kind that drain your energy before lunch even hits. Teachers talk. Pens scratch away. The clock hangs there, unmoving, as if it's got a personal grudge against everyone stuck in the room.

Jace and I skip the next lesson silently, exchanging just a look that says enough.

We cut across the oval and duck behind the old sheds where no one ever bothers to check. It's our spot. Out of sight. Out of mind.

We smoke. We talk. Sometimes we just let the silence do the talking.

Not many people know much about Jace and me.

We keep our lives quiet on purpose. Smart mouths. Careless grins. Jokes sharp enough to slice through anything real before it gets too close. It's easier when people think they've got you figured out. Easier when they stop digging, stop asking, stop noticing the cracks.

Noah knows some of it. Enough to understand why Jace and I behave the way we do. Why we don't trust so easily. But he doesn't know the whole story. He goes home to Ken, to a place that feels secure, to a dad who genuinely cares and shows it every day. Food on the table. Stability. Someone who shows up. Noah has a version of life where adults don't let you down over and over.

Jace and I don't have that.

Jace knows my shit because I know his. We don't sugarcoat it. We exchange truths the same way we pass joints, no judgment, no pity. Just understanding. That kind that comes from surviving similar messes.

He lives in an old trailer dumped out the back of his aunt's place, rusted and cramped and barely holding together. She's the type who smiles sweetly in public, all generous and selfless, telling anyone who'll listen how she took him in. Behind closed doors, she's a real cunt. Cuts him down every chance she gets. Reminds him he's unwanted. Ensures he knows he's a burden she never asked for.

Same story, different packaging.

People reckon she's a saint. Jace knows the truth.

My old man is a prick in a subtle way. Not loud about it. Not obvious. The kind you don't notice from the outside unless you know where to look.

He sort of gives a shit. There's always food in the house. Cans in the cupboard, something frozen if you're desperate. The lights stay on. Rent gets paid. He heads to work every morning without fail, steel-toed boots by the door, lunch packed, routine locked in. On paper, he does what he's supposed to. The basics. The bare minimum that lets people say he tried.

But he'd rather drink himself numb than build a relationship with his son. Always has. The bottle takes what I don't—his patience, his attention, any warmth he might have had to give. By the time he gets home, he's already halfway gone, eyes dull, voice short, shutting the world out one drink at a time.

It's been that way for as long as I can remember.

I don't even know what happened to my mum. I don't remember her. Not her face. Not her voice. Nothing tangible. Just a blank space where something important should be, a hole you don't notice until you hit it. He never talks about her. Not once. Not a name. Not a memory. And I learned early that curiosity wasn't welcome.

I remember being a little kid, standing in the kitchen, asking where she was. Just a kid wanting an answer, nothing more. The room turned cold. His face flushed red. The smell of alcohol hit me before the yelling did. He grabbed me by the collar and threw me onto the floor so hard I couldn't catch my breath.

Told me to shut the fuck up.

So I did.

I learned quickly. Realized that some questions aren't worth the pain they cause. That silence keeps you safer than curiosity ever could.

When the bell finally sounds, we head back up to the cafeteria, smoke still clinging to our clothes, heads a little quieter than before.

The halls are already loud—lockers slamming, voices bouncing off the walls, everyone spilling out all at once.

We calmly make our way through everything and head to our usual table.

Noah's already there with Aubrey and the rest of the girls, bags dropped, laughter easy and familiar.

This is the part that fucks with me more than it ever should.

This is why Sam now runs deeper under my skin than she ever did before. Being so close to her is a problem I didn't see coming.

Back when we sat at our old table, watching the hierarchy unfold each day, she was distant. A flash of red hair in the hallway. A presence I noticed without meaning to. Even though I always had a thing for her, it was manageable. I could look, file it away, lose myself in someone else, and forget about it by the end of the day.

Distance made it easier. Now there is no fucking distance.

She's right there. Across the table. Close enough that when she leans forward, I catch the faint scent of her shampoo. Close enough to hear her laugh. It does something to me every time. Tightens something in my chest I can't quite name.

It's changed now. And it's worse.

I can't pretend she's just a passing thought when she's sitting five feet away, when her knee bumps into mine under the table. I can't bury it because there's nowhere to fucking hide from it.

That's how it is for me right now.

Sometimes I miss our old table because of this constant pull, but when I look up and see Tia and Nicole holding court, asserting their fake dominance with smiles and whispered poison, the nostalgia quickly fades. The drama of it all is draining. I wish the two bitches would have a proper fight and finally end it. See who comes out on top and save us from this never-ending circus.

Jace often tells me that they should get down into their bras and panties and let the crowd decide.

I always find that funny because even if one of them lost, it wouldn't change a thing. The loser would still have a fucking problem. Still be jealous that the other has a leaner body, better hair, more attention. Some petty, warped shit that never actually goes away. There's always something else to compete over, some new angle to twist it into. That's just how it is.

Jace sits down, eyes already drifting to Lola's lunch bag. He squints at it, then at her. "What'd you bring today?" he asks, tone casual.

Lola rolls her eyes, but a smile teases her lips as she scavenges around. "Why do you always want my food?"

"Because you always have better food," he says easily. "And because I didn't eat breakfast."

"That sounds like a you problem." She pushes the container towards him. "Pasta salad. Homemade. Don't get excited."

He leans closer peering in. "Looks good."

She laughs. "Because it is. Now, are you going to try it or just stare at it all day?"

"Fuck yes," he says instantly.

She hands him her plastic fork. "If you complain, you're cut off."

Jace takes a mouthful, chews slowly, then looks up at Lola with that crooked smile he only ever wears around her. The one that doesn't try too hard.

"It's actually good," he says, like that surprises him.

"Told you," Lola says, snatching back the fork.

The rest of us watch them, with that mixture of curiosity and amusement, as if they're witnessing something they don't fully grasp.

I hardly notice any of it.

My attention never leaves Red.

She's sitting there pretending the room is more interesting, eyes drifting everywhere except where I am. She'd prefer to watch the doors. The windows. The clock. Anything but me.

I lean back in my chair, eyes fixed on her unapologetically.

She knows I'm watching. I can tell by the way her shoulders tense just a little.

Noah squints at us from across the table, brows pulled together. "Where were you two? Whitman was doing that head tilt thing she does when she's pissed."

Jace doesn't even look up. He takes another mouthful of pasta, chewing slowly. "We skipped."

"The period would have been boring as shit. It usually is," I say.

The moment the words leave my mouth, I feel it.

The stern look Red gives me is both furious and fucking beautiful at once. The kind of anger that sharpens her features instead of softening them.

I know exactly why it hit a nerve.

Sam is all about school. Grades. Futures. Structure. She believes in earning her way out of this place. Skipping classes is everything she hates. Careless. Wasteful. Proof that some of us don't give a shit about the things she works so hard for.

Jace reaches across the table and yanks the fork straight out of Lola's hand.

"Hey," she snaps. "What the fuck?"

"You're taking too long," he says, already stabbing another bite.

"That's my food."

"You offered."

"One bite."

He grins. "I'm on my third. Deal with it."

She lunges for the fork, misses, then scowls at him. "You're such an asshole."

"You love it."

She scoffs, shaking her head and muttering something under her breath about putting poison in the next thing she brings to school, but she's smiling despite herself.

Sam doesn't look at me again.

Not once. She laughs with Lola, talks to Noah, and it eats away at me.

Every second she pretends I don't exist, it digs deeper, clawing under my skin in a way I can't shake.

Fuck, I'd even take another slap if it meant she'd acknowledge me.

By the time the bell rings for the day, I'm more than ready to get the hell out of here. My patience has run out. My head is pounding. Everything feels tight in my chest, in a way I don't want to unpack.

I'm leaning against the lockers, waiting for Jace to grab his shit. I have no idea what the fuck he's doing in there when he hasn't pulled a single book out of his bag all day. He's rummaging around like he's lost something important, which is bullshit because nothing in that locker has ever been important.

I scroll through my phone, not really reading anything, just passing the time.

I feel it.

That shift. That awareness that doesn't come from sound or sight. Pure instinct. The air changes. My spine straightens before my brain catches up.

Red.

I lift my head as she approaches, clutching her books close to her chest like armor. Her eyes lock onto mine, sharp and furious, with no softness in them.

She stops right in front of me, close enough to see the tension in her jaw and the faint flush high on her cheekbones.

No hello, how are you? Just coldness.

"We need to work on the assessment," she says, flat and clipped. All businesslike. "I don't care about you, and I wish I didn't have to work with you at all. But I care about my grade. So this is happening whether either of us likes it or not."

Each word lands clean and precise, like she's rehearsed it.

I shrug, relaxed on the outside even though I'm watching her too intently. "You worry too much."

Her eyes flash. "I am not failing because you think school is a joke."

I tilt my head, take my time examining her. The tight grip on her books. The way her shoulders are squared, ready for a fight. "You really care about this."

"Yes."

No hesitation. Only the truth. It catches me off guard more than it ought to.

"Fine," I say finally. "We'll work on it."

The relief flashes across her face before she can stop it.

"When?" she asks.

I shrug again. "I don't know."

"Oh my god, you are so frustrating."

I smirk. "Tomorrow afternoon. But you'll need to come to my house."

The words barely leave my mouth before she stiffens.

"I am not going to your house."

I smirk, knowing this is the moment it clicks for her that I'm not giving an inch. "Then I guess we fail."

Her glare could cut glass. She hates that I've cornered her with the one thing she can't walk away from.

And that only makes it sweeter.

She lingers there for a moment longer, jaw clenched, eyes burning into my face before spinning on her heel and storming down the hall. Red hair swinging as she leaves.

A gentle sense of satisfaction settles in my chest as her boots echo down the hallway.

"Did she say yes?" Jace asks, slamming his locker shut as if he actually pulled something useful out of it. Which he didn't. He never does.

I push off the locker and roll my shoulders. "She didn't say no."

Jace snorts. "That's not the win you think it is."

My eyes remain fixed on the end of the hall where she vanished.

"She'll come," I say finally. "She wants that grade more than she wants to hate me."

CHAPTER 5

SAM

I fucking hate that I have to go to his house.

The sun hangs low, burning gold against the rooftops as I walk the cracked pavement, my backpack digging into one shoulder. Every house I pass looks the same kind of perfect. Trim lawns. White fences. Garden gnomes smile as if they know nothing bad ever happens here. Wind chimes softly tinkle, the kind that sound as if fairies really live behind those front doors.

Reece lives at the end of the cul-de-sac, where the road curves and rules no longer seem to matter. His house feels isolated from the rest of the neighborhood, as if it never truly belonged here.

The front yard is cluttered. Overgrown grass blocks the path to the door, weeds scraping at my ankles as I walk closer. An old couch sits half-buried in the dirt next to a torn-apart engine block that looks abandoned. Rusted tools are scattered in a milk crate on the steps. I wonder if he's the one who works on it. If those hands that scribble dirty notes know how to fix things or if they only know how to take them apart piece by piece.

That makes sense. It has a poetic quality, in a way.

Reece is good at breaking shit. The rules, people, anything that gets too close.

And me most of all.

I stop at the bottom of the steps, irritation creeping under my skin because I hate how he dragged me here. I hate how my grades matter more than my pride.

I stare at the door a moment longer than I should, my heart pounding in my chest. I take a deep breath and knock before I can chicken out.

If he pulls another stunt like he did in class with those filthy words and notes, I swear to God I'll lose my shit. Completely. No filter. No restraint. I'll tell him exactly where he can shove his mouth, his cock, and every smug little thought in his head.

Even if reading them made my thighs tighten under the desk.

Even if my body betrayed me in ways, I'm still pissed off about it.

I still remember every word. Every promise, as if he already had me spread out beneath him. As if he knew exactly how I would sound when I stopped pretending I hated him.

And the worst part is that he meant them.

I clutch the strap of my bag, trying to stay grounded. I am not here for Reece. I am not here for his smart mouth, his hands, or the way he looks at me as if I am something he intends to take his time with.

I'm here for the assessment. That's all. Because I'm not that girl. And he's not the kind of guy you survive.

The door swings open, and I immediately regret every decision that brought me here.

He's shirtless. Of course he is.

It feels intentional. Calculated. Like he knew exactly how much this would mess with me and twisted the knife before I even stepped inside. His jeans sit low on his hips, worn and loose, with the waistband cutting a sharp line across skin I absolutely shouldn't be staring at.

A new scar cuts across his ribcage, angry and pink, as if it's fresh. His hair is wet, with darker curls than usual, water still clinging to the ends.

The faint smell of soap drifts toward me, and my stomach flips in a way I refuse to admit.

His eyes flick to mine, slow and assessing.

His mouth twitches, just slightly. He knows exactly what he looks like and how it's affecting me.

I hate how my body responds before my brain can catch up.

"Sam," he drawls, voice low, filled with that cocky confidence. "You showed."

There it is. That tone. The smug satisfaction that shows he never doubted I would.

I straighten my spine, lift my chin, and refuse to give him anything more. I am not here for this. Not for his chest, the scar. Not for the way his eyes scan over me as if he's undressing me in his mind.

I grit my teeth. "Put on a shirt."

I push past him and into the house because it's the only thing I can still control. If I stop moving, if I hesitate, I'll bolt. Or worse, I'll stand there staring at his chest and that scar and forget why I came at all.

The door closes behind me with a dull thud.

Inside smells harsh. Smoke. Sweat. Old energy drinks gone stale. The old heat trapped in walls that have seen too much and been cleaned too little. Something hums faintly nearby, a low electrical buzz that crawls under my skin. The carpet beneath my shoes is worn thin and frayed, fibers flattened by too many footsteps and too little care.

This place feels tired.

I follow him down the narrow hallway, keeping my eyes forward even though every instinct tells me to watch his back, his shoulders, the way he moves with that lazy confidence that never quite slips.

We pass a cracked mirror hanging crooked on the wall. I catch my reflection for a moment and see the cracks beginning to surface.

Then we get to his room, and chaos doesn't even begin to describe it.

Dirty laundry is strewn across the floor in careless piles. A mattress sits directly on the ground instead of a bedframe, with sheets twisted and half hanging off the sides. A football is wedged near the corner as if it was dropped and never picked up again. I know he played back in the day. He was good too. I remember watching him. But chasing girls to score seems more his sport now.

There's a guitar in the corner missing two strings, neglected but not forgotten. A pack of cigarettes sits on top of a speaker, crushed and half empty.

The desk is a mess of crumpled paper, scattered everywhere as if he tried to write something and got pissed when it wouldn't come out right. Pens tossed aside. Ink smudges on the surface.

I glance at the crumpled notes before I can stop myself.

I wonder if they're just more of the same crap he handed me in class. Filthy. Provocative. Built to get under someone's skin and stay there. The thought makes heat crawl up my neck even as I scowl.

This room makes sense in a way I dislike.

Messy, angry, half-finished.

Just like him.

"Are you coming in or just judging from the doorway?"

His voice drifts over my shoulder. I step inside without answering, because engaging him on his terms is a mistake. I drop my bag to the floor and pull out my notes, stacking them neatly on my lap as if order might keep him from getting into my head.

"I don't have time to waste," I say. "So keep your comments to yourself."

"Relax," he says. "I haven't even said anything yet."

"Good. Keep it that way."

He grabs a hoodie off the bed and pulls it on, as if he's doing me a favor and knows exactly how much I hate that he gets under my skin without even trying.

We sit on the floor, knees spaced carefully apart. Just worn carpet beneath us and the scent of his cologne cutting through.

"Don't fuck this up," I say, meeting his eyes. "This is worth almost half our final grade."

"I got it."

"No," I say flatly. "You don't. You don't care about any of this."

He shrugs easily, unbothered. "Maybe I care about some things."

"Not school."

His eyes lock onto mine. "You care enough for both of us."

The audacity of it makes my jaw tighten. "Don't flatter yourself."

He leans back on his elbows, stretching out with a relaxed posture, watching me as I pull my laptop from my bag and place it between us. I sense his eyes on me, following every movement of my hands.

"Are you always this angry?" he asks. "Or is it just me?"

"It's you," I say without hesitation.

The corner of his mouth lifts, and the fact that he's smirking like he enjoys that answer just makes me more pissed off. Because even sitting here, surrounded by his mess and trying to focus on what truly matters, I'm painfully aware of how close he is. Of how easily this could go wrong. Of how much I want to prove I'm immune to him.

I open my laptop and remind myself that this is just work.

I repeat it to myself even as his gaze burns into my skin, and I know deep down that nothing about this will stay simple for long.

I don't allow myself to look at him. I keep my eyes trained on my notes, the screen, or anything that isn't his mouth, his hands, or the way he fills the room effortlessly.

Because if he wasn't who he was, this arrogant, reckless fuck boy who thinks he can coast through life on a smile and a reputation, maybe I could like him.

But he is who he is.

And I won't like him. Not now. Not ever.

"You can't just wing this," I snap, fingers moving as I pull up my outline. My voice is tight, clipped, already exhausted. "There's a structure. If we don't hit the criteria, it doesn't matter how smart the content is."

Reece leans back on his elbows, his long legs stretched out with boots still on the carpet, as if my grade isn't on the line. "You worry too much."

"I am not failing," I shoot back, heat rising fast, "because you think school is optional."

That does it.

He quickly sits up in one smooth motion, the laziness vanishing instantly. His eyes narrow, and his posture shifts to something alert. Dangerous. "You think I'm stupid."

The room becomes silent in a tense way that makes my skin prickle.

"I think you don't care," I shoot back, the words sharp enough to cut. "There's a difference."

He lets out a laugh. "You sure about that?"

"Yes."

He leans forward, forearms resting on his knees, bringing himself closer without actually touching me. His gaze remains fixed. It's steady. Too steady. The kind that makes you feel seen in ways you didn't agree to. "You wouldn't be here if you didn't think I could do this."

"I'm here," I snap, "because I don't trust you not to mess it up."

His mouth curves slowly. "Same thing."

"No."

We glare at each other, the air thick with it. Heat buzzing in the small room, tension snapping tight between us. His music plays from a speaker in the corner, the bass vibrating through the floor and into my bones. I force my focus back to my screen: bullet points, sources, headings. Anything that isn't his eyes or the way he's angled toward me like a challenge.

He moves closer. Not touching. Not yet. Just close enough to invade my space, close enough that I can sense his presence pressing in on all sides. I can smell him—soap, smoke, and something darker underneath.

"Are you always this intense?" he asks.

"Only when it matters."

"And this matters."

I ignore him and start explaining the thesis again because talking feels safer than thinking. I point at the screen. I speak quickly, loudly. I talk because if I stop for even a second, I'll notice that his attention isn't on the work but on me. On my mouth. On how my hands move when I get worked up.

"Here," I say, jabbing the trackpad harder than needed. "We split the sections. I'll handle the analysis. You do the case study."

He hums. "Bossy."

"Competent."

He laughs quietly, a sound that lingers in my chest whether I want it to or not. "Same thing."

I keep my eyes on the screen because I refuse to look at him. Refuse to give him anything.

Then he fucking shifts.

This time, his thigh presses against mine. It's solid, warm, and way too close. It's not an accident, and we both know it. My sentence stumbles halfway through a word, and I hate myself for it and how my body reacts faster than my pride.

"Sorry," he says, voice smooth and unrepentant. He remains still. "Is that better?"

"No."

"Tell me to move."

My throat tightens. I swallow. "Move."

He doesn't.

Instead, he leans over my shoulder, bracing one hand on the floor on the other side of me, trapping me. His chest brushes against my arm. Heat seeps through the thin fabric of my shirt. His breath ghosts my neck, and I freeze, every nerve firing at once.

"Relax," he murmurs, close enough that his voice slips over my skin. "I'm just looking."

Bullshit.

His fingers catch the end of my hair where it curls over my shoulder. He twirls it once, casually in a manner that feels dangerous. As if he doesn't realize he's doing it.

My pulse kicks hard. Loud and embarrassing.

I suddenly become very aware of the space between us and how it's not enough. I notice my own breathing, how badly I want to push him away, and how much worse it would feel if he pulled back on his own.

I push myself to keep talking, even though my voice sounds weaker now. "You need to focus. This isn't a joke."

His mouth moves closer to my ear. "Neither is this."

I close my eyes for a moment and hate him for noticing everything.

I open my eyes again, determined to put an end to this.

"Don't," I say.

He doesn't move or pull away. His fingers remain tangled in my hair. "Don't what?"

My voice sounds thinner this time. "Touch me."

"Do you always get this tense?" he asks, fingers still touching my hair.

I lurch forward, tearing free of him so quickly I lose my balance. My cheeks flush, heat spreading across my face. "What is wrong with you?"

"Plenty." He grins

"I am serious," I snap. "You don't get to do that."

"Do what?"

"That." I gesture wildly in the space between us, hands shaking despite my best effort to steady them. "Do not invade my space. Play with my hair. Act like this is some kind of game."

Something in his expression shifts. The grin fades, not completely, but enough. His eyes darken, sharpen.

"You're the one who came to my house," he says.

"For school."

"Sure."

"I mean it," I say, firmer now. "This isn't whatever bullshit you think it is."

He watches me for a long second without speaking. The room appears smaller. Quieter. Even the hum of the speaker seems to fade, leaving nothing but the sound of my own breathing.

"You're shaking," he says finally.

"I'm not."

"You are."

I press my palms flat against my thighs, trying to stop the tremor. Or at least I try to. "Let's get back to the assignment."

He doesn't reply right away. Instead, his gaze stays fixed on mine, as if he's trying to peel me apart layer by layer and figure out where I'll crack. I hold his stare even though every instinct tells me to look away.

I guess he's not used to a girl saying no to him.

Most girls allow him to invade their space and touch them as if resistance is just part of the dance.

But I don't soften.

I don't back down.

And I see it land.

Something flickers in his eyes, then he leans back, creating distance between us.

"Fine," he says. "Professor Carter. What's next?"

The tension doesn't go away. It just lingers.

I exhale slowly and force my shoulders to drop.

We work this time. No baiting or touching. No crowding my space.

And annoyingly, he actually listens.

He asks questions. Genuine ones. Even pushes back on a few points in ways that make sense, not just to be difficult. He challenges my logic, and I have to pause, reread, then grudgingly admit he's right. I hate that he's smarter than he pretends to be and prefers to hide it behind jokes, arrogance, and that reckless grin.

Time passes by without me noticing.

My phone buzzes on the carpet as I glance down.

Lola: Are you alive? Blink twice if you need rescuing.

I snort before I can stop myself and turn the screen black.

Reece catches it, of course he does; he sees everything. "Your friends worried?"

"They know you're a problem."

His mouth curves, as if he's pleased with my answer. "Smart girls."

We finish outlining the sections, the core structure laid out clearly. I close my laptop and slide it back into my bag, my heart still pounding for reasons that have nothing to do with deadlines or grades. I fucking hate this.

"I'll send you the outline tonight," I say, standing. "You need to actually do the work."

"I will." No sarcasm or smirk. Just a promise.

That bothers me more than the teasing ever did.

I swing my bag over my shoulder and turn for the door, already halfway gone in my head.

"Sam."

I stop with my back to him, fingers gripping the strap until it cuts into my palm. I do not turn. I will not give him anything.

He walks around until he's standing in front of me, close enough that I have to lift my chin to look up at him. I notice his eyes drop to my lips. The way he focuses on them feels intimate, even though I didn't agree to it.

"No goodbye?" he says. "You just walk out?"

My thoughts scatter. I hate how easily he can do that.

I meet his gaze directly. "Move."

His mouth curves into a smirk, and I know without a doubt he's enjoying this.

For a heartbeat, I think he won't move, that he'll keep pushing, testing that line again.

But he steps back, giving me space to leave before I do something stupid. Before I stay... or worse, soften.

Sleep refuses to arrive. The room is dark and quiet, but my mind is anything but. Every time I close my eyes, I'm immediately back there. On his floor. In his space. Too close. Too aware.

My mind keeps replaying everything I don't want it to.

The heat of his thigh pressed against mine, grounding in a way that felt wrong to notice. The weight of his presence at my back, close enough that I could feel him without touching. His fingers twisting in my hair as if they belonged there, as if my body had already agreed to something my brain was still fighting. His breath brushing my neck, soft and infuriating, sending my pulse into chaos like it didn't know how to behave around him.

I stare at the ceiling and swallow hard.

I hate that it stays with me. That it followed me home, crawled under my skin, and now refuses to come off. I dislike that my body remembers it so vividly, as if it's recorded every moment and won't let it fade.

And I hate myself the most for the thoughts I can't turn off, for wondering what would happen if I stopped fighting them.

CHAPTER 6

REECE

The moment she steps through the school gates, I'm already tuned in.

She's wearing that red skirt again. The one that flares when she walks, the one that should be harmless but isn't. My fists clench because I know she doesn't mean to fuck with me, which only makes it worse. But, fuck, it does something to me.

I watch her, books hugged tight to her chest, held there ready to raise if anyone gets too close. Her red hair pulled back in a ponytail, soft as sin. I know it fucking is, because I touched it yesterday. I couldn't help myself. Those red locks were a temptation I didn't try to fight. I just had to touch them. I can still feel them sliding through my fingers, still remember how my chest tightened when she froze under my hand.

Sam Carter is sunshine and sweet-girl energy with teeth. All control, hiding beneath flawless skin. Every glare she throws my way sinks into me and stays there. My blood runs hotter when she's near. My heart kicks into overdrive. My dick gets harder too, no matter how much I tell myself to rein it in.

Fuck, what I would do to her if she ever gave me the chance.

Never has a girl had my head this twisted. Never have my thoughts been this locked on to one chick. I'm supposed to be wired for chaos, for easy distractions, for moving on. Instead, I'm stuck walking around half feral, dick hard, ready to rub one out the second she crosses my line of sight.

She hates me. I can see that every time she looks through me instead of at me.

She's the one thing I shouldn't want and can't stop fucking wanting, anyway.

She pretends she didn't feel what happened yesterday in my room. The way she burned under my hands. The way she melted and then ran.

Her pulse fluttered under my touch. Her breath hitched when my thigh brushed hers. She wanted to pull away but didn't. Not right away.

And it's been fucking with me ever since.

She disappears into the building, and I don't even hesitate.

I pass Jace the blunt we're sharing, fingers brushing his as I shove it into his hand, already pushing off the wall. He calls after me, some smart-ass comment I don't bother catching, because my focus is already locked in one direction.

Her.

I have her schedule memorized. Better than I should. English. Bottom floor. Same room every Wednesday morning. No one hangs around down there this early before first period.

But I know Sam.

She always goes early. She gets there before the noise, before the chaos, before anyone can distract her. She sits, opens her bag, lines her shit up neatly, and gets organized as if the world won't fall apart if she's prepared enough.

Her head is down. She has no idea I am behind her.

I slow my steps and let my eyes do what they want. They wander freely. Those long, fucking legs built to wrap around me if she ever stopped pretending she didn't want to. I imagine it without asking. Her ankles crossed behind my back. My hands sliding over the skin she keeps hidden.

She pauses, thumb flicking over her phone screen to check something. It gives me the chance to close the gap.

There's no one else down here yet. Just the hum of the lights and the quiet she always seeks.

I move up slowly, hands shoved deep in my pockets so I don't give in to the urge to touch her—to grab her waist and see how real this pull is up close.

I stop right behind her. Close enough, but not touching.

"Morning, Saint," I murmur in her ear.

She stiffens immediately.

But her breathing shifts. I notice it in how her back rises and falls, sharper now, less controlled.

She turns slowly, as if she's forcing herself to do it, like she thinks it's a bad idea and can't help herself anyway.

Her eyes flash. "Don't call me that."

"Why not?" I lean in just enough to feel her heat, my gaze dropping to her mouth because I can't help myself. Because I want it turned on by me instead of against me. "It suits you."

I move closer to her, allowing her to sense it before she realizes she's running out of space.

She unintentionally backs up.

One step.

Then another.

Her shoulder hits metal.

Her books slip from her hands and scatter across the floor, pages splaying open as if they're as shocked as she is. She gasps sharply, and I move with her, shifting just enough so my palm rests against the locker beside her head.

She's pinned now, caged in by steel and my body, close enough that I can feel the heat radiating off her. See the pulse throbbing in her neck.

"Move," she hisses.

I don't.

One step closer, and I'd be pressed against her. She's aware of it too. I see it in her eyes, that storm brewing behind her perfect lashes.

"You know, if you weren't such a fucking saint," I murmur. "I'd have my fingers down your panties right now. Pressed up against your locker while I made you come so hard you'd forget what subject you had next."

Her breath falters. It hits my chest. Her pupils dilate wide. Her lips part, caught off guard. And fuck. My cock presses against the front of my jeans as if it's desperate to get closer to her.

I'm hard and drowning in her. The flushed anger on her cheeks, the wild heat in her eyes. She looks like she wants to slap me and kiss me at the same time. And I'd let her. I'd take both.

"You're disgusting," she spits, but her voice trembles at the edges, and it comes out more breath than bite.

I lean in, letting my nose brush against her cheek, just enough to see her shiver. My breath ghosts soft over her skin, and she jerks beneath it, her chest rising fast. I don't even need to glance down to know her nipples are hard beneath that shirt. She's fighting it. Resisting me. But her body's already made its choice.

God, she's stunning. The kind that burns you when you get too close. The kind that fucks with your head and ruins every girl who came before.

"You hate me," I murmur. "But your body doesn't."

Her chest rises again, sharp and shallow. One step closer and I'd feel the press of her tits against me. One more filthy word and I bet she'd either melt against my mouth or slap me again. And fuck, I want her mad. I want her feral. I want her so far gone she forgets why she ever wanted to hate me.

She moves before I can react, and her hand snaps up.

Crack.

Her palm strikes my cheek, snapping my head to the side. Heat rushes through my skin, sharp pain. My jaw aches, but my arousal remains firm. I don't bother hiding the smile curling at my lips.

She glares at me, fury burning across her face. Her chest rises and falls; her lips are parted perfectly. Those eyes flash with something fierce and unspoken.

She looks at me as if she wished it had left a scar.

And, fuck, part of me wishes it did too. Because then maybe I'd stop coming back for more.

"You do that again, I swear to God—"

"You'll what?" I turn my face back to her with a grin that's full of defiance. "Slap me harder?"

She doesn't answer. Just ducks under my arm, quickly gathering her books from the floor with trembling hands. Her face is flushed, mouth pressed into a thin line, fury radiating off her in waves. She doesn't say another word, simply rushes into the classroom before I can get another breath in.

I stay frozen for a beat, hand braced on the locker, cheek still stinging from the hit. And I grin because she'll never forget that moment.

And neither will I.

The sting doesn't fade. It stays on my skin. I touch it, feeling the throb beneath the surface. The kind of pain that reminds you that you're alive.

Pain has never scared me. Not when it's wrapped in flushed cheeks and trembling hands. Not when it's delivered by a girl who looked me in the eye and meant it. The beautiful that burns.

She didn't slap me because she hated it.

She hit me because she sensed it and was unsure how to handle everything passing between us in a moment. Her breath on my skin, the spark in her spine when I leaned in and said what I said.

She's fierce under pressure. The girl who'd rather draw blood than admit she wants me.

But I felt it in the shake of her hand after she hit me and the heat still rolling off her skin.

That's the part that'll haunt her.

The breath she gave me. It was the look in her eyes that drew attention. The stutter in her chest when I told her what I'd do if she weren't such a fucking saint.

It'll keep running through her mind for days.

I hear footsteps and turn my head, seeing Lola and Aubrey walking down the hall. They say nothing to me; they already know who and what I am. What I do when I get bored.

I slide my hands back into my pockets and walk toward them, shoulders relaxed, heart still racing as if it's caught in her orbit.

I head down the hallway, looking for noise, distraction, something easy. Maybe to find Jace or some girl who will give me that look that says she wants to be fucked and won't expect more afterward.

Either option works. I'm not picky.

I notice how Aubrey glances at me as I pass. The way Lola nudges her, both of them sharp-eyed, reading me in a way that irritates me.

They know exactly what the fuck I'm doing down here.

It all relates to Sam.

And no matter who I find next, no matter whose lips are on me, whose nails dig into my shoulders, whose moans fill the silence—

I'll be thinking of Sam's name when I come.

The face I see when I close my eyes.

The reason I grip harder, fuck deeper, chasing something that only she could ever give me.

CHAPTER 7

SAM

I practically throw myself into the classroom as if the hall is on fire.

"I hate him," I mutter as I step inside, the words struggling out of my throat. I slump into my chair and shove my bag onto the floor with more force than needed. I toss my books onto the desk, still haunted by him. His cock pressed where it shouldn't be, that filthy mouth brushing my ear, his voice low, smug, and intimate in a way that makes my stomach flip.

And God, that fucking smirk. The one that dared me to react.

My fingers curl into fists. I can't slow my heartbeat. My skin still pulses where he touched me, and where he didn't even have to touch me to ruin me. God, I should've slapped him harder. Made it sting longer and wiped that look off his face for good.

Aubrey and Lola walk in a second later, laughing about something that dies the instant they see me.

Both of them zero in, concern snapping into place. They cross the room fast, chairs scraping as they pull closer.

"Are you okay?" Aubrey asks, eyes searching my face. "You look—"

"I swear to God," I cut in, my voice shaking with rage I can barely contain, "if Reece Wilson comes near me again, I'll rip his fucking dick off."

That instantly grabs Lola's attention.

"Whoa." She leans forward, resting her elbows on the desk. "Okay. What happened?"

I run my hand along my ponytail and stare down at the scarred surface of my desk because if I glance up, I might actually scream.

Or cry.

Or do something worse.

"What didn't?" I mutter, dragging my bag onto my lap and digging through it as if I've actually forgotten something important. I haven't. I just need to keep my hands busy before I lose my shit. "He fucking pinned me against those lockers out there."

My fingers close around a notebook, but I don't pull it out right away. My chest tightens, heat rushing up my neck as the memory floods back in full color.

"And he..." I trail off, swallowing hard. "He said shit. Filthy, disgusting shit, right in my fucking ear."

"He, what?" Aubrey says, her whole body tensing up.

I yank the notebook free and slam it down on the desk harder than needed.

"He just stood there," I snap. "Boxed me in and let me feel him." My voice drops. "With his cock pressed against me, like he wanted me to feel it." I clench my jaw. "And I did. Trust me, I did."

"Oh my God," Lola breathes, eyes going wide. "Was it... you know, big?"

"Lola." I shoot her a glare.

"What?" Lola shrugs, completely unapologetic, lifting one shoulder as if we're talking about the weather. "Just asking. It's Reece."

"Exactly." I snap the word like it's a weapon. "Reece. Fuck boy of the century." My hands curl into fists on the desk, nails biting into my palms. "I swear that boy lives to piss me off. That's his entire personality. He doesn't give a shit about school, or rules, or consequences. He only cares for whatever girl is stupid enough to fall for his bullshit."

Lola opens her mouth, likely to argue, but Aubrey beats her to it.

"You better be careful, Sam," she says softly, before exhaling slowly, like she does when she's choosing her words carefully. "Guys like him don't just mess around. He'll ruin you if you let him."

The words hit harder than I expect. My spine straightens, anger flaring hot and fast. "I'm not letting him ruin anything."

Aubrey raises an eyebrow, unimpressed. "You sure about that? Because for someone who's supposedly not interested, you're giving off major I've-thought-about-him-naked energy right now."

My mouth opens automatically. "I haven't—"

The lie dies in my throat.

"Okay. Maybe once." I swallow hard. "In the dark. When I couldn't sleep. But I was stressed. And it didn't count."

Lola's lips twitch.

Aubrey just stares at me.

"Stressed," Lola repeats.

"Yes, I had a lot going on," I snap, even though my heart's pounding. "And it was brief. And stupid. And I didn't enjoy it."

The silence that comes afterward is deafening.

They both stare at me as if I've totally lost it and are waiting for me to finally tip over into madness.

I probably have. Because even now, with my face burning and my pride in shambles, all I can see is him smirking with me against the locker, hearing his voice in my ear, and all I can think is how badly I wish I'd hit him harder.

Aubrey tilts her head, studying me the way she does when she's piecing something together. "At first," she says. "I wondered what the hell was going on with you guys. Why he calls you Red like it's his favorite word." Her mouth twists. "As if it actually means something."

"It doesn't mean anything," I mumble, eyes dropping to my workbook. I pick at the corner until it starts to bend, then bend it some more.

"It kinda does," Lola sings, way too cheerful for where this is headed. "The way he looks at you—"

I whip my head toward her so quickly that my neck twinges. "Don't."

She ignores me. Of course she does.

Lola turns to Aubrey instead, smile bright, voice light, completely fucking oblivious to the grenade she's about to toss. "Reece was her first kiss."

Aubrey's eyes widen. "Wait." She blinks, then blinks again. "Reece was your first kiss?"

"Lola," I grind out, heat rushing to my face, my stomach dropping out from under me. I glare at her, furious and embarrassed, wishing I could undo the last ten seconds of my life. "Why would you say that?"

Aubrey gasps, her hand flying to her chest as if she's just received the juiciest piece of gossip. "Oh my god, Sam. He was your first?" She leans in, eyes sparkling with curiosity. "You have to tell me everything."

I let my hands fall on the desk and groan, then drag them back up to cover my face. This is my worst nightmare—public humiliation, served right before the first period of the day.

"It wasn't a big deal," I say into my palms, muffled and miserable.

"That's a lie," Lola adds, snorting softly. "Liz said you didn't shut up about it for three weeks."

I drag both hands down my face, palms pressing firmly, as if the sting might erase the image that flashes too easily in my mind.

"It wasn't," I mutter, dropping my hands and staring at the desk. "And it doesn't matter." My voice turns flat and defensive. "He just wants to mess with me. That's all this is. A stupid game."

"Sure," Aubrey says, not buying it for a second. "But even if it is, you're already playing."

I open my mouth to argue, then close it again.

Lola lights up. "So tell me," she says, leaning forward, elbows on the desk, eyes bright. "What does he taste like? I've always wanted to know." She nods to herself. "I bet when he kissed you, he tasted like sour lollies and rebellion."

Aubrey chokes on a laugh. "Jesus, Lola."

"What?" Lola shrugs, completely unapologetic. "I want to know." She looks between us, waiting. "Well."

"I can't remember," I say quickly, eyes dropping to my books. I start rearranging them, stacking and unstacking, lining the edges up perfectly so I don't have to look at either of them.

It's a lie because I remember everything.

I remember how awkward it was, being too close and not close enough at the same time. The way my heart pounded so loudly I thought he'd hear it. How his mouth brushed mine first, tentative and unsure. The way I froze for half a second before kissing him back, clumsy and inexperienced. I was fourteen and believed the moment mattered more than it ever really should have.

I remember how I couldn't stop smiling afterward, replaying it over and over in my head.

I push the memories aside and keep shifting my books around, pretending none of it exists.

"I call bullshit," Aubrey says softly, but her tone makes it clear she knows.

I don't lift my eyes, because if I do, I might admit that it used to matter, and even worse, that some foolish part of me is still afraid it does.

I don't answer. I just sit there, straightening my books on the desk for the third time, even though it's already neat. I can feel their eyes on me. Watching. Waiting. Like if they stare hard enough, I'll crack.

When I still don't look up, Aubrey's voice softens. "Are you okay?"

"Peachy." I exhale and finally lift my head, forcing a half-smile. "This is exactly why I don't get involved in shit like this. Boys. Feelings. Drama." I shake my head. "It's all pointless."

Lola hums next to me. "Yeah," she says. "But it's also kind of fun."

"Fun?" I bark out a laugh, sharp and disbelieving. "You call being manhandled against your locker fun?"

She doesn't even hesitate, just grins. "Depends who's doing the manhandling."

Aubrey snorts, then bursts out laughing, covering her mouth as if she's trying to behave but failing miserably.

I groan and roll my eyes. "You two are no help."

They're still smiling when the bell rings, cutting through the moment. Chairs scrape against the floor. Voices rise in excitement. The classroom begins to fill with bodies, noise, and the familiar chaos of first period. People push past desks, bags hit the floor, and laughter echoes off the walls.

The English teacher walks in a second later, heels clicking, with a stack of papers tucked under her arm. "Alright," she says, clapping once for attention. "Settle down. Books out. We're continuing with poetry analysis today."

Poetry. Of all things.

I open my notebook and try to lose myself in it. I highlight headings that don't need it. I rewrite the date even though it's already there. I tell myself to focus on the assessment—on anything that isn't the cocky, chaotic mess of a boy who has somehow invaded every unguarded thought I have.

I try.

But all I can think about is him.

His breath in my ear. That heat pressing into mine. The rough edge in his voice when he said what he wanted to do.

My thighs tense up under the desk. I shift in my seat, rage sparking because the aftereffects of it linger against me. My body remembers something my brain is trying to reject.

It makes me furious.

This isn't me.

I don't daydream about boys. I don't fixate on someone who only cares about getting off and causing trouble. And I sure as hell don't obsess over pretty boys with good hands and bad intentions. Boys who smile like trouble and talk as if they already own you.

I don't.

Except I do.

I stare at the board as the teacher begins talking about metaphors and symbolism, her voice drifting across the room. I nod at the right moments. I even jot down a few words. But it all sounds like white noise. Background static. Because my mind is still pinned against those lockers.

Still trapped in that narrow space with him.

I tighten my grip on the pen, knuckles turning white, as I struggle to stay still.

English blurs. The classroom fades.

He's not worth my time, I tell myself. I repeat it in my head, like a mantra. Reece is not worth the spiral. Not worth the tight chest or the restless energy buzzing under my skin. But when the second class ends, and I step into the hallway; my resolve shatters. My eyes betray me instantly.

I search for him.

It isn't a choice.

It's instinct.

A pull I don't want to admit exists.

My eyes scan the crowd automatically, passing over familiar faces, lockers, bodies too close together. Then I find him.

Reece is slouched against the wall near the science wing, one shoulder pressed against the brick, hands in his pockets. He looks relaxed, lazy, yet dangerous in that effortless way that makes my stomach sink. His eyes are already on me, dark and focused, as if he knew I'd be searching.

My heart pounds so hard it almost knocks me off balance.

For half a second, the hallway vanishes. The noise dulls. The movement becomes blurry. It's just him and that look, fixed on me with a certainty that makes my stomach twist.

Heat floods my chest, spreading quickly enough to steal my breath. My pulse races again, pounding too hard, too loud.

He doesn't smile.

He just watches me.

Waiting. Knowing.

That's what really gets to me.

The fact that he's already looking directly at me the moment I step into view, as if this moment always belonged to him and he depended on me doing exactly what he expected.

My fingers tighten around the strap of my bag. My shoulders stiffen. I stay completely still because if I move, if I relax even slightly, I'll break everything I'm trying to keep hidden.

I break eye contact first because I have to; if I don't, I'll stay there too long and let it turn into something else—something dangerous that he'll interpret as permission.

And I refuse to give him that.

I turn down the hall and walk fast, boots pounding the floor harder than necessary. My spine stays straight. My face remains blank. I shape my expression into something calm and unaffected, even though my pulse is still tripping over itself. Every movement is controlled, as if I'm holding myself together by sheer force of will.

I sense his gaze on my back, anyway.

It's physical—a weight pressing against my shoulder blades. My skin itches, nerves buzz, awareness edging beneath my clothes. Even with him behind me and out of sight, my body remains alert to him, tuned in, waiting for something I can't bring myself to name.

The hallway goes on, too long and crowded, with bodies brushing past me from all sides and voices echoing off lockers and walls. There's no place to hide in it.

I keep my head held high and my stride steady, even though my chest feels tight and my skin still tingles. I am painfully aware of myself—how I'm walking and how absurd it is that a single look from him can affect me this way. That I can feel off balance in the middle of a crowd that doesn't have a clue about what's playing out inside my mind.

Get your shit together, Sam. You don't fall apart over boys. You don't spiral in hallways or replay moments that should already be dead and buried. You breathe. You walk. You move on.

So I square my shoulders and keep moving, pretending I don't feel him lingering behind me or that this hasn't already gone deeper than I want to admit.

CHAPTER 8

REECE

The hallway is too loud. Not because people are shouting, but because I can hear everything all at once. Lockers opening and slamming shut. Metal against metal. Sneakers squeaking on the floor in uneven rhythms. Someone laughing too hard near the science wing—that forced laugh that goes on a second too long.

Everything crashes together inside my head.

The buzz beneath my skin won't settle. It never does, but today it feels tighter. Meaner. Coiled. Every nerve feels alive, stretched thin, waiting for something to snap.

I roll my shoulders once, jaw clenched, teeth grinding just a little. My hands curl and uncurl at my sides, knuckles itching for something to do. Something physical that hurts enough to shut everything else the fuck up.

The air is heavy. Warm in that exhausted school way that reeks of sweat and cheap deodorant and the lingering trace of cafeteria grease. It attaches to the back of my throat.

I walk faster.

People move around me in clusters. Girls huddle together, whispering behind cupped hands. Guys slap shoulders, shove each other, and laugh too loud. Someone bumps into me and mutters an apology without looking up. I don't respond.

My focus is off.

It has been all morning.

My mind keeps drifting, sliding back to shit I don't want to think about. Things I can't unfeel.

Get a grip, asshole. It's just another day.

Still, my chest feels tight.

I take a slow breath through my nose and exhale just as slowly. It doesn't help.

My eyes keep moving regardless.

Scanning more by instinct than deliberate choice. My brain catalogs everything whether I want it to or not. I see Jace near the lockers by the stairwell, laughing at something on his phone. His grin is easy and carefree, which pisses me off a little, though I don't know why. Maybe because he looks so comfortable in his own skin.

I walk toward him.

Halfway there, a sound pierces through everything else.

A laugh.

It hits low in my chest and detonates.

My stride falters, even if just for a brief moment.

It's enough to catch my attention and really annoy me.

That laugh comes softer this time, but it still happens.

I turn my head and see her there.

Sam's leaning against the lockers, hair loose, mouth curved into a relaxed smile. It's a genuine smile. She's laughing at something a guy says, and it hits me quickly, sharp as a blade under my ribs.

I know who he is.

Bryce fucking Andrews. Everyone knows who he is. One of those clean-cut boys who never sneaks out, never drinks, and never gets caught doing anything worth remembering. The type teachers smile at. The type parents point to and say, "Why can't you be more like him?"

The type Sam smiles at as if he's something safe.

My jaw locks up.

She tilts her head, smiling wider, eyes shining. Her hand lightly brushes his arm. It seems casual, probably nothing, but I still feel a twinge in my chest until even breathing becomes hard.

I force myself to move before I storm over there and rearrange his fucking teeth for smiling at her.

Every step toward Jace feels like running a marathon.

My temper radiates so loudly it drowns out reason. I keep my head down, eyes forward, pretending I'm not aware of every second Sam's laughter follows me down the hall.

When I get to Jace, he looks up.

"Hey man."

I don't respond. I just lean back against the lockers, my shoulders hitting them hard on purpose. The impact sends a dull jolt up my spine, giving me something solid to focus on instead of my constricted chest, which makes it hard to breathe normally.

Jace watches me for a beat. I can feel his eyes on my face, waiting for something. A reaction. A joke, anything that lets him pretend this is just another moment, another hallway conversation that means jackshit.

Then his gaze shifts.

He follows my stare, tracks it effortlessly, because I haven't moved my eyes since the second Sam laughed again.

I hate how she makes me feel this way without even looking at me.

I hear Jace snort a laugh next to me. It's quiet, full of meaning. That sound alone makes my damn skin crawl.

I grind my teeth until they hurt. The locker presses harder into my back as I shift my weight. The cold metal grounds me before I do something that would get my ass dragged into the Principal's office. My fists curl at my sides, fingers flexing, knuckles tight, anger buzzing hot and restless under my skin.

A kid steps into my line of sight.

"What?" I snap.

The word comes out sharp, already loaded.

He flinches.

I clock it instantly.

The nervous half-smile and the way his shoulders pull in, making himself smaller without realizing it.

"You're in front of my locker," he says.

His voice cracks just enough to irritate me more.

"Fuck off," I say, patience already burned down to nothing.

I watch him hesitate. I can see his thoughts flicker across his face—whether he should argue, if the books inside are worth it, or if today is the day he learns a tough lesson about picking fights. He lingers there a moment too long, caught between pride and self-preservation.

I keep staring.

All of this anger isn't really for him, and I know it. But it's rolling off me because Sam is still laughing across the hall, and I am still here, stuck in my head, losing my shit over it.

He chooses wisely. He turns and walks away.

Good.

Jace drops his attention back to his phone, thumbs moving quick, probably lining up some girl to keep him busy later. Same shit, different day.

"Still think you can fuck your precious redhead by the end of the year," he says, confidence dripping off every word. As if he is already claiming the win.

I shove my hands deep into my pockets before walking over to Sam and doing something stupid. My temper doesn't do well when my brain checks out.

I turn my head when someone calls my name.

"Reece."

The sound cuts through the noise, enough to grab my focus whether I want it to or not.

I pull my eyes off Sam and focus on the guy a few feet away.

It's Marcus.

We used to play defense together back when I still showed up to practice and pretended football was just football. He looks rougher than the last time I saw him. Tired in a way sleep doesn't fix. Thick white wrapping tape peeks out from under his shirt, covering one shoulder. He's limping, not enough to draw attention, just enough that you notice if you know what you're looking for.

"What," I say.

"Coach sent me," he says, straight to the point. No easing into it. "Tyler blew his knee last weekend. Out for the season."

I blink. Once. Twice.

A memory slips in—Friday nights under the lights, pads cracking, Tyler cursing when drills went long. He called me an asshole every time I laid him out in practice.

"Okay," I say finally. "Sucks for him."

It comes out flat. Detached.

Marcus shifts his weight. "We're short. Coach wanted to know if you'd be interested in coming back."

I almost laugh.

"Not happening."

Jace straightens beside me. "Why not?"

"Because I quit."

"Yeah," Jace says easily, shrugging. "Doesn't mean you sucked."

"That's not why I quit."

Marcus watches me carefully now. Not pressuring, just observing. Examining me as if he might notice the flaw if he looks long enough.

"You were good, man," he says. "Better than good. Coach still talks about you."

"Coach talks about anyone who doesn't fuck up drills," I snort.

Jace shakes his head. "Bullshit. You were solid. You only stopped because your dad made it his thing."

The words land and stick. For a second, I say nothing. Because it's the fucking truth. I quit only because of him.

At first, I thought my dad was proud of me.

I really did.

The first season I played, he actually showed up. He sat in the stands, watched the field, and asked questions on the drive home. I remember thinking, this was it. This finally mattered enough to make him see me. Not just the kid who always fucked things up.

Football was the bridge. That's what I believed.

It turns out it was never about me.

It was all about winning.

The more I played, the less he talked about anything else. School didn't matter. Friends didn't matter. I didn't either. Just stats, plays, and the things I did wrong. Every missed tackle or bad read. Every second I was half a step too slow.

He never said, "Good job."

Not even once.

If we won, it was because the team pulled it together. If we lost, it was my fault. I should have held the line better. I should have seen it coming, or I should have wanted it more.

He pushed me harder each week.

More drills. More lectures. Winning meant everything to him, and losing felt personal, as if I had just embarrassed him by simply existing.

I stopped being his son somewhere along the way and became just a position. I remember sitting in the car after a game. We had lost by three points. He wouldn't look at me, only stared straight ahead and told me, "You cost us that."

Us.

That was the moment something broke, because it was never "us"; it was just football. And when football was gone, there was nothing left between us. No conversation. No effort to know who I was when I was not wearing pads and bleeding for a fucking scoreboard.

I quit because I got tired of chasing approval that only appeared when I was winning and vanished the moment I wasn't.

Jace goes quiet.

That alone says everything.

He understands how much football meant to me—how it was the one thing that made me feel alive, like I was good at something that mattered more than just getting by every day. Jace also knows exactly why I had to walk away. Why quitting was the only way to break free from my dad's grip before it shattered whatever was left of me.

Marcus scratches his jaw, shifting again on his bad leg. "Well, Coach just said to ask. No pressure."

I nod once, not trusting my mouth.

My eyes then drift, as they tend to do, to that fiery redhead. I don't intend for it to happen, but it does anyway.

Sam is still across the hall, leaning in close to Bryce. Her head tilted slightly, a gentle, personal look even from this distance. Her eyes hold that warmth again, the kind she never shows me.

Jealousy is a cruel thing. It sinks in deep, scrapes along bones, and refuses to let go. My chest aches in a way that has nothing to do with breathing. My fists tighten again, nails digging into flesh as if that might bleed some of it out.

The decision hits hard, driven by anger, jealousy, and a need to control something. I'm pissed at her. At the way my body reacts when she smiles at someone else. At how my heart refuses to listen when I tell it to shut the fuck up.

I straighten up away from the lockers.

"Okay," I say. "Where's Coach?"

Marcus blinks, clearly surprised by that. "Uh, field house."

"Are you serious?" Jace's eyebrows lift, surprise flashing across his face.

I don't answer him, as I'm already moving before I can think better of it, boots scraping against the floor, pulse hard enough to feel it in my throat.

The field house smells the same the second I push through the door. Sweat. Old rubber. Grass that has been ground so deep into the concrete it never really leaves. The air is familiar with years of effort, frustration and boys trying to prove something to themselves and everyone watching.

Memories hit me right in the chest, so hard that I slow down without meaning to. Pads. Helmets. Coaches screaming until their voices are hoarse. My name called out across the field.

I hate how much of myself still remains here.

My boots echo against the floor as I walk down the narrow hall toward the offices. Every step feels heavy. My shoulders straighten automatically, muscle memory kicking in, posture snapping into place just like it always did before practice.

I stop outside the door with COACH REYNOLDS written on it.

I breathe out before knocking.

"Come in," says a voice from the other side.

Coach Reynolds looks up from his computer as I enter. His eyebrows lift, surprise lighting up his face before it softens into something warmer.

"Reece," he says with a smile. It's genuine, not forced. "I didn't expect to see you so soon."

"Yeah," I say. "Well, here I am."

He gestures toward the chair across from his desk. "Please, sit."

I stay rooted where I am, hands relaxed by my sides, weight evenly on the balls of my feet. Standing feels safer. More honest.

Coach's eyes flick down, quick and assessing, catching my boots, my stance, the way my shoulders are set. I see the recognition there. The quiet approval. He knows this posture. He should, because he taught it.

"You're here about the team," he says.

I nod once.

"I'm not promising anything," I say. "But I'll play."

Coach's smile widens. "I'm glad to have you back."

Something tight in my chest loosens, only a little, but enough that I notice it.

I nod again and turn before he can say anything else, before I can think about why I agreed to this.

By the time the last bell of the day rings, my head is a fucking mess.

The adrenaline that pushed me through the afternoon has worn off, leaving a dull, steady ache behind my eyes.

Regret gradually sets in.

What the fuck did I just agree to? And worse than that, how is this going to go when my father finds out I rejoined the team?

Later, Noah, Jace, and I end up at the basketball courts. Noah's idea—something to burn off the leftover edge before heading home.

I play half-focused. My body knows what to do, but my mind is somewhere else entirely.

Noah sinks a shot and jogs back, bouncing the ball easily at his side. He looks relaxed. Focused. The way he always does when everything in his life makes sense. It irritates me more than I want to admit.

Jace, on the other hand, cannot shut the fuck up. He's riding some high, words spilling out of him fast, energy crackling under his skin. He dribbles once, twice, then grins wide, flashing that smug look.

"So get this," Jace says, dragging it out, enjoying the moment. "Reece is back on the football team."

Noah turns his head and looks at me. His eyebrows lift, surprise sharpening his normally calm expression.

"Really," he says.

"Yeah." I shrug, keeping it small and casual.

Noah nods. "That's good."

"Told you," Jace says, snatching the ball from Noah.

Noah doesn't even glance at him. His focus remains on me.

"You were great at football, Reece," he says. "It's good that you're back. Not because of the team. Because it's yours again. It should've always been yours."

The words hit me square in the chest.

Coming from Noah, it matters more than anything. He isn't one to hype shit. Doesn't hand out compliments for fun. He says exactly what he means and nothing more.

If Noah believes it, maybe I wasn't crazy for signing back up.

"We'll see," I say, shrugging it off fast, before it can dig in deeper.

The ball thuds against the concrete as Jace fumbles it, muttering a curse under his breath. The noise pulls us back into the moment.

It's late by the time we get into Noah's car.

Jace rides shotgun, still buzzing with that restless energy he never seems to lose. I take the back seat, lean my head against the seat, watching the streetlights streak past in blurred lines as the night settles in around us.

Noah drops Jace off first.

Jace twists around in his seat, grinning. "Don't screw it up," he says. "I expect front row seats on Fridays."

"Get the fuck out," I tell him.

He laughs and swings the door open. It slams shut behind him as he keeps talking shit.

I watch Jace disappear up the driveway until he's gone, swallowed by the darkness.

Noah pulls away from the curb and looks at me in the rearview mirror. The streetlights briefly flash over his face.

"Are you okay with it all?" he asks. "You know, going back onto the team."

I hesitate, long enough for the truth to press against my ribs. Then I nod. "I think so."

He studies my reflection for a beat. "What about your dad?" he asks. "What if he wants it to go back the way it was?"

"Then he can fuck off," I say.

Noah's mouth quirks. He nods, accepting the answer for what it is.

When he pulls up in front of my house, it's dark.

"See you tomorrow," Noah says as I open the car door.

"Yeah," I reply.

I step out into the night and gently close the door.

Noah waits until I'm clear, then drives off, taillights fading down the street until there's nothing left but silence.

I stand on the curb for a moment, staring at the empty street long after he's gone. The silence quickly closes in, heavy and relentless. The weight of the day hits me all at once: football, my father discovering I rejoined the team, Sam laughing with that jerk. All of it knots together in my chest until it feels too tight to breathe.

I take a deep breath, straighten my shoulders, and head toward the house. Sleep is going to be tough.

But just standing here won't change a damn thing.

I slip quietly inside, dropping my bag by the door and kicking my shoes off. The TV hums in the living room, some rerun playing. My dad is passed out again on the couch. Bottle on the floor. Mouth open. Still breathing. Barely.

I stand there in the room for a moment and watch him. I wonder if letting him know I'm back on the team would stop the way he's been slipping farther away each day. If football could still reach him. If it could pull him back the way I once hoped it would.

Then, another thought interrupts.

What if it ends up the same as before?

The tightness in my chest worsens, and I push the thoughts aside before they can creep in any further. I've been down that road before, and it always ends the same way.

I turn away and head to my room, shutting the door behind me, choosing distance over hope because hope has fucked me over enough times already.

As soon as I get inside, I cross the room and stop in front of the cupboard on the far wall.

It sticks when I pull it open. I yank harder, and the door gives way with a soft crack, dust puffing into the air. It hangs there, floating and settling on my skin as if the past is trying to remind me it never really left.

The gear is pushed into the back corner.

Helmet. Pads. Cleats.

All of it is just waiting. I haven't touched any of it in over a year. Not since I decided I was finished chasing approval that only appeared when I was hurting for it.

I crouch down and drag everything out onto the floor.

The weight immediately rests in my palms, a familiarity that tightens my chest.

The smell hits next: sweat, grass, and old effort soaked so deep into the padding that it never washes out. It smells like training sessions, bruises, and wanting something so badly you break yourself for it. It smells like a version of me that used to believe in things.

I sit on the edge of the bed and pick up my boots.

I lace them up slowly, fingers steady, heart anything but. The leather creaks as I pull the laces tight.

They still fit. That shouldn't matter, but it does because it means a part of me never really grew out of this. It never let go, not even when I told myself I was finished.

I lie back on the mattress, arms folded behind my head, staring up at the ceiling fan that hasn't worked in years. It hangs there, useless, blades frozen, a perfect match for everything else in this house.

I agreed to this.

For Sam and what I saw in that hallway, the way jealousy lit me up and pushed me forward before I had a chance to think.

Lying here with these boots still on my feet, the room silent except for my breathing, I wonder if that's the whole truth. If I really did it because of the way she smiled at that asshole.

Or if I said yes to myself, for the version of me that once believed he was good at something.

For the kid who believed effort mattered and still yearns to feel that adrenaline again, even if it's clothed in pain.

I stare at the fan until my eyes burn, knowing there's no taking it back now.

Whatever the reason was, I opened that door myself. And tomorrow, I will find out what it costs.

CHAPTER 9

SAM

The library is dead quiet. I sit across from Reece Wilson, a thick textbook open between us, pretending it's the most interesting thing I've ever seen. My pen taps against my notebook in a slow, uneven rhythm. I haven't written a damn thing in the last five minutes.

Neither has he.

He hasn't said a word since he dropped into the chair opposite me, long legs stretched out, those fuck off broad shoulders taking up more space than any one person has a right to. His mouth is curved into that usual lazy smirk.

I avoid looking at him. I refuse to give him that satisfaction. But fuck, he's close.

Too close.

Every time Reece shifts, his arm brushes against mine. His knee bumps into mine when he stretches. Each small touch sends a spark straight through me, lighting up spots I really wish would calm the fuck down.

And his cologne.

God.

It's wrong for a school library. Something earthy and out of place among dusty shelves and old carpet. The smell wraps around me. It sinks into my lungs and settles somewhere dangerous. Each inhale fucks with my head.

This is supposed to be project time.

Research. Notes. Boring, safe, normal shit.

I've highlighted the same sentence three times. I know because the page is almost glowing at this point.

Out of the corner of my eye, I see Reece lean back in his chair, one arm draped over the backrest, his posture loose and frustratingly relaxed. He looks comfortable. It's as if this isn't torture for him. He seems blissfully unaware of how close his thigh is to mine or how his presence fills my space, making it impossible to breathe normally.

I risk stealing a glance.

Huge mistake.

His eyes are already on me. Dark. Focused. Amused in a way that makes my stomach flip and my pulse stutter. His smirk deepens, just a fraction, as if he caught me mid-thought and liked what he saw there.

Heat rushes low in my body. My pussy clenches traitorously, and I almost laugh at myself for it. Because my body has never listened to my brain where Reece is concerned.

I sit up straight in my chair, creating space where there isn't any. My pen taps faster now, irritation replacing nerves.

"Didn't peg you for the silent type," he says finally.

I lower my eyes to my notebook. "Didn't peg you as academically inclined."

He laughs softly to himself. "Touché."

I grip my pen tighter, knuckles turning white, eyes fixed on the page even though the words no longer make sense. I can feel him still watching me. It's a physical presence, a weight pressing into my awareness until I can't ignore it.

I dislike what it does to me.

It makes me squirm in my seat. Makes my blood run hotter than it has any right to over a stupid study table in a library.

He feeds on it.

The tension... the way my shoulders stiffen when his voice drops. The way my breath catches when his eyes flick to my mouth for a split second too long.

"Relax," he murmurs. "I'm not going to bite."

I snort softly. "That's not reassuring."

His eyes gleam. "Wasn't meant to be."

Before I can respond, he leans forward, elbows on the table.

Close enough to count the lashes around his eyes, see the faint scar on his cheek—pale against his skin, as if it's something he's earned.

Close enough to notice the way his mouth tilts when he speaks, crooked and knowing, as if he's always halfway through a secret he hasn't yet shared.

I swallow and finally glance up, meeting his gaze head-on.

And fuck me if his eyes aren't already burning straight through me.

"What's the deal with you and Bryce Andrews?" The question spills out, blunt and uninvited.

"Excuse me?"

Reece shrugs, radiating lazy confidence and calculated indifference. "You two were talking yesterday. It looked cozy."

I gaze at him. Really stare. And then it hits me.

Jealousy.

That doesn't make any sense. Reece Wilson doesn't get jealous. He cycles through girls like seasons, never staying long enough to care who's standing next to whom. He moves on before feelings even have a chance to breathe.

So, this isn't that.

This isn't about Bryce.

It's about control.

It's about the stupid fucking bet he made with Jace. The big statement. The one where he decided my pussy was a prize. And now he's pissed because I won't give him an inch. Because I won't stumble and fall into his lap and make this easy for him.

"We were discussing the assessment we have to work on," I say coolly.

His eyes flick to my mouth again before he looks back up. "I don't like it."

I let out a short laugh. "I don't care what you like."

Reece's smirk doesn't fade. If anything, it grows deeper—the kind that shows he's enjoying this way too much.

"Sure," he says. "Just didn't know you were into guys who button their collars to the top and call their parents sir and ma'am."

"That says more about you than him," I snap, heat flaring fast. "And for the record, I'm not into anyone."

The lie tastes thin the moment it leaves my mouth.

"That right?" Reece says, smirk firmly in place.

I shift in my seat, my spine stiffening. My mouth goes dry, my tongue feels heavy, and every instinct urges me to create distance between us.

"You can go back to pretending I don't exist now," I say, aiming for dismissive, but it comes off more defensive.

"I never pretended that," he murmurs.

The quiet presses in around us, and every sound suddenly feels too loud. There's the scraping of a chair leg somewhere behind us. Someone coughing. None of it breaks the tension wrapped tightly around my ribs.

He's too close.

The subtle shift of his body. His knee angles in. His presence dominates my surroundings, making my skin more sensitive, with every nerve ending fired up and screaming.

Then he leans in closer.

My breath catches.

His voice dips again, the kind that should come with a warning label. "You know you shake when I get near?"

I go still, heart slamming hard enough it feels violent. I try to breathe, but my chest locks up, lungs refusing to cooperate. Heat floods low in my body, my pussy clenching like it's got a mind of its own.

He watches me. Devours me.

His eyes darken, hungry in a way that makes my skin prickle.

I force my chin up.

"I do not."

"Yes you do," he says quietly. "Your fingers tremble."

I look down unintentionally and curse myself when I see it. My hand isn't steady.

"Your breath hitches, too," he continues, eyes flicking to my chest, tracking every shallow inhale. "You freeze."

My pulse thunders in my ears.

"Then you run."

Those three words linger between us, heavy and way too fucking accurate.

I swallow hard, because I hate that he sees me this clearly.

My hands tighten into fists as I force myself to sit back into the chair, creating space between us. My body protests as the distance grows, even though my head knows I need it.

"I only run because you piss me off," I bite out. "And I hate it."

The silence that comes after is harsh.

Too honest... too exposed. The truth that slips out when your guard drops for half a second too long.

Fuck.

I want to take it back. I wish I could shove the words back into my mouth and pretend I never said them.

But it's too late.

Something shifts on his face.

The smirk disappears, wiped clean as if it never existed. His pupils darken, spreading fast, swallowing the gold in his irises until his gaze turns heavy and intent.

The tension between us grows stronger, transforming the silence into something threatening.

He reaches out.

Just one hand. His fingers brush my hair back from my face, putting it behind my ear with a care that seems lethal. The touch is soft, barely there, but it detonates anyway. His fingertips trail along my cheekbone, lingering just long enough to make my breath hitch.

I freeze.

Every instinct screams to move, to pull away, to remind him he doesn't get this. But my body is frozen in place.

I don't move, blink, or breathe.

The room suddenly feels smaller, with the shelves closing in and the quiet pressing tightly around us until it becomes intimate. My body locks up completely, caught between fight and flight, neither one prevailing.

He's breathtaking in a way that can ruin you if you look too long.

Prominent cheekbones that seem sculpted rather than naturally formed. Messy hair that never stays in place, falling into his eyes as if it knows it belongs there. And that mouth. Filthy, cruel, unforgettable. A mouth that knows how to say all the wrong things just the right way.

The kind of beauty that destroys good girls.

The kind mothers warn you about and leave scars instead of memories.

And I could fall. God, I could fall so easily if I let him in.

If I allow myself to believe that the intensity in his eyes is about me, not conquest. If I let myself pretend this heat curling low in my belly means more than instinct and lust, and a body that doesn't know how to protect itself.

I despise the part of me that still desires him even though I know better. That envisions what those hands could do if they weren't so carefully hovering at my face. A part of me wants to surrender. It wants to end this ache.

But I won't because I understand who he is.

Mainly because I heard what he told Jace.

That fucking bet.

The memory hits me suddenly, catching me off guard. My stomach twists tightly, so sharp I almost gasp.

Is this all part of the act? The way he crowds me in this silent library and wants to destroy me from the inside out. Is he still playing that game?

Still chasing the win instead of the girl sitting right in front of him, trying not to fall apart.

Anger slices through the heat, hot and furious, giving me just enough strength to move.

I quickly stand up from the chair before I do something I can't undo.

My chair loudly scratches the floor. Heads turn. Whispers begin. I don't care.

I grab my bag, breath coming too fast.

I refuse to be a bet.

And I refuse to let him be the cause of my breaking.

He straightens up, blinking. "Sam—"

I shove my notebook into my bag, fingers clumsy and shaking, pages catching where they shouldn't. The zipper fights me, and I nearly rip the damn thing off in my rush. I sling the strap over my shoulder and turn away.

I don't look back because if I do, I'll stay.

I walk out of the library fast.

Too fast.

My heart is lodged in my throat, pounding so hard it makes me dizzy. Blood roars in my ears, drowning out everything else. The hallway feels endless, too bright, too open. My skin still hums from where his fingers touched me.

I keep walking until I slip into the girls' bathroom at the end of the hall and push the door open forcefully enough that it bangs against the wall.

It's empty.

Thank fuck.

I stumble to the sink and grip the edge with both hands, knuckles whitening as I lean forward. My reflection stares back at me, eyes too bright, cheeks flushed, lips parted like I've just run a mile instead of barely escaping something I wasn't ready for.

God. He's a fucking disaster.

Everything about him screams bad decisions. Trouble wrapped in filthy confidence. The guy you warn your friends about over coffee. The kind your mother would hate on sight and be right about.

And yet, it still works. Whatever this thing is, it works.

It shouldn't. Not on me. Bad boys have never been on my radar. I like safe, predictable, and knowing where I stand.

Reece Wilson is none of those things. He's chaos with a mouth that knows exactly how to undo me.

He shouldn't have that kind of power over me. Not with a look that lasts too long or a touch that barely counts but still burns, anyway. Not with a few quiet words spoken too close in a library full of people pretending not to notice.

But he does.

And that truth sinks deep into my chest, heavy and terrifying.

This isn't just about a stupid bet anymore.

He makes me feel reckless without even trying. And that scares the shit out of me more than anything he ever said to Jace.

CHAPTER 10

REECE

It's the last class of the day, and I'm balls deep in it with Chloe in the third-floor bathroom, trying to get the ghost of Sam out of my mind. My hand grips the sink as I thrust into Chloe from behind, the mirror shifting slightly with each movement.

"Oh yeah, baby," Chloe moans. "That's it. Just like that."

She throws her head back, her voice echoing off the tiles, with her mouth open, moaning louder.

Usually, I like it when girls get loud. I feed off it. But today, it's fucking infuriating.

Because every sound she makes reminds me she's the one beneath my hands, not Sam.

I grit my teeth, jaw clenched as I slam into her, trying to silence the voice in my head that keeps flashing images of Sam bent over the sink instead.

Chloe moans again, this time louder, and something inside me breaks. "Shut the fuck up," I growl.

I grasp her hair and pull her head back firmly enough to make the point clear. She gasps, startled, but she doesn't resist. I don't want her voice or reactions. I want complete silence.

I close my eyes and fuck her like I'm losing my mind. My hips snap against her ass, rough and relentless. My grip tightens, and in my mind, the blonde hair in my fist darkens. Softer. Red. Not stiff with product. Not fake.

Sam.

I picture how she froze when I touched her. The way her breath caught. How her mouth opened just a little, like she didn't know what was about to happen next. I imagine sliding my cock between those parted lips, that pause between us, her hesitation before she finally gives in.

The heat rises quickly. Too quickly.

My abs lock up, my balls draw tight as I chase it, pounding into Chloe with no rhythm, no care. I spill into the condom with a low curse, still fucking her through it until there's nothing left in me. Until I'm empty, pissed off, and breathing hard.

I slow down before coming to a stop.

When I open my eyes, the fantasy vanishes immediately. Blonde hair slips through my fingers. Not red. She's not Sam.

I let go of Chloe's hair and pull out my cock, not caring that she didn't finish. She probably fakes it anyway. The loud moans and breathless gasps—all fake to make herself feel wanted.

I walk to the trash can and throw away the condom.

Chloe adjusts her hair and waddles over with her underwear still bunched around her knees, completely unbothered.

"What's the matter, baby?" she asks. "You don't seem like yourself."

That word "baby" makes my blood boil.

After I tuck my cock back into my pants, I grab my bag from the floor and walk past her.

"You don't get to call me that fucking name, for starters," I tell her.

I ignore the hurt on her face, push the door open, and leave, ignoring the way she snaps my name behind me, pissed off and sharp.

All I can think about is Sam.

And the fucked-up truth is, Chloe, didn't help at all.

The bell rings, so I head to practice with my jaw clenched and chest buzzing, anger and desire tangled so tightly I can't tell where one ends and the other begins.

Every step toward the building feels heavy. I keep wondering whether the team already knows I'm back or if I'll get to walk in and see it register on their faces in real time.

The locker room provides that answer for me.

The second I walk in, a few heads turn.

A brief moment of silence, then it shatters.

"Wilson."

Someone grins. A couple of guys I used to line up beside get to their feet without saying a word, fists already raised. I tap them back; the contact sends a jolt through my arm. Welcome back. No speeches or bullshit. Just acknowledgment.

Some guys stay on the bench. The ones who aren't too happy about my return. A few guys I've put in place outside these walls watch me with flat expressions. I can tell by the way they don't move that they would rather watch me die than rejoin the team.

Good.

I don't need their fucking permission.

I drop my bag on the bench and sit down, shoulders tense, fingers already working on the laces and straps. I strip off and put on my gear piece by piece. Pads. Jersey. Cleats. The routine comes back quickly. Automatic. My body knows this even if my mind is still a mess.

The field hits me the moment I step outside.

Cut grass. Something welcoming underneath it all. The sound alone lights me up. Pads slamming together. Cleats tearing up turf. Coach's shouts floating through the air. It's loud, violent and honest in a way the rest of my life never is.

Coach Reynolds doesn't go easy on me.

"Wilson," he barks, clipboard tucked under his arm. "Defense drills. You're running last."

A few guys glance back at me. Testing. Curious.

I nod once.

Ten minutes in, and my lungs are on fire. Each breath grates on the way in and burns on the way out. My legs feel heavy, muscles screaming, but my body remembers what it used to do, even if it's pissed at me for stepping away. Muscle memory kicks in.

I was good once. Strong. Fast. Angry in a way that worked for me instead of against me.

Now every sprint is earned. Every drill costs something. Sweat stings my eyes, runs down my back and soaks into my pads until they feel twice as heavy. When I take a hit, it rattles my bones hard enough to knock the breath from my lungs.

But through everything, I welcome it.

Every shove reminds me I'm still here. Still standing. Still able to handle the punishment and send it right back.

I line up across from an asshole I put in his place about a month ago for running his mouth about Jace and I. He freezes when he realizes it's me. Half terrified. Half thrilled. Like he gets to tell this story later, no matter the outcome.

Bad fucking luck for him.

The whistle blows, and I don't hesitate.

I drive straight into him, shoulder low, legs pumping, giving it my all with the hit. Bodies crash loudly enough to turn heads. He stumbles back, eyes wide open, barely able to stay on his feet.

Good.

That message lands clean.

Coach watches from the sideline. He nods once. No praise. No commentary. That's all I get. And somehow it's enough.

Defense drills grind on.

Relentless. Repetitive. Brutal.

Sweat pours down my back, soaking my shirt until it sticks to my skin like a second layer I can't peel off. My lungs burn every time I breathe in. My legs move slower than they used to. Heavier. I miss tackles I shouldn't and get shoved harder than I expect. I get up more slowly than I want to.

It pisses me off.

So I push harder.

I take the hits. I give them back. My bones shake. My muscles scream. Every drill is a fight I have to win all over again.

But I don't quit because quitting would leave too much room in my head, and that space is dangerous.

That space fills quickly with the way Sam Carter looked at me in the library. The way her breath hitched and how she bolted as if she was afraid of what might happen if she stayed.

So I run again and again, hit harder, and dig deeper. I let the violence burn everything out of me for a few seconds at a time. Because if I stop moving, if I stop hurting, every thought I don't want of her comes rushing back. And right now, my head belongs to this team, not Sam.

By the time practice ends, my arms are trembling and my lungs are screaming as if they have something personal against me. Sweat drips off my chin. Everything hurts. Everything feels earned.

Coach claps his hand on my shoulder.

"Not bad for a comeback," he says. "You keep this up, you'll earn your spot."

Earn.

The word hits harder than any tackle I've taken today.

Earn means nothing is given. It means I don't get to coast on who I used to be. Earn means every day I show up, bleed a little, prove I deserve to stand here.

I take off my pads in the locker room and sit on the bench, lingering longer than I need to. My hands rest on my knees. I look at them as if I don't recognize them. Dirt under my nails. Knuckles scraped raw. Skin split and stinging.

Something about this feels right.

Purpose doesn't settle in clean. It never does. It hovers just out of reach—restless and unfinished. But purpose sits closer than it has in a long time, and that matters more than I want to admit.

I don't go home.

Instead, my feet move on their own and carry me back across campus, muscles sore, body heavy, mind quieter than it has been all day. The late afternoon air cools the heat clinging to my skin as I walk.

That's when I remember my notebook.

Still sitting at one of the tables in the library—the one covered in all my notes, with Sam Carter's handwriting in the margins, tied to a project I can't escape and a girl I haven't managed to shake all damn day.

The library is quieter this time. Not the tense, skin-tight quiet from before. Instead, it's more gentle. Afternoon light filters through the tall windows, pale gold and dusty, slicing across the room in long beams. Dust motes drift lazily in the air, slow and unbothered.

My boots sound too loud against the floor.

The librarian sits at her desk near the front, glasses resting low on her nose, fingers moving through paperwork with practiced boredom.

She looks up when I approach, her eyes flicking over me, lingering a second longer on my gear bag slung over my shoulder.

"Did anyone hand in a notebook?" I ask. My voice comes out rough, still scraped raw from practice.

She looks at me over her glasses. "I'll just have a look," she says, already bending down to check under the counter.

"It's a black one," I add unnecessarily as she opens a drawer and scans the contents.

As she looks, my attention drifts around the room, and there she is.

Sam is sitting at the same table we used earlier.

Her hair is pulled back this time, tidy and out of her face, revealing the curve of her neck. Her sleeves are rolled up, with her forearms resting casually on the table, her posture relaxed and loose in a way I've never seen directed at me.

A kid sits across from her. He's a freshman. Books are spread out between them, highlighters scattered as if he's drowning in coursework.

Red is leaning in, listening, with her pen tapping lightly as he talks.

And she's smiling.

The smile that softens her entire face. She nods along as the kid talks, says something I can't hear, and he laughs, shoulders relaxing, relief evident on his face.

She's helping him.

She looks happy.

And for some fucked up reason, that makes it harder to breathe than anything that happened on the field tonight.

"Is this the one?" the librarian asks, holding out a black notebook. The corners are bent. The spine is worn from months of being shoved into my bag and dragged back out again.

"Yeah. Thanks," I say, already reaching out.

I take the notebook from her and move without thinking, my feet already guiding me toward Sam.

She's explaining something with her hands, fingers moving as she talks, visualizing it in the air.

The kid across from her nods, eyes shining, shoulders relaxing.

I take another step closer.

"So this part," she says, tapping the page in front of him, "you're overthinking it. You've got the right way of adding it up. You're just doubting yourself."

He squints at the paper, then looks back up at her. "So you're saying I'm not bad at math. I'm just bad at believing in myself."

She smiles. "Exactly."

He grins. "Wow. I came for numbers and got a therapy session."

She laughs.

It's warm and unguarded. No edge. Just easy and natural.

Fuck.

The sound hits low in my stomach and spreads quickly. My fingers automatically tighten around the notebook without me realizing it.

She says something I don't catch. The kid nods again and looks down at the workbook.

I clear my throat. "Careful, Red. Your halo is showing."

The nickname slips out before I can stop myself.

She glances up, surprise flickering across her face before she masks the reaction. The smile she was wearing disappears, replaced by something guarded.

"I'm helping someone," she says, calm but pointed. "You should try it sometime."

The kid's gaze flicks between the two of us, brows furrowing.

I open my mouth, ready to say something that will make her bristle and restore the space to where it belongs. I've got a dozen lines queued up and waiting. Sarcastic. Cutting. The kind that usually hits the mark.

But it catches in my throat because of the way the kid looks at her with gratitude for helping him.

A timer goes off, and Sam shifts, her attention breaking as she reaches for her phone and turns off the alarm. The sound feels loud in the quiet.

"Thanks, Sam," the kid says, sincere as hell. "I think I actually get it now." He packs up his books, shoves them into his bag, and slings it over his shoulder. "Seriously, thanks." He gives her a quick wave and heads out.

The library settles again.

The quiet rushes back in to fill the space he leaves behind. And I'm still standing there, way too close. Holding my stupid notebook in my hands like an excuse to stay, giving me a reason to be in her space when I don't know what the hell to do now that I am.

She turns back to her table and starts stacking her things. Neat. Methodical.

Tension fills the space between us now. The kind that hums softly and refuses to shut the fuck up no matter how hard I try to ignore it.

I should say something. Anything.

Crack a joke.

Say something sharp. Walk away like I'm supposed to.

Every option exists right in front of me, and I choose none of them.

She helped that kid by showing up and making things easier for someone who needed it.

Watching her makes me feel stupid for every half-assed move I've made on her just to win that stupid bet with Jace.

I should fucking walk away, but I keep lingering.

Seeing her help that kid made it clear. I can't ignore it anymore after seeing that.

She deserves better than this asshole version of me.

CHAPTER 11

SAM

I don't know why I agreed to meet him here. Every step toward Reece Wilson's house feels wrong, like I'm walking straight into a bad decision with my eyes wide open and my pride duct-taped to my mouth. The path crunches under my shoes, each step sounding louder than it should be, as if the universe is narrating my stupidity in real time.

I tell myself it's about the assessment. The marks I need and not letting him derail my future just because he treats school like a joke and girls like a hobby.

If he pulls another smart-ass stunt or answers the door shirtless again, I swear I will lose it loudly and in a way the neighbors will remember for years.

I pause at the door and knock. One steady, confident knock.

The door opens.

And there he is.

Not shirtless. Not smirking as if he planned this moment in advance. He leans against the frame, shoulders relaxed, hair messy in a way that should be illegal, with that infuriating calm locked into place. His mouth curves into a half-smile that hits straight at places it has no right hitting.

"Hey, Red," he says.

The nickname hits softer than it should. I square my shoulders anyway, because I might be standing on the doorstep of a terrible decision, but I won't let him see that I'm affected.

My eyes flick to his face before I can stop myself.

There's a fresh split along his cheekbone. A thin red line cuts across skin that shouldn't look that good up close. It's small. Nothing dramatic.

"What happened to your face?" I ask, the question slipping out before I remember I'm supposed to be annoyed. Or guarded. Or smart enough to turn around and leave.

His smile tilts. "Football."

"You're playing again?" I ask.

I heard the whispers back when he quit. The way people talked about it in the hallways was like it was gossip instead of something that clearly wrecked him. I saw it too. The way he stopped looking like someone who knew where he was going and started looking like someone killing time instead.

I never asked why he quit. It never felt like my place. Plus, we didn't really talk, not that we do now.

He doesn't answer my question, just steps back, opens the door wider, wordlessly inviting me in.

I hesitate for half a second before I walk past him.

The house is quieter than before. No blaring music or chaos spilling out of every room. No sense that I've just wandered into a frat house with worse impulse control. It seems almost... normal.

That alone makes me nervous.

I move down the hallway, shoulders tight, already bracing myself for the comments I got last time. The sly swagger that usually rolls off him with every breath. The jokes about me being a good girl that are loud enough to stick under my skin and stay there.

They never come.

I step into his room and halt suddenly.

It's clean.

Not just shoved-under-the-bed clean. Actually clean. The bed is made, sheets pulled tight. The floor is clear. No trail of discarded clothes, crumpled papers, or empty bottles. No evidence of the chaos I fully expected to find.

Instead, there's a bag in the corner with football gear spilling out, cleats peeking through the half-open zipper. His books are already open on the bed, pages marked and bent, pens scattered as if he actually plans to use them. One notebook sits open, a page filled with notes in messy but purposeful handwriting.

I stare a second too long.

He sees me noticing.

"Shocking, I know," he says. "I can be house-trained. Who would've thought?"

I move further into the room, relaxing slightly. Some of the tension leaves my shoulders. I set my bag on the bed and reach for the open notebook, curiosity overriding caution.

He's actually been working on it. There are references, notes in the margins, thoughts that connect instead of drift. He's annoyingly smart—the kind of smart he keeps quiet because it doesn't fit the version of him everyone expects.

"That's a bit of research I did," he says, casually, as if it doesn't matter.

It does.

I sit down on the edge of the bed, still reading, still processing. "Who are you?" I ask, laughing now, "and what have you done with that annoying asshole Reece Wilson?"

I glance up.

And there it is.

The smile spreading across his face, dimples locked in—the kind girls whisper about. Paired with that infuriating smirk that says he knows exactly what effect he has and couldn't care less.

My stomach flips. I quickly glance back down at the notebook before he can see it, because if I stare too long, I might forget why I came here in the first place.

He sits beside me, close enough that the mattress dips and heat seeps through the gap between us. It shouldn't matter. But it does. My body reacts to him instantly, nerves flaring up in a way I hate. In a way that feels disloyal to every plan I've ever made for myself.

I hand him the notebook and turn slightly, digging through my backpack for my laptop—anything to keep my hands busy and my mind focused.

"So," I say, mostly to fill the silence before it swallows me whole, "you're back on the football team."

"Yeah." He nods.

"Why now?"

His jaw tightens for half a second. It's subtle, almost nothing. Next, he shrugs, as if it doesn't matter. "Seemed right."

That answer is vague enough to be a wall. I clock it. File it away.

I open my laptop and spread everything out on the bed. Papers. Notes. His notebook. I slip into familiar focus, outlining points, assigning sections, mapping arguments. It feels good. Normal. This is the version of me who knows what she's doing.

Apart from one thing.

Every time I shift, his eyes follow. They slowly roam over my skin. When I speak, his attention locks on my mouth, lingering a moment too long before I see his jaw tighten. As I reach for my pen, his gaze drops to my fingers, tracking the movement. When I frown at a sentence that won't cooperate, he doesn't look away. Instead, he watches me think.

I pause mid-note and turn my head.

His eyes stay fixed on me, dark and focused.

Heat rises up my neck. My heart stutters, and speeds up, rapid and deceitful. I shift again, pretending I need a better angle on the page, and his knee follows mine without touching.

He's not hiding it. He wants me to know he's watching.

I snap the laptop shut enough to get his attention. "Are you going to contribute?" I say, sharply, "or just stare holes through me?"

His grin appears. "You get cute when you're bossy."

"Reece."

The way I say his name shouldn't sound like that. It does anyway, and he hears it. I know he does because his eyes lift, catch mine, and something unreadable settles there.

"Alright, alright," he says, leaning back and raising his hands in surrender. "I'm working."

He isn't. His notebook remains open but untouched. The pen stays between his fingers, unmoving. His eyes drift back to me the moment I turn away, following the line of my arm as I reopen the laptop.

It's happening again. That constant pull. The weight of his attention rests exactly where my skin is most aware.

I type a sentence and backspace it twice. My focus slips. My breathing goes shallow. I tuck my hair behind my ear and catch his reflection in the screen watching the movement, his mouth curving.

I clear my throat. "If you're not going to help, I'm leaving."

That gets him.

He leans in, close enough that the mattress dips again, close enough that the air between us warms. He points at the screen, finally. "That paragraph. Your argument's good. You just buried it under too many words."

I blink. "You read it."

"Twice," he says. "You always do that thing you know when you're nervous."

I don't bother asking him what he's talking about, and I shift my head to glare at him. "I'm not nervous."

His eyes flick down to my hands, to how my fingers curl around the edge of the laptop. "Sure," he mumbles.

That's it. He's starting to get to me.

I snap my laptop shut and stuff it into my bag along with my notebook and pens, sliding off the bed in one quick motion. Papers crinkle as I force them into places they don't belong, my hands no longer steady enough to care.

"This is pointless," I say, voice tight. "You don't care. I can't afford to tank this because you think it's fun to fuck with me."

He straightens immediately. The lazy posture disappears, shoulders squaring, attention snapping into place.

"That's not what this is."

"It always is with you," I fire back, the words tumbling out now that the dam's cracked. "Everything is a fucking game. A joke. A way to get a rise out of people so you can feel powerful for five minutes."

I sling my bag over my shoulder and head for the door, chest burning with frustration.

"Red," he says, behind me, but I keep moving.

His hand grips my wrist. Not rough, but firm enough to halt me.

The contact triggers something inside me. A jolt runs up my arm and settles in my chest, stealing my breath and making my knees threaten to give way. My skin tingles where he touched me, my pulse racing as if I've been caught doing something wrong. I hate my body for betraying me when my mind screams to run and my feet refuse to move.

"Let go," I say.

He doesn't.

Instead, he steps closer, close enough that I feel his warmth against my back and catch his breath ghosting through my hair when he exhales.

The room suddenly feels smaller, as if the walls have leaned in to see what's going on.

"You walk away every time it gets real," he murmurs. "That pisses me off."

I spin around to face him, anger blazing. "This isn't real," I snap. "This is you being a smug fuck boy who thinks he can get whatever he wants because you smile and girls forget their names."

His thumb shifts, brushing the inside of my wrist where my pulse is racing wildly. My heart betrays me instantly, pounding harder, faster, making my blood roar in my ears. Every nerve sparks under that single point of contact, my body reacting before I can control it.

"You're shaking, Red?" he whispers, circling until he's in front of me, watching me way too closely. "Or is that just me?"

I rip my hand free and stumble back a step, the floor feeling hot beneath my feet. My cheeks burn. My skin hums everywhere he touched, as if it's still happening.

"Stop it."

He stays still, watching silently with dark eyes fixed on mine, breathing slow and steady while mine comes out uneven and hurried.

"Make me."

The words land heavily. Loaded. They sit between us and drain all the oxygen from the room.

I should leave. I know that. Every rational thought I have is screaming at me to grab the door and run before I do something I can't undo.

Instead, I stay there, my heart pounding, anger and desire so tightly knotted I can't tell which one's holding me in place.

He steps into my space again.

"You hate me," he says.

"Yes."

"Good." His mouth curves. "Means you feel something."

A laugh slips out of me. "You're unbelievable."

His gaze drops to my mouth, lingers there. "You have no idea."

"I wasn't talking about sex, asshole."

His eyes flick back up, as if I handed him something dangerous without realizing it.

"Oh," he says softly, "I know."

The words settle into me, causing my thoughts to scatter. I notice it happening, that familiar unraveling—the way my carefully arranged rules begin slipping away the moment he's this close.

My body betrays me first. It leans forward before my brain can catch up and pull it back.

I hate how every sensible thought I have when I walk into this room gets pushed out the door the moment he looks at me like that.

And worse than all of it? I don't want to stop him.

Not when his hand lifts to my cheek, when his touch is gentle, careful, nothing like the guy I've been fighting for weeks.

His voice drops lower. "You always run?"

I force a swallow, buying myself another second.

"Maybe it's because today you were staring at me the whole time and not doing the work."

A corner of his mouth lifts. "Maybe you were worth staring at."

"You're not funny." My throat goes tight.

"I wasn't trying to be."

We're too close. My chest can't expand properly. His eyes shift to my mouth, and I recognize that stare. I've seen it before; I've never stood still long enough for it to land.

"Don't," I whisper.

The word is weak.

He hesitates briefly before leaning in.

It's slow and unhurried.

As if he's giving me every chance to stop him and already knows I won't. His hand lingers on my cheek, thumb brushing my skin once before his mouth finds mine.

The kiss lands gently.

Not rushed. Just his lips fitting against mine with devastating certainty. Heat floods through me instantly, a dizzying rush that steals my breath and knocks every thought straight out of my head. My knees go weak. I grip his shirt without realizing I've moved, fingers curling tightly as if it's the only thing keeping me upright.

Fuck.

This isn't how I remember it.

The memory from when we were fourteen flashes and burns out just as quickly. Too fast. All teeth and nerves and no idea what to do with any of it. That was a kiss you survived.

This is a kiss you feel.

His mouth moves against mine, as if he knows exactly how to break me down. He kisses me deeper without asking, and my body responds immediately. My lips part, and he takes that opening, his tongue brushing mine in a way that sends sparks straight through my spine.

My head spins.

The room tilts. The air disappears.

There is only him. The taste of him. His body's heat pressing closer. The quiet sound he makes in his throat when I kiss him back without thinking, without holding anything back.

His hand slides into my hair, fingers tangling, holding me steady as the kiss deepens into something slow and consuming. My knees go weak, and I let myself sink into him, logic evaporating, resolve cracking clean in half.

This kiss is everything I acted like I didn't want. Everything I told myself he couldn't give me.

My bag slips from my shoulder and hits the floor with a soft thud that I barely notice. My hands clench his shirt, gripping tighter, nails digging into his chest as if I need proof he's real.

"Fuck, Sam." He groans into my mouth.

He lifts me as if I weigh nothing. His hands slide under my thighs, and instinct takes over before my brain can catch up. I wrap my legs around him, pulling myself closer, feeling the hard press of his cock against me as my breath breaks into uneven pulls.

The room tilts again. Everything narrows down to him.

He leans back slightly to look at me, forehead pressed to mine, eyes dark but steady. His hands remain steady, not moving to places they shouldn't.

"Say stop," he murmurs. "And I'll stop."

I know I should. I can feel every rational part of me screaming that this is the moment to step back, to remember who I am and what I want for myself.

But all I can think about is how right this moment feels. How every place where we touch seems to hum.

I don't say it. I drag in his scent instead—heat, him, and trouble—while my fingers knot in his shirt, and my heart pounds reckless and wild. Want crashes through me, sharp and dizzying, a craving humming beneath my skin. I want his eyes on me, his hands steady and claiming, the way he makes the world go quiet until there's nothing left but us.

That realization hits as hard as the kiss. Wanting him isn't the problem anymore. It's how impossible it feels right now to let him go.

The moment his lips press against mine, I fall. There's no gradual start, no slow buildup—just fire and desire. His tongue slides along the seam of my mouth, craving more. I open for him, and everything changes.

The kiss turns reckless. Teeth, tongue, and breathless fucking hunger.

He walks, his hands gripping my hips, guiding me toward the bed without breaking the kiss. In the next heartbeat, he's got me flat on my back. His weight presses into me, his mouth never leaving mine.

Our tongues tangle, messy and hot, as we chase air we don't care about. He groans low, a sound pulled from deep in his chest, and it vibrates through me.

He grinds against me.

My whole body arches sharply. A jolt of pain shoots through my core, and my mind goes blank. It's fortunate we're lying down because otherwise, my legs would have collapsed. My stomach tightens, and I struggle to breathe.

I feel him.

His hard cock. Thick. Pressed against me through his jeans. My thighs shift restlessly, craving more. The heat between my legs pulses, already aching, already soaked from how fucking good he feels even with the layers still between us.

He pulls back slightly, just enough to truly look at me. His eyes follow my face slowly and purposefully, as if he's memorizing every detail.

I should tell him to back off. I should push against his chest and remind myself why this is a stupid idea.

But, I don't.

I can't move. I can barely breathe.

His hand comes up, thumb brushing my cheek, rough and gentle all at once. His touch steadies me even as it unravels everything inside me.

"Jesus," he murmurs. His voice is low and husky, scraped raw, and it lands straight between my thighs. "You have no idea what you do to me."

My breath stutters. My skin is too tight, too sensitive, every nerve lit up and waiting.

"You're fucking beautiful," he says quietly. Like it's something he's been holding back and finally lets himself say.

His forehead presses briefly against mine, his warm breath near my lips. I feel his burden, the restraint he's struggling to maintain.

"I don't just want to kiss you here," he says.

His lips brush mine, soft and teasing, barely there. It's enough to make my head spin, enough to make my body arch up into him without thinking.

His mouth shifts, grazing my jaw, cheek, and ear. His lips brush against the sensitive skin underneath, and I shiver hard, a broken sound slipping out of me.

"I want to kiss you everywhere," he whispers.

The words slide straight through me, setting my whole body on fire. Every bit of control I thought I had fractures.

I know exactly what he means.

And God help me, I want it too.

My eyes flutter shut as his mouth trails down my jaw. Each kiss dragging another shallow breath from my lungs. His lips are slow, wet heat against skin that is too tight, too exposed.

One hand slides beneath my shirt, fingers grazing up my torso. My nipples turn to glass, stiff and aching the second the fabric lifts. Both hands spread across my ribs, thumbs slowly slipping beneath the edge of my bra.

It's a struggle to breathe.

His touch brands me. My back arches into him, desperate for more, my pulse thudding everywhere at once. He could ask for anything at this moment, and I'd give it to him.

His head drops lower, settling under my breasts, breath pouring over my skin in hot, broken pants.

"Your clothes are in my way."

Fuck, my body lights up from the inside.

"I need them gone," he says, his fingers already inching the hem higher. "I need to look at you."

The words shouldn't hit as hard as they do. But they do. Because it isn't only about touching. It's about seeing. About knowing. About stripping away every barrier and letting him take all of me, even the parts I don't know how to give.

Oh God.

My heart hammers in my chest, the thrum of it filling my ears. My hand trembles slightly as I lift my arms above my head, and he helps me pull the shirt off, slow and careful, like unwrapping something precious.

I'm bare to him.

Almost.

His eyes never leave mine, not even for a second, and it kills me. I can't hide. I am vulnerable, every bit of skin burning under his stare. My breath comes shallow as his fingers trail up to the clasp of my bra.

Nerves twist sharp in my belly.

Regret claws at the edges.

I should've worn something else. Something lace. Something black. Anything that said I knew what the fuck I was doing. Not this—plain white cotton. The kind you buy in a multipack. The kind that makes you feel twelve. Functional. Safe. The kind no one dreams about.

Panic prickles in the back of my throat.

This is where it ends. This is where he realizes the truth: I'm not the girl he thinks I am. I'm not sexy, dangerous, or mysterious. I'm boring. I play it safe. Even my damn underwear screams it.

But—

He looks.

And not with disappointment. Not even curiosity.

He looks at the plain white bra as if it's the sexiest thing he's ever seen, like it's lace or silk. It's as if what's underneath is a gift he longs to worship.

His eyes drop to it, and something flashes across his face—dark, hungry, reverent.

My breath catches because, even though it's simple and nothing special, he looks at me like I'm the most beautiful thing in the world.

He unclips the bra with one hand, smooth and confident, as if he's done this a thousand times before. Which I am sure he has. I lift slightly, heart pounding, as he pulls it from my body and tosses it somewhere across the room. I don't see where it lands because I'm too busy staring at the ceiling, trying to swallow the sudden rush of humiliation crawling up my spine.

My cheeks burn.

I know what he sees.

Flat chest. Small breasts. The body you hope he doesn't notice, or worse—pretends to like out of politeness. I've hated it forever—the way clothes hang, the way bras gape, the way I never fill out the space I'm supposed to.

I want to push him away. I want to pull the blanket over my chest and mutter some excuse about needing to stop. My hands twitch at the thought.

But before I can move, his mouth is on me.

He closes his lips around my nipple, and the sound that tears out of me is helpless. Humiliating in how desperate it is. A strangled gasp that betrays everything I was trying to hide.

He groans softly in response, a husky rumble that echoes against my skin.

"I had a feeling you'd like that," he says, his voice rough enough to send shivers down my spine.

Next, his tongue flicks over the peak again, repeating the motion as if he wants to study every reaction he draws from me. The suction intensifies, with long, deep pulls that drag heat straight to my core.

And when his free hand moves to my other breast, cupping it gently—his palm rough against the sensitive skin—I almost whimper. It's too much and not enough.

His touch brands me. His mouth owns me. My brain is scrambling, and my body is gone.

I should be thinking. But everything I experience is his mouth, his hand, his breath against my skin, and the sick, undeniable truth that no one has ever made me feel this wanted.

Not until him. Not like this.

His growl cuts through me, a deep, animalistic sound that races straight between my legs. Heat floods my lower belly. I squirm beneath him, gasping when his mouth moves to my other nipple, sucking hard until he pulls away with an obscene, wet pop that leaves me trembling.

His lips trail down the center of my body, open-mouthed kisses pressed into every inch of skin from my ribs to my stomach. It's slow and possessive, as if he's tasting what already belongs to him.

When he reaches the waistband of my tights, he pauses long enough to make me ache. Before his fingers hook into the sides and tug, dragging them down my legs with deliberate care. The fabric sticks to my thighs, and he lets out a breath as he peels them off.

"Christ," he mutters, his voice frayed. "These have been driving me crazy."

He tosses them, along with my shoes, onto the floor without looking. His mouth drops to my hipbone. His teeth graze across my lower stomach, and I jolt, thighs tightening.

"I can smell how bad you want me."

Oh. My. God.

I want the floor to swallow me whole. The embarrassment burns through me until his tongue slips along the waistband of my panties and his breath hits my skin like fire.

"I can't wait to taste it," he rasps.

My hands grip the sheets. My whole body feels like it's on fire. His voice carries that kind of tone that makes promises no one's ever kept, except him.

Reece is going to kill me tonight.

And I'm going to beg for it.

Hooking his fingers into the sides of my panties, he begins to ease them down. Slow, teasing, as if he's unwrapping something far more interesting than the plain, slightly too-worn cotton panties currently ruining my life.

I regret everything.

I wish I'd worn the black lace ones buried in the back of my drawer. The ones I save for days I think I might be hot. Not these. Not the boring white pair that screams responsible and washes her delicates with the gentle cycle. Nothing about them says, "fuck me senseless". They say "Target, three for twenty," but right now he doesn't seem to notice or even care.

He groans as he lowers his head, pressing his face firmly against the damp cotton. My breath catches in my throat as he inhales, as if it's the most wonderful smell he's ever encountered.

I cry out, my body jolting from the sudden intensity of it.

Panic grips my chest. My legs lock up. My hands jerk. I've never been touched like this before. Never had someone's mouth so close. And now, with his face buried between my thighs, all I can think about is how the hell I'm supposed to respond.

Do I moan?

Stay silent?

Say something?

What if I do it wrong?

I wish I were one of those girls—the ones who know how to arch their backs, tug at hair, and whisper dirty encouragements with perfect timing. The confident bitches in the steamy college books I read. But I'm not them.

I'm the girl who wears basic underwear and overthinks her breathing patterns while a guy goes down on her.

Still, when he finally pulls my panties off and throws them on the floor, he doesn't hesitate. His eyes darken as they move down, locking onto my pussy as if it's the last meal he'll ever get.

"Jesus," he mutters, voice gritty, a crooked grin playing on his lips. "Look at you." His gaze drags up, and I swear he actually looks awed. "Fucking perfect."

I blink. "Perfect? In my grandma panties?"

His grin widens. "Especially in those. Makes unwrapping you even better."

Oh my God!

Reece is insane.

I have so many flaws. Too many.

He's just being nice. That's all it is—a way to use sweet words to get what he wants.

His eyes follow every inch of skin as if I'm the most flawless thing he's ever seen. And it messes with my head.

My chest rises, my ribs expand too much, and the defenses I built brick by brick begin to crack.

His finger trails down the center of me. Featherlight over my slit.

"Open for me."

Tiny shivers run across my stomach. My legs shift. I hold my breath. I should say something, stop this from going any further. But I want to see what he'll do.

I spread my legs.

Barely.

His eyes darken.

"Wider. Show me everything."

Heat prickles across my skin as I obey, lifting my knees up and apart, fully exposing myself to him. Every inch of me bare and trembling.

"Good girl," he murmurs. The words fall over my skin soft as velvet. Then, his eyes flick to mine.

"If you want me to stop, you tell me. You say it. Do you hear me, Sam?"

I nod, but it's still not enough.

He leans in closer. His breath brushes against my inner thigh.

"Say it."

My voice barely gets past my throat.

"I'll tell you."

His eyes never leave mine as he lowers his mouth.

And I forget how to fucking breathe.

He shoots me a look that's completely predatory, the kind that says I won't escape unscathed. His lips brush the inside of my thigh, as if tasting the anticipation bleeding out of me.

"Has anyone ever kissed you here before?" he asks, breath hot against my skin.

I should respond, but my brain short-circuits. All language vanishes. There's only heat, pressure, and the way his mouth hovers so close it makes me twitch.

I shake my head.

That's all I can give him.

His lips curl into a wicked smile. "I'm gonna make you come so fucking hard."

That's the only warning I get before his mouth is on me.

My body jerks. My hands shoot to the blanket, clutching it as if I might fall through the mattress at any moment. I twist beneath him, unable to stay still, my mind scrambled from the first swipe of his tongue.

He licks me slowly at first, just enough to tease and make me ache, before he sucks—firm and hungry. My hips buck against his face.

He groans into me. The sound vibrates through my core as it sends another wave of heat crashing down my spine. My thighs tremble. My head drops back. I make a noise I've never made before in my life.

His tongue flicks over my clit quickly and precisely, then slows into a long, dragging circle that leaves me gasping. He knows exactly what he's doing—and worse, he understands the effect it has on me.

Greedy sounds burst from him as he pulls me into his mouth, each wet stroke ending with a filthy flick of his tongue across my clit. He groans against me, as if he's the one falling apart.

I arch into the sensation, my spine bowing off the mattress. He's relentless. Unforgiving. His mouth works me until I belong to him completely.

And damn, maybe I am his.

If this is what it feels like... if this is what those girls experience when they crawl into his lap and moan his name in the hallway, no wonder they keep coming back. No wonder they can't help themselves. Greedy little whores. And now I understand.

He teases me cruelly, repeatedly pushing me to the edge only to pull back just before I fall. My breath comes in ragged bursts. My fingers clutch the blanket tightly, and my thighs tremble, but I still can't stop myself from chasing it.

Then his grip tightens.

Fingers digging into my thighs, he pulls me closer, his mouth covering my clit. His tongue circles, then sucks—long, slow pulls that leave me gasping.

Instinct takes control. My hand moves, pressing on his head, holding him in place, craving the pressure. The sound that escapes me is part moan, part desperate plea.

"Fuck yeah," he growls, pulling my clit into his mouth again. He suckles hard, the sound obscene, wet and so fucking perfect. "Keep making those sounds for me."

And I do.

I can't stop.

Every time I do, his tongue dips deeper, licking through my folds. My hips move into his face, chasing every flick, pulse, and rush of heat.

Then... fuck... he adds a finger into the mix.

It slides in smoothly, his mouth still locked on my clit, his finger pumping in sync with the rhythm of his tongue. I cry out, legs jerking, everything inside me clenched tight.

It's both too much and not enough. I need more of everything.

A garbled noise escapes from my throat as he slips in a second finger, curling them inside me. He withdraws them, then pushes back in, filling me completely. The pressure, the stretch, the way his mouth keeps working—it's all too good. I can't think. I can barely breathe.

I buck against him, frantic. "Reece—" My voice breaks. "Oh my God." I twist my fingers in his hair, pulling hard as a wave of pleasure slams through me. "I'm...gonna—"

He doesn't let up. He shifts, kissing my pussy the way he kissed my mouth earlier. I whimper as he builds it again, and somehow it's worse this time. Better. More intense. Each pass of his tongue wrings more sound out of me.

I'm panting, writhing, fisting his hair as my thighs shake.

"Fuck, Reece... I'm so close."

"I know you are." His voice is a dark, smug rasp. A slow, wicked smile pulls at the corners of his glistening mouth.

He gives me one long, lazy lick.

"Eyes on me."

Wet sounds fill the room as he settles into a rhythm that makes my head spin. His mouth works me with relentless precision, tongue dragging, sucking, circling, never letting up. I lift my head enough to watch him, and, fuck, it's the sexiest thing I've ever seen. His face between my thighs. Mouth glistening. His focus locked on me as if nothing else exists.

"Reece," I gasp, my voice thin and broken.

Oh God, please.

I'm right there, so close it feels almost dangerous. My body is humming, buzzing, stretched tight with need, and if he doesn't let me come soon, I swear I might actually combust.

Something dark flashes in his eyes. He sucks my swollen clit harder, unapologetic, and then pushes another finger inside me, curling them just right. The pressure hits so deep I cry out, my whole body jolting.

I grind against his jaw, desperate, chasing the knot of pleasure he's built inside me as it coils tighter and tighter. There's nothing careful left in me now. No good girl. No restraint. Simply this version of me that wants to come so badly it borders on feral.

I don't care how it happens.

I don't care how loud I am.

All I want is to fall apart, to give in, and to see just how far Reece Wilson can push me.

It feels so fucking good.

Sounds tear from me, my thighs trembling uncontrollably as his fingers and tongue hit spots that turn me inside out. I can't stay still. I can't think past the heat surging through me.

A sharp cry slices through the air.

God, I'm so loud.

But I can't stop it. I don't even try. I'm beyond caring, beyond shame, beyond everything except the way my body is chasing release with reckless determination. I grind against his mouth shamelessly, using him, riding the pressure, until the tension snaps.

I explode.

Pleasure crashes over me like a violent wave, overwhelming and intense, as my back arches and the orgasm rips through my body. I seize up. My voice breaks. Everything turns white as I fall apart on his face, helpless and trembling, completely undone.

And even as it tears through me, one thought cuts through the chaos.

I am never going to be the same after this.

CHAPTER 12

REECE

Her cunt's still fluttering from the aftershocks, but her face tells a different story. Cheeks flushed, mouth parted, eyes wide like she doesn't know what the fuck just hit her.

Good. She shouldn't, because that wasn't forgettable. I was getting high off her pussy like it was the first hit of something I knew would ruin me.

I've never done that before. Never buried my face between a girl's thighs and let her ride until she climaxed.

But Red?

Fuck. I wanted to.

The moment I saw that pretty pussy begging for attention, I lost all control I had been pretending to hold.

And now she's lying there trembling, fists clenched in the sheets as if she's afraid to let go, trying to remember how to breathe. But her face gives her away.

She's embarrassed. Ashamed. Probably thinking she was too loud, too needy, too fucking raw.

That's the part that really pisses me off because there's nothing wrong with the way she came or the way she gave that to me.

She's fucking beautiful. That pussy, those sounds.

I kiss my way up her thighs, dragging my lips across her stomach while I feel her eyes on me. She's tense, caught between losing herself in the pleasure and wishing she hadn't.

I stay silent until I'm level with her again. My thumb brushes the damp edge of her jaw as I rest my forehead against hers.

"You're beautiful, Red, you know that?" My voice lowers now, less cocky.

Her eyes flutter shut, and I press my mouth to hers, slow at first, the kind of kiss that makes you forget how to breathe. My heart races in my chest.

"Are you scared, Red?" I ask, voice low, hoarse from everything I'm holding back.

Her hands slip into my hair, nails brushing my scalp as she pulls me closer. "I'm fucking terrified," she whispers, then kisses me as if she's not.

It's not sweet.

It's pure chaos.

Tongues clash, teeth catch, lips bruise. The kiss that tastes like lust, pain, and every unspoken thing between us. She doesn't pull away. She kisses me as if she's trying to win something.

I match her heat, that raw edge behind it, grinding against her as I take her mouth. My cock's straining, demanding friction. I need her. Need to be inside her.

"Keep making that fucking sexy sound," I groan against her lips, breathless as she moans into the kiss. That desperate, needy whimper makes my hips jerk forward.

Her fingers move to my jeans, fumbling with the button, and I lose whatever patience I was pretending to have. I grab her wrist, stopping her. Her pupils are dilated, her lips are swollen, her cheeks are flushed, and for a moment she hesitates.

"You made me come," she says, her voice a little shaky. "Now it's your turn." Then, more softly and uncertain, she adds, "If you want."

What the fuck kind of question is that?

My mouth drops to her throat. I nip at her skin, leaving a mark. "You think I don't want to bury my cock in you after that? You think I didn't nearly come in my jeans watching you lose it on my mouth?"

I move up onto the bed, slow and careful, keeping my damn mouth shut for once because this isn't about me. It's about her. About the way her eyes flicker with nerves and want, about the way her body still trembles from what I did to her. I give her space to decide what happens next. She doesn't need me pushing, doesn't need me running my mouth like I always do. She needs to know she can call the shots.

I lean against the headboard, watching her closely but not too intensely. I don't want her to think this is something I expect. Damn, I don't even know if she's done this before. She doesn't act like a girl who's been passed around, and I've never seen her with anyone who looked like they knew what to do with her body. Only those geeky guys who stumble through every sentence when she looks their way. I don't think any of them would have the balls to try. I've seen how they eye-fuck her when they think no one's watching. I've also seen how she never gives them an inch.

And maybe I should have kept my distance. But I didn't. I've watched too much. Thought too much. Wanted too much.

Now she's here, and I'm really trying not to ruin this moment.

Her fingers brush my knee as she crawls up beside me. I stay still, let her take the lead, set the pace. Her breathing is shaky. Her eyes flick down to where my cock strains beneath my jeans, then back to my face. She's nervous.

I reach up and tuck a strand of hair behind her ear. "You don't have to do anything you're not ready for," I murmur.

Her lips part, but no words come out at first. Then she swallows and says, "I want to. I just... I don't know how far I want to go yet."

"That's fine, Red," I say. "We'll go as far as you want. No more."

She leans in again, and her kiss is slower this time—less frantic, more focused. Like she's decided. When she pulls back, I can't stop watching her. My pulse thunders in my ears as she reaches down, fingers brushing my stomach, then lower. She pops the button on my jeans and eases the zipper down, the sound too loud in the quiet room.

My body goes still.

Her hand slips inside, and my throat tightens like a damn vice the second her fingers brush against my cock. My hips jerk instinctively, and I bite back a groan. She wraps her hand around me, curious, careful, but there's nothing gentle about the effect it has on me.

She pulls me out, but all I see is her—the way she looks at my cock.

She says nothing.

She simply stares.

I don't know what the fuck she's thinking. My stomach knots up. Is she overwhelmed? Scared? Turned off? My chest aches, and I almost say something, but then her fingers drift down the underside of my cock and—

"Fuck," I grit out, a hiss dragging through my teeth as my head hits the pillow behind me.

Her touch is featherlight, tracing the vein with the tip of her finger. It is not even pressure, only exploration. But it undoes me.

She looks up at me, lips glistening, eyes wide and dark with heat. But there's also a smugness there—a flicker of pride. She enjoys this. The way I'm falling apart for her, how I can barely breathe when her hand slides down my cock.

The air thickens, heavy with desire and her scent. She shifts closer, lowers her head again. Her tongue flicks out, tasting me. Before she wraps her mouth around the head and sucks me down hard and fast. Too fast.

She chokes on it.

"Jesus Christ," I growl, grabbing her shoulders. Her mouth slips free with a wet sound, and she coughs once, wiping her lips with the back of her hand.

Her eyes flick up to mine, embarrassed.

"I'm sorry," she says quickly. "I thought... that's what guys like."

That's the moment it all clicks.

When I fucking know.

She has never tried this before.

I sense it. The apology in her voice. That uncertainty in her touch. The way she tried too hard, as if she was mimicking something she saw, not something she's ever done.

Sam is a virgin.

I trace the edge of her jaw with my thumb, slow and steady, grounding her. "Just do what you were doing. But softer. Slower." My voice is rough, coaxing, not commanding, and yet still lined with authority she clearly responds to.

Her breath trembles, but she nods, biting her lip as she looks down at me. Her hand shakes just slightly as she wraps it around the base of my cock again, fingers tentative but eager.

"Kiss it," I tell her, my tone dropping lower. "Right on the tip."

She leans in and does just that, pressing her mouth to the shiny crown. My abs tighten at the contact. Her lips are soft, uncertain, but the effect is immediate.

"More," I rasp, my voice catching on the heat curling low in my spine. "Kiss it the way I kissed your pretty little cunt earlier."

Her cheeks flush, but she obeys.

She opens her mouth and licks slowly across the tip, slow this time, letting her tongue swirl around the head with the lightest pressure. The kind that fucking wrecks me. A small drop of pre-cum glistens, and she laps it up, her tongue flicking out again to taste me.

A soft sound escapes my throat. I give myself a slow stroke, guiding her through it.

"Good girl," I murmur, my voice ragged.

I gently press my hand at the back of her head and guide her forward, enough for her to take the head into her mouth. Her lips stretch around it, tentative but willing.

"That's it," I grunt. "Give me more of that tongue."

She hums against me, swirling her tongue as if she's trying to memorize the shape of me.

And fuck, if she keeps doing that, I won't last long. Not when I'm showing her exactly how I like it.

"Fuck," I groan, head dropping back for half a second. It's like I've gone to cock heaven.

Her mouth's so wet and tight, lips stretched wide around me. I pull back with a grunt, almost all the way out. The sight of her, on her knees, eyes glassy, lips slick with saliva and me.

Christ.

"Do you know how fucking sexy you look right now, Red?"

She pulls away, but I thrust into her mouth.

My body coils tightly. My control begins to unravel.

"Christ, I want to fuck your perfect face," I grit out, jaw clenching. "You'd let me, wouldn't you?"

She doesn't respond. Instead, she just looks up at me with those wide, innocent eyes as her mouth moves around my cock—lips slick, tongue teasing.

And that look... damn, that look nearly destroys me completely.

She likes this. Watching me lose control.

A feral sound tears out of my throat as I reach down and twist her hair around my fist, pulling it tight. The messier she gets, the more fucking perfect she looks.

"Hold still," I growl, voice breaking. "Let me use that mouth."

Her lashes flutter. She follows my commands.

That's the only warning I give her before I slam my free hand against the wall behind her and fuck into her mouth like I own it.

Hard.

Relentless.

My hips piston, using that pretty mouth the way I've dreamed about a hundred fucking times. But no dream ever came close to this. No fantasy was this good. Nothing compares to her lips stretched around me, spit pooling at the corners of her mouth as she gags and moans as if she wants it rough.

I realize I should slow down.

I should ease up. Be gentle. This is her first time.

But I can't.

She's got me fucking unhinged.

"Shit, Red," I grind out, muscles flexing. "You feel so fucking good."

I glance down, and, fuck me, the sight is enough to end me. Her throat works around the head of my cock, her hands gripping my thighs for balance, nails digging in when I go deep. She takes it. All of it. Letting me claim her mouth the same way I've dreamed of claiming her pussy.

And yeah, I've dreamed of this. Her lips wrapped around me. Her cunt soaking my cock. Her whimpers echoing off my walls. I've fucked my fist to that image more nights than I can count.

But this?

This surpasses anything I had imagined.

"Fuck, you're perfect," I growl. "So fucking perfect for me."

She gags slightly when I thrust too deep, and I curse again, panting hard.

"Breathe through your nose," I tell her, pulling back slightly.

Her mouth relaxes, and I take every damn inch she offers.

She lets me use her as I fuck her mouth deep, and fuck me; she's a natural. Her cheeks hollow around my cock, eyes locked to mine, begging for more even as tears streak her pretty face.

"Jesus," I say, fisting her hair tighter. "You like the taste of my cock, pretty girl?"

She moans, and it vibrates through me. Saliva drips down her chin, mixing with the mess already coating her lips, and she nods, eyes glassy and blown wide.

"Fuck," I rasp, chest heaving. "Show me how much."

She shifts on her knees and pulls me in further.

No girl has ever made me lose control like this.

She sucks harder and faster. My hips twitch forward on instinct. I groan, letting her know how fucking good it is. How much I want to blow in that mouth and watch her swallow every drop.

"Good fucking girl," I grunt. "You want me to come for you? That it?"

She nods again.

"Then keep going," I growl. "Make me come, Red. Make me fucking lose it for you."

She moans around me, mouth locked tight, suction deepening until I'm fucking undone.

"Fuck...Red."

The orgasm hits like a freight train. My hips jerk. My head drops back. A strangled sound escapes as I spill down her throat, hot and messy.

She doesn't flinch. Just keeps swallowing every drop while my cock throbs between her lips. A strangled sound tears from my throat. I've never come this hard. Never encountered anything like this before.

I look down at her—face flushed, lips swollen, mouth ruined from where I fucked it. Her eyes flick up.

"My dirty girl," I murmur, brushing a thumb across her slick chin. "You're my fucking dirty girl."

She releases my cock with a wet pop, saliva stretching between us, chest heaving as if she just ran a marathon. And shit, maybe she did.

Perfect. Beautiful.

Always so in control. But right now?

She's mine.

"You enjoy tasting me?"

She nods once, still breathless.

I lift her by the waist until she's straddling me, her knees pressed against the mattress.

"You're perfect, Red," I rasp, eyes locked on hers. "So fucking perfect."

I roll us fast, hard, taking the top so I can take the weight of her beneath me. My cock settles right against her pussy, and fuck, a shift of my hips would put me inside her. I could take her the way I've always imagined.

She crashes her mouth against mine, open and desperate, and wraps those legs around me. Hips grinding up like she's starving for the friction, as if she's trying to pull me in, force the inevitable.

"Fuck, you need to stop," I grit out, pulling back just enough to breathe, forehead pressed to hers. "Christ, Red. I'll fucking slide in if you don't."

Her eyes are wild, mouth swollen, breath jagged.

"I want these off," she growls, yanking at my jeans.

The corner of my mouth curls into a grin as I roll off her, sprawled out on the bed beside her. "I'm not stopping you," I murmur, voice thick.

She shifts as her fingers tug my jeans down, followed by my boxers.

Her hands are trembling. I can tell how nervous she is.

"Red," I say. "We can stop if you want."

She moves closer, climbing over me until her lips are mere inches from mine. "Kiss me." Her voice wavers, and so do her lips. But beneath that, there's something firm—something hungry and certain.

I kiss her softly at first—tender and slow, giving her every chance to pull away. But she doesn't. She deepens the kiss, her mouth becoming firmer and bolder.

"Fuck me," she breathes against my lips, "and make me yours."

I groan, tightening my grip on her hips, and suddenly she's on her back beneath me, her hair splayed across the pillow, eyes wide and shining.

"Are you sure?" I ask, my voice hoarse. I'm hanging on by a fucking thread. "Red, I swear, if you say no now, I'll stop. But if you say yes..." My jaw tightens. "I'm not holding back."

She bites her bottom lip and nods. Fuck, that look... those eyes, the blush creeping down her neck. It's the hottest fucking thing I've ever seen.

Who knew the girl who's had me twisted in knots for months could tease like this? Could flip me inside out with just one damn nod.

"Have you done this before?" I ask, trying to stay grounded.

She looks away.

I hold her chin and make her look at me. "Don't lie to me, Red. I need to know. It changes the way I fuck you."

"No," she whispers. "I haven't been with anyone else. I want it to be you."

That faint whisper of truth unravels something deep inside my chest. Something primal. Possessive. Feral.

She wants me to be her first.

I brush my lips across her jaw, down her throat. "Good," I growl. "And for the record…" I pull back just enough to meet her gaze. "You're already mine."

I reach across and grab a condom from the drawer, rip it open with my teeth, spit the foil to the floor, and roll it over my cock one slow stroke at a time. My hand works up and down the length of me, and I feel her stare burn into every fucking inch.

When I look up, her eyes are on my cock, and, fuck, that makes me harder.

"I'll take it slow," I mutter, voice rough with restraint.

Truth is, I've never taken it slow. Never needed to. Never wanted to. I fuck to forget, to get off, to wipe the slate clean. It's always been fast, hard, and dirty—as if it's a goddamn competition to finish first and walk away without remembering a name.

But this?

This isn't about getting off.

It's about her, and I'm not going to ruin her first time by treating it like every other fuck.

I shift between her thighs, grip my cock, and guide the tip to her pussy. She tenses a little, but I feel it. Her breath catches. Her thighs tighten.

"Breathe, Red," I say, my voice softening as I slide the head of my cock through her folds. "I'm not gonna hurt you."

Her lashes flutter. Her chest rises and falls with shaky breaths, and fuck, she's so beautiful in this vulnerable state. Trusting me to be her first.

I press in, slowly and carefully, just the tip, and her warmth wraps around me like a fucking vice. I bite back a groan.

Fuck, it's tight.

Gloriously fucking tight.

My cock throbs as I watch the head push in, swallowed inch by inch by her warm, untouched pussy. I lift my gaze to her face because, as much as I want to get lost in what she feels like wrapped around me, this isn't about me. It's about her. About Red.

Her brows are pinched, lips parted, and her breath is shaky.

"Does it hurt?" I ask, voice hoarse from holding back.

She shakes her head. "No... it just feels strange."

My thumb traces her hip, anchoring us both. "So you want more?"

"Yeah," she breathes. "But slowly."

I nod and grip her hips, anchoring myself there as I push in another inch. Then another. Her pussy squeezes around me, hot and slick, still so damn tight every nerve ending sparks. Every cell in my body screams at me to thrust, to bury myself to the hilt and fuck her like I always do—rough, fast, no strings, no thought. Simply sensation.

But this isn't that.

This isn't some forgettable fuck.

This is Red. My fucking Red.

The girl who kissed me once when we were kids and rewired my whole damn brain. The girl who's been living rent-free in my head ever since — smiling, laughing, haunting me with everything I never thought I'd want.

I move slowly and deeper until I'm almost fully inside. Her hands grip my arms, nails digging into my skin. I lean in and press my forehead against hers, my chest rising and falling.

"You're doing so well," I whisper, barely holding it together. "So fucking good."

She nods, her eyes glossy and her lips trembling. When I finally bottom out, fully buried inside her, I swear I see stars.

I give her some time.

Not just for her body to adjust, but because if I even think about moving right now, I'll blow my load like a teenage rookie and embarrass myself. It's that tight. That perfect. That fucking dangerous.

My arms tremble with restraint. I breathe through my nose, counting backwards, trying not to picture the way her pussy's gripping me, because if I do, I'm finished. This will go down faster than my first time, and that disaster barely lasted ten thrusts before I was apologizing and blaming it on excitement.

So, I wait.

I keep my eyes fixed on her face, watching for every flicker of emotion and each flutter of her eyelashes.

"You okay?" I ask, my voice hoarse.

She nods.

I still don't move. "Words, Red. I need your fucking words."

Her eyes meet mine.

"Yeah," she whispers. "I'm okay."

I move slowly, even though every inch of my cock sliding out of her pussy feels like hell and heaven tangled together. It takes everything in me not to lose control, not to fuck her the way my body is screaming for. I stay focused.

I pull back a little, her heat clinging to me, and ease back in. It's slow, measured, so it doesn't hurt her. Then I pull out again, slower this time, going a little deeper before easing back into her, letting her adjust to the rhythm. My cock throbs, begging for more, but I keep the pace steady, letting her body learn me inch by inch.

She relaxes beneath me. I feel it in the way her pussy opens, takes me deeper. I watch her face as I fuck her slow, the tension easing from her brow, her lips parting on shaky breaths. She's so fucking beautiful it hurts.

"Christ," I murmur, my voice low and rough. "You feel so good wrapped around my cock."

Her eyes flutter, and I thrust deeper, making sure she feels every part of me.

"Fuck," I growl. "I could stay right here in this pussy forever."

I move easier now, her body no longer tense from nerves or hesitation. She's experiencing it.

I shift my hand down between us, finding her clit with my thumb, brushing over it lightly—testing. Her gasp is instantaneous. Her eyes flutter shut, lashes fanning across her cheeks, and her lips part on a moan that makes my spine arch.

That sound... well, fuck me, I'd kill to hear it again.

Her hips shift, chasing the pressure, and that's when I know. She wants it now. Her moans grow louder, needier. She's no longer nervous; she's getting greedy.

I press more firmly on her clit, and her entire body jerks.

"Good girl," I breathe, fucking mesmerized. "You feel that? That's your pussy getting addicted to my cock."

She whimpers, and fuck, I swear I'll be jerking off to this moment for the rest of my life.

"Eyes on me, Red," I growl, never slowing the rhythm of my cock fucking into her.

Her moans are pure, fucking music, each sound pulling me closer to the edge. I want her to break first. I want to see what she looks like when she falls apart for me.

"Come for me, Red. Let go. Let me feel it."

"Reece," she whimpers, voice shattered, body trembling.

"I've got you," I say.

My rhythm shifts without meaning to. Slower. Deeper. Every thrust is a promise, a claim. Her body rises to meet mine, hips lifting with each thrust. I lean down and drag my mouth over the column of her throat, tasting her skin, inhaling the soft, warm scent of her hair as it fans across the pillow.

One more thrust and she breaks.

Her mouth drops open in a silent gasp before it crashes into a cracked, desperate moan that tears right through me. Her brows pull together, lashes fluttering, her whole face twisted in something so fucking beautiful it knocks the breath right out of me. Her back arches, thighs trembling, her cunt gripping my cock as she comes undone.

I don't even chase my release.

It crashes into me the second she falls apart—hot, fierce, and unstoppable. I groan, hips snapping forward as I spill into the condom, but my eyes never leave her.

She's still trembling. Still gasping. Still lost in the aftershocks of what I just did to her.

And I can't stop.

I keep fucking her through it, trying to etch the memory into my bones. Her eyes are glazed, her body soft, red hair wild, and every twitch of her pussy makes me want to drag it out a little longer.

When I still, I run my fingers over her face. Soft. Careful. She's quiet beneath me, skin warm, eyes wide.

"You okay?" I ask.

Because, fuck... this might be the best fucking day of my life.

She doesn't respond. Instead, she gazes at me.

A single blink. Then another. Slow and almost... distant.

Something on her face begins to change. Not a full recoil, just enough to make something cold cling to my chest.

"Red," I say again, this time more firmly.

She doesn't look away, but she's not really focused on me either. Her mouth parts as if she might speak, then closes again.

And that's when the panic hits.

An unwelcome surge of anxiety that cuts straight through me.

"Red," I say again. "Answer me."

She nods.

But it's a lie.

She's not the same girl who was beneath me ten seconds ago.

I kiss her once more, trying to anchor her to the moment. To me.

It doesn't.

I pull out, grab the condom, tie it off, and toss it in the trash. When I turn around, she's already getting dressed, snatching her bra off the floor and putting it on, tugging her shirt down with shaky hands. Her back's to me, but I can see it in the way her shoulders hunch.

I remain where I am, still naked.

"Sam?" My voice sounds rougher now.

She doesn't answer. She tugs on her boots and crouches to grab her phone, and her belongings and shoves them all into her bag. The silence lingers. It's too heavy, too loud. It's not the kind that follows something good. It's the kind that begins to rot.

I run a hand through my hair, trying to understand what's happening. We just shared everything. She let me in, and now she's shutting me out so quickly I can feel the walls closing back in.

"Talk to me, Sam." My voice catches on her name.

She's gone out the bedroom door before I can even get my fucking boxers back on.

Her footsteps echo down the hallway. They're sharp, fast, and panicked, but it's the silence after the front door slams that really wrecks me. I sit on the edge of my bed, staring at the space she filled. It's still warm where she was. Still smells like her. My chest splits open, as if something's pouring out—something I can't put back in.

I run my fingers through my hair, trying to figure out what the fuck happened.

One minute, she was beneath me, holding on as if she never wanted to let go. Now she's gone, just like I had imagined the whole thing.

And the worst part. She took every part of that moment with her and left this ache in my chest I don't know how to fucking fix.

I drag my hand down my face, my fingers trembling slightly. I never meant to fall this hard. But somehow, she got in.

And now she's out there, running away from me like I'm the worst mistake she's ever made. And maybe I am.

Maybe this was never real to her, but it was to me.

Fuck, it was.

CHAPTER 13

SAM

I don't sleep. Not really. I close my eyes, and I'm pulled right back into his room. Into his bed. Into that fucking moment that rewired everything I believed about my body.

It comes in flashes.

The weight of him pressed between my legs. His mouth on my skin. No chance to hide behind the girl I pretend to be. He stripped that mask off with his tongue and left me exposed.

There was only heat and desire.

And it hasn't let up since.

The echo of him remains. The way his cock filled me so deeply it took my breath away. The sound that escaped my throat when he slid inside was raw and guttural. It wasn't pain. It was surrender.

My pussy still aches from him. The way he moved, knowing exactly how to wreck me without even trying.

I remember how he watched me come, with that razor-sharp focus that made it obvious I was something he wanted to destroy slowly.

And he did.

I wake up soaked and panting, legs tangled in the sheets, chasing the memory of him—his mouth, his hands, his cock.

Fuck.

That's the part that haunts me.

It's how easy it was to fall apart for him.

How quickly he learned exactly where to touch and where to stay, how he made me feel owned.

And now?

Now I'm standing at my locker with books clutched in my hands, glaring at the metal door as if it personally screwed me over. My body feels like a mess. My head is a battlefield, and my heart is furious because it knows exactly who did this to me and still wants him anyway.

I slam the locker shut and take a breath that doesn't help steady me.

Fuck him.

And fuck me harder for wanting him to take me there again.

"Okay, spill," Aubrey says, sliding in beside me and immediately squinting at my face. "You're doing that thing with your mouth."

"What thing?" I mutter, shoving textbooks into my bag with zero organization and a lot of aggression.

"That thing where your lips go all tight," she says. "The one you do when you're pretending you're fine but your brain is actively lighting itself on fire. You're spiraling."

I pause.

"I'm not spiraling."

"You're twitching, then."

"I am not." I adjust the strap on my bag, tugging it a little too hard. "I'm fine."

Aubrey tilts her head, unimpressed. "You're never truly fine when you say you are. That's just your way of sounding calm while everything's falling apart."

I shoot her a look. "You're dramatic."

She grins. "And you're one bad decision away from a full emotional breakdown. So, again." She pulls at my arm. "Spill."

I lean towards her, keeping my voice low. "What do you want me to say, Aub? That I did something monumentally stupid? That I let the school's resident fuckboy turn me into some wide-eyed, gasping cliché?

That I can't stop thinking about him, even though I'm pretty sure I hate him?"

She stills. Her eyes widen. "You slept with him."

I don't answer because I don't need to.

"Sam..." her voice is quiet now. Careful.

"I don't need the speech," I whisper. "I've already delivered it to myself five times before breakfast, complete with dramatic pauses. And don't you dare tell Lola about this, because she'll have it trending by the end of first period."

I turn and walk away, with Aubrey falling into step beside me.

The hallway is noisy. Voices overlap. Lockers slam shut. Girls laugh loudly. Somewhere down the hall, a phone drops, and someone swears. It should all feel normal.

But it doesn't.

Everything sounds distant and muffled beneath the static screaming inside my head. My skin feels tight, and my shoulders stay high as if braced for an impact that hasn't arrived yet. Every laugh feels like it's aimed at me, and every group of girls makes my pulse race.

I'm waiting for the whispers. The "I-heard-Reece-totally-nailed-her" ones. The smug looks. The knowing glances. Waiting to hear that he had won. That the bet with Jace paid off. I brace for it with every step.

But nothing happens. No one looks twice or snickers when I pass by. No one leans in to whisper anything behind their hands. Conversations continue as if I don't exist at all.

I swallow hard and keep walking, my heart pounding, knowing it's not a matter of if it will happen. It's a matter of when.

I see him at the end of the hallway before he sees me.

He's with Jace and a few other guys. Shoulders loose. Heads tipped together. Laughing as if nothing in the world has weight. Reece stands a little taller than the rest, hands shoved in his pockets, that smug fucking grin carved into his face. He throws his head back at something Jace says, laughter rough and easy.

I slow down unintentionally. My mouth becomes dry.

I wonder if they're congratulating him. If Jace is patting him on the shoulder, calling him a legend, demanding details. If Reece is casually feeding them pieces of me, like guys do when they think a girl is just a story. I picture him talking about my mouth, my sounds, the way I lost control. About how easily he made me forget my name.

The thought makes my skin crawl.

He shifts.

Our eyes meet.

Just for a second.

Long enough for my chest to hurt.

Then he looks away.

He laughs at something Jace says and nudges his arm, casual and familiar, as if I don't exist. He turns fully back to his friends and keeps talking, shoulders relaxed, grin back in place.

And somehow, that hurts more than all his teasing ever did.

Aubrey catches it instantly. Of course she does.

"He's ignoring you," she mutters.

"I noticed."

"He's a fucking asshole," she says.

I swallow hard, my throat dry, as shame climbs up my neck and makes my skin tighten. "Don't say anything about this to Noah," I mumble. "Please, Aubrey. I know you two share everything, but I'm asking you. Don't tell anyone."

She glances at me.

"I just—" My voice wobbles before I can stop it. "I thought I wouldn't feel this stupid. That maybe I wouldn't just be another girl he fucked."

The words come out tasting terrible. Too honest. Too raw.

We start walking again, weaving through the bodies clogging the hallway, lockers slamming, voices bouncing around us like none of this matters, like my chest isn't caving in on itself.

"I won't say anything," Aubrey says firmly. "I promise."

She looks at me. "Are you okay?"

I don't even bother pretending. "No."

The truth feels heavy and bitter on my tongue, so I let it sit there because lying would hurt more.

"You know, I thought that if I gave away that part of myself," I say quietly, "it'd be to someone who—"

"Deserved it?" Aubrey finishes.

I nod, my throat tightening.

She exhales, looping her arm through mine to ground me when my feet feel a little too light. "It meant more to you than it did to him."

"I knew that going in," I say. "I know who he is."

We slow down near the courtyard, sunlight spilling across the concrete, voices drifting from outside. Lola's coming toward us, unmistakable even from a distance, full of her energy, opinions, and zero subtlety.

"I hate him," I mutter, the words bitter.

"You don't."

"I want to."

"Wanting and doing are two very different things," Aubrey says, squeezing my arm.

I swallow, watching Lola get closer, knowing Aubrey's right and hating her a little for it.

Wanting him is easy. It's the walking away that is the part I don't know how to do anymore.

Lola barrels toward us, ponytail swinging, phone already in her hand as if she's mid-broadcast. "You will not guess what happened to me this morning," she announces, eyes bright, grin feral. "My coffee betrayed me, my bus driver hates joy, and my skirt blew up. I'm ninety percent sure I flashed Mr Carver as he got out of his car."

She stops.

Her grin flickers as she surveys us. Me with my jaw clenched. Aubrey too silent. The atmosphere all off.

"Oh," Lola says, lowering her phone. "Never mind. Read the room, Lola. What's wrong?"

I sense it then. The weight of it. The moment when, if I open my mouth, everything spills out and I fall apart in front of everyone.

"Sam." Her tone softens completely. "What's going on?"

I swallow and shake my head. "Nothing. I just need to go to the bathroom before first period."

I don't wait around for an argument.

I turn and walk, quickening my pace, eyes fixed ahead. I push through the crowd, past the laughter and the usual hum of a morning that doesn't pay attention to me.

I don't stop until I'm in the last stall, door locked behind me.

My chest heaves. My palms sting from where my nails dug in too hard. I sit on the lid and fold over, forehead pressed into my knees like I can make myself smaller, quieter, invisible.

I am so fucking stupid.

I let him in. Past every wall, past every lock. I handed him pieces of myself I swore I'd keep guarded. Let his hands explore where no one else ever has. He kissed me as if I mattered. Fuck me like he truly wanted me.

I believed it all because of the way he looked at me, as if it meant something. That the way my body reacted showed we were speaking the same language. That for one reckless night, I wasn't just another girl passing through his hands.

And now?

Now he stands in these halls as if I don't exist.

Chapter 14

REECE

I can't stop thinking about the way she came for me. It doesn't matter what I do to drown it out. It doesn't matter how many laps I run until my lungs feel shredded or how many times I grip the bar and bench until my chest screams and my arms shake. None of it touches her. I can't sweat her out.

Her scent still lingers.

On my skin. In my mouth. In the part of my brain that's short-circuiting and glitching the fuck out.

I replay it without permission.

The sounds she made when she broke apart—those wrecked, breathless gasps. Her back arched, her mouth open, those pretty fucking whimpers spilling from her throat as if she didn't know how to hold them in. That soft little sound she made when I pushed in slowly, then harder, testing her, feeling her open up for me. Those desperate little fucking sounds that made my cock twitch before I was all the way buried.

Tight. Slick. Fucking heaven.

Jesus.

The way her pussy took me. Her mouth opened as if she couldn't breathe unless it was through me. The kind of heat that rewires your mind. That makes you forget every other body you've ever touched.

Fuck.

Red was heaven soaked in heat and sin, and now she's poison in my veins, already burning me from the inside out.

And then she fucking ran.

That part is stuck on repeat. She pulled her clothes back on with shaking hands and bolted as if she couldn't get away fast enough. Left me lying there, breath still fucked, heart pounding, staring at her as if I had been the one who had been used.

Guess that's karma.

I've walked away from girls many times after getting my dick wet. Left them with nothing but a memory and a sore body. I never thought twice about it.

Turns out I don't handle it very well when I'm the one left behind.

Not when I cared. Or that I was still inside her a minute before she ghosted me.

I slam my locker shut so hard that the hinge rattles and a few students jump.

Good.

My head's pounding from lack of sleep and too many swirling thoughts about her. Everything's too damn loud. There are too many people around. And there she is again in my mind, her voice cracking as she moaned my name.

Fuck. This is what I get. I treated girls as temporary side notes, and now the girl I truly desire won't even glance at me.

Jace stands next to me and pats my shoulder. He snaps me out of my spiral.

"Jesus, you look like you haven't slept in a week. What chick did you hook up with this time?"

I grin automatically, muscle memory kicking in. I don't answer because I don't want him to know it's Sam who has fucked me completely.

Jace leans back against the lockers, grinning at a girl in a skirt too short to be legal.

"Damn," he mutters. "You see that bounce? Fuck, this year's buffet just keeps getting better."

I grunt, distracted.

"You're grumpy," he says, grinning. "You finally tapped that cherry girl or what?"

"No," I say too quickly, eyes darting down the hall so he can't see the lie all over my face.

He laughs. "What the fuck is stopping you, man? You usually have girls folded in days." He leans closer, voice dropping. "No way you're gonna tap that frigid bitch."

My fist curls before I can stop it.

Heat surges through me, sharp and ugly. One more word, and I'd happily rearrange his damn face for talking about Red like that. For turning her into something cheap and laughable when he has no idea what she felt like.

Jace keeps talking, unaware that I'm one step away from punching him.

"Bring on the two hundred. Fuck, I could really use that shit."

I hate myself for the bet. That my ego couldn't handle the rejection when she shut me down repeatedly and that I needed to prove something instead of walking away.

And now all I feel is trapped in it.

Across the hall, Tia's high-pitched voice sounds.

Here we fucking go.

"I don't give a damn if you wore it last week, Nicole," Tia snaps, chin held high, voice sharp enough to cut. "This is my color. You're obsessed with me, and it's getting weird."

Nicole scoffs, arms crossing tightly over her chest. "Please. Just because your dad bought you fake Chanel doesn't mean you own the color red."

A few gasps ripple through the crowd.

"Oh honey," Tia sneers, smiling venomously. "I own everything. Including the spot at the top. You should remember that before you start dressing for a throne that was never yours."

The circle tightens around them, with people leaning in and feeding off the energy. Phones are half-raised. Whispers buzz. Drama hits this place like blood in the water, and the sharks are starving.

Most people don't care about who wore what or which label their dad bought. But it's loud, chaotic, and entertaining. It's the chaos that helps everyone forget about the real shit simmering underneath.

Then my body becomes tense.

I sense her before I see her. A tingling sensation slides down my spine, and my focus snaps to the side without warning. Red is nearby. I don't know how. I just know.

And suddenly the noise fades, the yelling blurs, the crowd becomes background static. Because it has nothing to do with Tia, Nicole, or their petty little screwed-up war.

It all comes down to the girl who walked away.

My eyes remain fixed on her.

She's standing with Liz, who's crying over something I couldn't care less about, but Red's the one holding her as if she's trying to glue her back together. Gentle, quiet, and warm. The opposite of everything I am and everything I can't stop wanting.

She hasn't looked at me once. Not when she walked in today or when she crossed the quad. Not even now, when I know she damn well feels me watching her.

That same ache gnaws at my chest. It's bitter and sharp. She's avoiding me. Like yesterday, she walked right past me as if we were strangers and I hadn't had her gasping my name with my cock buried deep inside her.

I didn't have a clue what to do when I saw her yesterday. Still don't. My brain goes static, all that cocky bullshit I wear like armor slipping off the second she's close. This girl has threw a fucking grenade into my chest and walked away as if nothing had happened.

She hugs Liz tighter.

And then her eyes flick to mine.

It's not long. Maybe a second or two. But it's enough to knock the breath clean out of me. My stomach flips, heart stumbles like a rookie. I don't move. I can't.

Someone steps into my line of sight, and I want to shove them out of the way just to keep watching her.

Maya.

Blonde bombshell who you don't get to speak and tits that defy physics. Her personality's about as real as her moans, and I've heard both... twice. Possibly three times. It was never about her. It was about getting off, forgetting the fucking noise out of my head for a few minutes.

She hones in, moving forward, teeth sunk into a pout like she's in heat. Again.

"Hey, stranger," she purrs, hand splaying across my chest like she owns it.

I stare down at it. "What the fuck are you looking for, Maya? Validation?"

She laughs, all breathy and fake. "You've been quiet lately. Thought we could fix that."

She presses in, her tits squished against my arm, her mouth brushing my ear as if she's trying to narrate a porno. "Free period next. I've got an empty car. Want to come make some noise?"

It should be an easy yes.

It always was before.

She's hot, willing, and saying all the right things.

But all I see is Sam. All I want is red hair and the breathy way Sam said my name when I fucked her with my fingers.

I step back, untangling Maya's hand from my shirt.

"Go find someone else to suck the life out of. I'm good."

Maya blinks, all glossy lips and confusion flickering behind thick lashes. "Seriously?"

"Can't miss next class," I mutter, voice flat. "Coach'll rip my nuts off if I'm late again."

Total bullshit. If it were Red saying those words "empty car, free period," I'd already be peeling off her shorts with my teeth. But it's not Red. It's Maya. And I don't want fake moans and plastic everything.

She huffs, spins on her heel, and stomps off, looking for a guy with more brain cells in his dick than his head. It shouldn't be hard. Probably someone like Jace.

Jace slings an arm around my shoulder, grin cocky. "There's the Reece I know. Fuck 'em and forget 'em. Still, I would've taken her up on it."

I smirk. "Yes, I am aware. You'd fuck a reflection if it winked at you."

He leans in. "You're lookin' at me now."

"Fuck off. You couldn't handle my dick." I toss it out, smooth, cool as ever. Delivered with all the swagger I've built my name on. "Besides, I got action last night."

It's a lie.

Jace gives me a glance. That grin that says he knows how full of shit I am. But he doesn't call me out on it. He just laughs.

And I let him.

Because I didn't fuck anyone last night. Didn't even jerk off. I lay there in the dark, hard and wrecked and completely alone.

Every time I closed my eyes, I saw her.

The sheets still smelled of her.

I didn't jerk off last night because the thought of my hand felt pathetic and hollow. I sure as fuck wasn't going to insult it with some mindless tug while thinking about Sam.

I wanted the real thing.

But now she won't even look at me.

So, I do what I always do. Slap on a grin. Throw on the swagger. Pretend.

Play the role of the guy who doesn't care. Let Jace think I'm still that guy who can fuck a girl and forget her name ten minutes later. The guy who shrugs things off and laughs at feelings like they're a punchline.

And now I'm pretending not to care, even though every cell in my body fucking aches for the girl who walked away. Because if I reveal the truth, I'll have to admit what's really happening—that I'm falling for her and I don't know how to stop.

It's easier that way—to fake it, laugh it off. Lie through my teeth and hope no one notices the way she's tearing me apart from the inside.

By the time practice rolls around, I'm barely holding it together. Half-feral with need, frustration, and whatever the hell this ache is she left behind.

Coach yells for drills, and I'm already moving. First in line, body tense, fists clenched. I hit harder. Run faster. Tackle like I'm trying to bury the memory of her in the dirt.

Every grunt is a battle cry. Every hit is my attempt to shake her from my mind, to bleed her out through sweat and bruises.

It doesn't fucking work.

But it gets me noticed.

Coach lets out a low whistle after I slam one of the starting forwards to the ground.

"Well done, Reece," he says, eyebrows raised. "That was brutal. Keep it up and you'll be the first pick this weekend."

It's what I want. What I've wanted since the day I lost it. To claw my way back into that starting lineup. To prove I'm not just some loud-mouthed asshole who burns everything he touches.

Even if I'm only getting the nod because they're short on the team, it still all counts, and it fucking matters. It's something I earned—through bruises, sweat, and grit in my teeth.

I need this. I need to believe I'm still worth something, that I haven't lost every damn part of myself chasing a girl who won't even acknowl-edge me anymore. Because when I'm on the field, when I'm hitting, running, and getting knocked on my ass, this is mine, and for the first time in too fucking long, I don't feel hollow.

Chapter 15

Sam

I saw her. Maya. Lip gloss smeared on too thick, tits stuffed into a glittery top like she was auditioning for a music video no one asked for. She swayed right up to him in the hallway, every move choreographed, as if she were auditioning for the world's most obvious hook-up.

And Reece... he leaned against the lockers, that signature smirk pulling at his mouth. All charm and ego. A performance he's perfected.

I saw her hand on his chest. He didn't push her away; instead, he let her flirt, and I hated every second.

I didn't stick around to watch her drape herself all over him. Liz was crying, clutching her phone, mumbling about plane tickets, leaving, and how the world had gone unreal around her. I couldn't let her fall apart. Not after everything she'd done for me.

But it burned deep. God, it burned so badly.

Not Liz, but the way my eyes refused to stop tracking Maya, even as I crossed the hallway. The way my chest tightened when I caught Reece's expression. A part of me wanted to stay and watch, to see if he brushed Maya off or let her lead him somewhere out of sight.

But Liz needed me, and I couldn't be the girl who let her own heartbreak come before someone else's pain.

So I walked with her into that crappy school bathroom with the flickering light, the cracked mirror, and the paper towels that always runs out too quickly.

I locked us inside the last stall while she fell apart in front of me. I wiped her mascara-streaked cheeks with my hoodie sleeve and told her she'd be okay. I nodded through the ache in my throat because that's what friends do.

We bleed quietly. We break in silence so the other doesn't have to.

But the whole time, my mind wasn't in that stall. It was still out there. Trapped in that hallway. Stuck in the moment he smiled at another girl. Wondering if he'd go with her. Wishing he hadn't. Hurting at the thought that he did.

Lola and Aubrey arrived shortly after I texted them.

By then, Liz had splashed cold water on her face, dabbed it dry with a paper towel that fell apart in her hand, and tried, bless her, to smile through the pain. She wasn't fooling any of us, not with her red-rimmed eyes and blotchy cheeks.

So when Lola and Aubrey wrapped their arms around her shoulders, something settled.

We didn't bother attending class. The four of us bailed, piling into my car with the windows down, music low, and drove across town to that tiny ice cream place Lola swears has magic in every scoop.

Liz ordered bubblegum-flavored ice cream and made a face after the first taste.

Aubrey took a bite anyway, insisting it was gourmet.

Lola got chocolate with sprinkles and shared her cone with Liz, aiming to make her laugh.

I got strawberry and only realized the cup was empty when my spoon hit the bottom.

We sat under the fairy lights strung above the outdoor tables, letting the sugar do its job.

Liz didn't cry again.

Not in front of us, anyway.

But now and then, I'd catch her staring into the distance, eyes glassy, tongue worrying her bottom lip like she was trying to keep something in.

None of us spoke the words we were all thinking.

Sometimes life just fucking sucks.

The party is already feral when we show up. Bass shakes the floor, lights strobe hard enough to screw with your own heartbeat. Heat and hormones clog the air. Every couch has a couple draped across it, half-naked and not even trying to be subtle.

Jace notices us the second we walk in. He pushes off the wall, swagger in every step, plastic cup in hand, and that grin—the one that could make saints sin and good girls question their morals.

"Shots," he says, loud enough to cut through the music. "Come on, Bells," he turns his attention to Lola. "You're the only girl here who hasn't tried to fuck me yet. That clearly means you haven't lived."

Lola crosses her arms and stares him right in the eyes. "It's Bellamy, dickhead. My surname. Try using it correctly for once. I know that's a tall order with your limited brain function. And maybe I don't want to fuck you and catch whatever mix of herpes and bad decisions you're walking around with."

Jace smiles, clearly amused.

"Oh, and before you get all offended," she adds sweetly, "I know plenty of girls you haven't fucked yet. Most of them are smart enough to run in the opposite direction."

Jace clutches his chest as if he's been stabbed. "You wound me, Bells. Truly. It's not easy being this goddamn desirable."

"Shut up," Lola says, a smirk tugging at her mouth—the kind she doesn't bother hiding.

He puts an arm around her shoulders and grins as if this is the best part of his night. "You're alright, Bells. Total menace, pain in the ass, serial ego bruiser... but still alright."

She doesn't shove him away.

Instead, she rolls her eyes, grabs the plastic cup from his hand, and downs the shot like water.

"Keep dreaming, Jace," she says, wiping her mouth and leveling her eyes at him.

His grin widens, all teeth and trouble. "Oh, I will. Trust me, Bells, I'll dream about you tonight."

I stand beside Aubrey, watching this unholy fever dream play out in real time. Jace Cooper, king of cocky grins and casual fucks, the guy who flirts as a goddamn sport and racks up girls faster than he remembers their names, has Lola tucked under his arm as if this is the most natural thing in the world.

She doesn't swoon.

No hair flips. No batting eyelashes to make him want her. She rolls her eyes, mutters "dickhead" under her breath, and drinks his shot like it's her right.

And Jace consumes it eagerly. Which is crazy, because he hasn't truly respected a girl since he figured out what his cock was for. But somehow, Lola Bellamy, the clever, nerdy girl with zero tolerance for his bullshit, has become the only girl in this room that Jace doesn't see as a game.

And honestly? That might be the most fucked-up part of all.

I blink, and Aubrey leans in close, whispering exactly what I'm thinking.

"What the fuck just happened?"

"I have no fucking clue," I reply.

Their friendship slowly developed over the past two months, strengthening in the quiet moments between Aubrey and Noah's whirlwind. No one really saw this happening, least of all me. Jace is a complete asshole to the core.

Lola doesn't let him get away with anything. She calls him out when he's being an asshole. She laughs in his face when he tries to smooth talk her, but she also shows up with an extra sandwich tucked in her bag, plays it off as nothing, and tosses it his way at lunch while pretending the whole thing was an accident.

She knows he doesn't eat much. He never talks about his home life. But everyone knows about the trailer behind his aunt's house, the roof that leaks when it rains, the front steps held together with duct tape and hope — the frosty nights and busted water heater. The way Jace never asks for help, never expects anyone to care.

Aubrey told us more. Quietly. As if the truth was not supposed to be shared.

Lola just nodded and said nothing. The next day, she had a Tupperware container filled with leftovers and a witty comment about how she made too much. She told him he had to help her eat it in her own savage, sarcastic, eat-this-before-I-punch-you way.

And he lets her.

Because maybe, for the first time in a long while, someone is showing up without expecting anything in return. And that messes with him more than he wants to admit.

Jace never thanks her. But he never turns her down either. And for someone who acts like he doesn't need anyone, who's made a name for himself pushing people away, he definitely doesn't push Lola away.

She understands him like no one else does. Her, sitting beside him, teasing him until he grins and calling him out when he pretends he doesn't care.

And maybe that's why he's doing it.

She sees right through all the armor he's built and doesn't flinch at what's underneath.

I keep talking with Aubrey and Liz for another ten minutes, pretending the walls aren't closing in, that I'm not listening for any voice in the room that sounds like his.

Eventually, I can't take it. I murmur something vague and slip away, weaving through the crowd, my pulse chasing something I won't admit to.

The moment I step outside, the night air hits me instantly. Cool against my skin. I take a breath deeper than any I've had all night and lift my face toward the sky.

The moon hangs low over the trees, bleeding light into the backyard.

I close my eyes.

I try to breathe through the ache crawling up my spine. Pretend I didn't spend the last half hour scanning every corner of that party, hoping for a glimpse of Reece. Just to see if he's here. If he ever spares a thought for me, the way my mind can't let go of him.

Behind me, the door opens and slides shut.

I don't turn.

My spine straightens. Recognition hits me before I even think, a shiver racing down my back, skin prickling with awareness.

"Hey," he says.

That one word opens something inside me. I tilt my head just enough to see him standing under the moonlight, jaw glowing in silver-blue. That face, all sharp angles and quiet chaos. That messy hair falling into his eyes. And that mouth. God, that fucking mouth. The one that left me yearning for more.

Without saying a word, he shrugs off his jacket and drapes it over my shoulders. His scent lingers on the fabric, brushing against my skin. Warm. Familiar. Intimate in a way I don't quite know how to handle.

I freeze.

His smirk is faint, eyes flicking over me in a way that always sparks my nerves. "Relax, Red."

I push the jacket back onto his chest.

"I don't need your jacket." The words come out sharper than I intend. I'm being a total bitch, but I can't help it. I have no idea how to act around him anymore. Not after everything.

Before he kept his distance, before Aubrey and Noah changed the whole dynamic, I could handle it. I could watch from a distance, pretend he didn't affect me, let the occasional glance suffice. It felt safe. Controlled.

But now?

Now I've let him in... let him fuck me. Now, every second around him feels exposed.

"Keep it," he says, dropping his voice to something quiet that doesn't match the cocky version of him everyone else gets.

We remain silent, the space between us humming. Each breath feels too loud. Time seems to stretch endlessly.

I stare at him, and all I can think about is Maya. Her hands on him. Her mouth. Did she make him forget about me?

"I saw you with Maya," I finally say.

He doesn't blink. He doesn't move. He doesn't offer any slick excuse, and that hurts more than if he had.

I turn to face him, seeking an answer before I can stop myself.

"Why didn't you tell Jace about the bet?"

"No one needs to know."

"So it was nothing, right?" I forced the words past the lump in my throat. "Just another fuck."

His eyes sharpened. "I think you made that clear when you walked away from me, Red."

"What does it matter, Reece? You screw all the time."

He flinches.

For a moment, I think he's about to say something cruel. But then he drops his hands in front of him, and I recognize the familiar motion. He spins the silver ring on his thumb, the one he always wears. I've seen that habit a thousand times when he's anxious, but right now, the sight hits differently.

I brace myself for a brush-off, a cocky smirk, or some bullshit line to smooth over the sharp edges between us.

But it never arrives.

Instead, he slides the ring off his thumb and holds it, turning it over in his fingers. He moves closer and reaches for my hand.

My breath catches as he presses the cool metal into my palm.

"Keep it," he says, voice rough and almost unsteady. "I had it on that night. When I—" His jaw clenches, eyes darting from my mouth to my eyes and back again, as if he can't decide where it hurts less to look. "When I fucked you, Red."

The words hit like thunder, but he doesn't step back. He watches me, breathing heavily, his next words coming softer.

"Now I can't wear the ring without thinking about you. About the way you looked at me as if I wasn't some fucked-up, heartless piece of shit. So keep the ring. If you're done with me, if nothing meant anything to you, take it. That way, I can try to forget that this ever happened."

My fingers curl instinctively around the ring, but he keeps going, eyes blazing now, with no smirk in sight.

"But don't stand around and pretend nothing mattered. Not when you broke the second I touched you, or the way you said my name, because I haven't forgotten. Not for a second." He takes a breath and then adds, almost under his breath, "And no. I didn't fuck Maya because I didn't want to."

I stare at him, mouth parted, heart slamming against my ribs like it's trying to escape.

He doesn't say another word. He turns and walks back inside, leaving me there in this fucked-up mess of air and feelings, still wearing his jacket.

The silver ring rests in my palm, heavy as hell for something so small. Scratched, worn, nothing pretty. My fingers tighten around the ring in my hand.

Now it belongs to me.

And I hate that it signifies something.

Stupid. Sentimental. Real.

This really shouldn't matter.

But it does.

My heart's pounding against my ribs as if it has something to say. My head's a jumble of unfinished thoughts.

Reece Wilson doesn't talk like that. He hooks up, he pushes people away with that confident mouth and never sticks around for the consequences. But now I'm standing here holding his ring, and nothing makes sense.

I feel unsteady, like I've stepped off the edge of the world and haven't hit the ground yet. Everything inside me is tilted toward him, and I don't know how to claw my way back.

I open my hand.

That ring sits there like it damn well belongs to me.

"Fuck," I mutter, throat dry.

Part of me wants to throw it after him, slam it into his chest, and demand answers I'll never accept.

But my fingers close instead. Then I shove it into my pocket as if I've already made a choice, even if I don't know what the hell it is.

Chapter 16

REECE

Jace's trailer reeks of weed and stale energy drinks—the same old smell as always. The couch sinks halfway to the floor the moment I sit down, and there's a suspicious stain on the armrest that I don't ask about.

Jace is slouched across from me in a busted camping chair, one leg kicked up on the coffee table, wearing that permanently stoned grin that makes me want to throw something at him.

I'm not here to hang out. Just passing time between pretending I'm fine and showing up at Sam's place with notes I definitely didn't rewrite three fucking times. My head's still spinning from the way she came apart on my cock, then ghosted me as if none of it mattered.

I drag a hand down my face, jaw clenched, every nerve still frayed and raw. I haven't jerked off since before that night. Not because I haven't wanted to, fuck, I've tried. More than once. But every time my hand moves, she's there.

The way her lips parted when she came, her breath catching just before she shattered, the way she whispered my name.

And then I lose it.

My cock goes soft. I get angry because my hand's not her.

There's no heat, no taste, no breath against my throat. Just sweat, frustration, and a reminder that I'm alone.

No amount of friction can shake her loose from me. She's everywhere. Under my skin. In my sheets. In my damn bloodstream.

And now I'm stuck—hard for a girl who doesn't want me. Obsessed with a memory I can't replace, ruined by the only fuck that ever meant more than it should've.

A bottle cap hits my chest. I look up and see Jace grinning at me.

"You look like your dick got rejected and your puppy ran away."

I huff out a breath, dragging a hand across my jaw. "Fuck off, Jace."

He just grins wider, slumped back in his busted chair like he's watching the best kind of train wreck.

I don't give him the satisfaction of reacting more than that. My head's a mess, and he knows it. Hell, anyone would, with the way I've been walking around this week like my skin doesn't fit right.

I lean back, eyes fixed on the yellowed ceiling, trying to let the silence drown her out. It doesn't. She's there anyway. In every thought, every beat of my pulse, every fucking breath. I thought that coming here would shake her loose—kill the ache and ease the pain.

It's only worse.

Jace takes another drag and exhales. "You good?"

I don't look at him. I'm fucking falling apart, and the worst part is I let it happen. I let her get in.

Jace flicks ash into an empty Coke can and watches me, waiting for me to crack. He senses something's wrong. But I'm not going to give him the satisfaction of a confession, not when the truth sounds as fucking pathetic as I can't stop thinking about this girl who bolted the second I pulled my cock out of her. I'd never hear the end of it, especially from him.

He yawns as if he's bored. "Jesus, you've got that look. All fucked up over someone you're not supposed to be fucked up over."

I watch the smoke curl from the joint in his fingers. "Don't."

"Don't what?" he smirks. "Say the thing we're both thinking?"

"I didn't come here for therapy."

"Yeah, well, maybe you should've. You've been weird as shit ever since—"

"Drop it." My tone silences him, mostly.

A long moment passes. The couch creaks under me as I shift, elbows on my knees, eyes fixed on the stain near my boot. I hate how much I want to talk about her.

I run my thumb along the edge of my jaw and settle back in my seat. "What's the deal with you and Lola?"

He freezes.

Then he exhales a short laugh, dragging a hand over his mouth. "Is that a deflection, or do you actually give a shit?"

"I give a shit."

"Since when?"

"Since you actually listen when she talks. That's new."

He raises his eyebrows. "Look at you, getting all observant."

"Shut up and answer the fucking question."

Jace tilts his head back, eyes on the ceiling. "She's... I don't know. Not what I expected."

"You fucking her?"

"No."

I wait.

He glances at me. "I mean, not yet."

"But you want too?"

"Yeah, glasses or not, she's a fucking babe. But it's not just that. There's something about her, man. It feels different. She makes me feel... fuck, I dunno. Like I'm not just some stoner fuck-up with a big mouth."

I watch him for a second. The smug grin has disappeared. His tone is serious, perhaps the most serious I've ever heard from him.

"You really like her," I say.

"Don't make it a thing."

"It's already a thing, man."

He groans. "Fuck off." He flips me off, but there's no anger in it.

Jace shifts in his chair, foot still hooked on the edge of the coffee table, with one brow cocked in a way that signals he's about to stir some shit.

"So," he starts, tapping ash into the can, "what's the deal with Cherry Girl?"

My eyes snap to his. "Don't call her that."

"Touchy." He grins, wide and knowing.

"She's not a joke." I lean forward, elbows on my knees.

"Didn't say she was," he says, but his smirk softens a little. "I just meant... she's got you spun. I've seen you with girls, man. You're in and out before they know what hit 'em. But her? You're walking around like your soul left with her panties."

"Fuck off," I snort, even though he's not wrong.

He leans forward, elbows on his knees. "You're the one who made the bet, remember?"

"Yeah. I fucking remember." My jaw is clenched, regret tasting like blood in the back of my throat.

Jace shifts, watching me too close. Reading shit I'm not ready to admit.

"You tapped that already, didn't you?"

"No."

His brow rises. "Bullshit."

"I said no." My voice is sharper this time. I shift in my seat, stare past his shoulder at the busted blinds and peeling wallpaper, refusing to give him more. My chest feels too tight; lungs are stuck somewhere behind all the things I can't say.

His eyes drop to the bag at my feet. "What's with the schoolboy gear? You headed somewhere?"

"Yeah, Sam's. We have an assessment to finish."

Jace lets out a sharp bark of a laugh. "Assessment. Fucking hell. Is that what we're calling it now? You showing up all eager with your little backpack, hoping she'll reward you with extra credit? Maybe a gold star for effort—right before she wraps her pretty mouth around your cock?"

My jaw snaps shut. "I told you. I haven't fucked her."

He falls silent, eyes fixed on mine, as if he's peeling back skin and reading what's bleeding underneath.

I don't give him the chance to say whatever smartass line he's loading behind that smug smirk.

I grab the strap of my bag, slide it over my shoulder, and head toward the broken door.

"See ya later, asshole," I mutter just before walking out.

Jace calls after me. "Try not to bust a nut all over her textbook, Romeo!"

I slide the strap over my shoulder and walk down the long driveway that curves past the main house—white pillars, manicured hedges, a fountain that's more for show than function. It's the kind of place that tries too hard to hide anything messy. That money can mask rot. The house you look at and think picture perfect—if you don't know the shit buried underneath.

I spot her.

Jace's aunt, elbows deep in her rose garden, sunhat perched on her perfect hair as if she just stepped out of a fucking magazine. She straightens as I pass, hands covered in soil, but her eyes are hard. That stare, which strips you bare in one sweep, finds you lacking.

Her lips purse. Disapproval drips from every wrinkle on her face.

She looks at me the same way she looks at Jace—breathing reminders of everything she's tried to keep hidden behind ironed curtains and whitewashed walls.

I nod once, more out of habit than anything else, and keep walking. She doesn't need to say a thing. Her silence screams loud enough. I'm a piece of shit.

By the time I reach Sam's Street, the sun's high in the sky, glaring down as if it has something personal against me. Her house sits perfectly — not a blade of grass out of place. White curtains are drawn, flower pots are lined up neatly on the porch, each one screaming clean and polite. It's a place that smells like rules and casseroles. The kind that would eat a guy like me alive if I stepped too far over the threshold.

I knock once.

Then again, harder.

The door creaks open, and her dad fills the frame. Tall. Cold. Dressed in a stiff-collared shirt that probably never wrinkles or sweats. He stares at me as if I just keyed his car. Doesn't say a word, just scans me slowly from head to toe, dragging his gaze over my creased shirt, the strap of my bag, and the bruises still blooming across my knuckles as if they're the bad decisions I never learned from.

His jaw clenches.

I lift my chin, meet his stare, and pretend the heat crawling up my neck is from the sun rather than the fact that I already know I'm the story he hopes doesn't happen to his daughter.

I clear my throat, voice low. "I'm here to help, Sam. With the assignment."

His expression remains unchanged. He simply glares at me, with a stare that makes you reconsider every bad decision you've ever made. I half-expect him to grab a shovel and start digging my grave in the front yard.

"Sam," he calls out, voice sharp enough to cut right through concrete, eyes still locked on me. "Your friend's here."

Friend. That's fucking generous.

Sam rounds the corner, ponytail swinging. She spots her dad, then me, then there's a heavy silence between us. She moves quickly, reaching for my arm as if trying to shield me from a firing squad, and pulls me past him before he can load another bullet.

Her fingers tighten around my wrist.

I let her pull me in, not because I fear her dad, but because if she wasn't standing there looking at me like she needs me to move, I might've turned around and walked the fuck away.

We don't talk. Just move quickly.

Her fingers stay wrapped around my wrist, warm and firm, pulling me up the stairs like she's afraid I'll vanish if she loosens her grip.

She doesn't look back. I'm already watching her, tracking every step and sway of her hips in those black tights that make my cock twitch as if it has its own damn heartbeat.

The hallway hits, and she slows, but I don't. My gaze keeps trailing down her spine to the curve of her ass, the stretch of those tights doing criminal things to my self-control. My mouth dries out. I want to press her up against the nearest wall, let her feel exactly what she's doing to me. The assignment can wait.

Then—

"Keep that bedroom door open," her dad yells, voice sharp enough to cut through bone.

My dick wilts instantly. I grit my teeth so hard my jaw cracks.

My skin crawls with that itchy, creeping heat that hits when someone's watching too closely. Like he can see right through the floorboards. Through my skull. Through every filthy thought I'm trying not to act on.

Another adult who sees me as nothing but a walking red flag. A fuck-up. A cocky asshole with no future, no right to be near his daughter.

Maybe he's right. Maybe I am those things.

Still, that doesn't stop me from wanting her.

Sam doesn't let go until we're inside her room, her fingers slipping away slowly, as if she didn't mean to hold on to me that long but couldn't help it.

The door clicks halfway shut. Not fully closed, not fully open—just enough for plausible deniability. She's playing it safe with Daddy Dearest lurking downstairs, ears probably tuned to every creak in the floorboards.

She turns her back to me and moves toward the bed, those tight black leggings hugging her in a way that makes my jaw twitch and my dick stand at attention. I force my eyes up, but not before they trace the curve of her hips and the way her oversized tee knotted at the front does absolutely nothing to hide what it's barely covering. Fuck me. I'm not a saint. Never claimed to be.

"What are you doing here?" Her voice snaps.

She's standing near her desk, arms crossed over her chest. Her cheeks are pink again—always are when I'm around. It's like her body's in on something her brain hasn't agreed to yet.

My eyes drift to her lips. Plump, a little parted. She shifts on her feet, and for a second I think she's waiting to see if I'll do the same thing I did last time. My body remembers it better than I do... her mouth against mine, the way she gasped when I pressed against her, it hits me all over again.

I brush it off. I'm not here for that. Not today.

"I thought we could work on the assessment," I say, dropping my bag to the floor with a thud.

I sit at the foot of her bed, stretching out my legs. She doesn't move, still standing there, eyes narrowed like she's trying to solve some equation I've got no part in. I ignore her and fish the notes out, spreading them across the carpet between us.

Still, she doesn't move.

"Are you planning on helping or just watching me?" I glance up and catch her staring full tilt, no shame. Her mouth tightens, then she exhales as if she's finally made a decision.

We get to work.

Our notes are scattered across the floor in messy piles, highlighters and loose pages overlapping as if we've done this before, even though we haven't. I glance at her once, twice, and keep doing it like I don't know any better. She's already sitting cross-legged across from me, leaning over a handout.

Every time she moves closer, I get a whiff of her perfume. It's soft, citrusy. Fuck, it's addictive. It hits me right in the chest and sticks behind my sternum. It's insanely distracting.

She's quiet while we work. Not cold, not distant. Just... careful.

Her sentences are brief, her tone slightly clipped, as if every word passes through some filter in her mind. She's holding herself back, avoiding eye contact. Yet her cheeks have been flushing nonstop since I sat down, and I can tell she's thinking about it—about us—as much as I am.

She leans forward to grab a pen, and her long lashes sweep down, brushing her skin. I watch them too long, following the flicker of her eyes as they scan the worksheet. I should concentrate on the notes. I should ask about the assignment. But all I can think about is how stunning she looks when she's trying not to look at me.

Her voice breaks the silence. "This question on this old test is marked wrong, but I think it's right."

I don't answer right away; instead, I observe her face, the small furrow between her eyebrows, and the way she chews the inside of her cheek when she's deep in thought. I'm not even sure I care about the question she's discussing—I'm too busy watching her.

There's this moment when I almost ask, "Do you regret it? Did you mean it when you acted as if it meant nothing, or were you trying to make it hurt less?" But the words get stuck. I bite down on them and force my attention back to the paper.

"Yeah," I say instead, circling the answer with my pen. "You're right. They probably marked it wrong."

We keep working.

Our hands brush once when we reach for the same paper. She pulls back as if I burned her, but her fingers linger for a second longer than they need to.

We still don't talk about it. Not the kiss. Not the fact that everything's changed since then. But it's obvious in how her lashes lower every time I look at her, and how I pretend I don't notice.

Maybe that says more than any of us ever will.

I pack my stuff slowly, dragging it out because I'm not ready to leave this room. I've spent the last hour pretending her thighs aren't painted into those tights.

She finally stands, brushing imaginary dust off her legs, as if she needs a moment to gather herself, and then—fuck.

She smiles.

At me.

And not some polite, neutral, "thanks for the homework help" bull-shit.

This one's real. Soft, sweet, full of something I've never seen on her face when I'm in the room. She's never smiled at me like that. That's how she smiled at that dickhead by the lockers last week—the one I almost knocked the fuck out just for existing near her.

"You're not so bad at this," she says, and it's not about the assessment.

I stare at her, my bag on the floor forgotten, because I'm two seconds from crawling across the room and kissing that smile off her lips. "Don't tell anyone. I've got a reputation."

That makes her laugh.

That sound hits me straight in the fucking chest.

My feet move me toward the door, but I'm not sure if my mind is with me. She opens it before I can and steps into the hallway. Her shoulder brushes mine, and I don't step away.

The stairs creak as we walk down them together, and for one goddamn second, I allow myself to feel it. The potential that could exist between us if she weren't so busy hating me. If I wasn't so good at fucking things up.

Then I see him.

Her dad.

Posted up at the bottom of the staircase like a fucking guard dog. Arms crossed, face hard, gaze locked only on me.

His eyes drag over me, as if he's waiting for me to slip. I feel that stare settle into my bones. That distrust, that barely concealed hate. He doesn't see a guy trying to help his daughter with schoolwork. He sees a walking screw-up, a threat with a hard-on.

I keep my chin up. I won't give him the satisfaction. I've taken hits harder than a pissed-off dad. Still, it doesn't stop the cold, low burn from crawling up my spine. The kind that reminds me of where I stand and what kind of guy I'll always be in his eyes.

Sam stiffens next to me. She remains silent as she walks over and opens the front door.

"I'll see you tomorrow, Reece, and thanks for coming by today."

I nod because I don't trust myself to speak, not with her dad staring at me as if I'm something he scraped off his boot.

The door clicks shut behind me. I adjust the strap on my shoulder, ready to leave, when Sam's voice breaks through the silence.

"Are you serious right now? You stood there judging him as if he were nothing."

I stop without meaning to.

"He is nothing, Samantha," her dad snaps. "You think I don't see the way he looks at you? That kid is trouble. I won't have him dragging you down."

My jaw locks. No surprise there. Same verdict. Different day.

"You don't know him," she fires back.

"No, but I know his type," her dad says. "And his type never changes."

"That's bullshit," she shoots back.

Her dad finally says, "I don't trust him."

"That sounds more like a you problem," Sam snaps. "Not a him problem."

Fuck.

I don't wait to hear more.

I walk fast and hard, my boots hitting the pavement with too much force.

The street's quiet when I hit the curb, just the buzz of streetlights and the distant bark of a dog. Porch lights flicker on like little spotlights, reminding me how many people are safe in their homes, loved and wanted.

Anger quietly simmers in my gut, sharp and bitter.

The way he looked at me was as if I were filth dragged in on her shoes. Another adult dismissing me with a glance. A man who sees nothing in me worth a second chance.

I should be used to it. But I'm not, because tonight she stood there defending me. Someone as good as Sam could believe in someone like me after everything I've done and still see something worth standing up for.

I want to be that fucking guy.

The one she sees when she smiles. The kind of smile she gave me tonight without thinking. Soft. Unafraid. Pure fucking sunlight slicing through all the crap I carry.

I want to be the one who maintains her gaze when the world becomes harsh. The one who doesn't flinch when her father looks at him like he's dirt.

I want to be enough for the girl with fire in her voice and courage in her spine—the one who made me feel seen for the first time in years.

Chapter 17

SAM

I tell myself this is for Lola, because she made me pinky promise yesterday in chemistry that I'd show up. Well, that's the story I'm sticking to.

Not because Reece Wilson's name has been ringing through these halls all week. And not because the coach made him a starter for tonight's game and the whole damn school has been buzzing about it.

And most definitely not because I spent yesterday afternoon sitting in the library, staring out the window, pretending to do my work, while watching him run laps as if he was training for war. Earphones in. Shirt off. Sweat gleaming across his chest.

I didn't even open my laptop. I just sat there with my mouth half open and my thighs clenched, watching a boy I swore I'd hate forever make discipline look fucking sexy.

He was focused. Determined. Everything I pretend not to care about.

And don't even get me started on Dad. The way he spoke to Reece last week... I've never been more embarrassed or more furious. I called him out right there in the hallway after Reece left, telling my dad he was out of line and that Reece didn't deserve that shit. Maybe if he got his head out of his own judgmental ass, he'd see Reece is trying.

My dad hasn't talked to me since he went into full dictator mode. Honestly, I haven't spoken to him either.

Mom's been trying, asking about school and how my project on post-war economic decline is going. I ignore her too, which makes me feel like shit, but as soon as I open my mouth, I know I'll start yelling and never stop.

My little brother keeps glancing between us like he's watching a silent movie turn into a horror film. He asked the other night if we were fighting because Dad had forgotten my birthday. My birthday was four months ago. That's how tense it is; he's clutching at whatever explanation makes sense.

And me... I sit there, silent and boiling, pushing my food around as if it's responsible for everything wrong in the world. Because if I stop, if I let myself sit still, I'll remember how Reece looked when he turned away. How he stood there and took it all.

The moment I pull into the school parking lot, I regret everything.

It's chaos.

Horns blaring. Kids hanging out of windows. Guys shirtless, girls in crop tops and glitter. Everyone's high on pre-game adrenaline, energy drinks, and probably a ton of weed. It's like the whole school has lost its mind. There's nowhere to park without some drunk sophomore ready to smash my side mirror with a foam finger.

I snake my way past some asshole doing donuts in a crappy sedan and squeeze into a spot between two trucks blasting bass-heavy rap that rattles my windows.

This is typical high school behavior, apparently. I mutter something about testosterone poisoning under my breath and push the gear shift into park.

I sit there for a moment, hands gripping the wheel, watching the crowd move in waves.

Aubrey and Noah are out of town; Aubrey has one of her volleyball tournaments. The two of them doing the whole lovers getaway thing. Hotel room. Zero parents. Zero curfew. Probably a "do not disturb" sign dangling off the handle while they make heart eyes over overpriced room service.

She told me Noah's proud as hell of her. Says he sits in the bleachers and cheers louder than anyone else. Can't shut up about her blocks or serves or whatever it is volleyball people get excited about.

It's kind of adorable how Aubrey's his whole damn world now—especially considering he used to be the runner-up in the school's biggest fuckboy competition, right behind Jace.

I grab my phone and send a quick message to Lola.

Sam: Where are you? This place is a fuckshow.

Three seconds later, I receive a reply.

Lola: East gate side. Saved you a seat. Liz is already here. Hurry. You'll die when you see Tia.

That can't be good.

I slam the door, lock the car, and plunge into the chaos, elbows up as if I'm entering a war zone. There's a kid running in a full cougar mascot suit, some freshman twirling a glow stick in my face, and two seniors hot boxing in their car by the front gates. A cheerleader shrieks behind me—either from joy or a twisted ankle, I don't stop to check.

And underneath all of that?

My pulse is racing like crazy.

It's just us girls tonight—me, Lola, and Liz. The original trio. Probably the last time we'll get to cause chaos together before Liz leaves next weekend, and everything shifts into "remember when" territory.

Liz has no idea that Lola's planned a "surprise" sleepover sendoff next week. But knowing Lola, I'm not sure how the hell she's kept it quiet this long. Subtle isn't exactly her strong suit.

Noise pulses through the air. Every shout, every chant, every drumbeat from the band hits my chest.

I take a breath, push my way through the chaos, and try not to trip over a flattened soda cup or some kid's abandoned backpack.

The entire field is illuminated, with stadium lights piercing through the night.

I see Lola first, waving wildly from halfway up the stands, two hot pink scrunchies in her hair and a slushie that looks like nuclear waste in her hand. Liz is next to her, already mid-eye roll, but she's laughing anyway. God, I'm going to miss her.

I drag myself up the stairs, shoulder past a couple making out like it's foreplay for the halftime show, and drop into the space Lola saved between her and Liz.

Drums pound behind the cheerleaders, brass screaming from the band section, and every third kid yells something that makes zero sense.

I look over at the field.

The team's on the sidelines, jerseys clinging, all of them buzzing with that pre-game fire.

Reece Wilson.

Number twenty-seven.

Helmet in hand. That dark, messy hair is matted down from warm-up drills. Pacing the edge of the field like a caged animal. And suddenly, I'm not sure I remember how to breathe.

The announcer shouts the team name, and the guys rush out onto the field. The crowd's noise is loud enough to shake the metal bleachers beneath my feet. My chest pounds in sync with the racket, adrenaline rushing straight up my spine.

I briefly look away from the chaos when something catches my attention.

Nicole.

Tia's right next to her, both of them squeezed into cheer skirts that barely count as clothing, with smiles that are too tight and eyes full of tension. They're standing so close I'm surprised no one's drawn blood yet.

Tia throws a high kick that narrowly misses Nicole's face. On purpose. Of course.

Nicole yanks Tia's ponytail, fingers clenched. "Do that again and I'll break your ankle."

Tia laughs. "Please. You couldn't even break your calorie count."

Behind me, Lola snorts so loudly I feel it vibrate through the row. "Tell me you saw that."

"Tia's gonna choke her out before halftime," says Liz, already losing it, shoulders shaking, laughter spilling out.

I shake my head, eyes flicking back to the field where the boys are lining up, hearts pounding, bodies ready. Between the football, the cheerleader showdown, and the way my pulse keeps spiking for one cocky asshole in pads, this night is already a fucking lot.

Lola leans forward and digs into her bag, pulling out a sleeve of Sour Patch Kids. That girl could survive an apocalypse on snacks alone. She opens it and holds it out between us. I grab a handful. Liz does, too, sugar already dusting her fingers as the whistle screams and the game begins.

My eyes lock onto number twenty-seven.

Reece is crouched low, muscles tense, helmet tilted forward, every inch of him coiled and ready. Defense. His stance. His territory. As soon as the ball snaps, he erupts off the line and crashes into the guy opposite him so forcefully that the impact echoes through the crowd.

Fuck.

"Damn," Liz mutters. "He's out for blood."

Play after play, he's relentless. He tears through their line, shoulders leading, knocking back bodies with a brutal precision that feels personal. He gets to the quarterback once. Then again. The poor guy barely has time to breathe before Reece is there, full of force and fury, dragging him down onto the turf.

He's quick, angry, and in control.

And he's fucking beautiful.

My heart stutters every time he collides with someone and immediately gets back up. Every time he rolls his shoulders, resets, and lines up again as if pain is just a suggestion. Sweat darkens his jersey, clings, and outlines everything I shouldn't be staring at in public.

And then he looks toward the stands.

Searching.

I wonder if he's looking for me.

Halfway through the second quarter, Jace materializes out of the chaos and plants a hand on the back of a freshman's seat. The seat next to Lola.

"Move."

The kid scrambles so fast he nearly trips over his own feet.

"Charming," Lola mutters as Jace drops into the empty spot next to her.

He flashes that grin that has never once apologized for anything. "You love it."

"I really don't," she says, rolling her eyes so much it could count as cardio. "You're mean to literally everyone."

Jace leans back, stretches his arm along the bleacher behind her, claiming the space without touching her. "You're not everyone."

"Still mean," she replies, holding out the packet of Sour Patch Kids.

He glances at it, then at her. His smile slows, and he leans in close, voice dropping just enough to feel deliberate. "You're saying you don't want me to be?"

Lola snorts. "I'm saying you'd implode if you tried being nice for more than five minutes."

He plucks a candy from the packet anyway before saying, "Guess it's a good thing I've got you to keep me honest."

Liz nearly chokes on her drink. She leans in, eyes wide, and speaks softly so only I can hear. "I don't know what the fuck is going on between those two, but if they flirt any harder, I'm calling a medic."

Jace doesn't blink; he simply chews slowly. "You're always feeding me, Bells."

"It's Bellamy, dickhead," Lola snorts. "Try not to choke on your own ego. Although... honestly, you might be doing us all a favor."

Jace smirks, eyes locked on her with a quiet, cocky intensity that makes the air around them tighten. He says nothing, but his gaze isn't casual. It's the look guys get when they've already decided something's theirs.

I glance at Lola. She's rolling her eyes and muttering something under her breath, but there's a faint flush on her cheeks that wasn't there before.

And I can't help but wonder if she's about to become his next conquest.

Third quarter drags into the fourth, and Reece remains a relentless machine. His defense never pauses. His legs keep pushing, body tense and fierce, hunting anything foolish enough to cross his path. He appears unstoppable.

And then, the world snaps.

One second, he's tearing downfield, all cocky power and sharp precision, focus locked in as if the world doesn't exist beyond the end zone. A damn weapon in motion.

Next, he's blindsided. Helmet to ribs, full force, savage and sudden. No time to brace or roll. Just a sickening thud as his body twists, all that power suddenly helpless.

He hits the ground and the world shifts.

Everything goes silent, brutal, and wrong. There are no whistles, no cheers—just this fucked-up quiet that amplifies the panic.

Reece is down.

Not moving. Not even a twitch.

My lungs can't function. My throat feels like a clenched fist, and my chest caves in. I can't breathe, think, or do anything except stare at where he's sprawled, motionless.

Liz's nails bite into my arm. "Shit," she says, barely a whisper, but it cuts across my nerves like a blade.

Jace jumps to his feet immediately. Lola grabs his arm, with knuckles white and eyes riveted to the field.

Reece still hasn't moved.

A medic rushes off the sideline, with two more following. Coaches shout, and players kneel.

And I'm sitting here, waiting for him to get up. For him to shake it off, flash that cocky grin, and go back to being the reckless asshole I can't stop watching.

But he doesn't.

He lies there. Still. Silent.

And it fucking guts me.

Get up.

Please get the fuck up.

He finally moves.

Barely.

One slow twitch of his boot against the turf. The crowd holds its breath as if that will help. It doesn't.

Two teammates lift him up, each slinging an arm over their shoulders. His helmet's gone, and even from up here, I can see the blood on his lip.

He's fucked. Broken in ways that make my stomach turn.

But he's on his feet. He's standing.

He's battered, torn open, and held together by sheer fuck-you energy. But he's up.

He's walking, and it costs him everything he has.

From the sidelines, the coaches swarm, holding clipboards and ice packs, panicking. The roar of the crowd swells all around, chaotic and endless, none of them seeing what I see. The shake in his knees. The way his lip is split. How his gaze never lifts from the ground. It's as if he looks up, the whole world might open up beneath him.

The whistle pierces through the chaos.

Players move and the game picks up again. Reece goes to the bench.

The team is holding the line. Just barely.

Every play now feels desperate, with each movement driven by the momentum Reece left behind.

They push.

They fight, and somehow, they come out on top.

The stadium erupts.

Thunder cracks from the stands.

The final score flashes on the screen, forty-two to thirty-four. Students jump out of the bleachers, cheering, arms raised high, jerseys flying as they flood onto the field. It's chaos. Flags whip in the wind. The band goes wild, drums booming, brass blaring, cymbals crashing so loudly that the sound vibrates in my ribs.

A guy in a letterman jacket slides to his knees on the turf like it's a damn movie.

It's a war zone transformed into a victory parade.

But I don't move.

I can't.

My eyes won't leave the bench.

He's still sitting there.

The boy who played every part of this game until his body wore out.

Now he's at the heart of the chaos.

Students swarm around him, everyone trying to touch him, celebrate him, and shower him with glory.

Nicole tries to make it her moment—hand on his chest, hips angled, wanting to be the next thing he touches. He shoves her off without a word. Doesn't spare her a glance.

Half of the student section cheers his name as if he's their king.

But Reece?

There's no grin. No cocky swagger. None of that usual bullshit confidence he wears when he's untouchable. He barely reacts at all. He just stands there and lets the noise crash around him.

They don't realize what it costs.

They didn't notice him until he refused to quit. Didn't feel the weight of every hit stacking up until sheer fucking willpower was the only thing keeping him upright.

He didn't bleed for them.

I saw it.

I saw something break loose inside him out there. Saw how badly he wanted this. Not the cheers. Not the attention. Proof. A reason. A chance to be more than what the no-hoper people label him without even trying to understand.

Reece wanted to be something.

And tonight, it seems like it took something from him in return.

I sit there long after the cheers fade, long after the last drumbeat dies and the band packs it in.

The crowd thins out, gradually leaving the field in waves. People continue shouting, laughing, and buzzing from the win as if it didn't just cost Reece everything.

Lola and Liz have already left, taking Jace with them.

The field empties.

I stay rooted to the metal bleacher seat until the last drunk senior tumbles off toward the parking lot and the field finally quiets.

Only then do I move.

Quick steps, careful ones, my head ducked as I slide down the rows. I hit the ground and stay close to the fence, circling behind the goalpost and cutting across to the other side. I already know where he'll be, and that's the place I am going.

I wait in the long hallway. The locker room door swings open halfway, voices spilling out. Most of the team has already left, half-dressed, shoving each other around like gods who just saved the world.

None of them look broken.

I wait until the last of them leaves, until I hear no more voices. Until it's just me and the pounding in my chest. Only then do I slip inside.

The air hits like a fist to the face—sweat, testosterone, damp towels, and blood. The room hums with it.

Lockers line the walls, dented and scratched, some with numbers half peeled off. A couple are still cracked open, gear spilling out. The floor's a battlefield. Mud prints streak across the tile. A towel lies crumpled in the middle, soaked through and stepped on, abandoned without a second thought.

I see Reece at the far end.

He's sitting with his elbows on his knees, head lowered, and his jersey is gone, with shoulder pads dumped in a heap at his feet. His chest rises and falls slowly, skin flushed, marked with bruises spreading in angry colors across his body.

White tape is wrapped around his torso. He's not moving. Not in the cocky, wired way he usually does. He looks broken, as if hollowed out by pain alone.

Even so, he's beautiful in a rough, broken way.

The boy who doesn't bleed just for show.

He keeps bleeding because he doesn't know how to stop.

And I don't believe anyone has ever told him he doesn't have to.

My chest hurts as I watch him.

I almost turn around, almost let him have this—the quiet, the hurt, the mess. But he lifts his head before I can move, looking right at me.

"Red," he says. It's not sharp, smug, or loaded with that usual fire he throws at me when we're mid-argument, mid-flirt, mid-whatever the fuck we are. It's quiet. Hoarse. Honest. My name stripped bare on his tongue.

I move toward him before I can talk myself out of it. My footsteps are loud in the silence, but my heart is louder.

"Are you okay?" I ask, even though I already know the answer. It comes out softer than I want. Stupid and small. But that's all I've got.

"I will be," he says.

I sit down on the bench next to him, close enough that our knees brush. The shock that runs through me is immediate. Electric. Bone-deep. He notices. His breath shifts as his eyes drift down to my mouth before slowly going back up.

"You shouldn't be in here," he mutters.

"I know."

"Don't tell me the good girl's finally breaking the rules."

I smirk, heat rising in my throat. "Guess you're rubbing off on me."

A breath of laughter escapes him, but it twists into a wince halfway through. Pain flashes across his face, and I move instinctively. My fingers brush his arm gently. Flesh on flesh.

He stiffens.

Every inch of him tenses up, as if I've short-circuited something inside him.

Neither of us speaks.

His fingers graze my jaw, gentle enough to undo me, rough enough to remind me why I want him. There's a tremor in his hand that matches the one low in my stomach. That same ache I thought I had buried after the last time. The same one that left me ruined for anyone but him.

My breath catches on it.

His eyes darken at the sound, and for a moment, neither of us moves. We sit there, suspended in this charged space between memory and what still lingers.

Then he speaks.

"You're beautiful, Red."

This isn't a typical line from him. There's no smirk, no play behind it. Just truth.

My throat swells, and I have to swallow the lump before I speak.

"Even when I'm pissed at you?" I ask, trying to pull us back into safer territory.

His mouth quirks, pain flickering behind it. "Especially then."

"You're not supposed to say shit like that."

His hand slips from my face and rests on my thigh, claiming the space. The heat radiates instantly from his touch, spreading through me until my thoughts fray.

I have to bite my lip to stop myself from saying what I truly want.

And that means asking him to slide his hand higher, slip it under my skirt—do that thing he did at his place, the one that made my back arch and my voice vanish, the one that turned my legs to jelly and rewired my brain around his touch.

My body recalls before my mind can argue. It leans into him, betraying every sensible thought I came in here with.

I need to stop these thoughts. I should be smarter. But all I want is his hand back where it was that day. His mouth on my neck. Fingers making me fall apart.

"Kiss me."

The words leave my mouth before I can talk myself out of them, before fear, pride, or common sense has a chance to pull me back. I've never been this reckless or this honest, but I need him just as desperately as I need air in my lungs.

He blinks, unsure if he heard me correctly, as if the words haven't fully registered yet.

Then his hand tenses on my thigh.

"Say it again," he says, voice hoarse.

I don't. I just keep moving.

Swinging one leg over, I straddle him in a single, breathless motion, careful not to press too hard against his ribs. His breath punches out against my throat, his eyes darken, and his hands instinctively find my hips.

"Are you sure, Red?" he murmurs, all rough-edged restraint.

I nod. "Kiss me."

The moment the words leave my mouth, he closes the distance.

His lips meet mine with a scorching heat, rough and hungry, but beneath it all, there's a quiet message that he needed this just as much as I did.

I kiss him harder, fingers sliding into his sweat-damp hair. He groans, deep in his chest, and I feel it vibrate through both of us.

His body's worn out from the game. I can feel it in the way he moves, slower, more cautious, the wince that flashes across his face when he shifts. But he doesn't stop.

I grind down on his hard cock, and he swears, his hands flexing on my hips.

"Fuck, Red," he mutters against my mouth. "You're gonna kill me."

"Then die happy," I whisper back.

And I kiss him once more.

His mouth opens beneath mine, needy and rough. His hands slide under my shirt, palms pressing against my lower back, pulling me closer, pressing our bodies together until only heat and friction remain.

He winces.

His body tightens as one hand slips from my back to brace against his ribs.

Shit, fuck... don't stop," he growls when I begin to pull back. "It's worth the pain."

He watches me. I stay still, my lungs tight, as his hand slowly slides up my thigh. He doesn't rush. He draws it out, testing me, daring me to stop him.

I don't.

My skin prickles when he gets closer to where I need him most. Fuck, I'm already wet, aching, already too far gone to pretend I don't want this.

He's watching me, not the way a guy checks out a girl, but the way someone studies art, trying to understand how it exists. I stay quiet, but my chest rises faster, and my legs tense under his touch. His fingers pause just short of my pussy, eyes searching mine.

He's trying to read me—to see if I'll pull away.

I close my eyes, resenting how much I desire this and the control he has at this moment.

"Reece," I whisper, almost in a murmur.

When I look at them again, he's still watching me, eyes full of that same desperate hunger that I'm drowning in. It's not just desire, it's outright need. It's written all over his face.

And for a moment, that terrifies me more than anything else.

His fingers glide over the front of my panties, tracing the wet spot he's already responsible for. He doesn't speak or smirk, or even tease me with that cocky mouth. He just strokes up and down my slit back and forth. I know he can feel how soaked I am.

My breath stutters. My hips jerk. I bite the inside of my cheek to stop myself from grinding into his hand. Last time, I lost control. Rode his face until I shattered, and when I came back down, I'd never felt more exposed. But even now, knowing I should pull away, every part of me leans toward him.

I want to experience that again. The way Reece made me feel before. Needed. Wild. Untouchable. He's a fuckboy. Every girl knows it. And I'm not the exception. But there's something inside me that doesn't care. That still wants him anyway.

I whimper as he finally moves my panties aside and slides one finger inside me. Then another. My body tightens around him, slick and prepared, and he moves purposefully. Slow at first, curling just right, then faster, pressing in deeper until I have to close my eyes and breathe through the pleasure surging through me.

My head falls back, the world shrinking to the addictive pull of his fingers inside me and the heat rushing over my skin. I am gasping, overwhelmed by sensation, too lost in pleasure to care about anything else.

He lifts my shirt slowly, then winces as his body curls forward and his mouth presses against my skin. That hiss, the pain from the bruises on his ribs should remind me to stop. But it doesn't. If anything, it makes my chest clench harder.

He pushes my shirt higher, then leans down again. His mouth finds my nipple through the lace, and he sucks gently, tongue dragging over the thin fabric. A sound claws at my throat, and I bite my lip trying hard to keep it down. A slutty little moan that reveals way too much.

I can't keep my emotions in check. I never can when he's nearby.

Ever since the day he saw me in the worst underwear disaster of my life—the saggy granny panties and a bra that did nothing for my figure—I swore it wouldn't happen again. Not because I thought he'd get another chance to see me naked. Hell no. Reece Wilson was a mistake with a cocky grin and a reputation I had no business getting involved with.

But apparently my subconscious is a traitor.

Even though I told myself it was a one-time thing, an accident driven by weakness and hormones, I'm now wearing black lace that hugs my hips and makes me feel powerful. A bra that pushes up what little I have, as if it's auditioning for round two.

I didn't plan for this.

I wasn't supposed to want him again.

But here I am, dressed for war. Hoping he'll be the one to start the fire.

The warmth of his breath brushes my skin, and everything inside me tightens. I've never been this girl before. I was the good one. The tame one. But Reece Wilson flipped some filthy, godforsaken switch in me. And now, I swear, the second he's near me, I'm a fucking orgasm junkie.

My mind goes hazy, nothing but static and heat as his fingers move in rhythm. I can't think clearly. I can't think at all. I'm chasing it, right there, almost—

Then he pulls away.

A needy, broken sound tears from my throat before I can swallow it down. It's humiliating and honest. I try to catch my breath, but all I can do is blink at the bastard, who just grins at me.

The cocky bastard knows exactly what he's doing, which only increases my annoyance.

"You don't get to come unless it's on my cock."

His voice is low and rough—a mix of threat and promise. He brushes my hair over my shoulder, his lips gently grazing the side of my neck in a kiss so soft it makes my knees weak. I close my eyes, melting into the sensation of his mouth on my skin, every nerve alert and alive.

"If you want it," he murmurs, his breath a slow drag down my neck, "then fucking take it. Let go on my cock."

The filthy promise sends a fresh rush of heat spiraling through me. My nipples pebble beneath the lace, my body already aching for more. His hand finds the back of my neck, anchoring me as our lips crash together in a kiss that isn't sweet. It's savage. Desperate. All tongue and teeth and hunger.

It's not sweet.

It's a fucking storm.

I kiss him like I'm punishing him for every second he made me wait. My hands are already at his waistband, yanking at the fabric until I free his cock. He's hard. So fucking hard. My hand wraps around him, stroking slowly just to watch the way his eyes darken, his jaw clench, his breath stutter.

I don't fucking hesitate.

I rise to my knees, shifting my hips, and guide him into me. Inch by inch, he fills me, stretches me, and I swear I see stars. He grabs my hips, fingers digging in hard, his mouth parted, his eyes blazing with something dark and desperate.

"Fuck," he breathes, voice wrecked, head falling forward until his nose drags along the column of my throat. "You feel so fucking good. So fucking tight."

As I grind down on his cock, sensation hits me like a goddamn freight train. Every roll of my hips sends a shockwave through my body, that tight pull deep inside winding higher, hotter, meaner. I'm drunk on the feel of him, on the filthy, breathless sounds spilling from his mouth. That low grunt when I squeeze around him. The curse he hisses when I do it again.

He grips my hand, rough and possessive, fingers locking with mine as he uses it to steady me. Holds me there like he wants to burn this moment into memory. His stare pins me in place, dark, wild, and wrecked, and I fucking love it. I move faster, chasing that raw friction that makes my thighs shake and my pussy clench.

And then I find it. That spot. The one that makes me forget my name. The one that turns me into a fucking sinner.

I ride him harder, each thrust making me unravel. My moans turn into gasps, into broken cries, into a string of "yes, fuck, yes." Heat coils in my belly, tighter than before, until it snaps and I come hard. My orgasm rips through me, blinding and brutal, and I scream his name like a prayer I'll never take back.

I'm gone. Fucked out. Floating in it.

And I don't even want to come down.

With a rough grunt, he yanks tighter on my hair, hips jerking as his orgasm tears through him. Bliss shatters across his face, his mouth falling open as a deep, guttural sound claws its way out of his throat. His lips crash into mine, and I swallow the growl he spills straight into my mouth.

"Fuck," he rasps, voice torn raw.

I slow my hips, still keeping him inside me, but the pace shifts. He looks at me, and I see his face change. That tight, desperate edge softens into something vulnerable.

"You're not gonna leave me this time, Red, are you?"

My heart clenches so tightly it hurts. I blink.

"No."

He exhales and presses his forehead against mine.

"Good." He closes his eyes, just for a second. "Fuck!" His eyes snap open, full of panic.

"What?" I freeze.

"We never used a condom."

The room stills. My pulse pounds in my ears. But his arms remain around me.

In the heat of the moment, I didn't think twice. My body made the decision—desperate, frantic, starving. I was too caught up in the way he kissed me, in how good his hard cock felt in my hand to even realize we'd gone there. No condom. Just skin, sweat, and the kind of hunger that made me forget every rational thought I ever had.

I exhale, slow and shaky, his cock still inside me, the aftermath of my orgasm still ricocheting through my limbs.

"Fuck," he mutters, forehead resting against my shoulder. "We didn't use anything."

"I'm on birth control," I add.

My dad made my mom take me when I was fifteen. Said some teenage boy at school was looking at me with a hard-on and called it insurance.

Reece pulls back and looks at me. He smiles in relief, but it fades when I say the next part.

"But maybe we shouldn't have done it. You know, with everything." I don't know how the hell to say this part, but it needs to be said. "All the girls you've..." I trail off, staring at his face, our bodies still joined.

"Red..." he says, lifting his hand and brushing the back of his fingers against my cheek. "I've never been with anyone bare before. You're the first."

A rush of something stupid, ridiculous, and soft tears through my chest. I hate how much it matters to me. I hate that I smile. That some fucked-up part of me feels special for being the only one who's felt him like this.

God, I really need therapy.

He leans in and brushes his lips over the tip of my nose, and somehow that small gesture undoes me more than the sex did.

"Before you do your dramatic disappearing act," he murmurs, "come get food with me."

I blink. "Food? Like... with you?"

He quirks an eyebrow. "No, Red. I was planning to eat alone and just wanted to see if you'd walk me to the car."

I roll my eyes.

"Come on." His voice is softer now. "You just rode me like you owned me. The least you can do is let me buy you a burger."

"You really think this grants you dinner rights?"

He smirks. "I think the moment you moaned my name like a fucking prayer, you agreed to fries. Plus, I know a place that does those thick-cut chips you like. The ones you stole off Lola's plate that one time."

I pause. "You remember that?"

He shrugs, eyes now a bit too cautious. "I notice shit."

I exhale slowly. "Fine. But if the fries are terrible, I'm walking straight out."

He grins, full teeth. "Deal. But fair warning, once you taste those fries, you'll be begging me for more than just a side of sauce."

"Gross," I mutter, but I'm already climbing off him, trying hard not to smile.

Chapter 18

REECE

I can't stop thinking about it. The way she looked when she rode me. Hair a tangled mess from my hands, skin flushed and damp with sweat, that perfect mouth parted, those eyes locked on mine as if she was trying to burn herself into me. And shit, she did. Every grind of her hips ruined me. Every slow drag of her pussy over my cock felt like I was being split open and stitched back together with her name carved in my ribs.

She didn't just ride me. She owned me. Took what she wanted and left me a fucking mess.

And bare? That was a first.

I never go without, not even during my worst, sloppiest, blackout fucks. But with her, all that went out the fucking window. Every damn heartbeat inside that tight little body was worth it. Especially the way she looked at me when she came.

That sound she made when she did... fuck. That whimper. That stuttering cry. The way her nails dug into my arms and her thighs clenched around me. And I know I'll be replaying that over and over, cock hard in my hand, chasing the feel of her.

Sam is not just in my head. She's under my skin, wrapped around my spine, etched into every part of me that used to be hollow.

I glance over at her in the driver's seat.

She hasn't spoken a word since I got in and told her where to go. She simply keeps her eyes on the road, gripping the wheel tightly as if she's holding onto something other than the drive.

Maybe she's trying to outrun what happened between us in the locker room.

Or maybe she's already regretting it.

Regretting that she had taken my cock so deep, she screamed my name.

That's the part that breaks me. Because I fucking felt it when she fell apart around me. It wasn't just sex. It was something more. It always fucking is with her.

But now?

Now she's quiet. Her silence now feels like a punishment.

And me... I'm sitting here, hard again, watching her bite her bottom lip, and I'm wondering if I'm the only one still falling.

I'm so fucking gone for her. Wrecked. Ruined. Totally fucked.

We pull up outside Wes's burger joint. The place looks like it gave up on life ten years ago. The neon sign's flickering as if it's got nerve damage, and one of the letters is burnt out, so it reads "BUR ER."

The windows are still so slick with grease you could fry an egg on them, but I've eaten more burgers here than anywhere else on the planet. Looks like shit, smells like heaven. Grease, beef, toasted buns. Best in town, no contest. It doesn't matter if the seats are cracked and the lights buzz like they're ready to blow, it's got history.

Noah and I used to own a booth in the back. We'd spread out, talk shit, throw fries at each other while Jace sweat it out behind the grill.

Those days are gone now that Noah isn't pretending he's not in love with Aubrey anymore. He picks her up from work most nights, always waiting in his car with that goofy expression on his face, as if he still can't believe she's his. Sometimes he even gives Jace a ride home. Guess that's what love does. Makes you soft, turns your rivals into carpool karaoke buddies.

I hold the door open, and the smell hits me right in the face.

She brushes past me, and, fuck me, even with her hair a little messy and her lip still kissed raw, she steals the air from my lungs. I let her go first because I need a second to get my shit together. My knee throbs like a bitch from the game, my shoulder's wrecked, my ribs are fucking killing me, but nothing hurts as much as whatever the hell is happening in my chest when I watch her.

Wes's burger joint has no charm unless you grew up here. Booths are torn at the seams, with duct tape holding more than just the upholstery together.

We head to the counter, and I nod at the guy behind it, some burnout who probably hasn't changed shifts since high school. He barely looks up, and I don't blame him.

Posters line the walls from every era of music—some curling at the edges, some half-ripped, some faded by the sun. But no matter where you look, Broken Oasis stares back. Xander, the guy your girl dreams about while you're inside her. Ace's fuck-you sneer and inked-up throat.

They began here. Right here in this crappy forgotten town, eating these burgers and probably sitting in the same booth.

"Pick a booth," I tell her, trying to sound casual and failing, my pulse still crazy from the sex and everything tangled up afterward.

She chooses one by the window, red vinyl split and worn, the seat giving a soft sigh beneath her.

I drop in across from her, the table scarred, my hands restless against the wood. I'm trying to act normal while I'm sitting across from the one girl who has fucked my balance to hell.

"I can't believe you brought me here," she mutters, eyeing the cracked menu on the table.

"What, not impressed by five-dollar fries and a chair that's one ass cheek away from collapsing?" I grin.

She snorts. "Is that the line you use on all your dates?"

"This is my first date," I say, dead serious.

Her eyes widen briefly before she shifts her expression. "Bullshit."

"Swear on my cock," I grin. "You've fucked me, you know how sacred that shit is."

She shakes her head, but a smile plays on her lips. "You're impossible."

"Unbreakable," I say with a wink.

That gets me a full laugh.

"Unbreakable? That's what you're going with?"

"It's a good brand. Strong. Sexy. Marketable."

Her eyes soften, and that's dangerous. I'm already fucked six ways from Sunday. She doesn't need to look at me like that, either.

The server walks over.

A girl maybe a year or two older than us, dressed in black jeans and a diner tee that's seen better days. She doesn't bother pulling out a notepad.

"What can I get you two?" she asks, her voice flat but not unfriendly.

I glance at Sam before turning my eyes back to the server.

"I'll have a double cheeseburger. Extra pickles. Fries. Coke."

Sam examines the menu as if it's a final exam. "I'll have the same, but no pickles and a chocolate shake."

The server smirks. "Coming right up." She turns on her heels and disappears behind the counter.

I lean back in the booth, stretching one arm along the cracked vinyl, and let my eyes drift back to Sam. She's already looking at me, chin tilted, fingers tapping against the table.

There's a pause. Long enough for it to settle between us. The kind that hums with something unsaid. That dares you to say the wrong thing and mean it.

"You walk around acting unbreakable," she says, voice steady but soft in a way that hits harder. "But that's bullshit."

I lift an eyebrow, but she's already moving on.

"You think I don't see it?" Her mouth quirks. "The fuckboy swagger. The cocky grin. The whole I don't give a shit act. It's armor. Not confidence."

A breath slips out of me before I can stop it. A half laugh–half surrender.

"What if I told you I wouldn't know who the hell I am without it?"

She doesn't soften it for me. "Well, perhaps it's time you stopped hiding behind it and figured that shit out."

Fuck. This girl has a knack for saying exactly what I don't want to hear but really need to.

"I haven't a clue how to do that," I admit, dragging a hand through my hair, restless and exposed, because this is the most honest I've been with anyone in my entire fucked-up life.

"Why?" she asks, voice softer now.

"You messed me up, that's a fact?" I glance across the table, heat still lingering on my skin. "One minute I'm teasing you, trying to get a rise, thinking I've got all the control I always do. Then you look at me, or... you're on top of me, and I can't fucking breathe without you."

Her eyes stay fixed. She watches me fall apart, piece by piece.

"I have no idea how to be someone else," I admit, my throat tight. "This cocky, fuck-everything version of me. It's been all I've had for a long time."

She blinks, caught off guard—but she doesn't look away or make a joke to deflect. She sits there, elbows on the table, eyes fixed on mine.

So I continue. "My dad didn't see me. Not really. Not unless I had a helmet and jersey on. That was when I mattered. When I won or played through an injury. Or I dragged us over the line by sheer fucking force. That's when I existed. The rest of me didn't matter. None of that was worth shit to him."

"So when you quit—"

"I didn't stop playing because I hated the game. I stopped because every time I stepped on that field, it felt as if I was begging him to notice me. Every win, every tackle, every touchdown. It was me screaming, "Look at me, you piece of shit." And he never did. Not really. He just nodded, told me to tackle harder next time."

Her eyes soften again, but it's not pity. It's understanding.

"I thought when I quit, my old man would lose his shit, but he didn't. He stopped showing up. He stopped asking how I was. Didn't care when I passed maths. Started calling me soft, because I'm not killing myself for a game that made me more of a man, supposedly." I tap my fingers against the table. "He still calls me that name."

I pause, jaw tight. The words dig up more than I thought they would.

"You know, he used to drag me out of bed before dawn, toss a ball at me before I could blink. Had me running drills until my legs gave out. Told me boys don't cry, boys don't give up, boys fucking win. And I did it, all of it, every bruised rib and bloodied knuckle, simply to get two words out of him. One fucking "well done.""

I shake my head, my eyes fixed on the grease-stained table.

"But none of that ever stuck. The moment I wasn't his football star anymore, I was just a disappointment again. Some loser who didn't live up to the family name."

The server arrives, plates hitting the table, the smell of grease and salt cutting through the heat between us. I blink down at the food, as if I forgot we even ordered.

I grab a fry but don't bother eating it. Simply hold it in my fingers until the salt sticks to my skin.

"I never told him I was back on the team." My voice is low, as if saying it out loud might make it real. "Didn't wanna give him the chance to fuck it up again." I shrug, but it's a fake one. Heavy as hell. "I still love the game. Last year, when I was playing... damn, I wanted to go all the way."

Sam lifts her shake, straw near her mouth, but she doesn't take a sip.

She's watching me instead, not trying to fix anything or fill the silence—just sitting with me in it.

"You still could," she says, and it's so damn simple. Three words. That's it. No pep talk. No pity. Only belief. "You walked away from playing for him. Not from the game."

It hits hard. Too fucking hard. Knocks something loose I didn't realize I was still holding onto.

I don't say shit. Instead, I shove a fry in my mouth to keep it from running.

She bites into her burger, chews, swallows, and doesn't rush it before hitting me with,

"I'm going to Mayfair next year."

My eyebrows shoot up. "That's where Noah and Aubrey are going, right?"

She nods. "Yeah. Lola too. I got a full scholarship. Double major. Psychology and neuroscience."

I blink slowly. "You're fucking with me."

She smirks. "Told you I was smart."

And fuck, everything clicks into place.

That smug little look she gave when I half-assed the assessment. The way she kept pushing me to get my act together while I was clowning around, running my mouth just to see her lose it. And I didn't even notice. I was too distracted by the way her lips moved when she talked and how satisfying it was to get under her skin.

She takes a slow sip of her shake, keeping her eyes on mine.

"Mayfair has a team, you know," she says, voice low, not pushing, only putting down the notion. "Maybe you should see about that. For yourself this time."

I don't answer. Just stare at her, and for once I really see her— not the girl who drove me crazy in chem, not the one who talks back when I push too hard. Only Sam. The girl who sees things in me I've never taken the time to look for.

And it guts me a little because last year I dreamed about college ball. The ideal version. The one where scouts compete for me, and I get to step onto that field knowing I truly belong.

Still. Tonight was the first time in way too long that it felt right. Not for him or the crowd. Not to prove some bullshit point about being good enough.

For me.

To push myself until my legs give out. To throw my body into every hit and keep getting back up. So that the sweat really means something. To experience the bruises and know I earned every one.

But the idea of playing college ball… that's a dream I let go of long ago. I already wrote it off before I even got the chance. Scouts have already zeroed in on the big names. Their golden boys. Perfect stats. Clean records. Smiles for the cameras. Polished players with highlight reels and parents who care.

Sam goes back to her burger.

We sit in silence for a moment. As she eats, I mostly stare at my food and pretend I'm not spiraling.

She's leaving next year to pursue the future she worked her ass off for.

Fuck, I'm proud of her. Of course I am.

But there's this sharp ache in my chest I can't ignore. All I can think about is that I won't be there to see it. That sharp little ache doesn't ask for permission; it just settles in.

She finishes her burger and licks the sauce off her fingers.

My eyes fall to her mouth, and it hits low, my cock thickening fast.

Fuck.

That mouth owns me, and she is completely unaware of it.

I don't even think. I just blurt out the first thing that comes into my head.

"Do you really think you could ever date someone like me?"

Her fingers freeze mid-lick.

Fuck me, I have to shift in my seat because my cock definitely isn't sitting right in my jeans anymore.

She blinks slowly, as if she's trying to figure out whether she misheard or if I've truly lost my mind.

"I'm serious," I say, gaze locked on hers. "Would you?"

She pulls her finger from her mouth so fucking slow I nearly groan. Wipes her hand on a napkin as if she's buying time, but I see it. That flicker of something in her eyes.

"Someone like you," she says, tasting the words, "You mean the guy who fucked half the cheer team?"

My mouth twitches. "So you've been keeping tabs."

She rolls her eyes. "You weren't exactly subtle, Reece."

I lean in, elbows on the table, a cocky smirk slowly curling at the corner of my mouth. "You say that as if it bothered you."

She doesn't answer

So I say it for her.

"No, I wasn't subtle. I was loud as fuck. I acted like none of it mattered because most of it didn't. But with you, Red... you were never just another name or another body. You were always the one I noticed when everyone else blurred out."

Her lips part slightly. That perfect mouth stills as she lifts her head and meets my gaze.

"You were never part of the noise," I say, my heart pounding as if it's trying to break through my ribs. "You were the thing I wanted to protect from it. The only thing that ever made me want to be better."

Silence grows thick between us, hot and charged.

"I know I've fucked a lot of things up," I say. "But I don't want to screw this up. I don't want to be that version of myself anymore. Not when you're sitting across from me, looking at me like I might still have a shot."

My voice cracks a little on that last word, enough to make it real.

"I want you, Red. Not for the night or for a quick hook-up. This is for fucking real."

"I don't know," she says finally, voice soft. I watch her blink, trying to make sense of me. "You confuse me like crazy, Reece. One minute you're an asshole, throwing out bullshit to piss me off. Next, you're telling me stuff no one else gets to hear. Things that really matter. It's hard to keep up."

"I confuse the hell out of myself too," I admit.

Sam watches me. She is cautious, waiting for whatever disaster I'm about to create next.

"But I want to date you," I say, and fuck, it slips out so fast. No filter or safety net. Only the truth, crashing through my chest and into the space between us. "And yeah, I've never done that. But I want to try. With you."

Her lips part. She looks at me as if I've completely thrown her off balance.

"Reece..." she breathes, her voice soft and shaken.

"I know what you're thinking." My voice is firmer now. "That I'm that guy. I fuck around. That I say the right shit to get what I want and do the wrong thing. That I'm a dick. And I was. I won't pretend I wasn't. But not with you, Red. Not anymore."

She lowers her gaze, and it hurts to watch her fold into herself like that. I can tell she's uncertain whether to trust me.

"What about the bet?" she asks, voice barely there. "How am I supposed to trust this isn't just another game?"

I shake my head. "I've never told anyone we hooked up. As far as I am concerned, there's no fucking bet. Not anymore. Not for me."

She looks up again, and that stare... It pierces through every wall I've spent years building.

"I'm not asking you to forget what I've done," I say, voice rough. "I'm asking for a shot to show you I'm not that guy with you."

Her teeth catch her bottom lip, and I notice it. That flicker of hesitation. The part of her that's bracing for the punchline. Expecting me to turn this into another fucked-up joke or one of my bullshit games.

"I know my rep's shit," I say. "I've earned every rumor. Every name I fucked and forgot. I've been a dick. No arguments there. But I wouldn't fuck this up. Not with you, Red. Not when I've finally got something real in front of me."

She watches me like she's waiting for the cracks to appear, for me to flinch. But I don't.

Her fingers curl around her cup's edge. Her eyes remain on mine.

Then a gentle, hesitant nod. "Okay."

I blink. "Okay?"

She swallows and then lifts her chin.

"I'll date you," she says, and my heart fucking jolts. "But on one condition."

"Anything." It slips out, breathless. I mean it. I'd crawl across broken glass for a maybe with her.

"No one knows. Not yet," she says. "Not Jace or Lola. Not anyone. I need time," she adds. "To see if this is real. If you're true to your word. If I do this, I don't want eyes on us. I don't want whispers or bets or people waiting for you to fuck it up. I want to know you're choosing me because you mean it."

I nod, and this dumb grin pulls at my mouth before I can stop it. "Deal. I'll keep my mouth shut."

"Good, because if Jace hears he'll tell Lola. And if Lola hears—"

I interrupt, saying, "She'll announce it over the damn school inter-com."

She smiles. I laugh, and it comes out more easily than I expect. A real, full-body laugh that makes my chest feel too big for my ribs.

I'm buzzing. Heart pounding, blood hot, this wild happiness surges through me so quickly I don't know what to do with it. I want to climb onto the damn table. I want to shout it from the parking lot that she's my girl.

But I don't.

I keep it quiet, just like she asked for us.

Still, the grin won't leave my face. Because for the first time in my loud-as-fuck, fucked-up life, I don't want to be the center of the chaos. I want to be hers. Quietly. Completely. No games. No noise.

She grabs a fry, pops it in her mouth without realizing she just turned my world upside down.

"Okay, real talk," she says with her mouth full. "What the fuck is going on with Lola and Jace?"

I raise an eyebrow. "You noticed that too?"

"Please. They practically eye-fuck each other across the cafeteria. Tell me something juicy."

I lean in and lower my voice. "I'll tell you something if you keep it to yourself."

She narrows her eyes. "Spill."

"Jace has a thing for her."

Her jaw drops. "No."

"Oh, yeah."

"No," she says again, as if saying it twice will make it less true. "Jace. Mr. I Don't Catch Feelings. I don't kiss on the lips. Mr. I'd fuck a shadow if it stood still long enough?"

I smirk. "Well, apparently shadows aren't doing it for him anymore."

She shakes her head, stunned. "Holy shit."

"Dude's been acting weird for weeks. More moody than usual. Even for Jace."

She leans across the table, eyes wide. "Do you think Lola knows?" She grins, and damn, the way her whole face lights up, yeah, I'd hold onto this quiet moment forever if it means I get to be the one who makes her smile like that.

I take a bite of my burger, finally hungry now that the world isn't falling apart around me.

"I think it's Jace doing his usual player stuff," Sam says, popping a fry into her mouth. "Dropping charm and showing off that whole emotionally unavailable thing he thinks makes him irresistible."

She grabs her shake, swirls the straw with her finger, and keeps her eyes on me as if she's waiting for backup.

"It's his classic move," I say, smirking. "Works every time."

"Not on Lola." She shakes her head, grinning. "That girl's got a bull-shit radar that could bring down an aircraft."

CHAPTER 19

SAM

I still can't believe I said yes. That was close to a week ago. Seven days of sneaking around, lying to my friends, faking smiles while my pussy aches for another round.

We've mostly been hiding out at his place. Reece's room has become some kind of secret fuck room—four walls, one bed, and seemingly endless ways to make me forget my own damn name.

Right now, my orgasms are clocking more hours than I am. If they had a loyalty card, I'd be earning a free one by now. Probably two. Hell, maybe a commemorative plaque nailed to his headboard.

No one knows. At least I hope they don't.

We keep it low. Real low.

Tossing glances across crowded hallways. Brushing fingers when no one's watching. That kind of slow-burn tease that makes me want to straddle him on the cafeteria bench and ride him right there in front of the salad bar.

He'll brush past me in the hallway and mutter something filthy under his breath, some shit about my skirt, or what he'd do to me if we were alone, and I swear my legs go weak every time.

And when we're alone, that's a whole different story.

My body has been wrecked in the best fucking way. That boy touches me as if it's a skill he's mastered. He knows every switch to flip, every sound that leaves my throat before I even make it.

His filthy mouth whispers in my ear, telling me all the ways he's going to fuck me, stretch me, break me open until I'm begging. And I do. Every single time. He makes it feel safe to fall apart under his hands.

He's possessive in ways that should frighten me.

He tells me my pussy is his like it's a fact, not up for debate. That I was made for him, and he's just claiming what was always his.

And when he touches me... damn. Every thought vanishes. Every rule I ever followed, every line I said I wouldn't cross, all of it burns away in his hands.

Every time he pushes inside me, he rewrites how I understand pleasure. I become a full-body, mind-blanking, toe-curling wreck.

I forget how to think. I forget my name. All I know is his voice in my ear, his cock filling me, and the way my body responds to him before my brain can catch up.

I should be terrified of how deep this goes, but I only crave more because there's nothing soft about the way he moans my name when he's buried inside me. Nothing gentle about how his hands shake when I fall apart in them. Nothing superficial about the way he kisses me afterward, as if he's starving and I'm the only thing keeping him alive.

And there's definitely nothing simple about how I keep going back for more, even when I understand this whole thing could blow up in our faces.

I keep reminding myself that this is temporary. It's controlled and contained.

That it's something I can step away from before it drags me under. Because, let's face it, Reece is a fuckboy. A true one. The kind girls whisper warnings about while reapplying lip gloss in bathroom mirrors. The kind you drop in group chats with red flag emojis and a quick "don't go there." He takes what he wants, gets you hooked, then leaves you empty and aching, wondering if any of it was real.

And yet, last night, he stood in front of me with soft eyes and said he'd never hurt me. And I wanted to believe him.

Damn, I still want to believe him. The ache is so intense, it hits spots I didn't know could be sore.

That's the problem with wanting.

I'm not stupid. I know what happens when girls hand their hearts to boys who've never been taught how to hold anything gently.

I've seen the pain. Heard the stories through bathroom walls, seen the smeared mascara and shaky hands clutching phones that never light up again.

I know what happens when someone prettier shows up—when they're easier, louder. When some girl with perfect timing and no hesitation offers herself on a silver platter and asks for nothing but a fuck in return.

I know what happens when Maya bats her lashes and smiles up at Reece. When she intentionally forgets her bra. When her laugh becomes high and flirty, and she stands a little too close.

I know what happens when temptation walks right up and doesn't ask for anything but his cock.

And I can feel it approaching.

I'm just waiting for the moment he pulls away mid-kiss.

An excuse for when his eyes shift, stopping to scan the room for someone shinier. When I'm waiting for a text and he doesn't respond. The night he sleeps with someone else and calls it a mistake.

Every day, I dodge Lola, Liz, and Aubrey like it's my full-time job. I run through every excuse in the book—homework, family stuff I don't even bother to make convincing. They're still falling for it... for now, anyway.

And yeah, I regret doing that to my best friends.

Liz is leaving in a few days. I should be soaking up every second with her. Laughing too loud. Taking photos, we'll forget to print. Being the kind of friend who actually shows the fuck up.

Instead, I'm hiding out in Reece's bedroom with sore thighs and a pussy that can't stop craving him, chasing this high I swore I'd never want.

Every time I try to pull away, he touches me or says something dirty against my skin, and it's over. I forget the guilt, that the clock is ticking on Liz's goodbye. I forget everything but him.

Today, as I walk into school, I can still feel it. The aftershocks, the soreness. The memory of everything he did to me yesterday in that room of his. My thighs ache. My lower back's tight. My pussy… well, it's still throbbing if I shift the wrong way. Because Reece didn't simply just fuck me, he wrecked me. Bent me over his mattress, mouth filthy against my ear, fingers digging into my hips like he couldn't get close enough no matter how deep he was. Every thrust was a promise and a punishment.

I loved every second of it.

After he wrecked me, he ordered pizza and sprawled on his bed, half-naked and cocky as hell, ready to study. Except he didn't put on a shirt. Just those abs and that goddamn smirk.

So there I was, with my textbook open and my brain fried, trying to focus on the assignment while his chest flexed each time he moved. I was supposed to be summarizing the Industrial Revolution. Instead, I ended up having another orgasm. That's why I'm sore today and can barely sit down without clenching.

If my dad knew where I was going every afternoon, he'd lose his shit. He thinks I'm staying back for tutoring. That I am being my usual responsible self.

If he knew I was getting completely railed by the boy he doesn't approve of, he'd threaten to castrate him on sight, and he'd probably burn the school down himself.

I'm honestly surprised no one has figured it out yet.

The way Reece and I look at each other across classrooms and hallways, as if we're the only two people in the entire building.

One glance and my body already remembers what his hands feel like. One smirk from him and I'm completely screwed all over again.

It's a constant live wire between us.

Every second we're apart, we're still touching, just with our eyes.

I'll catch him staring while the teacher's mid-sentence, that lazy grin tugging at his mouth as he remembers what he did to me yesterday and exactly how sore I am from it.

And damn, I stare right back.

A blink too long. A look too loaded and somehow, no one notices.

It's become this quiet game. Us, buzzing with our own little secret, invisible to everyone else. And God, that might be the best part. Knowing it's ours. Simply ours.

By lunchtime, I already know I can't do it.

There's no way I can sit across from Reece and pretend I'm not thinking about how he had me gasping while he fucked me against his bedroom wall yesterday. I can't watch his fingers tap against the table without remembering how those same fingers were inside me less than twenty-four hours ago.

I walk into the cafeteria, and the noise hits me hard. Laughter. Tray clatter. That awful hum of everyone knowing something I don't.

Lola and Jace are at our usual table, fully in flirt mode—if you can even call it that.

Lola doesn't flirt in a typical way. She insults Jace with a straight face and no remorse. She drops savage one-liners that make Jace blink twice before he grins as if he's been given a challenge. That's their thing — verbal bloodsport with a hint of sexual tension.

I'm pretty sure that's the only reason Lola hasn't figured me and Reece out yet. Because if she weren't busy sharpening her tongue on Jace, she would have sniffed us out by now. Girl's a bloodhound for secrets. You so much as glance at someone for half a second longer than usual, and she's crafting a full conspiracy board in her head.

Aubrey's not far behind either. She plays sweet, but she's got eyes. She picks up on vibes fast. I'm sure she would've picked up on mine already if Noah weren't permanently attached to her like some giant, possessive limb.

So I eat fast with my head down, barely tasting anything, going through the motions while conversation buzzes around me and my pulse thuds way too loud in my ears.

I don't look at Reece.

I avoid his gaze like it's fucking radioactive... which, let's be honest, it kind of is.

The moment our eyes meet, it's over. My body begins flashing through every dirty memory it shouldn't revisit in the middle of a crowded school cafeteria. His hands. His mouth. The way he growled my name right before he made me come so hard I saw stars.

And yeah, I'm not doing that here.

I stand when I'm done, mumble something about needing to study for an exam. It's total bullshit. The kind of flimsy excuse that would fall apart in Lola's hands in under five seconds if she were actually paying attention.

It's weak, I know it. They probably know it too. But no one calls me out on it.

Reece understands what this signifies. It's a code. If he wants me, he'll track me down. He's done it every other time.

The library is quiet when I walk in. A few students tucked into their usual corners, heads down, lost in textbooks and glued to screens. Perfect.

No one looks up when I slide into my usual spot near the back, tucked in the corner where the security cameras don't quite reach.

I drop my bag and pull out my notebook and laptop. Pretend. Type a bunch of nonsense that doesn't even look like words to appear busy.

And after that, I hear him—the slow, confident stride that makes my stomach tighten before I even see his face. Reece moves with the cocky ease he was born with, all swagger and no apology.

I don't look up. I keep typing, pretending.

He sinks into the chair next to me.

"Hey, Red."

My pulse skips, and my thighs tighten.

I turn my head and meet his eyes. He's already smirking. Then I feel his hand, warm fingers sliding over the inside of my thigh. His touch is gentle, teasing, just enough to make my breath catch.

He leans in, mouth brushing the shell of my ear. "I've been thinking about this pussy all fucking day." A shiver runs down my back. My thighs part instinctively. A silent yes. A fucking plea. "I want you dripping on this seat before we leave."

His fingers slide higher, brushing right at the spot where I'm already throbbing. He presses there just enough to make my whole body jolt in my chair. I bite down on my lip to keep quiet.

His mouth slowly curves into a smirk, signaling he knows exactly what he's doing to me and intends to enjoy every second of it.

"I'm already dripping," I tell him. "Maybe you should've arrived sooner."

His breath falters afterward, a quick inhale he barely manages to swallow. His jaw tightens, control stretched thin, and fuck me if that isn't the hottest part, watching him fight himself because of me.

He pushes my underwear aside and runs his thumb through my folds. His touch is teasing and slow. He touches my clit lightly at first, almost mockingly, and my breath catches so hard I have to press my lips together to stay quiet.

My head dips. My fingers curl into my notebook so hard the paper crinkles.

He closes his eyes as he touches me, his dark lashes against his cheeks, and his mouth slightly opens on a sound he doesn't quite release.

Seeing it hit him like that does something dangerous to me. I'm not the only one losing control.

"You're soaked," he murmurs under his breath.

His thumb strokes my clit again, slower this time, more cruelly, and my entire body responds. Heat rushes through me. A shiver runs down my spine.

I tilt toward him without even meaning to, desperate, shameless and so fucking aware of how exposed I am.

He slides a finger inside me, and I have to bite down hard on my bottom lip to keep the sound in.

My whole body tightens around him. Heat spikes sharp and dizzying. My head dips, breath shaking, fingers curling into the edge of the table while I fight not to move.

He gives me just enough.

A slow curl. A gentle thrust. Pleasure rolls through me in thick, pulsing waves that makes my thighs tremble. His thumb brushes my clit once more, and I swear my vision blurs.

He stops. Pulls his finger out slowly.

The loss hits harder than the touch did. I suck in a quiet breath, chest heaving, eyes lifting to his.

He's watching me. Eyes dark, focused, hungry. His jaw is clenched tightly, as if he's holding himself together by sheer will.

"Open," he whispers.

I do, and he places his finger against my mouth, pressing it past my lips.

"Taste yourself," he murmurs. "See how fucking sweet you are."

I press my lips around his finger and suck, my tongue sliding along the pad.

His breath stutters. Eyes flutter shut for just a moment before snapping back open, wild and wrecked. His free hand grips the edge of the table, knuckles turning white. His throat works as he swallows hard, trying to hold back the sound threatening to tear out of him.

He leans in closer, his forehead nearly touching mine.

"Fuck," he breathes. Silent. Shattered. "You're killing me."

He watches me suck his fingers. His chest rises fast like he's fighting to keep it together in front of everyone. And god, that does something to me.

There's a high in it.

I live for this version of him.

The way he falls apart when he's with me. The way one lick of my tongue over his finger can mess him up so badly he has to clench his fists to stay quiet. No one's ever looked at me the way he does. No one's ever needed me like this. I've never felt power like this before. Not over anyone.

But here's the kicker—he has power over me too. One word. One look. One touch of his hand on my skin, and I forget my own damn name.

He leans in again, voice rough. "If we weren't in this fucking library right now, I'd have your legs over my shoulders and your cunt in my mouth right now."

I inhale sharply, my thighs squeezing together, still throbbing from where he touched me. Still aching from everything we didn't finish.

He leans in, breath hot against my jaw, voice nothing but a rough promise.

"I guess I'll have to wait until we're at my place to make a bigger mess of this pussy."

God, he says it so casually. So fucking filthy. And I swear I can feel it between my legs.

But I shake my head, holding back the moan building in my throat.

"I can't come over tonight."

His brows knit together. "What?"

"Lola's sleepover," I say, keeping my tone gentle as my heart races. "It's for Liz. Her last night before she leaves."

"Fuck," he mutters. "So I'm just supposed to spend the night hard, rubbing one out while you're off painting nails and talking shit with your girls?"

My knee brushes his. It's a calculated drag of skin that's pure tease. Enough pressure to let him experience it.

He stills as his eyes drop to my mouth. That familiar flicker of tension cuts through his jaw. He knows he's being played.

"You're evil," he mutters.

I tilt my head, acting innocent. "You like it."

He leans in again, his hand slipping under the table, stopping right at my knee this time.

"You know I'm gonna have to rub one out before next period now?"

I drag my teeth across my bottom lip, giving him that slow, mischievous grin, a look that I know drives him insane. "Poor baby."

His gaze darkens instantly.

"You could help," he says, voice dropping lower, filthier. "Come to the boys' bathroom and suck my cock like the filthy girl you pretend not to be."

I shut my laptop, hands steady even though my pulse isn't.

Reece stands without a word, his eyes locking onto mine with that stare.

That quiet command. The one that says, "Come with me."

He turns and walks toward the back of the library, not toward the busy main bathrooms. He heads to the small one near the archives with the flickering lights, the forgotten bathroom that no one ever uses.

I wait another second, pretending to scan my notebook before I look around. A couple of kids are still hunched over their textbooks, earbuds in. Nobody is paying attention.

I stand there, my heart pounding so loudly I swear it echoes.

Each step toward the back hallway sharpens everything. My breath. My focus. My hunger. The moment I go through the door, Reece locks it, and he is on me.

His hands. On my waist. My hips. My face. His mouth crashes into mine.

I gasp against him, my back hitting the cold tile as his mouth trails down my neck, teeth scraping my skin.

His breath is hot. Words even hotter.

"You're gonna get on your knees for me," he murmurs, tongue dragging over the curve of my throat. "Take my cock and let me fuck that perfect face."

His hand moves up my thigh.

"Bet you'll choke on it, Red. Fuckin' love the way you gag."

I shudder, hips arching into him, entirely captivated by the filth spilling from his mouth and the way his lips seal over my pulse.

I undo his jeans and drag the zipper down slowly, just to watch the way his jaw locks. My hand closes around his cock, hot and heavy in my grip, and I swear I feel the shift in him instantly. His breath stutters. Just once. Enough to tell me I've got him.

When I sink to my knees in front of him, my eyes lift to meet his gaze, making his whole body go rigid.

"Fuck," he mutters. "You have no idea what that does to me."

His gaze sears into mine. Possessive. Dark.

"You on your knees, looking up at me like that, holding my cock as if it belongs to you." His voice drops lower, rougher. "Makes me want to fuck you all day and night."

I let my thumb trace the head, watching his control start to fracture.

"Jesus, Red," he breathes.

His hand slides into my hair, steady and grounding. Not forcing. Claiming.

"Open that pretty mouth," he whispers. "I want to see you take my cock. Want to see how bad you want it."

My tongue teases the tip of his cock, enough to make him swear under his breath. Salt. Heat. Want. All of it hits me at once, and I don't hold back. I lean in, take him deeper into my mouth, and feel his whole body react.

His head tilts back, eyes squeezed shut, teeth clenched tightly enough to crack. He's fighting himself, struggling to resist losing control.

Every sound he makes only makes me braver. I keep my pace steady, hand and mouth moving with purpose, knowing exactly how to work him without mercy.

When he looks down again, and our eyes lock, I see it happen. That moment when he's gone.

"Fuck, Red," he gasps. "Don't stop. Don't you dare fucking stop."

And for the first time, I realize exactly how much control I hold over him.

His grip tightens in my hair, a growl roaring from his throat. He thrusts once, twice, shallow and teasing, testing the edge of control he's about to lose.

"Red..." His voice is strained. "You feel so fucking good."

Then it shifts. His hips jerk forward, deeper and rougher, as I let him take control. His grip tightens where he needs me as he fucks into my mouth, using my throat the way he's been craving since the second I dropped to my knees.

"Shit. That's it. Just like that. Take my fucking cock. Take all of it."

He's wild now. Fingers gripping my hair tighter. Eyes locked on mine. Thrusts becoming ragged, like a man falling apart when there's no chance to turn back.

Then he groans.

"Fuck... fuck, I'm gonna—"

His whole body stiffens. One hard thrust. Followed by another. And he comes, hot and hard, spilling down my throat with a filthy growl of my name. His eyes close, head thrown back, every muscle tense as pleasure takes over him.

His cock still rests on my tongue, twitching from the aftershocks, and I don't move. I stay right there, eyes locked on his, mouth wrapped around the thing that caused him to lose control.

"Jesus, Red," he mutters again, voice hoarse. "You're gonna ruin me."

His hand remains in my hair. Softer now, but still there. Still asserting itself.

I smirk around him before I finally pull back. A string of spit catches the light between us before I wipe it with the back of my hand.

"Pretty sure that was the point," I murmur, licking the cum off my bottom lip.

Reece's eyes drag down my body. Chest rising too fast. But then he smirks.

"You look so fucking perfect down there. You know that? All sweet and cock-drunk."

I raise an eyebrow, still on my knees. "Cock-drunk?"

He grins, full of sin. "Don't tell me you're not. You just swallowed every drop, baby. You earned the title. Go sit on the counter now."

He's not asking; he's telling.

My stomach flips, pulse racing, because I know exactly what that mouth can do. And let me tell you, the way that guy flicks a clit—mind-blowing doesn't even cover it. It's precision. It's filth. It's art.

My legs move before my brain catches up, as if my body has already made the decision and my mind is just along for the ride. I slide onto the counter, breath caught somewhere between anticipation and chaos, because I know that once he's between my thighs, I won't remember my name, let alone care about anything else.

He steps closer, hands on my knees, opening me up.

"Sit back," he says, voice low, mouth tilted in that cocky smirk that's got my pussy pulsing already. "Let me give this pretty cunt what it's been begging for."

He drops to his knees, and I swear my lungs forget their job. They just stop. Full shutdown.

The first touch of his tongue rips a gasp out of me. He is confident, greedy, and relentless. He goes at my pussy like he's been denied oxygen and this is the only way he survives.

One hand grips my thigh, fingers digging in hard enough to bruise. There's no gentleness in it. No hesitation. Only possession.

"Fuck," I whisper, already shaking, already losing the battle.

His tongue works on me with purpose. Slow where it hurts, fast where it wrecks. He knows exactly what he's doing and enjoys every second of watching me come undone. My vision blurs. My head tips back. My fingers claw at the edge of the counter until my knuckles ache, and my legs tremble.

His fingers slide into me, one curling perfectly inside.

I hiss at the first touch. A sharp inhale reveals how incredibly good it feels.

He grins against my pussy. The cocky, filthy kind of grin that says he knows I'm his.

"Fuck..." I choke out, breathless.

His tongue works my clit in relentless, filthy circles. It's fucking heaven. It's too much and yet not enough.

My legs start to shake. A moan punches out of me loud enough I have to slap my hand over my mouth, eyes rolling back as pleasure tears through me like wildfire.

He doesn't stop.

It builds fast. Too fast. No teasing edge this time, no slow unravel. Simply fire and hunger. Only him.

And when I come, it's violent.

My whole body locks around him, clenched and trembling, while his tongue continues to drag over my clit, as if he wants to overstimulate me.

And when he finally pulls back, his mouth glistening and his chin slick with everything he just pulled from me, he stays on his knees for a beat. Breath uneven. Hands still anchored to my thighs.

His eyes sweep over my body.

He looks proud of himself.

He should be. I'm a complete mess. Still trembling. Still trying to remember how to breathe.

Chapter 20

SAM

Lola's house hits me the second I walk in. Cinnamon candles, perfume and popcorn grease, the scent that clings to your clothes for days. It smells like chaos wrapped in glitter. So basically it smells like Lola.

Liz's laugh echoes through the hallway before I even see her. There she is—sprawled across the couch in fuzzy socks, legs tucked under her. Her nails are painted gold and glittery enough to blind someone if she waves too hard. Which she does.

"Finally," she says, grinning. "Took you long enough."

I force a smile. Not because I'm not happy to see her—I am. I'm still carrying too much memory of Reece after what he did to me to function like a normal human being right now.

I take off my shoes and set my bag by the door.

"I was helping Mom with dinner," I lie smoothly, as if I haven't been eaten alive in a school bathroom by the most dangerous boy I've ever met only three hours ago.

Liz clocks me halfway across the room and chucks a throw pillow at Lola, who's halfway through arguing with her.

The smoke alarm blares overhead.

"Oh my god Lola," Liz says, covering her ears.

Lola bolts for the oven in full chaos mode, yanks the door open, and pulls out a tray of cookies with a smoke-trailed behind.

"They're not burned," she yells over the alarm, waving a bright pink oven mitt in the air like its Exhibit A in a high-stakes court case. "The smoke alarm is being overdramatic. Look at them."

She marches into the living room, holding the tray out as if she's presenting fine art, completely unfazed by the piercing alarm still wailing in the background. The cookies are suspiciously browned and still sizzling.

"Look," she says, eyes wide. "Crispy on the edges. That's flavor."

Right then, the front door swings open and Aubrey steps in, a paper bag of snacks cradled in one arm with her brows furrowed.

"What the hell is happening here?" she asks, eyeing the smoke.

Lola lifts the tray higher. "Cookies."

"You're just in time," Liz adds, as she props her feet on the coffee table, with a fuzzy sock now dangling from her toes.

"For what?" Aubrey shouts as Lola, still in the middle of kitchen mayhem, grabs a broom and climbs up onto a stool. A second later, the smoke alarm shrieks even louder.

"Lola said blindfolded karaoke is happening," Liz yells.

We all turn instinctively toward the kitchen.

Lola stands barefoot on a stool, holding a broom as if fencing with the ceiling. The tray of burnt cookies now lies abandoned on the bench. She pokes at the fire alarm, muttering something about "drama queen electronics."

One last jab, and the alarm finally falls silent.

Lola lowers the broom, steps off the stool with a victorious shrug, and walks back into the room as if nothing happened.

"You're welcome."

"Wait," Aubrey says, pointing between Liz and Lola as if they've both gone crazy. "Back it up. Blindfolded karaoke... how is that even possible?"

Lola shrugs, totally unfazed. "You wear this blindfold. Someone else holds the mic. And if you want to make it funnier, you spin the person around until they don't know which way is up. Duh."

I laugh as Aubrey walks over and plops down on the couch next to me.

"This is gonna be one of those nights," she mutters, pulling a throw pillow into her lap. "I can feel it already."

"Lola doesn't do chill," I say, nudging her with my elbow. "You knew what this was the second you walked in and smelled fire and sugar."

Aubrey exhales a slow breath and moves closer to me, speaking softly. "Yeah, but you know what? Some part of me... the really naïve, stupid part of me thought maybe tonight we'd do normal people things. A board game. A face mask. Perhaps we'd talk about our feelings—"

Lola gasps suddenly, as if a lightning bolt of chaos just struck her brain, and darts back into the kitchen, nearly wiping out on a rogue sock skidding across the hardwood.

"Oh no," Aubrey laughs, watching her disappear with wide eyes. "She's sprinting. That's never good. Not in socks and not with that glint in her eye."

"Heaven help us," I mumble.

Liz sniffles beside me, dabbing at her eye with the sleeve of her over-sized hoodie. "I'm going to miss this," she says, voice thick with tears she's trying to blink away.

Aubrey shifts closer and wraps an arm around her, pulling her in gently. "Yeah," she says, her smile softening. "Lola's crazy. But she's sweet, funny, and somehow always gets away with everything. I swear, I've never been able to stay mad at her for more than two seconds." She glances back toward the kitchen and raises a playful eyebrow. "What part are you going to miss the most, Liz? The spontaneous combustion cookies or the risk of being knocked unconscious by karaoke?"

"All of it," Liz says, letting out a laugh. "The dumb stuff. The not-actually-singing competitions. The almost-burning-the-house-down bonding rituals."

"And the glitter," Aubrey adds with a mock shudder. "You know there'll be glitter."

Liz laughs harder this time, wiping at her cheeks. "There's always glitter."

"I swear to God, if she comes back in here with a piñata, I'm leaving," Aubrey says.

A loud crash echoes from the kitchen.

"Lola!" we all shout in unison, already bracing for whatever new disaster she's brewed up.

She reappears in the doorway, smiling brightly. One hand holds a ridiculously fluffy pink blindfold, while the other carries a bag of rainbow glitter.

"You guys," she says breathlessly, "I totally forgot I bought sparkles for this. Blindfolded karaoke just got a glow-up."

There's a moment of silence before we lose it.

Aubrey's head drops into her hands as she bursts out laughing, snorting. "This is how we die," she wheezes. "Smothered in sugar and suffocated by glitter."

Liz doubles over, gasping for air. "I can't... oh my God, I can't... " Her laugh turns into hiccupy little sobs, tears spilling freely down her cheeks.

I slide off the couch in a completely undignified heap, clutching my ribs. "I'm gonna pee," I manage through the wheezing. "I swear to God, I'm gonna pee."

Lola grins, completely unbothered, and holds up the pink blindfold again. "So... are we doing glitter karaoke or what? I also have glow sticks."

That sets us off all over again.

Liz slides down until she's lying on the carpet.

Aubrey crawls off the couch to join me on the floor, still snorting uncontrollably.

Through it all, there's this warmth—a reminder of why nights like this matter, because no one else understands us the way we understand each other.

Hours later, the chaos has finally eased into something quieter, softer around the edges.

The room has shifted in the quiet way that time does when you're not paying attention. When laughter fades and bodies settle into corners of the couch with fleece blankets draped over their legs, remnants of snacks are scattered across the coffee table. There's glitter on the rug. The karaoke mic lies abandoned upside down in the beanbag, and someone's stuck googly eyes on the popcorn bowl.

It's well past midnight, but no one is ready to call it. The energy has softened into something calmer now. Dim lights. Bare feet. The occasional yawn, muffled by a hoodie sleeve. One of Liz's socks is hanging off the back of the couch, and no one knows how it got there.

Lola sprawls across the floor, braiding Liz's hair without asking as Liz scrolls through her phone. Aubrey is curled sideways in the armchair, nursing a cold drink she should have finished hours ago. The steady hum of a mellow playlist plays in the background—quiet enough that no one really hears the words, just the mood it creates.

There's comfort in the silence now— that gentle hush where nobody feels the need to fill the space. The kind of quiet that is earned, full of contentment and unspoken things that don't need fixing.

It is the hum of friendship, that rare, sacred thing where you can let your guard down and just be. No performances. Simply girls on a couch, wrapped in a night that could go on forever.

And that's when the conversation starts.

Aubrey shifts in her chair, placing her cold mug on the coffee table, and glances at Lola, who's still lying on the floor, half-focused on the braid she's been working into Liz's hair.

"So," Aubrey starts casually, "are we ever going to talk about what's going on with you and Jace?"

Lola freezes mid-braid.

Liz snorts from the floor. "Oh my god. Finally."

"Nothing's going on," Lola says, too quickly.

Liz immediately snorts. "Oh, it's not nothing."

"Do you mind not outing me in my own house?" Lola says.

Liz raises her eyebrows, grinning. "Babe, it's not exactly subtle. You practically purr when he walks into a room."

"I do not—"

"You do," I cut in, smirking. "And don't get me started on the food thing. No one else gets to steal bites off your plate without losing a hand."

Lola groans and flops dramatically onto her back. "You're all seeing things."

"Please," Liz mutters. "You bring him snacks. And not the cheap ones either. The good stuff. You literally shared your last dumpling with him."

"I felt sorry for him," Lola says quickly, staring at the ceiling. "You know the kind of life he's had. It's not like he's got a stocked fridge waiting for him at home."

Aubrey's voice softens. "Is that why you're so good to him?"

"I just..." Lola shrugs. "I don't know. He lets me be myself. He doesn't get offended when I say dumb shit. He never shuts me down. It's not like that with most guys."

That part's true. Jace is the only one who lets her get away with the relentless teasing, the sass, the weird food combinations she forces on people. And he always takes it. Laughs. Sometimes even shoots it right back.

I glance at Lola, tempted to speak. I could tell them what Reece said. That Jace likes her. That it isn't banter for him. It's something more. But I promised Reece I wouldn't say anything, and for some reason, I want to keep that.

"I mean... he's cute. Obviously," Lola continues. "He's got that whole scruffy, brooding, stares-at-the-wall-too-long vibe. I've wondered about it, sure."

"So if he ever made a move?" Aubrey taps her fingers against the arm of the chair.

Lola raises her eyebrows. "You mean, if he ever actually tried something?"

Aubrey nods.

Liz leans in.

"I'd shut it down," Lola snorts.

"Why?" Liz asks. "You clearly like him."

Lola turns her head toward Liz. "Because it's Jace. He's hot, yeah. And he lets me get away with shit no one else does. But he's a fuckboy. The kind who chews girls up, spits them out and doesn't even look back to see if they're still standing."

Her words hit harder than I expected. And suddenly I start thinking about Reece—about how he's the same. The same swagger, reckless charm, and trail of broken hearts behind him.

"I don't want to be that girl," Lola adds. "One of many. No thanks."

"You're not the kind of girl anyone forgets," I murmur, more to myself than to her. But she hears me.

Her mouth quirks. "Damn right I'm not. But still, it is better to wonder than to regret."

Something about the way she says it hits too close, that sharp edge of honesty that sinks below my ribs.

Her words "Better to wonder than to regret," loop endlessly in my mind as Lola kicks her socked feet up and yawns. Liz shoves popcorn into her mouth.

I lean forward, pick up my drink from the edge of the coffee table, and take a sip.

"So... apparently someone fucked in the library today," Lola says casually, like she didn't just light a fuse.

I choke. Full-body cough. Sounding like a dying cat with a nicotine habit. "What?"

"Dead serious." Lola grins, absolutely thrilled.

Liz perks up, wide-eyed and eager for drama. "Oh, my god. Who?"

"That's the thing," Lola says, voice dropping low, eyes gleaming as if she's about to leak state secrets. "Shayleen told me someone got really loud in the library bathroom. You know, the ones no one uses behind the archive shelves. Apparently, it got loud. Like, full-on moaning and everything. But–"

She drags the word out, milking it for effect.

"She hasn't a clue who it is. Yet."

My stomach hits the floor. "Yet?"

"Yeah, apparently someone saw." Lola leans in, eyes gleaming. "Shayleen said a girl walked right past as someone was leaving. She saw who it was. But she won't say. Yet."

The word hits me hard. My grip tightens on the silly flamingo straw until it bends slightly. I loosen it before anyone notices.

Liz lets out a gleeful cackle. "Oh my God, I hope it was that sleazy student who keeps snapping girls' bras in the hallway. That boy deserves a public scandal."

"Anyway," Lola continues, "Shayleen's on it. The girl's got better instincts than a drug dog. She'd track your orgasm calendar if it meant breaking a story."

I force a laugh, brittle and too quick. My heart's still trying to climb out of my throat, and all I can think is: fuck.

Lola grabs a handful of popcorn and throws a few kernels at Liz. "I swear, though, if it turns out to be someone boring, I'm gonna be so pissed. This kind of gossip deserves a proper scandal. Give me a cheerleader and teacher. Or rivals from debate club hate-fucking between rounds."

Liz cackles again. "Honestly, I'd believe it. That debate captain has big "let me dominate you in the archives" energy."

They keep going, tossing theories and laughing like it's nothing more than juicy entertainment.

But my pulse keeps racing, and the back of my neck prickles every time I picture Shayleen cornering the girl who saw.

"Did Shayleen say who the mystery witness is?" I ask.

"No. But she said the girl who saw it talks to her when her brother plays soccer. She has to come to games to cheer him on or whatever. Shayleen's gonna corner her next match and drag it out of her."

My heart stutters.

I know exactly who that is.

Tara Evans.

Always there on the bleachers with a coffee and a bad attitude, pretending to care about her little brother's midfield skills. She's quiet. Observant. The kind of girl who notices everything and says nothing. The girl who makes eye contact and holds it too long, as if she's seeing all your dirty thoughts on a projector screen.

Fuck.

I glance at Aubrey. She's gone still, eyes narrowed, like she is thinking.

"Tara," she says quietly, confirming it.

Lola swings her head toward her. "You know her?"

"She's in my art elective," Aubrey says. "Barely talks. She sketches weird shit and watches people. She creeps me out a little, honestly."

Liz perks up. "Maybe she's the villain in this whole thing. You know, keeping her info close, waiting to make some power move."

"Or maybe she's just not a gossip," Aubrey mutters.

"God, I hate waiting," Lola says, throwing her hands up. "I need answers now. I need the scandal. And I definitely need to know who was getting their brains fucked out with Mrs. Clarke nearby."

I swallow over the lump in my throat; no one notices. If Shayleen corners Tara and gets her to talk—

"Whoever it is," Liz says, oblivious to my meltdown, "I hope they're smart enough to deny everything. Honestly. Take it to the grave."

"I don't think Tara's the type to gossip," says Aubrey.

"She's not," Lola shrugs. "But Shayleen's relentless. You all know how she gets when she smells a story. Tara won't stand a chance if she puts pressure on her."

"She might hold," I say, but it's half hope, half prayer.

"Yeah, well, I hope it wasn't you in there, Aubrey, with Noah," Lola teases, nudging her with her foot. "Or Shayleen's gonna have your sex life printed in the school newsletter before Monday morning."

They all laugh. I don't; I simply smile.

The edges of my vision blur a little.

"God, but imagine if it was someone we know," Liz says, eyes wide, practically glowing. "I'd die. Like, can you imagine if it was someone totally unexpected?"

Lola smirks. "Oh, you mean like you?"

Liz throws popcorn at her. "Shut up."

Lola yawns and stretches. "Whoever it was, I hope they had fun. Bathrooms are gross. But like, we should all be living more. If it is someone we know, I want full details. You can't just fuck in the library and not tell your girls."

Liz lifts her glass. "To whoever the mystery bathroom slut is. May her grades stay high and her legs spread higher."

They clink glasses.

I pretend to sip mine, pulse thudding hard behind my ribs.

Aubrey's the first to pass out, her mouth slightly open, one leg kicked free of the blanket, toes twitching now and then like she's fighting demons in her sleep or reliving blindfolded karaoke. It's hard to say.

Liz goes next. She's curled up in a nest of throw pillows, phone resting on her chest, still wearing that ridiculous rhinestone lip gloss.

Lola falls next. She knocks out quickly but dramatically, sprawling on her back with one arm over her face, hair everywhere, breathing deep and steady as if the chaos switch finally flipped to off.

And me?

I'm still wide awake.

I stare at the ceiling, eyes following the slow flicker of the string lights. They cast strange shadows on the walls—shapes that stretch, crawl, and whisper the same thing over and over: "You fucked up."

Every time I close my eyes, my thoughts spiral. Not soft or gentle. Full tilt.

I roll onto my side, then my back, then my stomach. I feel too hot, too wired, too full of every unspoken thought. My body is exhausted, but my mind keeps pounding away.

Because what do I even say?

Hey, Lola, guess what? That mystery girl who got railed in the library today? Yeah. That was me. Reece Wilson dropped to his knees and made me forget my name. Also, he called me baby. Also, my pussy is still sore from where he fucked me the day before, and my head is completely fucked because I think I liked it way more than I should.

Nope. Absolutely not.

I squeeze my eyes shut, my heart still racing hours later. The room is quiet except for soft breathing and the hum of the lights, but inside my head, it's loud. Messy. Dangerous.

I don't move again. I lie there, staring up at the ceiling, waiting for sleep to save me but it never comes.

Chapter 21

REECE

I haven't been with another girl. Not since Sam. Not since that first night in my room when she fell apart under my touch and then walked out as if she hadn't just shattered my entire spine and left it that way. Every chance since then has still come to me just like it always did. Easy. Willing. Loud enough to stroke my ego and nothing else.

And I feel nothing.

There's no spark left. No pull. No hunger. Just this dull, unending ache sitting low in my gut, whispering her name every time I close my eyes.

Red.

She's everything I want.

There's no doubt about it. No confusion. I'm in love with her, and that realization hits harder than any hit I've ever taken on the field. I've never felt this way about anyone. Not even close.

That's the part that really messes me up the most.

It pisses me off how quickly she got under my skin. How fast she transformed me. I built my whole reputation on not caring. On taking what I wanted, screwing who I wanted, and walking away before emotions ever had a chance to breathe. It was simple. Clean. Easy.

Until her.

Now I can't get hard for someone else.

It doesn't matter how attractive they are or how far they will go, my mind pulls me back to her.

I don't even recognize myself. Who the hell am I if I'm not the guy who lets go first?

Because here I am—watching every door, every hallway, every crowd of people hoping she'll be in it. Listening for her laugh in rooms she's clearly not in.

And if she told me right now that she wanted more, I'd fucking give her everything.

I'm early for practice. First one here.

The field's still soaked from the afternoon storm, slick under my boots, with the smell of wet grass sharp in the air. Coach isn't here yet? It doesn't matter though; I need to move. Run. To bleed some of the shit out of my system before I do something stupid. Something I'll regret.

It's been three fucking days.

Three days since I had my hands on her. Since I tasted her moan in the back of my throat and watched her come undone with my name broken in her mouth.

Three days without touching her, and it already feels too long. My skin itches from it. My cock stays hard at the worst times, aching for the girl who told me we needed to stop for now. My muscles burn from trying to keep it together, pretending I'm fine when all I want is to shove her up against the lockers and feel that little hitch in her breath again. Watch her pupils blow wide. Make her forget whatever the fuck Lola said.

But I can't. This matters to her. Someone saw us, so she wants to lay low.

She thinks it's Tara, maybe. Sam's not sure exactly, but it spooked her. She told me that morning after her night at Lola's. Her voice was too fucking soft for someone as strong as her.

She bit her nails. Her voice cracked at the edges. And I swear to God, I stopped breathing.

She tried to act cool, laugh it off, with that sarcastic little smile she wears like armor. But I saw her fingers twist in her lap. I heard how her voice went flat when she said we needed to back off. For now.

And that's the part that gutted me because I'd already been imagining what I'd do next. Where I'd take her on our next date. How I'd make her come apart again, slower this time. No rush. Just her spread out for me, mine to ruin all over again.

But she was scared, so I swallowed it. Nodded even though every cell in my body screamed not to. Now I'm stuck in this in-between hell, walking past her in the halls and pretending she's not all I fucking want. All I see. All I need.

There haven't been any whispers yet. No sly comments. No one in the locker room smirking or asking if she moaned my name. Not even Jace, who usually can't shut the fuck up when there's gossip in the air. If he knew, he'd already be printing flyers about the fucking bet I never should have made in the first place. His group chats would be full of GIFs, dick jokes, and "did you hear?" energy.

If anyone says one word that turns her into a punchline, I'll break their jaw for it. I don't care who it is. I'll knock out teeth before I let anyone talk about her like she's some easy fuck in a library stall.

Tara Evans with her tight ponytail. Always sipping on some overpriced iced latte, face set in that bored, holier-than-thou expression. The girl who acts as if she's above everything but still drags your name through the dirt without lifting a finger. She is judgmental as hell and acts too good for gossip until it's juicy enough to give her a sense of authority.

She's been talked about in the locker room before. A few of the guys have bragged about finger-fucking her in dark corners at parties, passing her around like a trophy.

So if it was Tara who saw us, maybe for once she's sticking up for Sam. Maybe she's keeping her judgy mouth shut because she knows what it's like to be the girl everyone talks about. The one who's only relevant when she's being fucked.

Or could it be she's just biding her time, waiting until she needs a distraction from the rumors that float around her.

But if she really lets it slip, that's when I'll have a serious problem.

This isn't just some hallway rumor. This is ours. And I'll defend it. I'll defend Sam. Every messy, fragile, beautiful part of her.

If Tara says one word, I swear to God I'll make sure she regrets it.

Coach Reynolds steps onto the field first, whistle already in hand. The rest of the team follows behind him, all noise and swagger—shoulders bumping, laughs too loud, the usual reckless energy they bring everywhere they go.

It used to settle into me easily. It used to feel like mine. Now it rubs me the wrong way. It doesn't sit right in my chest. It's too loud. It doesn't match the way everything inside me has shifted.

"Reece," Coach barks, walking over as I finish my second lap. Sweat's already soaking my back, my shirt drenched, but I keep moving. "You're here early again."

His tone is rough, but I see how his eyes catch on the dirt beneath my cleats. The way he nods once, proud without saying a word. He knows I'm all in this time. No skipping reps. No half-assing warm-ups or sneaking off early to chase a girl or punch someone in the parking lot. I'm showing up. Earning it. Bleeding for it. Every damn step.

We hit drills hard. Sprint sets first, back and forth, sharp turns, legs burning. Then tackling practice. Coach is pushing us harder than usual, shouting from across the field, voice cutting through the air. No room to breathe. No room to think.

Good. I don't want to think.

I want the pain. I want the bruises. I crave the ache in my muscles and the fire in my chest. Every time I hit the grass, I see a different face. One of the boys in the locker room cracking a joke. Tara fucking Evans smirking behind her cup. I hit harder. I hit angrier.

That's the fucked-up part. I've never protected anyone before. Not unless they wore my jersey colors.

But Red's not just anyone. She's the girl I've been chasing without realizing I was running. The girl I've loved in silence. In glances. In every reckless move I made just to feel something real. And I didn't even see it until she pulled away.

Coach blows the whistle and I drop into formation, heart pounding, dirt on my knees. I run hard as if it's the only thing I've ever been good at.

Dylan fucking James. Quarterback. Star boy. Walks around with a crown on his head and a hard-on for his own reflection. He always has a crowd, always high on praise and that dick-swinging swagger he probably jerks off to at night.

He shouts something across the field just as I finish the drill, his voice full of smug bullshit, fishing for laughs and throwing bait to his little fan club.

I don't accept it. I push past him forcefully, catching his shoulder.

He stumbles, catches himself, releases a laugh that's all bark, no bite. But I notice it. The flicker in his eyes. The one-second pause before the mask falls back into place.

Cocky fuck thinks he's invincible. Maybe he is, when his entire offensive surrounds him, guiding every move. But remove the blockers, peel away the ego, and all that's left is a loudmouth riding on everyone else's effort. So what if the guy can throw a ball? He wouldn't last a second without his wall of protection. He'd be on the ground before he could blink.

I don't pause to feed it. I'm not here for his mouth.

He'll get what he deserves.

Just not today.

Right now, it's the snap count in my head and the target in front of me. I read the offense, track every twitch in the line, plant my feet, and hit harder than the asshole across from me expects. I move with purpose, fists clenched, jaw tight. Out here, I don't question anything. Don't second-guess. It's the one place I don't feel fucked up, too much, or not enough. Out here, I just am. Solid. Ruthless. Grounded as hell. And for three perfect seconds, that's everything.

By the time practice ends, I'm a complete mess. Muscles trembling. Sweat soaked through every layer. My ribs ache, my shoulders hurt, and my legs feel like concrete blocks. My helmet hits the locker with a clang, and I peel off my pads, skin burning where the fabric's rubbed raw.

The hot water hits me in the shower, and I almost groan, leaning into it. Letting it slam into the back of my neck, shoulders, spine. My breath drags in slowly. Controlled. I count it out, trying to pull myself back into my body.

Then it hits me.

A memory from a few days ago. Sam in my shower, bare and dripping, steam curling around her hair, eyes locked on mine. The way her mouth parted when I ran the soap over her skin. The sound she made when I pressed her against the tile. The scratch of her nails down my back. How she tasted when I kissed her under the spray. I fucking hate how easily my mind goes there. How desperate it still is to live inside the seconds we stole.

I rest my forehead against the wall and mutter a string of curses under my breath.

Get it fucking together, asshole.

I stay in the shower longer than I should. Long enough for the noise to fade. Half the guys are already gone, and the locker room smells more like soap than sweat.

I turn off the water, towel off, and put on clean clothes.

I stuff my things into my bag, sling it over my shoulder, and head for the door, eager to get the hell out of here.

I'm nearly past the Coach's office when I hear it.

"Reece."

One word, and my spine snaps straight as if it's been yanked into place. I halt mid-step and turn my head just enough to see Coach through the open door. He's behind the desk, face unreadable.

"Come in and close the door."

Fuck.

My grip tightens on the strap of my bag as I step through the door. One look at Coach's face, and I realize this isn't about missing a block or half-assing a drill. This is deeper.

I already know what this is.

It has to be my old man.

This town can't keep its mouth shut for shit. Yesterday, I was shooting hoops behind the school with Noah and Jace, and some guy I've never talked to said, "Heard you had a killer game last week."

So yeah. The rumors are out.

The comeback. The stats. The whispers.

And my father, sure as shit, wouldn't ask me. He'd go straight to Coach and act like he's proud. Pretend he actually gives a fuck.

It wouldn't be the first time he crawled out of his hole when football gave him a reason to care. When I made him look good enough to talk about in bars.

Coach knows everything about it. Every flaw in that history. He's the one who told me to stop giving my future to a man who only shows up to control it.

"Play for you," he had told me. "Not for a ghost that's still breathing."

And I'm trying. Damn, I'm trying. But ghosts have long arms. And my old man still has a grip around my fucking throat.

"You've been putting in the work." Coach says. "You're not coasting."

"I didn't come back to coast."

He grunts. His chair creaks as he leans back, studying me. "Your old man know you're back?"

My jaw clenches before I answer. "I don't know. Probably." I don't add that he wouldn't ask me if I was playing.

"That is not why I called you in."

That gets my attention.

"Then why?"

He taps the pen on the desk again. Once. Twice. Then, he sets it down and folds his arms.

"There's a scout coming."

My pulse skips. Chest tightens. I force a breath.

"He's coming to check out West. Wants to see if he's got the toughness for their defense. But while he's here, he'll be watching."

"That's... not for me."

"Bullshit," Coach snorts. "You think I didn't see what you did out there today? Your footwork's cleaner than it's ever been. Your vision's sharp. You're reading the field better than half the damn league."

"I had my shot, Coach. I quit," I say, voice low. "I threw it all away."

"You think that's how this works?" he leans forward, forearms braced on the desk. "You think one mistake writes off the rest of your life?"

I glance away.

"Reece." His voice hardens. "You could go all the way. You've got that thing. The thing you can't coach. The shit that sets you apart when everything's on the line."

I blink hard. My palms sweat. My heart pounds oddly, not from running but from remembering what it felt like to be a kid watching those matches, dreaming of being on the field. Cleats cut into real grass. Lights. Roaring crowds. My name on the back of a jersey.

That dream got buried under fights, fuckups and fists slammed into lockers. Under girls who meant nothing and nights I still can't remember.

Now, it's no longer buried. It's clawing its way back to the surface.

"Play the way you did today," Coach tells me. "And this Mayfair scout won't miss you. He won't be able to keep his eyes off you."

The name alone hits me deep. Mayfair.

Top-tier. Full ride. Out of this town and every messed-up part of it. Away from my old man's bullshit, away from the memory of every time I got close to something good just to see it ripped away from me.

Mayfair means I get to choose who I am. It means I don't have to become him.

That means I get to be with Sam without this place looming over us. Noah and Aubrey will be there too.

Coach leans forward, voice low. "Think about it, Reece. You've got the talent. Don't waste this shot."

I push to my feet, heart slamming against my ribs. "Thanks, Coach."

He watches me for a moment longer, mouth set in that half-smile he saves for when he's proud, but not too obvious about it.

I nod once, then swing my bag over my shoulder and leave before that pride can slip away.

The hallway is quiet except for the hum of the vending machine and the sound of my boots hitting the tile. I pull out my phone, knowing there's only one person I want to tell.

Reece: Hey. Can we meet up? There's something I need to tell you.

I stare at the screen, thumb hovering, before I hit send.

A second later, the screen lights up.

Sam: Yeah. I'll meet you at your place usual time. We'll work on the assessment. And no, that is not code. Assessment only.

A smirk pulls at my mouth. There she is, all sharp-tongued and always two steps ahead.

I shove my phone in my pocket, chest still tight but a little lighter now. She's coming over. She's giving me that shot too, even if she's pretending it's about homework.

I've got one chance to fix everything. Football, get it back on track. Earn that Mayfair offer.

Sam, I'm fucking done with dark corners and half-truths when all I wanna do is grab her hand in front of everyone and make sure they know. She's mine. My fucking girl. My Red.

CHAPTER 22

REECE

I check the time, then check it again. Twenty-eight minutes. Not that I'm counting. Or that I've been planted at the kitchen bench this entire time with the same can of Pepsi slowly going flat in my hand. Not that I've opened the fridge, stared into it, shut it, then opened it again just to pass the time.

She's late. Not Sam getting distracted late with the sorry I got caught up grabbing a pen late. This is different.

It's the kind of late that makes my mind chatter.

Every worst-case scenario lines up, one after another, loud as hell.

Did she change her mind because it's not worth it, or did someone say something to her?

Or did something happen on the way here?

Did the fear finally win?

I hate how quickly my thoughts turn to shit when she's not where I expect her to be.

I run a hand through my hair and tell myself to calm the fuck down. She's fine. She'll walk through the door any second.

I check the time again.

Yeah, she'll be here. She always shows up.

We haven't put much effort into the assessment at all. Grades are important to her. Her future matters. She doesn't half-ass anything.

She'll bring her books, her highlighters, that determined little frown—but it's always her mouth I keep tasting. Her moan in my ear and her thighs around my waist. Her nails dragging down my back while I fuck her across every surface in this place.

I exhale sharply and try to push the nerves away.

I wonder what she'll say when I tell her there's a scout coming. That Mayfair might actually see me. Might actually want me.

I wonder if she'll want me there with her. If she sees me in her future, just like I'm starting to see her in mine.

Shit, listen to me. Acting like I already have the offer, as if the scout already has my name on the damn scholarship.

The doorbell rings.

I don't walk. I launch forward like I'm running a drill. My heart fucking jumps, nearly knocking the can out of my hand.

My hand hits the doorknob too fast. I yank the door open.

There she is.

Damn, she is beautiful.

Sunlight hits her red hair, and for a moment I forget how to breathe. That perfect shade of red that makes you think of fire, cinnamon, and sex. Eyes dancing as if she doesn't realize she already owns me.

"Hey," she says.

One word—that's all it takes—and I'm out. Cooked. Melted right into the damn floorboards. Heart doing backflips. Cock already half-hard.

"Hey," I manage.

She walks past me, her bag swinging low off her shoulder, hips swaying just enough to affect me. Her perfume reaches me next, sweet and alluring, before she smiles at me.

When I fumble while shutting the door because I'm too busy staring at her mouth, she laughs. That breathy, hit-me-in-the-gut kind of sound that makes my skin buzz.

We walk down the hall side by side, not touching. Still, my fingers twitch uncontrollably. Useless urges, always wanting more—wanting to curl around her wrist, her waist, and her throat.

But I don't touch her because she asked me to hold back until the shitstorm settles. And I want to be that guy. The one who respects her boundaries. Even when my body's burning to do the opposite.

"So," she says, breaking the silence as we reach my room. "What did you want to tell me?"

She moves over to the bed and drops her bag, as casual as anything on the floor.

I exhale a breath, grateful for the shift before I lose my damn mind.

"Do you remember what you said the other night?" I ask, as I drop onto the edge of the bed.

"You're gonna have to be more specific." She sits down next to me.

"The part where you said I could still try," I say. "For the team. For everything I thought I'd already fucked up."

Her expression softens. "Yeah, I remember."

My heart pounds again. Loud. Stupid. Honest.

"Coach pulled me aside after practice and said there's a scout coming from Mayfair." The words feel heavy in my mouth. "He's coming next weekend to watch West. But Coach said he'll be watching everyone."

Her eyes widen, then that smile appears. The one that gets to me every time. The one I crave more than air now.

"Reece," she says, leaning in closer. "That's huge."

"It is." I nod.

She studies my face. "But is it what you want?"

I don't hold back. Don't downplay it.

"Yeah," I say. "I want it. I want it bad."

"So we'd be there together?" she says.

"Yeah," I say. "If you want it."

The hesitation, the hope, the weight of everything we haven't said is all in the weight of her gaze.

"But fuck," I mutter, dragging a hand through my hair, "I haven't even been accepted yet. I don't wanna get ahead of myself."

"You'll get there," she says without missing a beat. "You were the best player on the field last game, Reece."

I gaze at her. Red hair catching the light, eyes sharp and steady. The girl I never should have touched. The girl I can't stop needing.

"You really think that?" I ask, my voice already cracking at the edges.

She lifts her hand and touches my face, brushing her fingers against my jaw as if she's been dying to do it but hadn't let herself until now.

"Yeah," she says, steady as hell. "I do."

And that's it.

The world comes to a halt. My thoughts fall silent. I pull her close until there's no space left to breathe, until only the scent of her skin and the gentle rush of her breath against my mouth remain.

Her lips are soft when I press mine to hers. She makes a quiet little sound in the back of her throat, surprised, and for half a second I think she might pull away.

She doesn't. Instead, she melts into me.

My hand slides to her waist, gripping tightly, fingers digging in. My other hand cups her face, thumb brushing her cheek, and damn, the smell of her floods my mind until she's all I can think about.

Her body presses against mine, heat soaking straight through my clothes, and my cock reacts instantly. I move my mouth to her neck, tasting her skin, breathing her in. She arches without thinking, giving me exactly the space I need, as if her body already knows how this goes.

Her hand fists in my shirt, tugging me closer, desperate and needy in a way that destroys me. She wants more. I feel it in the way she clings, the way her breath catches, how her hips tilt toward me.

Every kiss ignites. Every touch burns hotter. I'm trembling with it—longing for her, needing her.

"Please," I murmur against her skin. I pull back enough to look at her, my eyes dark, chest heaving. "Please let me fuck you."

I'm begging. I've never begged before. Never had to. But for her, I would. I'd beg. I'd lose my mind. I'd give her everything because she already has me—every broken, desperate, messed-up piece.

She pulls back, her eyes locked on mine, burning and fearless. Her hands reach for the hem of her shirt, and she yanks it over her head in one smooth, fierce motion.

Fuck.

She's sitting there in a red lace bra, confidence radiating from her. Every guy's fantasy doesn't even come close to capturing it. This is so much more than that.

Her fingers reach behind her back and unclip the clasp. Her bra slips off her shoulders and falls away, forgotten. My gaze follows it down, then snaps right back to her tits. Fuck, they're perfect. My mouth goes dry. I tongue comes out to wet my bottom lip.

I drop to my knees before her.

My hands reach for her boots as I take my time, sliding them off while savoring every second. She watches me, her breath shallow, chest rising and falling, fully aware of what she's doing to me.

When I'm finished, my hands are on her again. I guide her back until she's stretched out on the bed, hair fanned over the pillow, tits bare, eyes dark and waiting.

My cock is hard as hell, aching, but I don't rush.

I hover over her, palms pressed into the mattress on either side of her hips, and look down at her—the girl who wrecked me without even trying.

My fingers find the button on her jeans, executing that practiced flick to snap it open quickly. The zipper comes next, my knuckles brushing her skin as I pull it down. Then I grip the waistband, slowly tugging her jeans and panties down in one deliberate, punishing pull. My eyes remain fixed on every inch I uncover.

She shivers when the air hits her, but she keeps her legs open.

Good girl.

I toss the denim somewhere behind me. Not even sure where. My focus is fixed on the bare fucking heaven between her thighs. Smooth. Wet. So fucking perfect it makes my cock ache.

My tongue slides over my bottom lip, slow and hungry. I want to taste her and make her forget every damn name but mine.

"Goddamn, Red," I mutter, voice low and strained with hunger. "Are you always this eager for me? Or just when you know I'm gonna ruin that pretty, perfect pussy?"

My hands grip her knees and push them apart, wide enough to make her blush. I don't look away. My eyes devour every inch of her spread out for me.

Three days. Three damn days without touching her, without tasting her, and it's been pure agony. I've been crawling out of my skin, twitching for the hit, desperate for the fix only she can give me.

"You're fucking perfect," I growl, voice full of need. My fingers dig into her thighs, rough enough to make her gasp, to leave marks I'll make her see later.

"And I'm not rushing a single fucking second of this," I mutter, lowering myself between her legs, breath hitting her skin. "You're gonna feel it all. Every second. Every inch. Every time I make you beg."

And shit, I haven't needed anything more.

My fingers slide through her slick folds, teasing, slow and cruel. She arches off the bed with a hiss, hips chasing every touch of my fingers. I growl, the strain crawling down my throat because I know I should take this slow... but fuck, I'm barely hanging on by a thread.

"Shit," I rasp, voice like gravel. My eyes meet hers and lock, dark and hungry. My fingers go deeper, spreading her open, dragging her wetness across my skin. I smirk, all teeth and filth.

"You're so fucking drenched for me," I murmur. "This pussy's fucking desperate. Begging to be ruined."

I lean down and plant a kiss on her stomach. It's soft. Too soft for what I'm about to do.

"Lower," she says, her voice breathy and sharp.

That pulls a filthy grin from me. The good girl's gone. She knows exactly what she wants and, fuck, I'm going to give it to her.

I trail my mouth lower, pressing soft kisses across her stomach, slow and possessive as hell. My tongue drags across her skin, tasting her, marking her. My voice drops to a whisper, lips brushing just above where she needs me most.

"You're mine, Red."

Another kiss. A gentle lick.

"And I'm gonna take my time fucking you."

I slide a finger into her, slowly, and fuck me, she clamps around me so tight I almost lose it right here. Hot, wet, and fucking perfect. It's a chokehold. A goddamn vice.

"Shit," I say. "You're so fucking tight."

Another finger presses in, and I feel her stretch around me, inch by inch. Her back arches off the bed, hips rolling into my hand, chasing the friction with this frantic, dirty rhythm that makes my cock throb against my zipper.

Her lips part in a gasp. Her eyes flutter. Then she moves—grinding down, owning it. Owning me.

My thumb finds her clit and starts circling. Her whole body jolts under my touch, and it sends a shot of pure fucking lust through my veins.

"That's it," I murmur, voice low and edged with need. "Take it. Show me how much you fucking want this."

I curl my fingers just right, dragging against that spot that makes her hips jerk, her breath catch, her moans break open against the air. She's a vision. Writhing, needy, wrecked, and she hasn't even had my cock yet.

I lean in, breath brushing over her skin. My lips graze the inside of her thigh, just enough to tease. I breathe her in. She's ripe, sweet, dirty. She smells like sex and everything I need.

Then I flick her clit with my tongue.

She jolts — hips snapping upward, a cry ripping from her throat. And just like that, she comes alive.

"Reece," she breathes, that soft, needy whisper that fucks with my head in the best way possible.

God, I fucking live for that sound.

I flick her clit again, then suck hard enough to make her hips jerk. She moans my name a second time, all breathless and broken. I groan against her pussy, tongue relentless as I devour her. I lick. I suck. I curl my fingers just right, stroking her inside until she's shaking, right on the edge.

She's a mess. A damn masterpiece.

And I'm not stopping.

Not until she's falling apart with my name in her mouth.

"That's it," I growl, my voice rough and dripping with hunger. "Let go, Red. Let me fucking feel it."

And fuck, she does. She falls apart in the most intense way. Head thrown back, mouth open, face twisted in this perfect blend of pleasure and surrender. There's no holding it back. No pretending. Just raw, chaotic need. Her moans hit my ears like gasoline to a flame, every sound she makes fueling the fire inside me.

I can't look away. Watching her fall apart under my touch is the hottest fucking thing I've ever seen. Every shake, gasp. Every filthy sound spilling from her lips is addictive. I swear, I'll never get enough of this. Of her or the way she gives in when she trusts me to take her there.

Finally, when I ease back, her skin flushed and glistening, her breathing shallow and uneven, I lift my hand. My fingers glisten with her release. I lock eyes with her as I bring them to her mouth.

"Open," I say, voice rough, dripping with need. "Taste how fucking good you are."

Her lips part instantly. I push my fingers past them, and she closes around them, sucking hard. Her mouth alone is enough to make my cock throb painfully. Her eyes flutter shut, her tongue swirling over my fingers as if she's savoring every drop, and I can't take my eyes off her.

"Jesus, Red," I mutter. "You don't know what you fucking do to me."

But I think she does. That smug, satisfied, fucked-out look that screams she owns me.

When I pull my fingers free, I don't give her a second to catch her breath.

I'm on her before she can blink. Leaning in, crashing my mouth to hers in a kiss that's all hunger and heat and fucking possession. It's rough, messy. It's everything I've been holding back

"I'm going to fuck you now," I growl against her lips, my voice thick with promise. My forehead presses to hers for half a second, just breathing her in like I need it to stay sane.

Then I pull back.

Damn, she's a vision. Sprawled out on my bed, hair tangled against the pillow, cheeks flushed, lips kiss-swollen and parted as she fights to catch her breath. Her nipples are tight, her chest rising and falling. Her legs are open, her thighs slick with arousal, her entire body screaming for me to claim her.

My girl.

My Red.

I stand at the edge of the bed, looming over her, grabbing her knees and pushing them wider, just so I can take in every inch of what's mine. Her slickness catches the light, her folds glistening, pulsing with need.

I reach down and pop the button on my jeans, dragging the zipper down with one slow pull. The second the fabric loosens, my cock springs free, rock hard, thick, and already leaking. Her eyes drop, her lips part.

"See what you fucking do to me, Red," I rasp, voice rough with need as I wrap my hand around my cock, giving it one slow stroke. Her eyes stay locked on the movement, pupils blown wide, mouth still parted, chest rising and falling.

I pull my jeans the rest of the way down, step out of them, and walk over to the drawer. I yank it open, grab a condom, rip it open with my teeth. I roll it on, keeping my gaze fixed on her.

I return to her, kneel between her thighs, and press the thick head of my cock right against her entrance. But I don't push in. Not yet.

Instead, I drag the tip through her folds, letting it glide over her clit in slow, teasing passes. She moans, desperate for more. I keep at it, watching her fall apart from just this.

"Fuck, you're wet," I growl, touching her clit again with the tip. "You want it that bad, hey Red? You want me to fill this tight little pussy?"

She nods, her lips trembling, and her eyes plead.

I slam into her in one smooth thrust, burying myself to the hilt. Her back arches off the bed with a cry, her pussy clenching tight around me. The fucking grip of her knocks the breath from my lungs.

"Shit," I groan, fists gripping her hips.

I pull out slowly, then slam back in harder, my hips snapping forward, the sound of skin on skin echoing through the room. Her moans are loud and needy, and I lose any last shred of restraint I had.

I fuck her hard and deep, each thrust rougher than the last. Her body takes all of it, her nails dragging down my arms as she cries out my name.

"Reece... oh my god... fuck... don't stop."

Damn, the way she moans has a hold on me I won't ever break free from. It crests beneath my skin, sinks into my bones, and pushes every ounce of control out of my body. Her body shudders underneath me, legs trembling, arms thrown back, mouth parted in that perfect, fucked-out way.

"You love this, don't you?" I growl. My hands slide down, gripping her hips, holding her in place. "You're mine, Red. Fucking say it."

Her voice shakes, but she gives it to me, anyway. "I'm yours."

Fuck.

The way she offers herself to me so fully, it lights me up from within. I snap. I push into her harder, deeper, every muscle clenched, every part of me chasing the moment when we stop being two bodies and just become heat, sweat, and raw need.

I look down and fucking groan.

Her pussy swallows every thick inch of my cock. The sight turns me feral. I fuck her harder, deeper, nothing held back, nothing gentle. It's fast and filthy. I'm a lunatic, lost in it. In her.

Her back arcs, perfect and pleading. Her tits lift like an irresistible offering. I lower my head, my tongue flicking over her tight nipple until her sharp gasp turns into a moan.

I bare my teeth and scrape them against the swollen peak, just enough to hurt.

"Fuck, Reece," she cries out, breath broken, hand pulling in my hair. She tugs hard, and I love it. I suck harder, nip at her skin, claiming her. My mouth expresses the truth all over her body. She's mine. Mine to take, to fuck, to ruin.

My hips don't hesitate. I keep driving into her with a steady rhythm, every thrust smooth and relentless.

She begins to shake. Her moans turn into ragged, desperate sounds, her body tense beneath mine.

"I'm gonna come," she gasps, voice cracking.

"Good," I rasp, lifting my head to look at her. "Come for me, Red," I growl, my voice rough with the edge of breaking. "Show me how fucking beautiful you are when you do."

She screams my name as if I earned it.

Her orgasm crashes over her, wild and unstoppable, a goddamn masterpiece of chaos. Her body writhes, head thrown back, mouth wide open in a broken cry. I don't stop or give her a second to catch her breath. I fuck her through it, each thrust dragging out her pleasure until she's shaking all over, a mess of sound and sensation.

She's gone.

And I'm fucking close.

I drive into her harder, rougher, losing rhythm and sanity. My hips slam into hers, pace aggressive, my grip tight on her waist, pulling her down onto every inch of cock.

My body locks up, every muscle going rigid as my release detonates through me like a lightning bolt. It's brutal. Blinding. I keep moving with shallow, frantic thrusts, grasping at every ounce of sensation. Refusing to let it end. I pour every fucking drop I have into the condom.

Panting, I collapse against her, my chest pressed to hers, heart pounding like I just sprinted through fire. We're both exhausted—slick, trembling, and breathless.

I remain inside her, my cock still twitching faintly. My body still hums from the aftershocks. And damn, I could stay here forever. Right here. Buried deep in the only place I've ever truly belonged.

Her.

"You're so fucking perfect, Red," I murmur, my voice rough. I press a lazy kiss to her jaw, breathing her in, inhaling the scent of sex and her skin as if it'll keep me sane.

The aftershocks are still there, rippling down my spine, nerves shot to hell, every part of me still humming from how fucking good she feels wrapped around me.

I lift my head just enough to look at her. Our eyes meet. My hand brushes her red hair away from her face, fingers softly skimming her cheek.

Tell her, idiot. Tell her you're finished hiding. Tell her you want everyone to know she's yours.

But I don't say it. Instead, I lean down and kiss her slowly. Every filthy, fucked-up thing I don't say gets poured into her mouth.

Then I ease back and pull out. My cock slips free, wet and spent. I tie off the condom and toss it in the trash.

When I turn back around, I half expect to see her already halfway dressed, like she always is after we finish. But she's still there, lying on her back and staring at the ceiling.

I move back to the bed.

She begins to sit up; I grab her wrist. "Wait."

She freezes.

I climb onto the bed beside her and pull her into me, just needing her close. I've never done this before. Never wanted to. But damn, I want it now.

Her cheek rests against my chest. Her fingers trace lazy shapes on my skin. My whole body tightens, goosebumps chasing her touch.

"We're not going to get this assignment done," she whispers against my skin.

"Not a chance." I chuckle because every time she comes here to work on the assessment, we end up hooking up. "We'll get it done," I add, pressing a kiss to her temple and letting my mouth linger there longer than I should.

We lie there in silence. Every gentle stroke of her fingers sends shivers across my skin. I stay still and silent, just feeling her warmth, her breath and the weight of her body pressed against mine.

She fits there. Fuck, she fits too perfectly.

"I want to make this official," I say.

She stills beside me as if I dropped a grenade in the middle of the room. Her breath hitches.

"What?"

I prop myself up on my elbow so I can see her face. She leans her head back against the pillow.

"You heard me," I say. "I'm done sneaking around. All this hiding and pretending this is casual when it's anything but."

She opens her mouth, then closes it. Her lips part again, but nothing comes out. So I keep going.

"I don't give a shit who sees us, Red. Not the guys on the team. Not your friends or mine. I want to walk into school with you on my arm."

Her eyes dart across my face, searching for the catch, as if this is some cruel trick I'm playing just to see her flinch. But I don't blink. I mean every goddamn word.

She goes silent for a moment.

Finally, she speaks.

"Why now?"

"Because I'm tired of pretending, Red. And because I know what I want."

"And what happens when you get bored?"

"What?"

"You're used to girls throwing themselves at you," she says. "You're Reece Wilson. Fuckboy with a smile that ruins people." She swallows hard. "What happens when the next shiny thing shows up? Some girl with longer legs, no history and a willingness to blow you in the school bathroom. Do I just become the ex you pretend never existed?"

"Is that really what you think?"

She lifts her eyes to mine, and damn, there's so much in them—hurt, fear, and the vulnerability she doesn't show to anyone.

"I'm scared, Reece. If this becomes real, and I let myself fall into it, and then you change your mind... I won't survive that. Not with everyone watching, waiting for me to be the next name you erase."

I sit up, brushing her hair back from her face, my fingers trembling slightly under the weight of her words.

"Red," I say, voice low and deadly serious, "you aren't some passing phase. You're not a fling. You're not the next girl I fuck and forget."

She blinks, her lips parting as if she wants to say something but can't.

"You are the only person who has ever made me forget every other girl existed," I say. "You walk into a room and I forget how to breathe. You smile and I lose my fucking mind. You're the only one I see. The only one I want."

Her mouth trembles, and I notice it. All the parts of her she's kept hidden, rattling behind her ribs, waiting for a reason to trust me.

"You think I'd trade that for some hallway blowjob?" I ask, shaking my head. "You think I'd throw away everything we've done for a shot at easy?"

I press my forehead to hers, needing her to feel every part of me. Every ounce of this need, which has clawed its way into my chest since the second she walked into my fucking life.

"You're not easy," I murmur. "You're everything."

Tears burn at the corners of her eyes. "Reece—" she stops herself, swallows, and takes a deep breath.

"Say yes, Red," I whisper, my breath grazing her lips. "Just say yes."

I see the war in her eyes, the way she's weighing the cost of giving me her heart when she's still not one hundred percent sure I won't shatter it.

Her fingers lift, brushing my jaw with a touch so damn gentle it undoes me. "If I say yes... and you hurt me..." Her voice breaks. "That's it, Reece."

My heart stutters. I fucking feel it. The weight of her trust. The risk she's about to take.

"I won't hurt you. I swear to you, Red. I would rather die."

She studies me and then nods.

"Yes."

The word sounds soft and shaky.

I fucking lose it. I pull her mouth to mine and kiss her with everything I've got. Deep. Desperate. A little wild. My hand fists in her hair as I pull her closer.

I pull back just enough to breathe against her lips. "I'm the happiest motherfucker on the planet right now."

Her laugh is perfect. "Don't make me regret this."

"You won't," I promise. "You won't even remember life before me."

She rolls her eyes, but she's smiling now.

CHAPTER 23

REECE

I'm already leaning against the brick wall near the school lot when Red pulls in. Her small car coughing its way into the lot as if it's just as nervous as she is.

She texted me three times already this morning.

Sam: Are we doing the right thing?

Sam: Maybe we should wait.

Sam: People are gonna talk.

I didn't reply. Not because I didn't care. She was already lost in her thoughts, twisting herself in knots, dissecting every damn message. The last thing she needed was a text from me to make her overthink. What she really needed was me.

Right here.

Showing the fuck up and making it clear I'm not walking away from this.

I watch as she pulls into the space, kills the engine, and sits there for a second, hands still gripping the wheel. Her hair's caught in the light, the sun turning it to wildfire. All fire, trouble, and temptation.

When she finally steps out, her eyes scan the lot and lock onto me.

She pauses for a breath, then another.

Next she moves. Head held high. That stubborn chin lifted. Every step defiant. Fierce and absolutely gorgeous.

The noise fades as she approaches me.

I barely hear the laughter, the whisper. The low, drawn-out "fuuuck" from some loser who's staring too long. A few fuckers too slow to look away. I see one of them tracking her hips, and my hands curl into fists instinctively.

Don't they realize I'll tear their fucking eyeballs out?

I stop breathing as she walks to me. Her hair's catching fire in the morning sun, and every step she takes lights me up from the inside out.

She's a slow burn that becomes a raging inferno.

Her hair's half-up, some strands spilling loose. A black tank top hugs those curves I already know by heart. Faded denim shorts that make my brain short-circuit. Skin I want to taste, freckles I want to count, and I'm so fucking gone for her it's not even funny.

I don't wait. I meet her halfway, my hand sliding to her waist. She's warm under my palm, her body already leaning into mine, her breath catching the second I pull her close.

Her eyes flick upward. Her fingers grip my shirt.

"Hi," she says softly.

I grin. "Were you worried I wouldn't show?"

"No," she lies.

But she's already melting into me, and I'm already hard. Shit. This girl's gonna be the death of me. And I'll thank her for every second of it.

I kiss her like I fucking mean it. Deep and dirty. Tongue sliding in, hand running up her back to tilt her mouth closer, until there's no space between us. Just her lips, her taste, her body pressed tight against mine while I lose my damn mind.

We break apart, gasping.

She glances around, flustered, as she tucks her hair behind her ear.

"Let them fucking look," I mutter, dragging my thumb across her cheek, slow and sure. "Did you tell Lola or Aubrey?"

She shakes her head, teeth biting into her bottom lip. "No."

"Do you feel bad?"

"A little. Liz left yesterday, but still, they're my friends. I probably should've said something."

I don't answer.

I grab her hand and thread our fingers tightly, not giving her a second to overthink it.

Her fingers twitch in mine, but she doesn't let go. Not when the first heads turn or when the whispers start curling through the air.

It's almost nine, and this place is already crowded.

I can sense her nerves. Shoulders are tight. Her steps are quick. She's holding her breath too long. But I stay steady, anchoring us both through it.

The moment we cross the gates, everything changes. Every stare feels more intense. Every new glance cuts deeper.

And when we reach the hallway, it gets worse.

Eyes turn to us. Girls whisper behind their hands. Half of the football team pauses, jaws slack, heads turning. Nicole's frozen at her locker, mouth half open. Tia's caught mid-step on the stairs, staring as if we've broken something sacred.

I won't stop. Let them choke on it. Let them see what's really happening.

Up ahead, I see Noah and Jace in our usual corner, talking shit with Aubrey and Lola. Just another Thursday morning lineup... until the hallway goes quiet.

It's subtle at first. The kind of silence that sneaks in when something's about to happen. Heads turn. Voices quiet down. And that's all it takes to grab their attention.

Noah sees us first. His eyes land on our joined hands before flicking back up. That bastard's been watching every move I've made this week. Every glance. Every accidental brush.

Aubrey's next. Her eyes widen, her mouth parting in surprise. Then Lola turns, and Red stiffens next to me. Her fingers grip mine tighter, nails digging into my skin

Jace leans against the lockers, arms crossed. But I notice that spark in his eyes, the curl of his mouth. He's already got some bullshit locked and loaded.

The instant we stop in front of them, I feel it. Red's hand twitching in mine, her fingers stiff, her body going still.

Lola looks down at our hands. "No fucking way."

Aubrey stares. "You two…"

Jace lets out a low whistle, already grinning. "Well, fuck me. You finally dipped your cock in the Red Sea, huh?"

Red jerks beside me, eyes flashing to mine. Mortified. Pissed. Feeling a mix of both.

"Jesus, Jace," Lola snaps, stepping in front of him. "Do you ever stop being a giant fucking asshole, or is it your full-time personality now?"

He shrugs, completely unfazed, and tips his chin at me. "Pretty sure I owe this dickhead two hundred bucks."

Sam freezes.

I do too.

Aubrey's frown hardens. "What the fuck are you even talking about?"

Jace shrugs, all innocent bullshit and dead eyes. "We had a bet," he says, tipping his head toward her with a smirk that makes my jaw clench.

Red yanks her hand away from mine.

My stomach drops.

"There was no bet," I snap, heat rising under my skin.

Jace snorts. "Sure. I just imagined you asking for a bonus if you finger-fucked her on school grounds?"

Sam jerks back as if he'd actually slapped her. Her eyes flick to mine, and I see the hurt, the rage, all of it.

"That never fucking happened!" Fury tears through me like claws.

Jace raises his hands, smug as hell. "I'm saying I can't pay it all at once."

"Jace," Lola snaps, "shut the fuck up for once in your miserable fucking life."

But it's already too late. Red's walking away before anyone can stop him, jaw clenched, shoulders tense.

"Red," I call out, panic rising in my throat.

She doesn't slow down. She rounds the corner and disappears, yanking the air from my lungs with her, leaving me standing there feeling stupid, hollow, and completely alone.

I take one step after her, and then Jace opens his mouth again.

"So?" he calls out, loud and smug. "Is she any good?"

Something snaps.

I don't plan on it. I just turn and swing. My fist hits the bastard's face with a loud, brutal crack that echoes down the hall. He falls hard, his back slamming into the lockers, his ass hitting the floor. Blood pours from his nose, and shock is clear on his stupid fucking face as he stares up at me.

I stand over him, chest heaving, fists clenched, every nerve ablaze.

"You don't get to fucking talk about her," I snarl. "Ever."

He wipes the blood under his nostril with the back of his hand, smearing it across his skin, still grinning through it because he never fucking learns.

"Help me up, Bells," he mutters, hand reaching out.

Lola stays still.

"What is wrong with you?" she snaps, eyes blazing. "You open your mouth and somehow make everything worse. You don't get to joke about her, Jace. You don't get to fucking talk about her at all like that."

Lola turns away.

Noah's voice cuts in next. "You'll never fucking learn, will you, Jace? One day someone will not stop at one punch."

I'm already gone.

My feet hit the floor forcefully as I move, heart pounding, lungs burning. I don't care about the looks or the whispers flickering to life behind me. All I see is her face when she pulled her hand away from mine. She looked hurt, disappointed, as if I'd just confirmed every fear she ever had about me.

CHAPTER 24

SAM

I don't look back because if I do, I'll completely fall apart. Not just crack—I'll shatter into a thousand jagged, bleeding pieces of some stupid girl who thought she mattered to him.

My boots hit the tile with quick, desperate smacks. Loud in my ears, loud enough to drown out the sound of my heart breaking.

The looks on Aubrey and Lola's faces when they heard what Jace said. The sick twist in my gut when it landed.

Bonus if he fingered me on the school grounds.

I stumble into the bathroom, fingers scrambling for the first stall door. I slam it shut, lock it quickly, and drop onto the cold toilet seat before my knees give out.

It feels like my ribs are being pried open with a crowbar. Every breath has to fight through the pain. I squeeze my eyes shut, but the words are carved into the backs of my eyelids. Over and over. Each one a knife. Each one proof I was nothing more than a fucking game. A bet.

My nails dig into my thighs. I want to scream. Rip the door off the hinges. Punch a hole through every mirror out there until I don't have to see her anymore. That girl. The idiot who let him touch her. Who let him make her feel wanted, needed and fucking special.

And the whole time he was thinking about a damn bet?

I press the heels of my hands into my eyes so hard I see stars, but it doesn't stop the tears or the way my shoulders shake. And it sure as hell doesn't stop the heat burning through my skin from the inside out.

He touched me. Crawled into my head. Into my heart. Into my fucking pussy. First time I've ever had sex with someone, and it didn't mean a damn thing to him. Now I'm just some pathetic goddamn punchline.

I should've known. Hell, the warning signs weren't subtle. They were neon-lit and screaming, and I still walked right into it with open arms and no helmet. I let him in anyway.

Now I'm locked in a bathroom stall, mascara streaming down my face, chest torn wide open, while he stands out there, smug and golden, wearing that perfect fucking smirk.

Damn him for making it look easy.

And damn me for giving him the knife.

I gag, swallowing it before the sob can claw its way up my throat. God, I'm such a fucking idiot.

There's still this traitorous part of me that wants to believe him. That Jace made it up and Reece didn't sell me out for two hundred bucks and a high five.

But the words are there, hanging in the air, and I can't swallow them down.

Hoping it was all a lie doesn't change the truth I heard with my own ears—that night, at that party, those words he said to Jace. It doesn't erase what just happened in the hallway. It doesn't soothe the burning in my chest or stop the shame from crawling under my skin.

Footsteps echo across the tile.

"Sam... are you in here?" Lola's voice filters through the stalls, gentle and careful, as if she already knows I'm cracked right down the middle.

I stay quiet. Words are a luxury I can't afford at the moment.

A second later, Aubrey's voice cuts through the silence, razor-sharp.

"Out. All of you. I don't care if you're crying, pissing, or plotting your next fuckboy disaster. Get the fuck out."

Footsteps scatter. A few whine softly. No one dares to talk back. Aubrey's name still holds power after what she did to Tia.

But that's the thing about Aubrey. She's fierce, not cruel. She can be mean when she has to, but she's kind where it really counts. And right now, she's both for me.

A door slams shut, hard enough to rattle the hinges. Then silence. Thick and pulsing. The quiet built on girl-loyalty, fury, and the friendship that bleeds when you do too.

I exhale. The kind of breath that fights its way out, kept inside through heartbreak and humiliation.

I hear two taps on the stall door. Gentle. No force. Just a quiet backup waiting to catch whatever mess steps out.

My fingers tremble as I fumble with the lock. It clicks open.

I step out.

Eyes red. Pride in pieces. Heart barely hanging on.

But still standing on my damn feet.

Lola's face shows pure fury. Aubrey stands next to her, gentler but just as intense, her gaze sweeping over me as if she's checking for bruises that aren't visible on the skin.

Lola tilts her head, disgust evident in every word. "That motherfucker, Jace, he's a dick. You know that, right?"

A laugh slips out of me. "What because he said out loud what I already knew was happening?"

She stills. Completely.

Aubrey blinks, the color draining from her face. "You knew about the bet?" she asks, voice soft.

I nod once. That's all I've got.

Aubrey moves closer—careful, gentle, like you would when approaching something already broken. "Sam..."

"I heard them at Michaela's party," I say, lowering my voice because if I raise it, I might start screaming. "I was going to the bathroom. Reece didn't know I was there. He said something to Jace about a bet."

"That was weeks ago," Aubrey says, horrified. "Why didn't you tell us?"

I lift one shoulder. "I was embarrassed. Then, when we hooked up, he told me there was no bet. And when he didn't go around bragging that we fucked, I convinced myself..."

Lola doesn't hesitate. "You believed him."

I meet her eyes, shame burning hot in my chest. "Yeah," I whisper. "I did."

The bathroom door swings open again, and the air quickly turns rancid. Thick with cheap perfume and hostile energy.

Nicole struts in as if she's on a runway nobody asked for, her two backup dancers flanking her, both trying too hard and failing even more. She doesn't bother hiding the smirk ripping across her face.

"Well, well," she purrs. "So much for Little Miss Virgin."

My stomach flips over.

Nicole flashes a grin, all teeth and venom. "Or should I say... Reece's winnings?"

Lola tenses up next to me, anger simmering just below the surface.

But it's Aubrey who really steps up fast.

She marches straight up to Nicole, eyes blazing. "Get the fuck out. You and your crusty-ass lashes and whatever festering STD is leaking out of your mouth today."

Nicole blinks, showing a flicker of real shock before that smirk slides back onto her face. "Aw. How cute. Trying to intimidate me?" Her voice drips with sugar, but a hint of poison is evident. "Hate to break it to you, bitch, but I'm not Tia. She might piss herself when you raise your voice, but I don't scare that easy."

Aubrey's jaw snaps tight. Her fists curl, knuckles white, her whole body vibrating with the urge to launch Nicole straight through the damn mirror. But I know she won't touch her.

Aubrey still feels guilty about what she did to Tia. Even if Tia deserved every harsh word, Aubrey hated what it made her become.

Nicole lets out this high-pitched, try-hard laugh, tosses her over-processed straw-blonde hair, and struts out like she didn't just shit all over the floor and call it perfume.

Her small posse hustles behind her, heels clicking, trying to keep up but stumbling over their own egos.

They follow her like cheap perfume, clutching their phones, their drama, and whatever bits of mean-girl power she allows them to have.

Lola shakes her head, disgust clear on her face. "I swear that bitch is one tampon short of a crime scene."

A laugh slips out of me. It's small, shaky, hardly there. More breath than sound. But it's something.

Aubrey moves closer, her hand touching my arm.

"We should get to class," she says, eyes searching mine. "Are you okay, Sam?"

I open my mouth, but nothing comes out.

She pulls me into a hug, arms tight and firm. "Jace is an asshole for saying what he did," she murmurs into my hair. "Reece isn't any better, but at least he knocked Jace on his ass for running his mouth about you."

That's all it takes.

The burn climbs up my throat. My eyes sting, heavy with everything I've been holding back since the hallway.

I'm really not okay. Not even close.

But I nod anyway because if I stop moving, if I let myself really feel it, I'll collapse right here and I won't know how to put myself back together again.

We shove the bathroom door open, and the hallway hits us all at once. The noise, bodies, and the sharp sting of fluorescent lights on raw nerves.

And then I see him.

Reece.

Leaning against the lockers as if he's been there the whole time, waiting. His eyes catch mine instantly, the way they always fucking do. There's something there... regret, panic, maybe both, but I don't care.

My chest clamps down so fucking tight it pushes up into my throat, raw and burning.

He looks like shit.

Good.

"Sam," he says, voice rough and broken.

I don't stop. I walk right past him as if he's nothing more than noise I refuse to listen to anymore.

"Sam, fuck, wait—"

His hand wraps around my wrist.

I rip it away so quickly his fingers barely brush my skin. "You don't get to touch me."

His mouth opens, jaw working, but whatever he's trying to say dies in his throat. I don't wait for him to find his voice.

"You should walk away, Reece," Lola says, stepping in front of me, shoulders squared, eyes daring him to test her.

If I weren't hurting so badly, I'd be smirking at her because this isn't the same girl who used to shrink under Tia's shadow. This is new-Lola energy. Try-me-and-bleed-for-it energy. That mess-with-my-girl-and-I'll-bury-you look in her eyes—that almost makes me proud despite all the fucking pain.

Aubrey's already moving, slipping between Lola and Reece before things escalate. "Not now, Reece. Give her some space." She hooks her fingers around Lola's arm and pulls. "Come on."

Reece remains rooted to the floor, frozen in place.

I keep walking, even though something inside me still aches for what we almost became. For the version of him I allowed myself to believe in.

And fuck, I hate that it still hurts. And even after everything, some pathetic part of me still wants him to fix it.

By the time I reach class, I'm hollow. Scraped clean. Stripped down to nothing but skin stretched over what used to be a girl.

I settle into my usual seat in the middle row, spine straight, chin up, pretending I'm not falling apart at the seams.

Lola settles next to me, her presence a shield I didn't ask for but damn it, need. Aubrey slips into the seat behind me, claiming her spot beside Noah.

"Is she okay?" Noah whispers.

Aubrey doesn't answer, at least not aloud.

Then there's Reece.

One row ahead. Three seats over. Far enough not to touch me, yet close enough that I can feel every single moment of his gaze.

The teacher speaks in a monotone blur of dates and assignments. I don't hear a thing.

My only awareness is Reece's stare piercing into the side of my head.

Even so, I avoid looking his way.

Midway through class, my phone buzzes on the desk. The vibration rattles loudly enough to turn a few heads. I flip it over quickly, heart already pounding in my chest.

Reece: It wasn't like that. I swear to fucking God, Sam.

I don't move or breathe.

Another buzz.

Reece: I never said that shit. You weren't some bet.

My stomach twists. That voice in my head whispers, "What if he's telling the truth?"

I shut it up fast.

Buzz.

Reece: Talk to me, Red. Please.

My hand hovers over the phone. Just for a second. Long enough to wonder whether answering would fix anything.

Then I blink.

The words blur together, foggy from tears burning in my eyes.

I shove the phone into my bag so quickly I almost fall out of my seat.

I blink hard. Breathe deeper.

Then, I lift my pen. I force my eyes to the board, anything to anchor myself in something that isn't him.

The teacher's droning about ecosystems or equations or some shit I should probably care about. So I write it down, word for word. Not because it matters, but because focusing on the lesson means I'm not replaying his voice in my head.

I underline a heading, then write the date. Pretend it's just another day, and I'm not falling apart behind every word I write.

By lunchtime, he's sent me seven more texts.

Each one a digital scream, buzz after buzz, his name lighting up my screen. I don't open them. I already know what they'll say.

I didn't mean it. I swear. It wasn't like that. Please, Red.

I just sit there, watching the notifications stack up. All the while pretending my heart doesn't skip a beat every time his name flashes across the screen.

All day, the whispers follow me like shadows I can't escape. They cling to my skin, crawl under my clothes, and settle in the space between my shoulder blades. Every hallway feels longer. Every turn is sharper. I hear them behind locker doors, between class changes, and over the flush of toilets.

The stares hit harder.

Some land with pity. Eyes wide, soft, full of that sad-girl sympathy that makes me want to scream. Others are sharp with curiosity, trying to read the scandal on my face as if it's written across my cheeks. But the worst ones are the ones that laugh. The ones who treat my humiliation like a goddamn group chat joke. Passing comments in the hallway: "Guess she wasn't that innocent after all" or "Bet he didn't even have to try that hard."

A boy behind me snickers during biology. Another one whispers something to his friend in the hallway, and they both burst out laughing after I walk past.

They don't care if I hear.

That's the point.

Their words weren't meant to be secret; they are meant to brand.

And they do.

Every one of them sinks into my skin, poisons my blood, wraps around my ribs, and squeezes until I can barely fucking breathe.

And the worst part?

There's no escaping it.

We sit at our lunch table as if the world isn't tearing me apart with every whisper. Conversations buzz loudly in my ears. Fluorescent lights stab into my skull.

But we sit anyway, pretending my name hasn't become the punchline of every locker room joke and hallway rumor.

Lola sits to my right, and Aubrey to my left. They both check in with me in their own subtle ways. No grand gestures, just gentle glances and small touches. Their hands rest on my arm, or knees nudge mine. A steady rhythm of 'I've got you' without needing to say it.

And thank fuck for that.

They're the only reason I'm upright. The only reason I haven't grabbed my bag and bolted from the cafeteria like I'm on fire.

Reece takes his usual seat at the table, directly across from me.

The tension sticks to us, thick and uneasy. He says nothing. Not with Lola watching him like she's about to throw her juice box at his head. Not with Aubrey stiff beside me. And definitely not with Noah, glaring at him as if he's ready to swing if Reece so much as breathes wrong.

So he remains quiet.

And so do I.

We all sit there, pretending this isn't a goddamn mess, three girls trying to act normal while my heart slowly bleeds out beneath the table.

I keep my eyes down, fork digging into the pasta. I'm not eating it, just moving it around to look busy.

I see what Reece did to Jace. The bruises are still spreading across his face, deep purple and menacing. A perfect match for the filthy shit that crawled out of his mouth.

Lola hasn't said a word to Jace since he slid into his spot at the table, wearing that smug grin he's perfected. He practices the casual act, voice low, eyes gentle, and quietly says, "Hey, Bells."

Lola doesn't look his way or offer him any food like she usually does.

He keeps trying to drop that nickname, like it still holds weight.

Second attempt.

Third.

By the fifth, he's struggling, voice tight, ego bruised.

She still doesn't look at him, calmly sipping her juice with a disinterest that makes silence seem harsh.

He gets it eventually.

Jaw clenched, he stalks away, muttering something under his breath about bitches and whatever cock-measuring contest he's losing today.

He'll probably find some easy fuck behind the gym to remind himself that he still matters.

Reece remains silent the entire time, sitting there with his elbows on the table and his jaw clenched so tightly it's a wonder his teeth don't crack.

Ten minutes go by before he gets up and walks away.

Finally, I can breathe again.

Enough to take a sip of water without feeling like it chokes me.

By the end of the day, I'm barely holding it together with a grip that makes my fingers ache. My smile is a crack in concrete, and my voice is barely more than a breath. But hey, I'm still standing. Sort of.

Aubrey and Lola stay close to me.

We pile into my car. My hands tremble too much to drive, so I sit quietly with keys in my lap.

Aubrey slides into the passenger seat, and Lola takes the back.

No one speaks for a second.

Aubrey turns to me, her voice gentle but steady. "So, how long has it been going on between you and Reece?"

I swallow hard. "I went to his place," I say, staring at the steering wheel. "To do the assessment. You know... because of how my dad is with guys."

They nod. They know what that means.

"We had sex there," I say. "That was the first time."

Lola lets out a soft whistle from the back seat but stays quiet.

I glance at Aubrey then down at my hands. My voice barely comes out when I say, "And I was the one in the library. That was me."

Aubrey blinks, stunned. "Holy shit."

Lola gasps so loudly I almost jump. "Wait, your Library Girl?" Her eyes go wide in the rearview mirror. "I thought that was some senior skank with no gag reflex." She doesn't stop there. "Babe, I thought that was one of the cheerleaders. You know, the ones who moan when they sip Gatorade."

Aubrey snorts. "Lola—"

"No, seriously," Lola keeps going, now totally excited. "I told Jace the other day, it was probably some senior bitch who thinks sucking off the quarterback counts as team spirit."

That's it. I lose it.

A laugh punches out of me, so unexpected, that it startles all three of us. Aubrey's eyes snap wide before she bursts out laughing too, clutching her stomach and shaking her head. Lola's already collapsed in the back seat, wheezing so hard she sounds asthmatic.

And for a second, it's perfect.

Three girls in a car. Just ugly laughs, snorts, and the kind of joy that burns quick and hot.

The laughter gradually fades, thinning out between shaky breaths. My cheeks are damp, my ribs hurt, and for a moment I forget why I was bleeding in the first place.

Then I remember.

I wipe my eyes and look out the windshield, voice soft. "I have his jacket. And his ring." My hand forms a fist in my lap. "Can you give them to Noah?" My voice nearly breaks. "To give to Reece."

Aubrey nods.

Movement outside grabs my attention.

Across the parking lot, Tia walks confidently through the lot, Jace right beside her, hands in his pockets, head tilted toward her with that laid-back smirk. Her arm brushes against Jace's, and even that seems rehearsed.

"Are you ever gonna forgive him?" Aubrey asks, her voice directed at the back seat.

Lola doesn't respond right away. She leans her head back against the seat. "He fucked up," she says finally. "Said shit about Sam. So no. Not yet. Not until he earns it."

Aubrey looks back at her. "It hurt him today. With you ignoring him."

"He deserved it," Lola scoffs.

"I know. But still, when you ignored him, it hit him harder than you think."

"Maybe," Lola says, voice flat. "But he doesn't look hurt now."

We all look out through the front windshield.

Jace is laughing at something Tia says, his whole posture relaxed, casual, and at ease.

"He looks like he's got a sure thing with her," Lola says.

Then nothing. No more punchlines or sass from Lola. Just silence.

Lola sinks into the seat, eyes on the floor, shoulders tense.

And I catch it in the rearview mirror; her face falls, but it's enough to see that whatever she says, Jace means more to her than she wants to admit.

Aubrey moves next to me and raises her eyebrows. That look says it all. She saw it too.

I say nothing as I reach for the keys and slide them into the ignition. The engine turns over. I ease the car out of the lot. Jace and Tia shrink in the rearview.

When we pull up in front of my house, Dad's there, hosing off his truck. His flannel sleeves are rolled up, arms dripping with water, boots soaked from standing too close to the spray. He looks up when he hears us, eyes squinting against the sun.

"Hey, girls!" he says as we step out of the car.

"Hi, Mr. Carter," Aubrey calls out.

"Hey, Mr. C," Lola says.

He grins at both of them, before he looks at me. His eyes scan my face, lingering a little too long.

And there it is.

The falter.

That brief half-second crack in his smile. The way his brow furrows.

"You okay, kid?" he asks.

"Fine," I lie. The word barely makes it past my lips. "Just tired."

He nods, but I know him. He doesn't buy it, not for one second.

We head inside, take our shoes off at the door, and I hang my key on the hook. Routine. Habit. Something normal to hold on to.

I lead them down the hall, passing framed photos of better days—birthdays, camping trips, one of me and Dad at the track, both of us sunburned and smiling. Dad was right. Boys like that are bastards.

In the kitchen, I grab a couple of cans from the fridge and slide them across the counter to the girls. Aubrey cracks hers open immediately, leaning against the bench. Lola holds hers.

No one speaks as I lead them up the stairs.

When we arrive in my room, we drop our bags near the door. My room is generally clean, with a little clutter here and there. There's a stack of books by the bed and clothes that are half-folded on the chair in the corner.

Lola kicks her feet up on my bed, cracks open her can, and takes a long sip while half-sprawled across the pillows. Aubrey sinks into the beanbag by the window, sipping her drink as her eyes drift across the room.

I don't sit.

Instead, I walk over to my closet and take down Reece's jacket from the hanger. It still faintly smells like him. Then, I go to my bedside drawer. The ring rests inside, cool metal against my fingers as I pick it up, remembering how he used to spin it on his thumb during class.

I turn and walk over to Aubrey, clutching Reece's things in my hands. She looks up without a word, her eyes soft and steady. I hold them out to her. Two pieces of him I can't bear to keep anymore.

She takes them and tucks them into her lap. Somehow, it lifts, just a little — enough to breathe again, knowing nothing in this room belongs to him anymore.

"Okay," Lola says, standing up and dropping her can on my desk with a loud clunk. "Now, after the day you've had, I'm putting goop on your face."

I blink. "What?"

"Facials, bitch." She's already heading to the bathroom, her tone all business. "Healing energy. Minimal emotional scarring."

Aubrey chuckles and shakes her head.

I sigh and stretch out on the bed as Lola comes back with a tube in one hand and a stack of towels in the other, her hair up in a messy bun, sleeves pushed to her elbows as if she's getting ready for battle.

Fifteen minutes later, we all recline.

With me lying across the pillows, Aubrey curled up on my beanbag, Lola at the foot of the bed—green masks drying on our skin. Spotify is playing something soft and non-depressing.

We don't discuss Reece, Jace, or anything real.

We just sit and breathe, letting the silence suffice.

And for a little while, it is.

Chapter 25

REECE

J ace can go fuck himself. It's been four days since I put him on his ass, and my knuckles are still bruised enough to remind me it actually happened. Every time I flex my hand, it hurts.

Jace has been trying to talk to me ever since, cornering me in hallways, blowing up my phone, and acting confused about why I won't give him the time of day.

Honestly, I've had enough listening to his bullshit voice. He said what he did and fucked everything up. End of story.

I'm home alone, slumped on the couch, phone glowing in my hand as I scroll through nothing, trying to drown out the silence that's louder than anything.

All I want is to talk to Red. Tell her it's not what she thinks. I've tried everything—texted her more times than I want to admit, called until it just rang out and went straight to voicemail. I swear to God, I would've walked the highway barefoot if I thought it would make her hear me out.

But she won't. And that's on me.

I hate myself in a way I didn't know was possible. This isn't the usual guilt or regret I can fuck away or joke about. For the first time in my life, I don't want to be Reece the player. I don't want the looks or the rumors or the easy girls who don't ask questions. I don't want another mouth on my cock or another warm body that doesn't matter.

I just want Red.

It fucking hurts in that rip-your-chest-open, can't-breathe, punch-to-the-gut kind of way, because she doesn't want me anymore.

And I can't blame her for it.

Because if I were her?

I'd hate me too.

The knock hits hard. It's sharp. With no patience behind it—just fists and fuck-you energy—I haul myself off the couch, already pissed and muttering curses under my breath. If that's Jace, he can go choke on his own ego. One more word out of his mouth, and I'll make sure he never says a fucking word to me again.

I yank the door open, prepared to unload.

But it's not Jace. It's Noah.

And my chest hurts the second I see what he's holding.

My jacket.

The same one I wrapped around her that night at the party. She was freezing, but too damn proud to admit it. Arms crossed, nose pink, teeth probably chattering behind that stubborn silence. She wore it like she didn't need it, but, fuck, she looked good in it. Too good. I remember thinking I wanted her to keep it. Thought maybe it meant something if she did.

Guess not.

Now it's back in Noah's hands, folded in a way that feels final, as if she couldn't bear to see it in her room for another second.

Noah doesn't say a word. He simply holds it out, and I take it, with every part of me screaming at the weight of what it means.

She's fucking done.

I take the jacket, fingers curling around it as if it still holds a trace of her. It doesn't. It's just fabric now. Cold. Weightless.

When I step back, Noah walks in without asking. He heads straight for the couch, drops onto it, legs sprawled, arms draped over the back.

I follow more slowly, dragging my feet, each step a reminder of what's missing, as if my body has forgotten how to move without her.

Noah doesn't say anything at first. Just watches as I sit down on the couch beside him. He shifts in his seat before reaching into the front pocket of his hoodie.

He pulls out something small, clenched in his fist, then slowly opens his hand, fingers uncurling one by one.

My ring is sitting in his palm.

The one I used to spin on my thumb when my thoughts got too loud. When I couldn't sit still, breathe, or deal with the way she made everything feel too real.

The same fucking ring I gave her without actually saying the words. No label or promises of what I felt. Just a silent hope that she'd feel it and know. That she'd wear it and understand what I couldn't say out loud—that she was mine.

I stare at it a moment too long. Then I reach for it, snatch it out of his hand, and tighten my fist around the metal as if I could force the meaning back into it. If I hold it tight enough, maybe she won't be gone.

"She gave these to Aubrey," Noah says. "Asked me to give them to you."

I nod, jaw clenched, and swallow hard.

It fucking burns. Every inch of my throat feels scraped raw.

"Did she say anything else to Aubrey?" I ask, even though I already know the answer.

Noah shakes his head. "No. Not really."

That's it. No final shot at closure, just my stuff handed back to me.

"Fuck," I mutter, dragging my hands down my face.

Noah leans back and pulls a joint from the front pocket of his hoodie. Lights it up with zero ceremony and even fewer fucks.

He takes a hit, then passes it to me. "Figured you'd need it."

I take it without a word, bring it to my lips, and inhale deeply enough to feel it claw through my lungs on the way down.

"Thanks," I mutter, exhaling slowly and watching the smoke curl up toward the ceiling.

We pass the joint between us, silence heavy, smoke swirling through the air. My head spins, but I embrace it. Better to feel high than feel empty.

Noah leans back, eyes half-closed, voice quiet. "You care about her, don't you?"

"Yeah," I say, without hesitation. My throat's raw, not from the smoke, but from every fucking word I haven't said to her.

He takes the joint again. "Then I've gotta ask, because she's Aubrey's friend, and Aubrey's not gonna let me hear the end of it if I don't."

I glance over at him.

"Why did you do it?" he asks.

I look away and stare directly ahead.

"It wasn't fucking like that," I say.

He waits. Calm, quiet, giving me the rope and watching to see if I'll hang myself or try to climb out of the hole.

The silence lingers. The pain in my chest intensifies because the truth is, I don't even know how to explain it.

I scrub a hand down my face; the guilt crawling up my throat like it's got claws. "It started off as a stupid bet with Jace," I say, words dry and bitter. "She shot me down at that party so fucking fast I didn't have time to blink. So I ran my mouth. Said shit to save face."

I lean forward, elbows on my knees, hands hanging uselessly between them. "But it changed. Because I changed. She got under my skin so fast I didn't even notice it happening. One second I was playing the game, and the next I was falling, and I didn't know how to stop."

Noah stays quiet. He doesn't interrupt; he just observes.

"By the time I actually did the shit I said to Jace, I didn't tell him. I couldn't. Hated the fucking bet. Even when she asked me about it, I told her it wasn't a thing anymore. Lied to her face because I thought if I ignored it, it'd go away."

I exhale sharply, eyes fixed on the floor. "But it didn't. And when Jace opened his mouth, I was already in too deep. It was real to me. We were going to make it official that morning we walked in together. She wasn't some fuck to me or a bet." My voice drops lower. "I wanted her. All of her."

"Did you say it?"

My head jerks up. "Say what?"

Noah's eyes stay on mine, calm but sharp. "The shit Jace said. About extra points."

I shake my head hard. "I never fucking said that. I'd never talk about her like that. Not her."

He watches me for a moment. "Yeah. I figured. Jace has a mouth built for pissing people off. Shoots it off just to hear himself talk. I nearly flattened him a few months ago when he kept circling Aubrey like she was something to sink his teeth into."

I let out a laugh. "You should've."

"I might still," he says.

Another moment of silence lingers between us.

"She's not gonna believe you, you know," Noah says eventually. "Not for a while."

"I know." The words catch in my throat as they come out.

"And she's hurting."

"I am too."

He looks at me, one brow raised, eyes sharp. "Then do something about it. Get your head straight. She's not gonna wait forever while you sit here crying into your dick."

I don't respond, mostly because he's right.

He stands and pats me on the shoulder once before walking toward the door. He stops just before stepping outside.

"She cried when she gave Aubrey your stuff," he says, glancing back at me. "I think that counts for something."

Next he's gone. And I'm left alone again with my thoughts.

Me and the silence, and the ring I keep spinning on my thumb as if it has the power to rewind time. Like maybe if I turn it enough times, it'll take me back to the night I slipped it into her hand with every intention written across my fucking heartbeat.

The next day doesn't come any easier. If anything, it drags its boots across my chest and spits in my face for good measure.

Sam doesn't look at me. Not once. She just walks past me in the hallway as if I'm invisible. No worse than invisible because even air gets breathed. I'm nothing to her now.

I try to talk to her between classes when she's heading to her locker. I call her name, softly at first, then louder as she keeps walking.

This one time she stopped, and I thought maybe I'd get my chance to fix things. But when she looked at me, her eyes didn't blaze as they usually did; they were frozen.

"Go to hell," she says. It's cold now. Nothing soft remains, as if everything she used to give me—her laugh, her blush, her fucking heart—got locked behind a door I no longer have the key to.

She walks away, and I stay standing there, feeling every eye in the hallway on me. My hands itch. My chest won't fucking settle.

She's shut it off.

That light she used to give me? It's gone. The softness she used to show me when no one else was around? Gone too. The part of her that looked at me as if I was more than just a cocky asshole with a smart mouth that her father thought I was? Well, it's gone too.

Every second of silence, every cold glance, every clipped word is a debt I racked up and now have to pay.

She's fire turned ice.

And I'm the reason she froze.

I barely make it through the day without losing my shit. Every class feels longer than the last, and every encounter with her in the hallway hits me like a punch to the ribs. I can't think. I can't breathe. I can't get the look on her face out of my head when she told me to go to hell.

By the time training rolls around, I'm hanging on by a thread. I need to run, hit something, experience the burn in my legs and pretend I'm not coming apart at the seams. But before I can step onto the field, Coach calls me into his office.

"The scout'll be at the game," he says. "Confirmed it this morning."

I nod, the words barely landing.

Coach keeps going. "Your dad knows you're back."

My head snaps up. "Did he call you?"

"No," Coach shakes his head. "He showed up."

"When?"

"Two days ago."

I sit back in the chair, stunned, with my hands clenched into fists against my thighs.

Two days ago.

And he said nothing.

Not when we crossed paths yesterday, when I walked past him in the hallway and gave him a nod like some dumbass still hoping to be seen. He didn't assert authority, bark orders, or question me about why I was back on the team.

"Well, just give it your best shot out there tomorrow, Reece, and everything will work out," Coach says.

"Thanks, Coach," I say, pushing up from the chair.

But my head's a fucking mess.

By the time training begins, I'm so tense I can barely breathe. Every muscle in my body is on edge, ready to snap or explode—I can't tell which.

So I run.

Harder than I ever have before. I push until my legs burn, my lungs scream, and sweat pours down my back, soaking through my shirt. I take every drill like it's life or death, as if the scout's already watching, as if the ghosts in my head are chasing me down, and the only way out is to keep moving forward.

It's not about the scout or my dad, even though his silence still echoes in my ears. It's Sam.

If she never looks at me again, never speaks my name without venom, I still want to be the guy who deserved her. The one who should have fought harder. Who should have told her the truth sooner. The one who should have never let her walk away carrying all that pain alone.

Even if I never get the chance to fix it, I need to be someone she would be proud of.

It's the night of the game. The night the scout comes to watch West play, or anyone else worth betting on. The night I have to matter.

The field smells of freshly cut grass, an earthy scent that lingers on your skin. But tonight, there's something else in the air—something heavier. The smell of pressure, of too many broken promises to myself, and second chances already spent.

The bleachers are buzzing with so much energy. When the crowd roars, it hits the base of your spine and climbs. Saturday night under the lights. That means every fucking play counts.

I stand on the sidelines, helmet in hand, jaw clenched. The lights are bright and harsh, shining in thick beams, highlighting every movement, every mistake. No shadows to hide in tonight. No room for errors.

The scout's somewhere, watching and judging. Measuring every sprint, pass, and block against some invisible standard I'll never be told. He won't remember my name unless I make him. Give him something he can't ignore.

Coach pats me on the shoulder. "Play smart. Play hard. You've got this."

I nod, but my focus already narrows. The noise fades away. The crowd turns into background static. It's just the field now. The game.

Coach pulls his cap lower, the brim nearly covering his eyes.

"Listen to that crowd," he says, his voice gruff and loud enough to cut through the nerves buzzing under my skin. "Let it get into your blood. Let it fuel you. Take a second. Look up there to see who showed up tonight. They came because they believe in you."

I breathe through my nose before scanning the bleachers.

There.

Right in the middle, same seats as always. Noah. Aubrey tucked into his side, head leaning just enough to show they're solid. And next to them is Red.

High ponytail. Face locked in that stare she has when she's moments from shutting someone down with her words. And damn, she's gorgeous. Even with that don't-fuck-with-me look carved across her face.

Beside her, Lola is blowing bubbles with bubblegum as if she's sitting through a math test instead of a game that might determine the rest of my future.

Jace's seat is empty, and it feels wrong. He's always there—usually stealing half of Lola's food, running his mouth, pretending he doesn't care who wins. Seeing that space sit empty, even when I'm still mad at him, hits harder than it should.

The whistle blows, pulling me back onto the field. The boys jog over. Before I can step forward fully, Coach's hand presses down on my shoulder. It's strong. Solid. A weight meant to ground me.

He looks me straight in the eye.

"I believe in you, kid."

When he releases, I put my helmet on and sprint across the field, heart pounding. The crowd roars around us, a wall of noise and heat, and the boys are already hyped, shouting, slapping helmets, ready to go all out.

The first quarter kicks off with fire under my feet.

I'm locked in from the first whistle, every nerve firing, every muscle tuned. I don't just move; I hunt. Fast, aggressive, reading plays before they develop. My cleats rip across the turf, and every time the quarter-back thinks he's got a second too long, I'm already in his face, pushing past the line, teeth bared, body low.

First snap, I break through and hit him hard enough to make the crowd roar. On the second drive, I shut down a run that should've gone somewhere. Instead, it goes nowhere. I drag the guy down by the waist and bounce back up before the ref can even blow the whistle.

Every time there's a hit, it gets a cheer.

Every stop causes the bleachers to shake.

I hear my name shouted—once, twice, louder—chanting, "Wilson. Wilson. Wilson."

It doesn't even seem real.

But I don't stop.

I'm chasing every loose ball, barking orders, rallying the line as if it's my damn war to win. Coach is screaming from the sidelines, fist pumping. My teammates slap my helmet between plays, yelling shit I don't even register.

And then it happens.

West goes down hard.

One second, he's charging shoulder-first into the line. The next, he's crumpled on the turf, clutching his knee, his face twisted in a way that makes my stomach turn. The whole crowd inhales sharply. Silence falls over the field like a heavy blanket. He tries to get up but can't.

And just like that, the guy the scout came to see is finished for the night.

They help him limp to the sideline, his cleats dragging. It hits hard. West isn't only the best on defense; he's my teammate, and he wanted this as badly as I do.

When play starts again, I don't slow down. I flip the switch. Lock in harder. Hit meaner. Because fuck, if he stayed and still is watching?

I'll be everything he came for—everything he lost when the second West dropped. I'll leave him no choice but to notice.

And if this is my shot?

I'm fucking taking it.

Second quarter, I fucking snap.

I find the edge, the place where thought ends and instinct takes over. No more wondering if she'll ever forgive me. No more replaying the look in her eyes when she told me to fuck off. I silence the noise. Strip it down to muscle, rage, and motion. I play pissed.

First tackle, I drive the bastard back five yards. Next, I hit so hard he hits the ground with a thud. I don't check if he's okay. I don't stop moving, don't even flinch when someone's elbow slams my ribs. I want them flattened. Every single one of them. I want their quarterback dragging himself off the turf by his fingernails.

It's hot under the lights. Sweat burns in my eyes. My throat's raw from shouting calls, from screaming at the line to hold. My knuckles are busted, skin torn over bone, blood seeping into the tape. I don't give a single shit.

The crowd goes wild. They roar every time I hit, every time I move, every time I leave another guy gasping for air.

By halftime, we're up by seven. The scoreboard's glowing, the crowd's buzzing, but my chest's still heaving from the last hit. I jog to the sideline, drenched in sweat, jersey clinging, my ribs aching with every breath. I grab a bottle, chug the water—and spit it straight out. Tastes like metal. Like blood and heat and something else I can't name.

Coach is already barking plays, clipboard in hand, spit flying. The boys nod, fired up, shoving each other with that rough love that only comes when you're bleeding for the same damn goal. I nod too because I want this—bad. Not just for the team, not for the win, but for me. For everything I haven't said and everything I've lost.

I charge the line, read the play, dive for the tackle, and get completely leveled.

Air rushes from my lungs. I hit the ground hard, pain flashing through my side. For a moment, all I hear is ringing. Everything tilts. Players surround me, helmets and voices.

"You good?" someone asks.

I take a breath in. Another one follows. My chest burns, fire-hot, but I nod anyway. "Yeah," I rasp. "I'm good."

Then I'm on my feet.

The crowd loses its mind. Screaming. Roaring. Metal bleachers shake under the intensity. I barely notice any of it over the pounding in my ears. It sounds thunderous inside my skull. Every breath is raw, every rib protesting where the hit landed.

Next play, I line up again without hesitation.

It doesn't matter that I was face-first in the turf twenty seconds ago, lungs locked, vision filled with white. That moment is already gone. I leave it there with the dirt and the pain.

I burst off the line, driven by anger, desire, and everything I refuse to surrender.

I'm already fired up for the win.

Fourth quarter. Ten seconds remaining. One last chance for the opposition to take the lead.

The stadium's lost its mind. Coach is shouting himself hoarse on the sideline. The boys are yelling across the line, hyped and feral. Parents are on their feet, fists punching the air. The bleachers are shaking, metal rattling under the weight of too many bodies and too much hope.

I set my stance and drop low. Every muscle tightens. I wait.

The ball snaps.

And I go.

Hard and fast, fueled by muscle, rage, and every ounce of frustration I've been carrying all season. I punch through the line, meeting the runner head-on. Shoulder to chest. Pads collide. The sound is brutal and clear. Bodies slam to the ground and stay there.

The whistle shrieks.

Game over.

We held the line.

We fucking won.

The field becomes chaotic. The moment the whistle blows, the crowd erupts like a wave, crashing over the turf. Bodies push in from every direction. Helmets come off, boys scream, fists punch the air, and cleats stomp on the dirt. Sweat streams down my face. My chest still heaves from the last play. Every nerve is on fire. I'm not sure if I'm about to throw up or scream.

I turn and scan the crowd. Noah's in the bleachers, his grin wide and proud. Aubrey's got her arms around Red. They're jumping, shouting, losing their minds with the rest of the school.

But that's not what causes my stomach to flip.

It's the man in the black coat standing right behind Coach, frozen like a damn statue while the world erupts around him.

Nothing but sharp eyes follow every move I make, studying me with an intensity that exposes every choice I've ever made.

He doesn't push through the crowd. Instead, he waits until half of them wander off and the adrenaline crash hits me hard. I'm just about to throw up right there on the fifty-yard line.

He walks over, calm and controlled, as if he has all the time in the world. He pulls a card from his coat pocket and holds it out.

"Mayfair wants you."

That's all he says at first. No big speeches or hard sell. Just those three words, like a damn grenade dropped in my lap.

I stare at the card. Mayfair. The dream I'd buried so deep it almost stopped hurting.

I take it, fingers slick with sweat.

"Coach will organize a time," he says. "He'll talk to your parents. Then we'll lock in the details. I don't hand out cards for nothing. You've got something we don't see every day."

And just like that, it's real. I'm no longer a kid who nearly squandered everything. I'm wanted. Fucking Mayfair wants me. I stare at the card, at the name on it, the logo I've dreamed of since I was ten years old.

Then he's gone.

Coach walks up and slaps my back so hard I nearly stumble. "Knew you had it in you, kid," he says, voice rough. "Knew it all along."

I nod, but I can't speak.

All I want, more than water, or air, is to find my phone and call Sam to tell her I did it. That football's back on the table. That I didn't fuck it up this time.

And maybe, a part of me still hopes she'll answer.

CHAPTER 26

SAM

The energy from Saturday night still stays with me. It's beneath my skin, buzzing from what he did. Everyone saw it in every cheer, every held breath, every eye locked on Reece.

Reece tore through that field as if it owed him blood. He didn't hold back; he played with everything he had. Every hit and every bruise he's still carrying, he gave it all. Every part of himself, as if the game was the only way he knew how to express himself.

And maybe I resented him a little for that. For making me feel proud when I didn't want to be. For being that boy again—the one who gets under my skin and stays there no matter how hard I try to push him out.

I'm walking through the school gates. Lola's next to me, talking quickly, her voice rushing over itself with something about a broken nail or her cousin's party. I nod as if I'm listening, but I'm not. I'm somewhere else. Back on that field.

Watching Reece lift his helmet off, sweat-drenched and breathless, eyes scanning the crowd as if he was looking for something or someone. And at that moment, I wondered if it was me—if he saw me standing there with my heart in my throat, knowing I could never hate him enough to stop caring.

I haven't stopped thinking about it ever since—what it means that he still has the power to devastate me without laying a finger on me.

I should have been working on that damn assessment... the one Reece and I are supposed to be doing together.

But I couldn't.

I opened the document several times, stared at the blinking cursor, tried to outline arguments, and piece together paragraphs.

I almost messaged him just to say, "Hey, can you do your half of the assessment so we don't both fail?" But I didn't. Because if he replied... if he even said my name, I'd cave. I'd hear that voice and forget all the reasons I'm supposed to stay mad.

So I did nothing. I just sat there all weekend, letting the silence eat away at me as the deadline approached.

"Sam. Hello. Earth to heartbreak girl."

I blink and turn to Lola, who's staring at me as if I've grown an extra head. Her brows are raised, and her lip gloss is too shiny for this early in the morning.

"What?" I mumble, pulling myself back to reality.

"Are you still seriously thinking about that boy?" she asks.

I roll my eyes. "Shut up."

We barely walk through the doors, and it's already chaos.

Screams bounce off lockers, tearing through the air, bodies pressed so tightly it's a miracle anyone can breathe. Phones are out, mouths are open. Drama spills down the walls.

Lola yanks my arm, already stretching her neck like a bloodhound catching a scent. "Oh, hell yes. That's Tia's screech. I'd recognize it anywhere."

She squints through the crowd. "And unless my eyes are lying, which they never fucking do, that's Nicole's crusty-ass weave in Tia's hands."

She pulls me forward, weaving through the crowd until the main event comes into view.

Tia and Nicole. Full fucking carnage. Clawed hands, flying limbs, hair getting snatched like they're auditioning for some apocalyptic Real

Housewives spin-off. One of Nicole's nails hits the floor. Tia's got blood on her lip. Nicole's tit is a second away from making a guest appearance. It's savage, stupid, and everything this school fucking lives for.

The crowd converges like a pack of vultures fighting over the last piece of meat.

I should walk away. This isn't entertainment for me. Even if part of me wants to cheer when they rip each other's hair out, karma's a bitch, and they've both handed out enough poison to deserve it.

But then it hits.

That slow-burning heat creeping down my spine. That hum in my bones.

I don't have to look around to realize he's here.

I feel it in my chest, in the way my pulse skips, and how the noise around me fades into static.

And sure enough, when I look up, there he is. Reece Wilson. Leaning against the wall, all easy shoulders and smug smile, arms crossed over that broad chest that's wrecked more girls than gossip.

He is not watching the fight.

He is watching me.

He doesn't blink.

Neither do I.

He just stands there, drinking me in with those intense eyes, and I hate that my heart stumbles like some clueless girl in a YA movie.

He's still beautiful—stupidly, disgustingly beautiful—in that boy-who-breaks-hearts-and-doesn't-care kind of way. Messy hair. Sharp jaw. That crooked smile that wrecks good girls and dares them to thank him for it.

He wears pain like a damn crown. And I wish I didn't want to kiss him or ask what broke him before he ever reached me.

"Okay, break it up," a teacher barks, pushing her way through the crowd. "Tia. Nicole. Office. Now."

The crowd groans as phones are put away. The show's over.

Tia spits out a curse so filthy it'd get me grounded until I turn thirty. Nicole shoots back with something about banging someone's cousin. I don't know if it's true, but judging by the gasps of Tia's little wannabes, she hit a nerve.

Lola is practically vibrating next to me, eyes wide, voice hushed with excited horror. "That was better than reality TV. I swear, next time I'm bringing popcorn and dragging a lawn chair into the hallway."

She's absorbing the chaos, energized by second-hand bitch-fight vibes, until she notices my face.

Then she groans.

"Oh no. Not that look again."

I don't answer.

"That's the "he's ten feet away and your ovaries are still writing him love letters" look."

I tear my eyes away from Reece and head to my locker, pulling it open with a loud bang that makes it rattle. "What are you talking about?"

"The way you look at him is the same as someone dying of thirst looks at water."

"I do not."

"You do," Lola sings, way too pleased with herself. "It's giving tragic heroine energy. The kind who swears she's done but would still ride him into next week if he so much as blinked."

"Lola," I snap, giving her a glare that could trigger the fire alarms.

She just smirks and taps my shoulder. "Be strong, Sam. Or at least keep your panties on until lunchtime."

Then she struts off, leaving me in the wreckage of my dignity and Reece-fueled hormones.

Aubrey finds me by the lockers. I'm halfway through juggling my books and trying not to think about the look Reece gave me a moment ago.

"Sam!" she calls out. "Did you hear?"

I blink. "Hear what?"

She grins. "Reece. The scout from Mayfair called Coach this morning. Wants to set up a meeting."

It hits harder than it ought to. My grip on my books slips for a moment.

"That's... that's great," I say, forcing the words past the twist in my chest. "He deserves it."

He does, especially after everything he invested in that game the other night. And now he has what he wanted: his second chance, his shot.

But it fucking hurts because all I can think about now is that I'll see him around campus next year. Passing him on the grounds, him sitting with Noah and Aubrey. I won't be able to look away, I already know it. I'll still remember the way he kisses. The way his hands knew where to touch, the way he made me feel as if I were more than a good girl with a plan.

I don't know if I'll ever stop craving that.

Wanting him.

Even when he's the one who broke me.

"You should talk to him, Sam," Aubrey says.

I shake my head before she finishes. "No."

Her brows pinch. "Sam. He's trying."

She doesn't understand. "So what if he is?" I snap, and it comes out sharper than I meant, but fuck it. That's what happens when you give everything to a boy and he trades it for a two-hundred-dollar punchline. "He can be sorry all he wants. It doesn't mean I have to listen."

Aubrey flinches but stays firm. "Noah talked to him. He said he's a mess. That he's hurting."

I laugh, hollow and bitter, as something breaks in my throat. "Good. He should be."

She stays quiet, just standing there and biting her lip. She wants to fix this, to sew it all back together with enough thread to make it seem like it never tore. But I'm not some flat tire she can pump full of hope and send back into traffic.

"I can't let him in again," I whisper, voice cracking right in the middle. "Not after what he did."

"What if it wasn't what you think?" Aubrey's voice is soft and careful, but it still hits hard.

"But it is." I laugh. "He told me there was no bet, but there fucking was. And it doesn't matter what he says now. He made me feel different. As if I meant something to him, just to toss me in the same pile with every girl he's fucked and walked away from."

"You're not," she says. "You know that."

"Do I? Because it doesn't feel that way. I'm still there, Aubrey. Still lying in that pile, right on top, with his fingerprints all over me."

She doesn't look away. "But you're the one who walked away, Sam. Not him."

I stay still. I don't have an answer for that because she's right. I ran first. I told him to stay the hell away.

Aubrey takes a slow breath. "The good ones don't stop trying to fix their mistakes." Her voice trembles. "Noah says he's never seen him like this before. Not ever. He's hurting, Sam. He barely speaks. Reece is messed up over it, and it's not for show. He's gutted."

"Perhaps." My voice cracks again as I press a hand to my chest, trying to hold back the pain and keep it from spilling out. "But sometimes, trying isn't enough. Not when he's already shattered the part of me that trusted him."

I slam my locker shut harder than I intend to. The metal clangs loudly through the hallway, but I don't stop. I can't. Not with my throat burning and my chest tight. I leave Aubrey behind, even though my stomach twists with guilt for brushing her off. She was only trying to help. But I can't keep talking about him. Not when the wounds are still raw and bleeding beneath my skin.

I turn the corner and come to a full stop.

There he is.

Reece.

Leaning against the lockers further down the hall, that lazy smirk tugging at the corner of his mouth. Maya stands in front of him, hair curled perfectly, makeup sharp, posture radiating wit and that flirty vibe. She's tucking her hair behind her ear as if she's the star of some cheesy teen soap opera.

And for a moment, my heart stumbles.

He looks fine. Every bit the cocky, unfazed asshole who tore me apart.

I hear Aubrey's voice in my mind: He's hurting, Sam. He's not the same.

Yeah... Doesn't look like it.

Maya reaches out to him, her hand brushing his arm.

Then, it happens.

Reece recoils.

His hand snaps up, knocking her hand away. "Don't fucking touch me."

A few people turn to look.

Maya blinks, stunned. "What the hell's your problem?"

"You are," he says.

Maya huffs before storming down the hallway, heels clicking loudly, yelling something about him being an asshole, but I don't catch the rest. I've never seen him like this before. He has never pushed anyone away. He's always been the flirt, the tease, the smooth talker who knows exactly what he's doing.

But not today.

I stay there watching him walk away, his hands shoved in his pockets, his head down, with no prowling in his step. No swagger. Just a boy who looks heavy and worn down.

Aubrey slides up next to me.

"See?"

I don't answer.

"I told you Noah said he's not the same," she says, nudging my arm.

I watch him walk further down the hallway, shoulders hunched. That cocky energy has disappeared. Hands tucked deep into his pockets. Eyes fixed on the floor.

"You broke him, Sam," she says softly. "You need to see it. He's different now, and it's because of you."

I swallow hard, feeling my throat get tight.

Maybe I see it, but I still can't speak.

God, I want to believe that this change is real—that he's still trying, even when I won't let him.

But believing means tearing down the wall I built around the part of me that still loves him. I have to risk it all again—my pride, my heart, and the tiny, fragile piece of trust he already shattered once.

And I don't know if I'll survive losing him twice.

CHAPTER 27

REECE

C oach offered to come with me. He said he'd sit beside me and run interference if I needed it, especially if things got messy with my old man. I told him I'd handle it.

Now I'm sitting here wondering if I fucked that up, too.

The house is silent. The TV is muted, displaying a news anchor on the screen. It's quiet enough to hear every second pass. I'm slumped on the couch, phone in hand, watching the screen, hoping that this time it will light up and she will reply to one of my texts.

I already know it's a waste of time.

The last ten messages are still there—blue bubbles lined up in a row, each one a version of me trying and failing to get her back.

The last one said:

Reece: I'm sorry. I miss you.

Three days before that:

Reece: Please talk to me, Red. It's not what you think. Fuck, Red, please let me explain.

I gave up trying two days ago.

Not because I wanted to, but because I had to. Watching my messages sit there unanswered started feeling worse than being told to fuck off.

I don't know if she blocked me. My phone still delivers the texts, but there's no response. It feels final, as if she erased me without ever pressing a button.

It's not the knowing that kills me. It's the empty space where she used to be. The silence that stretches endlessly until it settles in my chest and makes a home there. I wake up reaching for my phone. I go to sleep staring at it. Every quiet second reminds me she's out there choosing to avoid me.

And the cruel part is I'm still fucking in love with her. Nothing shut that off. Not the shame or the regret over what I did. Or the way she looked at me when Jace said the words.

I throw the phone onto the couch cushions and press the heels of my hands into my eyes until sparks flash behind my eyelids. I should be riding the high right now. A scout from Mayfair wants me. I played the best game of my life. Coach has my back.

This is everything I've been chasing since I was a kid.

And all I feel is nothing. Nothing at all.

My chest is empty, hollow as hell. There's no rush or victory lap. Just this dull ache that won't go away no matter how hard I try to ignore it, because football isn't the only thing I want anymore.

I want her too.

The front door creaks open and then slams shut so hard it rattles the frame. Heavy boots thud across the floorboards. I smell the alcohol on him before I even lay eyes on him.

My father, carrying a six-pack.

He doesn't look at me as he drops his keys into the bowl on the bench or when he shrugs out of his jacket, muttering shit under his breath as if the world had personally wronged him on the way home.

I push myself up from the couch, throat dry, heart already bracing for impact.

"I heard you spoke to Coach," I say.

He grunts and keeps moving, not stopping until he drops into the recliner.

He places the six-pack on the floor beside him and pulls out a bottle.

"Yeah," he says. "I did. So what? You're back on the team and you couldn't fucking tell me?"

"I was going to," I say. My voice comes out tight, clipped. "I didn't think you'd care."

That grabs his attention.

His eyes flick to me—bloodshot, sharp, and evaluating. "Of course I fucking care. You think I put up with your shit all these years because I didn't believe you could do something with that talent?"

My fists curl at my sides. Nails bite into skin. "You mean football."

"What else is there?" he snorts, flicks the cap across the room, before taking a long pull from his beer.

The words hit hard. Familiar. Brutal in how normal they sound.

And in that, the truth resides—always lingering between us, decaying in the space we never discuss. The only version of me he's ever bothered to see.

"Jesus," I mutter, dragging a hand through my hair. "You only gave a fuck about me when I was flattening guys on the field."

His laugh's sharp, mean, soaked in whatever he's already knocked back. "I pushed you because you had talent. You needed someone to beat the weakness out of you."

"You mean discipline," I snap, stepping in. "You mean turning me into some fucking machine so you could brag to your work buddies that your boy was going pro. You tied my worth to tackles and bruises. You only saw me when I was bleeding for the team."

"And so what, now you're crying over it?" He shrugs and takes another swig. "You had the shot, hero, then pissed it all away. That's on you."

"I was fucking drowning," I shoot back. "But you never saw that. You didn't see me unless I was wearing shoulder pads and lighting up the scoreboard."

"You whine now, but you had it. You could have made it." He snorts, not even flinching.

"I still can," I say, quieter this time. "Mayfair wants me. The scout called Coach. They're setting up a meeting. I need you there."

That sobers him up. For a beat, he just stares in silence. Then his mouth shifts. Not a smile or anything soft, just that slow curl of pride. The kind he only ever reserves for wins and stats.

"Well, shit," he mutters. "Mayfair. That's big."

"I know."

He nods and brings the bottle to his lips. "Alright. I'll come."

I don't thank him. I'm not fucking stupid. That nod wasn't meant for me. It was for the jersey. For the kid who hits hard and keeps his mouth shut.

I walk out before he can utter another goddamn word. I go to my room, close the door, and flop onto my bed, pressing my knuckles into my forehead as if I can force the thoughts out of my skull. My head's a fucking warzone. Words I didn't say. Ones he'll never hear. That hollow, rotten ache where something close to love should've been.

My phone buzzes beside me.

Hope flickers quickly and fiercely in my chest. I reach for it before the screen lights up completely, praying with all my heart that it's her. That she finally gave in. That maybe, just maybe, she wants to hear me out.

But it's not her. It's Noah.

Noah: Party at Ryan's. Aubs and I might hit it. You should come. Could do you some good to get out for a bit.

I don't answer. I just toss the phone back onto the bed and lean back, staring up at the ceiling.

The party's already a mess when I arrive. Beer-soaked air fills the place and couples are pressed against the walls as if their hormones could burn the house down. Someone's already puked in the hydrangeas out front.

The place is crowded. Sweat, perfume, cologne, bad decisions—it's all here. Some guy I don't know shoulder checks me with a "Yo, man" and keeps walking. I don't bother responding.

Noah's in the corner, arm draped around Aubrey, both of them grinning at something on her phone. She nudges him with her shoulder, and he pulls her in closer. They're crazy in love. It should annoy me. Instead, it just reminds me of what I fucked up.

Lola's on the dance floor, grinding with a girl from the year below, her dark curls bouncing, a half-laugh caught in her throat. Her drink sloshes dangerously, but she owns the chaos. Some guy tries to cut in. She pushes him away with a smirk, winks at him, and keeps dancing.

But none of them are who I'm here for.

I scan the room, eyes piercing through the bodies, the crowd, and the noise. I exhale slowly when I don't see her. I scan the room again, just to be certain.

Red's not here. No flame-bright hair in the corner. No sharp eyes watching me across the room, as if she's already read every dirty thought I've ever had and still dares me to come closer.

My gaze drifts toward the corner near the back wall, and there he is, Jace. Smug prick with his mouth pressed to some blonde I've never seen before. She seems older, could be college age. Fake tan, white nails. Tight dress, too much lip gloss.

He catches me looking, pulls back with a slick grin, and flashes me a peace sign as if we're good. As if I never laid him flat on his ass and told him to keep Sam's name out of his fucking mouth.

For a second, I consider walking over and telling him the things I haven't said out loud—that it wasn't all on him. I was the one who made the bet, but what he said was low.

But I came here tonight to forget. I thought that if I drank enough, I'd drown the ache of missing the only girl I have ever loved. I figured it'd be easy. Shot of tequila. Some girl whispering bullshit in my ear. Her hands on my chest. My hands wherever I needed them to be.

But as I glance around, I know it's not working for me; none of it is.

Every girl here is wrong.

They're too loud, laughing at shit that's not funny. Too fucking confident in all the ways Sam never needed to be. They pout on purpose. Twirl their hair as if they've practiced it. They press to close, tits up, grabbing guys' attention.

And all I can think is she never had to try.

Sam walked in, and the whole room seemed to bend around her. She didn't need a short dress, a fake laugh, or to grip my arm like she was staking a claim. She just looked at me, and that was it.

So yeah, I might have come here to forget. But all I see is everything she's not. And every time someone leans in too close or licks her lips, I want to scream because it isn't Sam. And no amount of alcohol can pretend it is.

I leave the party without saying a word. I simply slip out, the cold hitting me harder than I expect. Music still thumps behind me. Laughter echoes. Glass breaks. Someone shouts out a dare. I don't look back.

I just walk.

I have no idea where I'm going. No plan. Just taking it one step at a time, hoping the distance will wear away something.

I pass a diner. Inside, a couple shares a basket of fries. She's laughing at something he said, while he's looking at her like he'd rather starve than see her stop smiling.

I feel the ache as I recall that night after my first game back on the team, her sitting across from me, smirking as she stole fries from my plate. I didn't care. I would've given her every last one if it meant she stayed with me a little longer that night.

I don't even realize where I'm going until my feet stop moving. Her street. Her house. I stand there before my mind catches up, heart already pounding as if it's been waiting for this.

I don't go to the door. I don't have the balls for that. Instead, I stay across the street, half-swallowed by the dark, hands shoved deep in my pockets. After a while, I sink down onto the curb, elbows braced on my knees, head tipped back as I stare up at her window.

Her bedroom light is on.

I picture her inside, brushing that bright red hair, sitting on her bed with her knees pulled up, chewing her lip as she pretends to read something, with music playing softly in the background.

I lose track of time. Minutes blur into something heavier. I keep waiting for something stupid. A curtain to twitch. A light to flick off. Some kind of sign that I'm not a complete fucking idiot for sitting out here in the cold.

My spine starts to ache. My legs go numb. And for a dangerous second, I almost convince myself to do it. To cross the street. To climb up to her window and beg. To tell her I'm sorry again. To promise her everything.

But I don't.

I stay exactly where I am because wanting her doesn't give me the right to hurt her again. Loving her doesn't mean she owes me forgiveness.

So I sit in the dark, staring at the light she hasn't turned off yet, and let the ache settle into my bones.

I finally push myself to get up and move because staying still feels dangerous.

When I get home, the house is dead quiet. My father is either already asleep or passed out on the couch.

I head straight to my room, grab my backpack from the corner and flip it upside down, everything spills out in a mess of crumpled papers, pens, and a half-crushed protein bar I forgot was in there.

And then the assignment lands last. That stupid, messed-up assignment we were supposed to be working on. The one we ditched for bathroom make-outs, my mouth on hers and deadlines forgotten.

I stare at the stack for a moment too long. Then I spread it across my bed. Pages crinkle under my hands, some still marked up in her handwriting. Her notes curl into the corners, little arrows, underlines, and the occasional sarcastic comment written in the margins that made me smirk the first time.

There's one sheet—our rough outline—where her writing becomes sloppy halfway through. I remember that night clearly. She sat cross-legged next to me, biting her lip, twirling the pen between her fingers, distracted. I kept bumping her knee on purpose, and she kept leaning in. The closer we got, the worse her handwriting became.

I take a breath, sit on the edge of the bed, and pick up my pen.

And I work.

Not because I give a shit about the grade. But because she does.

So I write.

Hard.

Fast.

Focused.

I fill in every gap, organize each bullet point, and clean up her sections without changing her voice. I review our references, cross-check every source, and tighten each sentence.

But I don't stop. I refuse to.

I work until the sky begins to bleed into morning and the first stubborn birds start making noise as if they've got something worth singing about. There's ink on my fingers, a dull ache in my back, and a burning sensation behind my eyes that won't go away.

But I finish it. The whole fucking thing.

Every word. Every carefully stitched-together sentence we planned when we still couldn't keep our hands off each other.

I make sure it's clean and polished. Better than anything we could have put together in class and what she expected from me because this is for her.

For us.

Even if there's no us anymore. Even if she never talks to me again.

I open the email draft, attach the document, type her name in the recipient box, and stare at the blinking cursor for a minute. My fingers hover over the keyboard, eager to type something else—something more.

But there's nothing left to say that she hasn't already ignored. Nothing I could write that would make this right.

So I hit send.

And then I just sit there.

Staring at the screen long after it disappears from view, long after the little whoosh tells me it's gone. I sit in silence, amid everything we were, hoping that maybe this one thing will matter.

That she'll see it.

That she'll know I still give a fuck.

Even if it's too late.

CHAPTER 28

SAM

The email arrives in my inbox before I choose what to wear.

Reece Wilson has shared a file with you.

I freeze, towel wrapped tight around me, hair dripping cold trails down my back. For a full minute, I stare. Part of me wants to delete it. To pretend I never saw it. Pretend he doesn't still live in the part of my brain that won't shut the fuck up.

But curiosity is a bitch, and I've never been good at walking away from things that hurt.

I click it open.

And there it is. The assessment. The entire damn thing.

Every heading and section are perfectly aligned. The tone is professional. He didn't just finish it; he poured himself into it. It reads like both of us—his voice, my notes, our ideas—woven together as if we were still working side by side instead of not being on speaking terms at all.

I scroll down slowly. My heart races with each paragraph.

He recalled everything.

Every conversation we had in the library and in his room before things got messy and we forgot how to be anything other than broken and bleeding. He used the structure we argued over for half an hour. The quotes I highlighted. The dumb shit I said about emotional language and contrasting perspectives that I was sure he wasn't listening to.

He listened.

He took everything we created and made it meaningful.

Honestly, I'd been drowning in panic over failing this assessment, and I still didn't reach out. I couldn't. Because if I messaged him about the project, then I'd be messaging him.

But he did it regardless.

Not for credit.

For me.

I bite the inside of my cheek and scroll all the way to the bottom. There's no note. No message. No "I'm sorry" tagged on the end. Just the work.

My heart aches because this is the most genuine thing he's ever given me. And it guts me.

I slam my laptop shut before the tears start falling.

I've spent all this time telling myself he never once cared about me. That I was nothing to him but a punchline, a two-hundred-dollar joke passed between guys who think feelings are for games, not girls.

But this, I don't know what the hell this is.

He didn't have to do it. He could've let the whole project fail, let me drown in it and struggle alone, or ask him for help that I wasn't ready to beg for. But he didn't.

He took everything and carried it alone, quietly.

Maybe that's who Reece truly is.

Not the cocky bastard with the fuck-you smile and the hands that know exactly how to ruin a girl's good sense. Because this isn't some fuckboy move. This isn't him trying to win points or slide back into my good graces with a wink and an apology. This is something else.

I don't know how to handle that version of him.

I sit still for a minute before I get up and go through the motions: get dressed, pull my hair into a high ponytail, hands trembling slightly.

The idea keeps looping in my mind. Should I thank him for it?

But the other voice kicks in. The one that reminds me of what he did—how the bet was real and how he let me fall without stopping it when it mattered most.

I grab my keys from the counter and slide into my car, the engine coughing to life. The drive to school feels longer than usual, even though I hit every green light. My mind's too busy. Every turn of the wheel brings another thought I can't quiet.

I keep thinking about how he did the entire thing without asking for anything in return.

By the time I pull into the parking lot, my hands ache from gripping the wheel too hard. I sit there for a minute, engine ticking, watching students stream into the building like it's just another normal day.

The day is endless.

In first period, I don't absorb a single word the teacher says. I keep running through fake conversations in my head—all the different ways I might say it.

"Thanks for the project."

Or, "You didn't have to do that."

Or even, "I saw what you sent."

But nothing seems right. Every version of me seems too fragile to risk breaking in front of him.

By second period, I am exhausted from overthinking.

And between second and third period, I see him.

He's standing by his locker, laughing at something one of the guys says. A few team members are gathered around him, exchanging their usual bullshit. He's leaning against the door, relaxed and effortless.

I pause for a second.

As if sensing me standing there, his eyes flick to me. They hold for a moment before moving away.

I swallow hard, fingers gripping the strap of my bag as I step forward.

I should say thank you. It's two simple words. But I don't.

I walk past without stopping, and whatever I was going to say slips away.

Nicole catches me between classes, stepping into my path. There's a bruise blooming high on her cheekbone from her fight with Tia, but she wears it like a trophy. Her hair is freshly straightened, lips glossed to the max, and that crocodile smile is plastered on her face.

"So…" she drawls, voice syrupy sweet with a bite beneath it. "How's it feel to be someone's prize, Sam?"

"Get fucked, Nicole."

She smirks, flicking her hair over one shoulder. "Already have. But thanks for the advice."

I walk past her before I do something I'll regret because if I open my mouth right now, I might scream until the walls crack. I might claw at the ache in my chest until it finally lets me breathe again.

She's not worth it. None of them are.

The rest of the day drifts by in fragments. I'm in class, but I am disconnected. Floating. Hollow. Moving through rooms filled with noise I can't grasp. Every hallway echoes with pieces of him. Every corner I turn seems like he might be there, until he's not—and it's the same lockers and the same reminders that I'm still carrying all of this alone.

Even Lola's usual chaos doesn't break through the fog. She tries. God, she tries. Pulls ridiculous faces in math, writes dirty things in the corner of my notebook to see if I'll crack a smile. Whispers that Nicole's hair looks more fried than her personality today.

But I can't laugh.

Not today.

The final bell rings, but I don't head to the gate. My feet seem to have a mind of their own, dragging me somewhere I know he'll be.

I sneak around the back of the gym, hugging the brick wall and keeping my head down. The metal of the bleachers is hot against my hand as I climb, each step ringing louder than the last. I reach the top and settle down, tucking my knees in and curling my arms around them.

I see Reece already on the field, helmet tucked under one arm, sweat darkening the collar of his practice jersey. Coach paces in front of them, barking orders, before they move. Drills begin, feet hit the turf, whistles pierce the air. Reece is faster. Meaner. Controlled in a way that feels almost dangerous.

His body is a weapon. Every move is precise and brutal.

I stay tucked away here in the shadows, watching. There was a time I thought his smirk was arrogance. That cocky tilt of his mouth, the kind that screamed I-own-this-place and knew exactly how handsome he was while doing it. But now? I believe it's the only armor he has. A lifeline. That smirk is the only thing holding him together and preventing him from falling apart.

They run another drill. Then another. Finally, Coach calls it a day. The team begins to scatter, helmets off, towels over their shoulders, slapping each other on the back. But Reece doesn't move. He stays put. Drops his helmet at his feet and starts running.

One lap. Two. Three.

His sweat clings to him. He drags the hem of his shirt up and wipes his face—and Jesus. My breath stutters.

Those abs. That body. All tan skin, sharp lines, and muscles so tight it makes my mouth go dry. Every inch of him reminds me of what I had, what I walked away from, and yet I still can't stop staring.

I know every inch of that body. Every scar, every freckle. I know how his hands feel pressed against my thighs and on the front of my neck when he fucked me, how his mouth sounds when he's groaning against my skin. I know the way he kisses—hard, hungry, as if he's starving for something he doesn't think he deserves. I know how he fucks, and how he destroys what he claims to care about.

I shouldn't be here watching. My heart shouldn't be fluttering and swelling for a boy who used me for a bet and made my world collapse without blinking.

But I don't move because deep down, beneath all the anger and shame, I am still that girl who wants him.

He bends at the waist, hands resting on his knees, each breath coming out rough and uneven, chest rising and falling. He rolls his shoulders back and tilts his face toward the sky, mouth parted, breathing heavily.

Then he jogs.

A few more steps.

Slower now as if his body is slowly winding down.

And then he looks up.

Right at me.

Fuck.

The shift happens instantly. The moment his eyes meet mine, the entire damn world shrinks to just us. That stupid invisible wire between us tightens until I can't breathe.

My pulse races, my stomach tightens, and every part of me screams to turn around and run.

But I don't.

My legs tremble as I get up. I walk down the bleachers, step by step, eyes fixed on his, hating that part of me that still craves that stupid smirk and the way he used to call me Red.

He stands there. His hair's a mess, damp at the edges, sticking to his forehead. His lips are parted, breath still rough. He looks beautiful in that fucked-up, raw, Reece Wilson way. Like a sin I've already committed and would do again just to feel something that real.

I stop a few feet away. Close enough to feel the heat rolling off his skin.

My fingers twitch at my sides, muscle memory firing off as it recalls his mouth on my neck.

He doesn't speak. He just stands there, chest rising and falling, dark eyes locked on mine. His gaze then slips to my mouth, quick but obvious. My pulse stammers and my knees start to wobble.

Fuck.

I swallow, my throat tight.

"Hey," I say, barely more than a breath.

He nods. "Hey."

Silence hangs heavy in the air, filled with all the unspoken words we refuse to say. I glance at the grass, at my shoes, anywhere but at him for a moment. Then I force myself to meet his gaze again. "I got the assessment."

His jaw twitches. "Yeah."

"I read it." I take a shaky breath. "Thank you. You didn't have to do that."

He shrugs as if it's no big deal, but the way his eyes flicker says otherwise. "You weren't gonna ask me for help. Figured it was the only way to make sure you didn't fail."

"Still," I murmur. "What you wrote... it was good. Really good."

His mouth curves, not quite a smile. Not even close. But there's something there. Something soft. Something vulnerable.

"I did it for you, Red." he says, voice low and steady.

That name.

God, that fucking name.

It hits me harder than it should. That nickname is the only one he's ever used.

My lips twitch before I can stop them. A flicker of a smile appears, and he catches it.

His whole expression changes. His eyes soften, shoulders easing just a little.

"I heard about Mayfair," I say softly. "Aubrey told me."

He nods, wiping his hand over his jaw. "Yeah. I've got a meeting tomorrow. Coach thinks I've got a shot at a four-year scholarship. But I don't know. I want to see what they're actually offering first. No point in getting my hopes up."

"That's huge." My voice is stronger now. "You deserve it, Reece."

"I want it," he says. "For a chance to be more than where I came from. More than who I was."

"You'll do great," I say. And I mean it. Every damn word. I've got a thousand more words on the tip of my tongue, but none of them are safe. "Reece..." I start, but I don't finish. The words catch in my throat.

He moves forward. "I miss you, Red."

It hits me in the chest. No warning. No mercy.

I close my eyes for just a second, trying to hold it together and not let those four stupid words undo everything I've built since he wrecked me.

When I open them, he's still watching me.

His gaze is soft

"I should go," I whisper, even though my body is screaming to stay right here.

"Right." His jaw tics hard.

I turn.

One step, then another, before I stop.

My entire body is trembling, just one breath from turning around, running straight into his arms, and pretending none of this ever happened. I almost say fuck it.

But I don't. I summon the courage to keep walking.

CHAPTER 29

REECE

I've never been this nervous in my life. Not before a game. Not even the first time I kissed Red.

My hands won't stop sweating. My heart's pounding so damn loud I'm sure Coach can hear it through the wall. I've been standing outside his office for over a minute, staring at the handle as if it might burn me. I should've gone in already, walked in confident, cocky, sure of myself.

But I feel frozen because this isn't just a meeting; it's my future.

Twelve o'clock sharp. That's what they said. This is the moment I sign with Mayfair—the shot I've been dreaming of since I was a kid tossing a football against my dad's shed.

"You can do this," I remind myself.

But there's the other voice. The one that whispers maybe they changed their mind. Maybe I'm not what they wanted after all.

I shake it off. That voice won't win today.

I grab the handle, nerves still running high, but I turn it anyway and step inside before I can back out.

Coach is sitting behind his desk, arms crossed, with his mouth set in that firm line he wears when he's not willing to give anything away.

To my left is the Mayfair guy—Collins, based on the card he gave me. Sharp suit, straight tie, hair neat enough to suggest he doesn't sweat. His eyes flick to me the second I walk in. He scans me from head to toe, as if I'm already secured. A product with the tags ripped off. Something he's already bought and boxed.

And there's my dad.

Slouched in the chair closest to the desk, legs spread wide, arms resting heavily across his chest. He lifts his chin when I enter, one brow raised.

"You're late," he says.

Coach doesn't hesitate at all. "He's not. He's exactly on time."

I nod once at Coach in quiet thanks and take the empty seat across from Collins. My palms are still sweaty. My throat is dry. I take a slow breath, but my leg betrays me. It bounces once, twice, quickly enough that I have to plant my heel to stop it.

Collins moves a folder in front of him and meets my eyes with that same tight smile that doesn't reach his. Corporate. Polished. Practiced.

"Reece," he says, voice smooth, like he's done this a hundred times, "we've seen everything we need. All that's left now is your signature."

He slides the contract across the table toward me. The pages land with a soft thud that still manages to make my stomach twist.

"You're being offered a full ride. Tuition, housing, training, medical. Everything's covered. Four years," he adds, tapping the paper with his pen. "Pre-season camp starts in August. You'll need to report before then for summer conditioning. Is that all good with you?"

I nod. "Yeah." It comes out rough but clear enough.

Collins shifts slightly in his chair and looks at my dad. "Are you both happy with that?"

My dad leans back slowly and lets out a low hum, as if he's weighing his options, even though we all know he's already made up his mind. He taps a finger against his knee, relaxed as ever, but there's something tough behind his eyes.

"It doesn't sound terrible," he says, dragging out the words. "Though I thought maybe Westbrook might have something better. They've got a stronger program... more exposure."

Of course he fucking did. Trust him to twist it. To take something good and beat it into the ground. To turn this into a consolation prize instead of the damn miracle it truly is.

My fingers tighten around the arm of the chair. I don't look at him because if I do, I'll lose the thin grip I have on my temper.

I'm fortunate to be sitting here, looking at a contract with my name on it, after walking away from the sport last year. And still, he can't simply say he's proud or give me a pat on the back or even a quiet "well done."

Nope. Not him. Because it's never enough. I'm never enough.

He leaves the sentence hanging there.

Collins shifts in his seat, trying not to react. Coach doesn't bother hiding his annoyance. His shoulders stiffen, and he shoots my dad a look so sharp it could cut glass.

"Mayfair is giving him a full scholarship," Coach says. "That's not nothing."

My dad shrugs. "I'm not saying it's nothing."

I clench my teeth.

Collins clears his throat and turns back to me. "It's a strong program. And you'll be a cornerstone in their new lineup. They're banking on you, Reece."

My dad scoffs softly, amused. "Let's hope he delivers."

The room falls silent.

I stare at the paper in front of me, seeing my name printed in bold at the space waiting for my signature.

This is mine. No matter what crap my dad throws at it or how many jabs he takes.

Coach hands me the pen, and I sign my fucking name. This is my decision, not my father's.

That's it. I'm heading to Mayfair.

I set the pen down. This is the first time in my entire life that I've done something this big. This one's mine.

I glance up when I hear Coach's voice.

"Proud of you, kid."

That one hits harder than I expected. I nod, swallowing past the lump forming in my throat. My eyes burn slightly, and fuck, I wasn't ready for that—not from him. Not today.

"Big day," Collins says, sliding the signed papers into his briefcase. He stands, smooths down his expensive jacket, and smiles. "Congratulations, Reece. We're excited to have you."

He pulls out a Mayfair cap and hands it to me. The weight of it feels unreal. He turns to Coach and shakes his hand. It's a firm grip and a respectful nod.

He turns to my dad.

"Mr. Wilson," he says, extending his hand.

My dad takes his fucking time. Simply leaves Collins hanging there like an idiot before finally lifting his arm and giving him the coldest, limp handshake I've ever seen.

"You better keep him in check," he mutters.

Collins doesn't bite. "I'll be in touch, Reece." He nods, turns, glances at Coach, and then he's gone.

The door closes, and silence falls over the room.

Coach leans back, arms crossed, jaw clenched. My dad avoids looking at him, just taps his fingers on the chair as if he has somewhere else to be.

"You could've dialed it back," Coach says after a second.

My dad snorts. "I don't coddle."

Coach raises an eyebrow. "No. You don't."

That silence returns, thicker now.

I sit there, cap still in my hand, feeling the weight of both of them pressing down on me. Coach's quiet defense. My dad's cold dismissal. The two of them couldn't be more different. One sees me. The other sees the version of me he wishes I'd be.

My dad stands, still wearing that half-disappointed look he always keeps in his back pocket. He stares down at me for a beat too long, to make sure I'm ready for whatever shitty parting words he's about to throw my way.

"Don't fuck it up," he says flatly. No warmth. Just pressure, like always.

Then he turns and walks out without saying another word, the door swinging shut behind him.

Coach exhales and gets up from his seat and walks around the table. "Reece," he says, calm but firm, "you don't owe him anything. You've earned this."

I exhale. "It's always been this way, Coach."

He nods. "I know. Perhaps it's a good thing you're leaving that house next year. That place hasn't been good for you in a long time." He points to the Mayfair cap. "This is your chance to figure out who you are. Not just a player. But a person."

"Thanks, Coach." I walk toward the door, cap in my hand.

The hallway is lively, buzzing like always during lunchtime, lockers slamming, sneakers squeaking on linoleum, voices echoing off the walls in a chaotic, messy rhythm that's just part of school life. I weave through the crowd, still riding the high. My fingers curl around the brim of the Mayfair cap in my hand, brushing over the stitched logo. It's real. It fucking happened.

But then I hear it.

"Guess he needed practice, huh?"

Sweet on the surface, rotten underneath. That voice could peel fucking paint off the walls.

Nicole.

She's standing dead center in the cafeteria, right under the harsh fluorescent lights, with her small audience gathered around her. Every eye in the room begins to turn toward her, feeding off the tension it always does.

Her voice rings out again, this time louder.

"Poor Sam. She gave up her virginity for a two-hundred-dollar bet and didn't even get a thank you."

Laughter erupts around her, ugly and harsh—the kind that makes your skin crawl.

I freeze in the doorway, my vision narrowing until all I see is her.

Red.

She's standing there, caught in the spotlight of every stare in the cafeteria. Frozen. Exposed.

Nicole is positioned directly in front of her, with all her minions surrounding Sam, blocking any escape routes.

Sam's face is pale, eyes wide, lips slightly parted as if she wants to speak, but no words come out.

And the worst part is no one is fucking stepping in or stopping it. They're all watching it unfold.

Nicole keeps moving, eyes fixed on Sam.

"Tell me, was he any good, Sam? Or was it part of the assessment, you know extra credit for cock?"

My stomach turns.

Nicole's minions laugh loudly and forcibly, as if it's the funniest joke they've ever heard. They soak it up, playing their role, eager for her approval.

But the rest of the cafeteria doesn't join in. They simply stare— silent and uncomfortable— because they all know exactly what Nicole is like.

And ever since Tia was knocked off her throne, Nicole has been worse. Meaner. Louder. Crueler in ways that aren't even subtle anymore, to remind everyone she wants to run the room.

This isn't gossip; it's a public execution.

I see Noah and Aubrey rushing in from the far side of the cafeteria, eyes wide with horror as they take in the chaos Nicole's created.

Aubrey's already moving, breaking into a run as she heads straight for Sam, her face etched with panic. Noah's locked in, his gaze focused on Nicole as if he's two seconds away from losing control. I've seen that look before. He's done acting nice. Done warning her to back the fuck off.

My feet are already moving, rushing across the cafeteria floor while every cell in my body hums with fury. The cap crumples in my fist, forgotten. My vision is filled with her—Red, frozen in the middle of this chaos, Nicole spinning around her, looking like the ground is about to give way beneath her.

"Enough." My voice cuts through the cafeteria, erupting sharply, loud and final.

Everything stops. Conversations jam. Laughter ends mid-breath.

The silence is abrupt and sharp, like a clean cut.

Every head turns toward me, necks stretching out, phones half-lowered, jaws slack.

Nicole turns slowly and smug at first, until she sees my face.

Her smirk falters.

Good because I'm not here for drama. I'm not here for another scene in the twisted little show she plays.

I'm here to put an end to it.

"You want attention, Nicole?" My voice stays steady, even as my hands shake. "Congrats. You got it. Now shut your fucking mouth."

She laughs, but it's softer now, unsure. "Oh, look who finally decided to show his face."

I take a step closer. Followed by another. Each step is deliberate. Controlled. There's nothing casual about how I move toward her now—only purpose and fire.

I've spent weeks pretending none of this mattered. I'm done pretending. And if this is the only chance Red will hear me, then it has to be now.

"You want a show, Nicole?" My voice deepens. "Fine. Here it fucking is."

Gasps break the silence.

"You're correct. There was a bet."

The noise is immediate.

Aubrey's eyes widen. She covers her mouth. Noah's jaw clenches so tightly I swear he might break something. Lola rushes in and stands next to Aubrey. But Sam doesn't move. She watches me, wide-eyed and shattered, her entire world breaking apart all over again right there in front of me.

Her pain devastates me.

"Yeah," I keep going, even when it burns. "It started with a fucking bet. I threw down a two-hundred-dollar bet to Jace, saying I could get her to fuck me before the end of the year. Thought it'd be funny. Thought she was easy."

I turn my head, and my eyes lock on Nicole.

"You know, like you."

The impact of my words hits harder than any physical punch. Nicole flinches, her face twisting, but I keep going.

"And I made that bet," I say, voice hoarse, chest burning. "Because I was a piece of shit who couldn't handle the fact that she didn't want me. That she looked straight through the mask and saw every fucked-up part of me I tried to hide. That she shut me down without blinking."

My voice cracks, and I don't bother to fix it.

"She wasn't easy. She wasn't a game. She was fucking everything."

I look at Red, and the words spill out of me as if they've been clawing their way up for weeks.

"She's smart, brave, and sharp as hell. She walked into my world and tore it apart. All that fire, fuck-you attitude, and stubbornness as sin. She called me on every lie, didn't fall for the charm, didn't laugh at the lines, and didn't melt like every other girl did. She stood there, unshaken, making me want more and feel things I didn't have words for."

My hands shake. I let it all show. I let it bleed.

"I fell for her."

My eyes remain fixed on Red's, while every wall inside me is already breaking down.

"I fell for the girl I was supposed to fuck and forget. Not in some fake-ass high school way where you say it to get her back. I mean really fell. Hard. Fast. No parachute. No plan. I fucking fell."

I swallow hard, my throat tightening.

"And yeah, I never told Jace there wasn't a bet anymore," I say, voice raw. "Because if I had, he would've known I lost. And I wasn't about to make a joke out of what we had. Red, you are not some punchline I could laugh off at lunch. You are the only real thing I've ever felt."

Her mouth parts. Just barely. Her eyes lock onto mine.

I keep going.

"And yeah, I fucked it all up. Lied through my teeth. Broke your trust. Took something pure and cracked it right down the middle. I hurt the only girl who ever made me believe I could be more than the shit I've always been. More than just another asshole with a smile and a game plan."

My voice lowers, stripped down to the truth.

"But I need you to hear this, Red."

The entire room remains silent. No one dares to move, or even breathe.

"I love you," I say. "I'm in love with you. I think I was from the second you told me to fuck off in that hallway."

I step closer, heart pounding against my ribs, fists clenched at my sides. But my eyes, fuck, my eyes are only on her.

"You don't need to forgive me. You don't have to talk to me either. But I will tell you one thing: I will never let anyone treat you like you're disposable again. Not even me."

Every nerve in my body is stretched tight, pushed to the limit.

Sam doesn't say a word.

Part of me expects her to turn and walk away, to throw my words back in my face, to spit the truth I already know—that I broke us, that I lit the match and let it burn. That she owes me nothing, and walking away would be the strongest thing she could do.

And if she did, I would let her.

Because it would be her decision.

Her eyes glisten, catching the light, holding the weight of everything we've never said and everything I've already destroyed.

Then she moves.

Not away. Toward me.

One step and then another.

The air in the cafeteria is thick with silence. Everyone holds their breath, waiting and watching. The entire world seems frozen in this impossible moment.

She stops inches from me, close enough for me to see the tear slide down her cheek.

My fingers twitch, aching to reach out, to wipe it away, or hold her the way I should have from the start. But I don't move.

Her gaze slides over my face, slow and searching, as if she's trying to decide whether I mean every word or if I'm still the same asshole who broke her heart.

And she hits me.

A solid punch to my shoulder. It's not hard, but enough to make me stumble back a step.

"You asshole," she whispers, her voice trembling. Then she grabs my shirt with both hands, fists clenched in the fabric, pulling me toward her as if she's finally done holding back.

Her mouth crashes into mine.

And fuck.

It's everything.

Fury. Relief. Fire and forgiveness. All teeth, lips, and that kind of kiss that hurts in the best fucking way.

I kiss her as if I'm coming back to life.

My arms wrap around her waist, pulling her close. I kiss her with everything I have—every breath, every ache, every damn apology I can't find the words for.

When she finally pulls back, her breathing is uneven, her chest rising quickly against mine. She doesn't let go, simply presses her forehead to mine, lips parted, eyes closed.

"You broke me," she whispers.

The words hit suddenly. Sharp. Honest.

"I know," I say. No excuses. Just the hard fucking truth.

Her eyes open, and the intensity behind them almost knocks me over. "Don't do it again."

"Never."

My voice cracks when I make the promise. I mean it with everything I've got. Everything I am.

Applause erupts all around us. It shatters the silence, and it takes me a second to realize what's happening. Someone whistles from across the room. Another person yells out something about finally.

Eventually, we turn slightly, still wrapped up in each other. I glance around the cafeteria. It's full of students watching two idiots find their way back to each other.

I see Noah leaning against a nearby table, his arm around Aubrey's shoulders, his face soft in a way I've never seen. Aubrey wipes a tear from her cheek, trying to hide it, but she's smiling too. That quiet, full-hearted kind of smile that says she never stopped hoping we'd figure it out.

Sam notices them too. Her fingers still curled in my shirt, grounding us both.

I glance back at her. Her eyes still sparkle with something that hints this isn't the end of our story. And this time, I'll fight like hell to keep her mine.

Not ready to let Reece and Sam go just yet?
See where they land **three weeks on** in this exclusive bonus scene.
Grab it at
https://storyoriginapp.com/giveaways/376f0340-021c-11f1-8e7b-631
087c278ee
Cruel Promises is next. Jace and Lola's story.
Cruel Truths – ISBN- 9781923416277

About the

Author

Eve Campbell writes gritty, emotional romance that rips your heart out and makes you beg for more.

Her stories are raw, sexy, and full of angst, featuring bad boys with ruined pasts, fierce girls who don't back down, and love that's messy, hot, and unforgettable.

When she's not writing, you'll find her juggling real life, cuddling her pets, inhaling coffee, or plotting new ways to ruin you with her next emotionally intense book boyfriend.

Don't miss a release, sale, or exclusive bonus scene —

<u>Sign up for her newsletter at:</u>
https://evecampbellauthor.myflodesk.com/thaq2q59or

Connect with Eve Online

<u>Join My Facebook Readers Group</u>
facebook.com/groups/915383006946541

<u>Instagram</u>
https://www.instagram.com/eve_campbell_author/

<u>Facebook Page</u>
https://www.facebook.com/Evecampbellauthor

<u>Book Bub</u>
https://www.bookbub.com/authors/eve-campbell

<u>Goodreads</u>
https://www.goodreads.com/author/show/49004938.Eve_Campbell

9 781923 416277